The angry girl walked defiantly up to Jane Scarlett.

"What are you doing here, anyway?" she screeched. "I wonder, do they know who you are?"

Jane turned a bewildered look at the woman of the world, who raised her voice higher.

"Haven't I seen you selling goods in Windle's store? Answer me!"

"Why yes," Jane said with poise. "Certainly. Why? Did you want me to use my influence to get you a job?"

Jane had stood up to her tormentor—but had she gone too far?

Bantam Books by Grace Livingston Hill
Ask your bookseller for the books you have missed

Grace
Livingston
Hill

Homing

BANTAM BOOKS
Toronto • New York • London • Sydney

HOMING

*A Bantam Book | published by arrangement with
Harper & Row, Publishers Inc.*

PRINTING HISTORY

Lippincott edition published 1938

Bantam edition | October 1971

2nd printing	...... October 1971	6th printing	.... June 1973
3rd printing	...... January 1972	7th printing	.... June 1974
4th printing	.. September 1972	8th printing	.... April 1976
5th printing	...... January 1973	9th printing	.. September 1981

ISBN 0-553-14813-3

Published simultaneously in the United States and Canada

PRINTED IN THE UNITED STATES OF AMERICA

18 17 16 15 14 13 12 11 10 9

I

THE day had been intensely hot. There didn't seem to be a breath of air stirring anywhere. Even in the great wide store that was supposed to be "air-conditioned" the sultriness of the fervid August day had penetrated.

Jane Scarlett had been working hard all day. Of the two girls who usually helped her at the button and clasp counter, one had been taken sick that noon and gone home, and the other had gone to a picnic. That was Nellie Forsythe. She was pretty and popular with the heads of the department and would get away with it without losing a cent from her pay. Jane shut her lips hard and fanned herself with her handkerchief, after carefully mopping her face. Not many times today had she been able to get enough respite from work to do even that much. It seemed as if there had always been somebody at the counter wanting to look over the whole stock. Not that she had had so many sales, for people weren't buying buttons and clasps in August, unless they saw a particular lovely bargain.

The fourth girl who usually served at that counter was on vacation. She would return in three more days, that is if she didn't have to take a few more days' sick-leave to get over her holiday.

Vacation!

Jane's lip curled. Well, *she* was supposed to have a vacation too, but she wasn't going to take it. She didn't have to, of course, if she was willing to give it up and go on working. One got a little more money if one worked during vacation time, and she needed the money. She had practically told Mr. Clark, the head of the department, that she wouldn't balk at staying if he needed her. Why should she go on a vacation anyway? She had no place to go. Of course one could go any place at all just for a rest, but why bother if there wasn't any place you really wanted to go? If you had to go among strangers? Also, she hadn't any vacation clothes. She was making last

1

year's things do, because she really needed a warm coat for winter. Though today in the heat a warm coat seemed less desirable than a summer organdie.

Well, August was almost over, and then the winter's work would begin. Perhaps if she worked all summer she might get a promotion or something, and that would be nice. She drew a deep breath and gave a tired fagged look around, and then sighted a girl with a button in her hand coming straight toward her. And just at that very minute came the bugle for closing time! It *would* work out that way, a girl with a button to match at the last minute, on a day like this! Of course she must stay and wait on the girl even if she didn't buy half a button. That was the rule. She must be polite to late people. She couldn't put on a distant reproving air and say "I'm sorry, madam, it's closing time!" and slam the last drawer back into place as if she had been insulted. They gave lectures to the girls now and again on an attitude like that, and she knew just what happened to girls who persisted in such behavior in spite of the instruction. Of course some of them could get away with it by lying, or acting innocent and smiling judiciously. But she scorned an attitude like that.

The girl with the button hastened her steps and arrived definitely at the button counter now, smiling ingratiatingly toward Jane. The bugle gave the last clear note for closing, but Jane shadowed forth a weary smile, with a hope in her heart that the request might be for something she didn't have.

"I wonder if you can match this button?" said the customer pleasantly.

Jane accepted the button and saw at a glance that she had it. Just a common black gutta-percha button.

"Yes, we have it," said Jane swinging briskly around and reaching with accustomed fingers to the little drawer where such buttons were kept.

"Oh, I'm so glad!" said the other girl with a relieved sigh. "I came in town just on purpose for those buttons, and then I almost forgot them! I'll take a dozen. And if you have a smaller size, about right for sleeves, you can give me a dozen of those, too."

In silence Jane hunted out the smaller size and showed

them to her customer, and then with her sharp little scissors cut in half the card that held two dozen.

"It's terribly hot, isn't it?" said the customer.

Jane summoned a semblance of a smile and agreed. Her swift fingers were putting the buttons into a bag and accepting the right change, while her mind leaped forward to her freedom.

"I'm ashamed to have kept you a minute longer than closing time," said the customer as she accepted her package. "I suppose you are just dying to get to your home and put on the coolest thing you own."

Jane smiled then.

"Oh, that's all right," she said. And then, following a sudden impulse she added:

"You see, I haven't any home! I never have had. And I guess after all this store is cooler than the little third-story-back room where I board."

"Oh! I'm sorry!" said the other girl. And then added earnestly: "Come on down with me to the shore. I'd love to have you. We have a cottage right close to the beach and there's a big cool guest room overlooking the ocean. I know mother would welcome you. Will you come?"

Jane felt something unaccustomed like a sudden rush of tears near the surface, and a little blaze of glory came into her pale face.

"Oh, thank you! I couldn't! But it was dear of you to suggest it. Just the memory of your asking me will quite cool me off for the evening."

"Well, I wish you could come. I'd like to get to know you. When I get back to the city I'll look you up. Maybe we can plan something nice together. I'm really grateful to you for being so nice when I kept you after hours. May I know your name?"

"Oh! Why, it's Scarlett. Jane Scarlett!"

"What a lovely name. I won't forget that. Good-bye. I'll be seeing you again sometime in the fall."

Jane watched her as she walked away, a lovely graceful girl in expensive clothes, with a beautiful summer home by the sea, and probably a lovelier one back in the city. But why had she answered her that way? Blurting out to her that she had no home, and never had had one? What a silly thing to do! Sob stuff, that was what it was. The kind of thing she just loathed. She had been guilty of that! She was aghast at herself.

Abruptly she turned and put the card of buttons back in its drawer, slammed it shut, drew down the gingham covers over the whole section and went on her way, hurrying her steps to make up for the loss of time.

And Audrey Havenner, the girl with the parcel of buttons, took a taxi to the station and boarded the bridge train to the shore. In due time she arrived at the lovely place beside the sea and got herself into charming filmy garments for evening.

"Did you have a very uncomfortable time in the city, dear, this hot day? I understand the mercury fairly soared in town."

Her mother said this conversationally at the dinner table after the meal was well under way.

"This certainly wasn't a very good day to select for shopping," remarked her father with a lifting of his eyebrows. "I wouldn't have gone in town if I hadn't had to."

"Nor I," said Kent her older brother emphatically. "You women never do know when you're well off."

"It wasn't so bad," said Audrey cheerily. "The stores are air-conditioned, you know."

"Yes? Well, for all that, I'd have stayed in a cool place by the sea if I'd had my choice."

"So would I," said Audrey amiably, "but you see I didn't have my choice. I went in town to see a friend who is in the hospital and is deadly lonely, and incidentally I did the shopping for the family. By the way, dad, I got your coat buttons that you are always talking about. I almost forgot them too, and went back at the last minute. Came near losing my train in the act. And mother, I nearly brought a guest out with me."

"Why didn't you, dear? Who was it?"

"Nobody I ever saw before. She waited on me for coat buttons after the bugle blew and was as sweet as she could be."

"They have to be or they'd get fired!" said Bruce the fourteen-year-old brother importantly.

"Oh, but this was a different kind of sweetness, brother," said Audrey lightly. "This was really courtesy."

"Heavens! Courtesy in a button salesgirl!" exclaimed Evalina Harrison, a self-invited second cousin who had been with them all summer. "Is that the kind of guests you pick out to land on us? I'm glad you restrained your impulses. This cottage is already overcrowded."

"Why, I didn't restrain my impulses," said Audrey. "She did it for me. I did invite her. You see I realized I had kept her overtime, and I apologized and told her I knew she was just dying to get home and get into the coolest thing she had and rest. She looked terribly warm, and utterly tired out. But she just smiled and said that was all right. She hadn't any home and never had had. And then of course I really tried hard to make her come. I told her mother would have given her a lovely welcome. But she wouldn't come."

"Heavens, Audrey!" said Evalina. "Haven't you any discretion? And don't you know her at all? I don't think that was being very kind to the rest of us. She might have been an awful nuisance. You really ought to think of your brothers, Audrey. A girl like that would be very likely to get notions in her head about Kent, think he was in love with her and all that!"

"Yes, Audrey," put in Kent solemnly, "you really ought to protect my tender impressionable youth!"

Audrey laughed.

"But really, Audrey, I mean it. A sister should be careful about strange girls. You don't even know her name, do you?" persisted the cousin.

"Oh, yes, I do!" said Audrey with a comical twinkle in her eye. "She has a lovely name. I asked her what it was and she told me. I told her I wanted to get acquainted with her sometime when I got back to town."

"Audrey!" said her cousin. "That's just like you! Have you no discretion at all? Cousin Mary, I hope you'll forbid an acquaintance like that. A mere button-saleswoman! The perfect idea!"

"What was her name, Aud? Kent is all ears to hear it!" grinned the fourteen-year-old wickedly, his eyes on the elderly cousin.

"Her name is Jane Scarlett!" said Audrey with a twinkle at her young brother.

"Jane Scarlett?" said Kent looking up in amazement

and dropping his fork on his plate with a sharp clash. "You don't mean it!"

Audrey looked up with a startled expression.

"Why? Do you know her, Kent?" A shade of half fear crossed her face, lest after all her cousin would really think there was some ground for her insinuations.

"Great Scott!" said Kent excitedly. "Jane Scarlett! No, I don't know her, but I've been hearing her name almost all day long. She's been more talked of in our law office than any other one person today. Great Caesar's ghost! Jane Scarlett. If I could really locate her I'd get the attention of the office turned to my humble self, I guess! She's very much wanted, and nobody knows where to find her. But then, I don't suppose she's the right one."

"Yes," said Cousin Evalina, "I *thought* so! Some criminal, I suppose! What's she done? Killed somebody?"

"No!" said Kent crossly. "Nothing like that! Just a matter of when she was born and a few dates. You wouldn't understand."

"H'm!" said Evalina offendedly. "She's probably trying to break a will or something. I told you, Audrey, that you should never make up to strangers. You can't tell what they'll turn out to be!"

Kent opened his lips with a glare toward Evalina and then closed them firmly and drew one corner of his mouth down in a quiet amusement.

"You're wrong again, Cousin Evalina, but I'm not telling any more about it. This isn't my business, it belongs to the office, and I've no right to go around discussing it. Which store was that, Audrey? Stevens and Drake?"

"No, Windle and Harrower."

"You *see!*" said Cousin Evalina. "The mischief is done. Now if anything happens it will be *your* fault, Audrey!"

The brother and sister twinkled their eyes at one another.

"My sins be upon my own head!" said Audrey comically.

Then there was a momentary cessation of the conversation as the dessert was brought in, and as callers came in for the evening the subject was not again taken up. The young people hoped their cousin had forgotten.

But Evalina never forgot. She came into Audrey's room

late that evening while she was preparing to retire, and told long gruesome stories of young men who had made unfortunate marriages that might have been avoided, until finally Audrey was driven to get into bed, and her pleasant regular breathing soon proclaimed that she was asleep, so that Evalina was forced to turn out the light and retire to her own room.

Audrey was up quite early the next morning and walked with her brother to his train.

"Kent! What is this you are going to do to the girl I discovered yesterday? Because I won't stand for anything happening to her. She's fine! And I shan't tell you where she is if—"

"You've already told me!" he laughed. "Have you forgotten?"

"Kent! I protest! You shan't do anything to her. You shan't get her in any jams. I saw the dark tired circles under her eyes and if you give her any added troubles I'll feel that it was all my fault. Why can't you just ignore what I told last night? Forget it! You haven't any right at all to take advantage of my confidences. I was just talking for the benefit of my family, and it's disloyal to take what I said and make trouble for someone I like who did me a real favor. I tell you truly, Kent, if you go and hunt up that girl and put your old law firm on her track I'll telephone her before you get there and tell her to make tracks for Nowhere and hide till I give her the high sign. I really will. I mean it, brother!"

"Say look here, kid, what do you think I am?" laughed the brother. "A sleuth? Or a gangster? I'm not even a detective. I wasn't hunting for this girl myself, but I knew the whole office force was put to it to find her whereabouts, and it's such a peculiar name I couldn't help but notice. Of course I shouldn't have *said* a word, not before the highly respectable cousin anyway. But you needn't worry about that girl. If she's the right one, which I very much doubt, because they are searching for her up in New England at a school, nothing will happen to her except what is perfectly all right. I don't know just what it is, but you needn't think I'm going to hurt your protégée. They'll only ask her a few simple questions, what her father's name was, and where she was born—things like that."

"It'll scare her to death!"

"Not at all. They'll tell her it's for some statistics the law firm is getting out, and if she is the child of the wrong father they'll beg her pardon and buy a few buttons and take their way out of your old store, and nobody any the wiser."

"Are you being square with me?"

"I sure am. Now, will you be good? And for Pete's sake don't tell a word of what I said to the cousin with the gimlet eyes. Let her marry me off to a few heathen maidens or whatever she likes, but just laugh."

Audrey gave her brother a long level look.

"All right, brother, when you look like that I know I can trust you. I just wanted you to know that this girl is an all right girl, and I won't have her pestered."

Her brother grinned wisely.

"All right, kiddo. You win," he said gravely, "but it beats me how you found all that out in ten minutes while you bought coat buttons. I know you have pretty good hunches about people and they usually come out right, but I just want you to be sane, and realize that you couldn't be trusted in a casual glance like that to sift out a possible criminal. Some of them are pretty slick, you know."

"Yes, I know. But this girl is a real lady."

Her brother studied her for a moment and then he said: "Oh, yeah?"

"Well, wait till you see her yourself—*if you do,*" said Audrey sharply.

"Yes—*if I do!*"

II

MOST of the other girls with whom Jane occasionally walked part way had already gone, and when she came out of the store after selling Audrey the coat buttons, her own footsteps lagged as she reached the hot pavement. What was the point in her hastening to her stifling little third-story-back bedroom? It would be unbearable there now, and hard enough to bear after dark. It was too hot to light her tiny flame of an oil stove and attempt any cooking. Even a cooked cereal would heat up the place so she couldn't sleep afterward, and to heat a can of soup would fill the room with the smell of onions. Besides, she didn't want anything to eat. She wished she didn't have to eat. It was too hot to eat. But of course she must eat. Well, probably ice cream would be the best. Ice cream and a cracker. Maybe not even a cracker. She had crackers in her room she could eat later if she got hungry. Perhaps she would just get some ice cream now, and then go around by the little park and sit there on a bench. Perhaps there would be a breath of air and she could get cool. Anyway it would be pleasant to walk past the trees and shrubs and hear the fountain splashing, for it wasn't likely she could get an empty bench at this time of day.

So Jane turned her steps toward the place where she could get the best ice cream for the smallest money, and after she had eaten it slowly, she wandered out toward the park. But to her disappointment she found her worst fears justified. Every bench in the whole place was occupied by tired discouraged-looking people. Some of them were dirty people, with indiscriminate garments, coatless and hatless, men in shirt sleeves, women in dresses of a bygone day, with straggling hair, a few more smartly dressed but with such a look of utter hopelessness upon them that Jane could not bear to look at them. Not one of them looked as if he had a home, or a family who cared, much less a home by the sea like the girl who had come

9

to buy buttons. That old woman over there with the run-down shoes, and eyes that looked as if they had wept till there were no more tears, what would she say if she were invited to spend the night in a pretty room in a cottage by the sea? Suppose she had such a cottage and could go up to that poor old creature and ask her to come and spend the night with her? Or that young thing over there with the tattered dirty green frock and the three whining children, one of them a babe in arms? Didn't she have a husband? Where was he? Why didn't he take care of her? Well, perhaps he was out of work! Oh, this was a hard world!

She walked briskly on past them all, feeling that in spite of her homeless lot and her little hot third-story-back room, she still had something to be thankful for. And she definitely didn't want to sit down there in the park with that tired discouraged mess of people and class herself with them. Not unless she could do something to relieve them. Doubtless they all had some kind of habitation even if it wasn't worthy of the name home, and they were just out here to try to get cool the way she was. There! There was one who had some sense. Another little mother with two children. She had a clean dress on. To be sure the sleeves were cut off above the elbow, and the neck turned down for coolness, but even the children were clean. They were sitting on the grass against a sheltering clump of shrubbery, one child kicking its bare feet lazily and chewing on a crust of bread, the other sound asleep by an empty bottle. Jane Scarlett wished she might find a sheltering bush and lie down and kick her feet too, she was so tired, and it did seem a little cooler here among the green things. The sun had definitely gone down now, and there was perhaps a trifle of breeze coming up from the river way. Or was it just the sound of the splashing fountain that made her think so? Well, she had better get back to her room. She had some stockings to wash. That would cool her off for a few minutes perhaps, and if she could just get to sleep it would soon be morning. Morning was always a little relief, even in hot weather. And besides she had that invitation to spend the night at the seashore to think about. If she went about it in the right way she could really imagine herself as perhaps accepting it sometime.

As she walked on up the street of closed offices with dim lights in the distant depths, her thoughts went back in her life, and she tried to imagine what it would have been if she had ever had a real home where she belonged.

Then she saw a familiar figure approaching. Who was it? Somebody she ought to know? Why did he stir an unpleasant memory? Oh yes, the new floor-walker in the next department. Stockings! His jurisdiction was just across the main aisle from the buttons. He had only been with the store a couple of days but she couldn't help seeing him often, although she had never had words with him. Just yesterday she had seen him in intimate conversation with Nellie Forsythe. She had inadvertently caught a snatch of a sentence and it disgusted her. He was good looking, with hair that must be a permanent wave, and long golden eyelashes. But she didn't like his mouth. It didn't seem trustworthy. Jane wasn't a girl who lost her head over young men. There had been a mother in her life who had spent time warning her mite of a girl who was presently going to be left alone.

However, it didn't matter what his mouth was like. She didn't know him and wasn't likely to, though every other girl in his section was wild over him and made it quite apparent. He wouldn't ever have time to notice her of course. Not that she cared.

Then suddenly the young man turned his head, looked her full in the face and stopped.

"Oh, I say, aren't you somebody I'm supposed to know?" he asked engagingly.

Jane gave him a level look and answered coolly:

"I'm afraid not." Her tone was distant.

"Oh, but you're from Windle and Harrower's, aren't you? I'm sure I've seen you in the store. You're not from perfumes and sachet, are you?"

"No," said Jane matter-of-factly, "only buttons. I'm on the other side of the middle aisle. You wouldn't have met me." There was no encouragement in her voice.

"Oh, but I've noticed you. Yes, I have. Buttons of course! I've watched you on the side. I've noticed how well you do your work, and how people seem to like you.

Noticed your smile, you know. You're a good sales-woman. And buttons aren't easy, either. It takes patience to be a good button salesperson. You had a late customer tonight, didn't you? I noticed you were charming to her. It takes a real lady to be patient and smile the way you did to a late comer on a hot night like this. But she didn't keep you all this time surely!"

"Oh, no. She kept me only a minute or two. I stopped on my way to get some dinner."

"Dinner? Oh, that's too bad. I was going to ask you to have some dinner with me. Well, how about a movie then? I'm not keen on dinner myself tonight. It's too hot to eat. But you and I must get together and get acquainted."

Jane lifted an independent young chin.

"Thank you," she said, "I'm busy tonight. I have work to do."

"Goodness! Work on a night like this? Have a heart, lady! Don't you know this is the time for relaxation? Well, then, how about tomorrow night?"

"Thank you, no," said Jane coolly.

"Now, Beautiful, that's no way to behave. What have you got against me?"

"Nothing whatever," said Jane crisply. "I am not in the least acquainted with you, you know."

"Oh, is that it? High hat? Well, next time I'll try and bring my credentials with me. But how about having at least a cool little drink with me somewhere? I might be able to find a mutual friend if we had the time."

"Excuse me," said Jane, "I'm in a hurry," and she smiled distantly and marched on, her proud little lifting of her chin, and her dignified carriage, covering a sudden tendency to tremble.

So he thought he could pick her up as casually as he did those other girls in the store. Well, he would find she was not so easily picked. Of course it wasn't that he was exactly a stranger. He was employed in the same store with herself, and she had happened to hear his name called by cash girls and saleswomen in his department: "Mr. Gaylord! Oh, Mr. Gaylord! Will you sign this sched-ule for the customer please!" He was just not the type of person she cared to companion with in any way. A young man who had his hair marcelled and talked to a girl that way the first time he ever spoke to her! It would have been different perhaps if she were in his department and had been formally under his management. It would even have been different if he had been in the store for some time and had been formally seeing her in their regular business gatherings. But she definitely didn't like him anyway. She had seen him stroking Isabel Emory's hand fondly just before the girl with the button came.

She hurried on trying to put him entirely out of her mind, but there was a distinct uneasiness concerning him. His bold gay eyes darting into her quiet life disturbed her strangely, as if there were some undefined alarm connected with him, and that was absurd of course. He had nothing whatever to do with her, and never would have if she maintained her aloofness, as of course she would.

With a sigh she entered the dingy boarding house where she resided. The atmosphere was of numberless dreary meals lingering at the door to meet her, the aroma of greasy fried potatoes, of ancient fried fish, of unappetizing meats, and onions, of pork, and spoiled fat that had burned. It smote her in the face on the breath of the heavy heat of the day, and made her suddenly dead tired and heartsick.

She climbed to the third floor to her gloomy room where the evening sun was scorching in at the single window, pricking through the worn old green window shade, burning every breath of the air out and intensifying the dusty breathlessness of the apartment till it almost seemed unbearable.

Jane shut the door despairingly because the smell of the burning fat was even worse up here than down in the hall. Taking off her hat she flung herself down across her bed and let hot discouraged tears pour out of her tight-shut eyes.

Suddenly it came to her what a fool she was. Here she had been offered a chance to go down to the shore and spend a night in a lovely cool guest room by the sea, and also she had been asked to dinner by a personable young man; she could have had an appetizing meal in gay company, she could have attended a movie in a room that would have been air-conditioned and cool, and she had declined them all! But she still had her self-respect! Why bother about smells and breathlessness? She had this quiet place and her self-respect, even if the air wasn't good. Someday perhaps she might be able to afford a better spot. Till then she had better be content.

She lay a few minutes getting the ache out of her tired feet, and then she got up and washed her face in the tepid water that had stood all day in her water pitcher. It was good to get her face wet, and her wrists and arms, and summer didn't last forever. There would be bitter cold in the winter, with no fire whatever in her room and the necessity of opening the hall door to take the intense chill from the air.

There was cabbage coming up the hallway now, and fried apples, but she knew just how they would look, little gnarly apples, with specks in them. She was not going down to dinner at all tonight. The ice cream she had eaten was enough. She couldn't bear the thought of the dinner that would be served in that house.

She took her water pitcher and went down one flight to the bathroom to fill it, and then got out some soap flakes and washed a pair of stockings and some underwear. After that she was so tired she lay down and went to sleep. The drying clothes broke the dry heat of the August night and made a little moisture in the room, and by and by she had a dream. She dreamed that she had gone to the shore with that lovely customer, and was lying in a beautiful soft bed with a great cool breeze blowing over her, and the smell of the sea in the air. But after a time she suddenly woke up again and the room was terribly hot and breathless, the ham and cabbage were lurking on the edges of the ceiling, and a fire siren was blowing with all its might.

Jane lay there panting with the heat and thinking how hard things were in her life. It was harder now than she ever remembered it before.

She had been a very little girl when her father died. They were living at the time in a tiny apartment in a western city. Jane could remember the many stairs they had to climb, because her mother always had to stop and rest between landings. It seemed that she had always been climbing stairs.

Dimly she remembered the two rooms where she and her mother lived next, and her mother took in sewing. Her mother wasn't well. She coughed a great deal and had a pain in her side, but she was always there when Jane came home from kindergarten, and then from grammar school. And nights when they went to bed early to save light her mother would talk to her, and give her many precepts and principles, wrapped in engaging stories, which she told her were to be remembered for life. And Jane had asked questions and gained a pretty good idea of life and the way it should be lived.

But she never remembered any time when the place they had to live in was so unbearably hot as this little room of hers. Perhaps she ought to give up saving for a nice winter coat and change her room for a cooler one. Perhaps—well perhaps she should have accepted that invitation to the shore for the night and got really cooled off and rested for once. No! She never could have done that of course. They were strangers, and she was only a poor girl whom they would have felt sorry for and despised. Probably the girl's mother would have been cross if she had brought her home, too. Of course she could not have gone with a stranger!

Well,—perhaps—was there any possibility she ought to have put her pride in her pocket and gone with that manager of the stocking department? Got a good dinner and had a little laugh and a restful time, and perhaps been able to sleep afterward? That was what other girls did, unless they had homes, pleasant comfortable homes, where there was some way to get cool in such intolerable heat.

No, she couldn't do that! Not if she died of starvation and heat would she go with a man who had a permanent wave, and held hands with all the pretty girls in the store, not even if she knew him. She couldn't respect a man like that.

Had her mother been right in giving her such high standards of taste and principle?

Yes, of course! There was no question about that.

After a time she got up and looked out her window. There wasn't much satisfaction in looking. She could only see a limited number of red brick walls and tin roofs and chimneys, with a high red distant glow as if the fire must have been a very bad one.

She touched her meager wash hanging across a string from the bureau to the post of the bed and found everything dry. That was a comfort anyway. She could wear fresh garments in the morning. One was always cooler after a bath, even if it was only a sponge bath, if one could put on fresh garments.

So she crept back to her hard hot bed, and finally fell asleep again, but woke in the morning only half refreshed. She could smell the breakfast fumes rolling up from the open kitchen window. Codfish on a morning like this! Blistering hot! And it was spoiled codfish too, it smelled that way! They had had it that way once before. The landlady always bought enough for two days of anything like that. Well, she would ask for a hard boiled egg. She would not take codfish!

If this heat lasted she must find a better place to board. It was unbearable to think of staying here any longer.

Then her little alarm clock whizzed out a warning and Jane got sadly up and went at the work of dressing.

Another hot day ahead of her, hard work, and nothing to relieve the monotony! Of course there was young Gaylord, the stocking manager. She might smile at him if she were that kind of girl, and perhaps he would ask her again to go out to dinner and somewhere for the evening. She was so utterly sick of the monotony of life in this awful little hot hole of a room, with no cheerful contacts anywhere except such as one could find among her department store customers.

Well, of course that was all nonsense! She wasn't going back on the principles her mother had taught her. She was going to go steadily on trying to do as nearly right as possible. And perhaps some day God would give her a break!

That sounded rather irreverent too. Mother wouldn't have liked her to talk like that. Mother always wanted her to go to church. But she had gotten out of the habit when mother was so terribly sick.

Then there had been the time after mother died, when great aunt Sybil, a widow who lived in Connecticut and had two summer places, one at the mountains and one at the shore, had sent for her and looked her over for a few weeks, finally fitting her out with some indiscriminate garments belonging to her two daughters who needed more fashionable wardrobes, and sent her off to a queer stupid school in the country where you worked for your board and learned very little. But great aunt Sybil had married again, and had shunted Jane off by getting her a place to do kitchen work on a farm where they kept summer boarders. The two daughters had meantime married and passed out of the picture. Then when fall came and the summer boarders had departed, the farmer and his wife bought a trailer, and left for Florida. Jane, obviously de trop, took matters in her own hands and hiked by slow stages to this city where she finally got a job in a department store where now at last she had a small foothold, faithfully doing her best, and working up from cash girl to notions, and from notions to buttons.

But this morning with the heat over everything, and the smell of the unappetizing breakfast coming up the stairs, Jane groaned within herself. Of course she was glad she had made some progress, but oh how long at this rate would it be before she ever had a decent place to call home? Would she ever have a home, a real home? Probably not. Other girls expected to get homes by marrying, but Jane felt she would never be willing to marry the kind of man who might ask her. She wasn't at all pretty, she told herself, as she gave a disapproving look in her mirror and slicked her hair coolly back. It was only pretty girls who attracted nice refined men who could provide comfortable homes. Homes where on a morning like this one could go calmly down to breakfast expecting to find cool melon set in ice, or thin glasses of orange juice, delicate hot biscuits, cereal with real cream, and coffee that was a joy to drink.

With a sigh Jane fastened the buttons of her thinnest shirtwaist dress and went downstairs to begin another hot day.

III

KENT HAVENNER walked into the office that morning and went straight to the senior member of the firm.

"Well, I've found a Jane Scarlett for you. Whether she's the right Jane or not I don't know, but she's a Scarlett, anyway. At least she says she is."

"You don't say!" said the senior lawyer who was J. Waltham Sanderson and quite well known and respected in the world. "Now how in the world did you go about it to find one after all our combing of the country failed?"

"Well, you see I didn't go about doing it at all. It wasn't my business of course. But I heard the name mentioned so many times in connection with that case that I couldn't get it out of my head, and when I heard my sister mention it quite casually last night it clicked of course."

"Your sister! Why, Havenner, does your sister know the girl?"

"Well, no, she's not a personal acquaintance at all, but she bought some buttons of her late yesterday afternoon at Windle and Harrower's."

"Why, that's most extraordinary! Had she known her before?"

"No, I think not. The girl looked tired and hot and my sister is always picking up friends in the most unexpected places. You see, she took a notion to the girl's looks or something and she asked her name. Or perhaps she was afraid she might have to return the buttons. Anyhow she asked her name, and it was so unusual that she told us about it when she got home."

"Well, that's most extraordinary!" said Mr. Sanderson. "Of course she may not be the right one as you say, but even at that it is encouraging to have found a Scarlett, for she or her family may be able to put us in touch with some other branch of the family. Scarlett, after all, is a most unusual name. And then again she *may* be a daughter or a niece of the Jane Scarlett for whom we are searching. Have you told Mr. Edsel?"

"No, I just got in," said Kent.

"Well, he ought to know at once. Edsel!" he called lifting his voice a trifle, as a man about forty-five entered the outer office. Mr. Edsel came in and stood beside the desk, a tall stern man with keen eyes, and hair silvering at the edges.

"Havenner here tells me he has found a Jane Scarlett," announced the senior lawyer.

The keen eyes searched Kent Havenner's face.

"Sure she's the right one?" he asked.

"Not at all," said Kent. "I haven't even seen her yet, only heard there is one."

"Well, I won't have time to do any investigating today. Not till I get back from Chicago. Why don't we let Havenner handle this himself?" he asked, looking at Sanderson. "I think he could find out what we want to know as well as I could."

"I was just going to suggest that," said Mr. Sanderson. "You really can't delay that Chicago matter even a train, and I think it is quite important that we find out at once whether this person is the right one, else she may vanish from our sight while we delay."

"That's all right with me," said Edsel. "I'll give you all the papers, Havenner, and I wish you good luck. If you find it is a false lead it won't be the first one we've had. I never supposed any color as bright as Scarlett could be so hard to find in broad daylight." He said it with a twinkle in his eyes. "I'll get you the data, Havenner, and if you can discover anything on this case nobody will be gladder than I."

So, a few minutes later, Kent Havenner, armed with the necessary credentials, and a paper containing questions that must be answered, started out to find Jane Scarlett.

He went to Mr. Windle first. He knew him personally, and moreover the name of the famous law firm which he represented would have given him a hearing anywhere in the city.

Mindful of his promise to his sister he was most careful about what he said:

"Mr. Windle, I'm not going to take your time. I know you're busy at this hour of the day. I've just come to you for permission to see one of your employees for about

five minutes. I think she may be able to give us a few
dates and names that will help us in our search for somebody. I won't keep her but a very few minutes. We just
want to make a contact with her."

"Delighted to serve you in any way we can, Mr. Havenner. What is her name?"

"Scarlett. Jane Scarlett. I have been told that she is at
the button counter. I could have gone there and searched
of course, but I wanted your permission to speak to her
during working hours. And we do not know her address
so we cannot go to her elsewhere."

Mr. Windle turned to his secretary.

"See if we have a Jane Scarlett at the button counter,
and ask them to send her up here. You know, Mr. Havenner, some of our salespeople are on vacation now at this
slack season. I hope she is here."

"I was told that someone saw her there yesterday. But
Mr. Windle, don't let us trouble you here. I can go down
and speak to her at the counter. It's only a few simple
questions I want to put to her."

"That's quite all right, Mr. Havenner. You can see her
as long as you wish right in the next room there, and it
won't upset our routine here in the least. Just step in
there and be seated and I'll send her in if she's in the
store today."

A moment later Jane Scarlett, white to the lips with
fear, presented herself at the chief's office.

She had turned faint with apprehension when the telephone call came for her to go at once to Mr. Windle's
office, and she had waited upon the customer she was
attending with frenzied haste, left the sale in the hands
of Nellie Forsythe who was languid and apathetic after
her picnic, and hurried wildly up the stairs, not delaying
even to wait for the elevator.

What could Mr. Windle want of her except to find
some fault with her work, or to dismiss her perhaps? And
what would she do if she lost her job? This time of year
jobs were almost impossible to find.

Her hand trembled so that she could scarcely open
the door.

But Mr. Windle was very affable. Could a man look
like that if he were going to fire a girl, she wondered?

"Are you Miss Jane Scarlett?" he asked, and his keen eyes seemed to search her face.

Jane took a deep breath and nodded. She couldn't summon her voice to speak.

"Well, Miss Scarlett, just step into this side room," he said. "A friend of mine wishes to ask you a few questions. He won't keep you long."

Jane turned wild eyes toward the strange young man and gripped her slender fingers together to quiet their trembling. Her lips were trembling too. She wondered if others could see that.

"Mr. Havenner, Miss Scarlett. He is of the law firm of Sanderson and Edsel."

Mr. Windle bowed and left them, partly closing the door behind him, but if he had just set up a machine gun before her for the young man's use he could not have frightened her any worse. A lawyer! What had she done that they should set a lawyer on her? Her quick mind reviewed all possibilities and her heart sank. Perhaps something valuable had been stolen and they suspected her. If they did what could she do? There wasn't a single person in this part of the country whom she could call upon to take her part or even give her advice. Even that poor little pauperized school where she had worked for her board, and where they might have given her a character, was not in session. She wouldn't know where to reach one of the teachers, or the dreary old principal.

"Oh God!" her heart cried wildly, and then she realized that she hadn't been keeping in very close touch with her mother's God and how could she expect Him to help her? So she stood there trembling.

But the young man was speaking courteously.

"Won't you sit down, Miss Scarlett," he said, and his eyes studied the girl before him in a veiled surprise. There was something fine in her face just as Audrey had said.

Jane gave him a startled look and sat down on the edge of a chair close at hand, her hands clasped nervously and her eyes alertly watching the stranger.

Kent Havenner smiled.

"You don't need to be disturbed," he said kindly, "I'm

only here to get your help in the matter of a few statistics. At least I'm hoping you'll be able to help."

Jane's mind darted about again through the unknown. Was someone else in trouble, and they were wanting to check up through her? But her anxiety was by no means relieved.

The young man was calmly taking out a notebook and pencil.

"Your name, please, full name, and residence?"

Jane answered in a quiet voice, that had in it such evidence of breeding that the young man lifted his eyes with a brief glance to her face, and there came to his own voice a touch of almost deference. He was recognizing that it was this quality in the girl that had attracted his usually particular sister.

As he wrote down her quiet answer he paused at the street address she had given, and looked up again before he set it down.

"Is this your home address," he asked, "or only where you are staying?"

Jane Scarlett answered quite impersonally in a disinterested colorless voice.

"It is a boarding house," she said.

"Then you are not living with your own people, your family?"

She gave him a swift searching glance, as if to wonder why he asked that question, as if almost to resent his trying to pry into her personal affairs. There was almost haughtiness in her reply.

"I have no family. They are all dead."

A kind of shame came into Kent Havenner's face.

"Oh, I beg your pardon! I'm sorry!" he said, and then wondered why he had felt that way. She was just a working girl, yet she seemed to have the power to make him feel himself an intruder in her affairs.

She gave him a level look and then her gaze turned toward the open window.

"This routine business of statistics leads into annoying questions sometimes, I'm afraid," he apologized. "But now would you be so good as to give me the names of your father and mother?"

Jane's voice was steady as she answered:

"My father was John Ravenal Scarlett, and my mother was Miriam Warrener."

"Would you happen to remember dates, or approximate dates of their births, marriage and deaths, and where they were living?"

Her brow was instantly thoughtful, and slowly, with careful pronouncement she gave the answers.

"Thank you," said the questioner, "that helps. And your grandfather Scarlett. Do you remember his name?"

"Josiah Scarlett," said Jane easily. "He lived to be ninety-two. I can just remember him when I was a child. He must have been born about—" she hesitated and then gave a year. "I'm sorry I can't be accurate about it."

"Oh, that is near enough," said Kent Havenner, his pen jotting down the items in his notebook. "Now, was your father an only child or were there other brothers and sisters?"

"There was a sister Jessica who died when she was a child, and a younger brother Harold who left home and went abroad somewhere after my father was married. He lived abroad for several years, but after my father died my mother read one day in a paper that he had returned to this country."

"You don't know where he lived when he came back?"

"No," said Jane. "We never heard."

"Then you were not in touch with him? You couldn't give give a clue as to where we might hope to communicate with him?"

"No," said Jane. "I do not even know if he is living. I only know he did not go back to the old home. It might have been sold. I do not know. And anyhow my mother said he would not be likely to live in a plain country place. He liked gaiety."

"Your mother never tried to get in touch with him?"

"Oh, no," said the girl, her chin lifting with just that shade of haughtiness again. "My mother was proud. And she had never known him very well. She went back to the west where she had grown up. I'm afraid that's about all I can tell you of the Scarletts. I've sort of drifted off by myself since mother died."

He gave her another keen approving glance and smiled, and in spite of her she liked his smile.

"You've given me quite a lot of help," he said pleasantly. "If I need anything more I'll come back. There isn't any other cousin or relative that might give me information about that Harold Scarlett, is there?"

Jane thoughtfully shook her head.

"I don't think so. There's a great aunt, Sybil Anthony, the child of grandfather's second wife but he had a quarrel with her. Still, she always seems to be able to find out things. She's married again. She is Mrs. Anthony. I can give you her address."

"Suppose you do," said the young man. "Write it here in my notebook."

Jane wrote in a clear hand, and the young man watched her while she did it, studying the sweet profile, the lean line of cheek and lip and chin, the dark circles under the big tired eyes. If ever a girl looked as if she needed someone to care for her this one did. Why, she would be beautiful if she weren't so pale and tired looking. He hoped Audrey would not forget her threat to bring the girl out to the shore and show her a good time. He had a feeling that he was under obligation to her for having put her through this questionnaire, and yet of course that was absurd.

She handed the book back with the address. "That's where she was when last I knew," she said, and lifted her eyes for an instant to his, wondering why he dimly reminded her of someone who had left a pleasant memory.

"Well, I thank you," he said rising. "You've made my work easy."

She allowed herself a faint little impersonal smile.

"I'm glad if it helped," she said perfunctorily, and wondered why she had a feeling that this was a pleasant little interval. This man was a gentleman, and it rested one to come into touch with real gentlemen.

"And now," said Kent, "may I call on you again for help if other questions develop?"

She lifted startled eyes.

"Why, of course," she said simply, and turned away back to her button counter again, a vague alarm stirring in the back of her mind.

IV

THE floor manager of her section had arrived at the button counter with an irate woman calling loudly for salesperson number fifty-one, just as Jane came back. The glint in the floor manager's eye warned Jane that he was due to misunderstand her if he possibly could. "Miss Scarlett, did you sell this lady this set of clasps yesterday?" he asked fixing a severe glance upon her and showing by his manner that the lady in question was a most important person and not to be angered or annoyed in any way.

Jane gave a quick look at the woman and recognized her as a trying customer who had insisted upon seeing every clasp in the place before making her choice. She glanced at the clasps and saw that one was broken clear in two. Now, what was this woman trying to do? Those clasps had all been perfect when they left her hand yesterday morning.

"Yes, Mr. Clark, I sold the lady the clasps," admitted Jane quietly.

"Well, how do you account for this broken one in the lot? Mrs. LeClaire tells me that when she took the clasps out of the box this one fell apart.

Jane lifted honest eyes to her floor manager's face.

"Those clasps were all perfect when they left my inspection, Mr. Clark," said Jane honestly.

"Oh, yes, of course I knew she would say that!" exclaimed the lady. "The truth of the matter was she was impatient to go on talking with one of the other saleswomen, impatient because I took so long to decide. You see this wasn't at all the style of clasp I was looking for. I wanted something far better, more smart looking you know, but this girl insisted she didn't have anything better, and kept persuading me that these were the very latest. To tell you the truth I had a feeling all the time that she was simply too lazy to look for something else and wanted to get rid of me. And she certainly must have known this clasp was broken."

Jane was white with anger but her lips were untrembling.

"Have you forgotten, madam, that I laid the clasps out for you in a row on your piece of goods so that you could see how they would look? Don't you remember that they were all perfect then?"

Jane's eyes were very dark and they looked straight into the eyes of the other angry woman.

"You're mistaken," said the customer. "You only laid two of the clasps out. The rest were in the box."

Jane met the other angry eyes an instant and then she lifted her gaze to the floor manager's.

"I had them all out, Mr. Clark. You can ask Miss Forsythe if I didn't. She came and looked at them and admired them on the material."

"Yes, that's right," said Nellie Forsythe softly, nodding to Mr. Clark. "I counted them."

"Oh yes, those two would stick up for each other!" sneered the customer. "I never saw it to fail."

"Besides, the wrapper would have gone over each one carefully, Mr. Clark," reminded Jane.

Mr. Clark gathered up the sales slip and clasps and went back of the counter to consult with the wrapper, and Jane slipped into her place behind the counter and went to work, waiting on another customer, uncomfortably conscious of the snort of disapproval and the sneering expression that the woman of the clasps cast upon her. What was the matter with this new day? Everything was the matter! And it was going to be another scorcher, too! Oh, everything was wrong!

The floor manager came out from behind the wrapper's counter apologetically, and led the irate clasp lady aside for an earnest talk, his face suave but firm. Jane could catch a word now and then.

"They are lying of course, both those girls!" said the clasp woman furiously. "They ought to be dismissed, both of them!"

Jane lifted cold tired eyes and gave one glance at the woman. What hell on earth one misguided mistaken woman could make for a poor salesgirl. She didn't care for herself. She could pay for the clasp, though she knew the woman herself must have broken it, but she couldn't stand the thought that the little wrapper would have to bear the expense. The wrapper had a sick mother and a baby brother with a curvature of the spine, and her tiny salary was sometimes all that came into the household from week to week. Hilda shouldn't have to bear it anyway. She shut her lips in a firm determined line. She would go to Mr. Clark after this pest of a woman was gone and tell him all about how hateful the woman had been, insisting that there must be something different hidden away that they didn't want to bother to show her. She would offer to take the blame rather than have Hilda have to bear it. Poor Hilda. She could see the fear in her eyes, and a furtive tear, as she passed the little alcove where Hilda wrapped packages all day long.

The other girls at the counter cast pitying glances at Jane's grim countenance.

"You should worry!" said Nellie Forsythe as she brushed by her to get the drawer of white pearl buttons. "Don't let that old Clark get your goat! He's only trying to toady to that high flier. Isn't she the limit! I've seen her kind before. She just wants to make trouble. She's no lady! I'll bet she broke it herself and didn't want to pay for it. Some of those millionaires are just too stingy to live. I'd like to see 'em poor themselves for a little while."

Jane cast a fleeting pale smile toward her unexpected champion and went on her busy way through the morning.

At noon she sought out the floor manager.

"Mr. Clark," she said a little breathlessly, "I came about that broken clasp. I didn't break it and neither did Hilda, but if anybody's got to stand for it I will, not Hilda. She can't! She's got a sick mother and little brother to support and she's half starved herself."

"Somebody broke that clasp, Miss Scarlett," said the cold hard tones of Clark. He was new in the department and trying to show what good discipline he could establish. "Somebody has to pay for it."

"Yes," said Jane with that almost imperceptible lifting of her chin that gave her a patrician look, "somebody evidently broke it, but it was not broken when I gave the

package to Mrs. LeClaire. I know that for I stood beside
Hilda while she inspected each one. The lady was in a rush
as she always is and I waited to take it right to her. And
I know those clasps were every one perfect when they left
this house. But Hilda shan't stand the blame, anyway.
She's crying her heart out this minute and won't be fit to
work tomorrow if this goes on. And she can't afford to
stay at home!"

The cold hard eyes of the floor manager studied her
sharply and the tight line of his lips relaxed a trifle.

"Very well, Miss Scarlett, I'll speak to Mr. Windle
about it. You understand that Mrs. LeClaire is a very important customer. But of course somebody has to pay for
that clasp."

Jane gave Mr. Clark a despairing look and bowed,
trying to choke back her rising indignation.

"Very well, Mr. Clark. In that case I'll pay for it!"

She turned away quickly lest the telltale tears would
appear in her eyes, and hurried off leaving him looking
after her, wondering over her erect carriage, the patrician
way in which she held her shoulders. Somehow she impressed him even more than the irate customer whom he
had to humor because of her millions. Still, if Jane Scarlett
broke that buckle she ought to suffer for it.

So Jane went out and bought a five cent package of
peanut butter sandwiches, although she loathed them because she had eaten so many of them exclusive of other
fare, and took a good draught of ice water afterwards,
and determined to eat five cent lunches for a couple of
weeks to make up for the price of that crystal clasp.

But there were too many tears in Jane's throat to make
a dry lunch like that very palatable just now and Jane,
after a bite or two slipped her package in her little cheap
handbag and went around on what she called a window-
shopping expedition, just to take her mind off the unpleasant things.

She went to the coat section and took another look at
the green coat with the brown beaver fur collar that she
so hoped to be able to buy before it was gone. She
wouldn't get on very fast saving for it at this rate, not
with paying for expensive crystal clasps. There! She must

forget that. Why in the world couldn't she put it out of her mind entirely and just be comfortable?

It was just then she realized that there was something else on her mind besides that broken clasp. She searched probingly for it and found it was the visit of that young man searching for statistics about the Scarlett family. The more she thought about it the more she became alarmed at the thought that he might be coming after her again. Why hadn't she made it plain that she had told him everything she knew about the family? Oh, what else could he possibly be wanting? Was there something dark and sinister in the history of the family and were they trying to pin it to her branch? Were they possibly trying to pin something upon herself?

Her mind went quickly back over her brief life since her mother died. Was it conceivable that somebody at the school or the boarding house where she had worked had missed something valuable and fixed upon her as the one who had taken it?

But how ridiculous! It was just because of that unpleasant happening about the clasp. She must be all wrought up, to get up ideas like that. And that pleasant young man hadn't suggested any such thing either. What had he said, anyway? Something about collecting statistics about the Scarletts. But a lawyer's firm wouldn't be getting up a family tree, would they? Oh, it was all a mix up. And what could she do about it?

She turned languidly away from the lovely green coat. Why had she thought it so desirable anyway? How hot the cloth looked! And fur around one's neck! Ugh! She closed her eyes and drew a deep quivering breath. Suddenly she seemed to have reached her limit. Everything had gone against her. If only her mother were living and she could go home and put her head down in her lap and cry it out, and tell her everything!

Well, of course it was idle to think of that! It only meant she would be unnerved for her afternoon's work. Oh, how her head ached and how faint she felt! She must manage to eat another bite or two of those crackers, or drink some more water, or something.

Just then she came face to face with the young head of

the stocking department, and his greeting was most effusive.

"Now, look who's here!" he exclaimed. "Could anything be more delightful! I was just looking for a companion to help me while away my noon hour."

"Sorry," said Jane in her most businesslike tone, "I'm just finishing mine. You'll have to look farther."

"But surely I saw you just leaving the button counter not five minutes ago!" protested the young man.

"Are you quite sure you know me from the others?" asked Jane impishly as she turned and slid into an elevator.

As the elevator slipped smoothly down out of sight Jane made a mental resolve to watch herself when homing time came at night, and not be in this young man's way. She didn't want her life further complicated at this stage by this doubtful stranger. She wasn't at all sure she would care to have him around at any time.

So she entrenched herself behind her counter and kept her eyes strictly on her customers of whom there were plenty. She didn't even see young Gaylord when he arrived back at his precinct. She was trying her best to keep so busy that she would not think nor puzzle over her perplexities.

"Oh, are you back already?" welcomed the next girl whose turn it was to take lunch time. "Why, you haven't had your full time."

"I wasn't hungry," said Jane evasively. "Yes madam, we have crystal buttons. What size?"

"Oh, do you really mean it?" questioned the other girl in a whisper. "I was just counting the minutes. A friend of mine has something to tell me and she was afraid her noon hour would be over before mine began. Do you mind if I go now?"

"Go on," said Jane with a satisfaction in her voice that would easily pass for a smile. Jane had forgotten to take the second bite of those neat dry crackers. The faintness that was enveloping her now and then was something primitive, something to be fought and kept under. After all, why should she miss one little meal? She had often gone without several without feeling it much. One got used to going without food. "Yes madam, we have a smaller size of the same button."

The customers were coming in droves, it seemed to her. Why did everybody want buttons on such a hot day? She tried to focus her eyes on a woman who was questioning her, and realized that she was dizzy. What was the matter with her? She wasn't ever dizzy. Was everything getting her? Was she going soft so that she'd be unable to cope with life as it presented itself to her day by day? Of course she hadn't eaten much that morning,—that sickening smell of spoiled codfish over everything! Ugh! She could smell it now! Or was that the lobster she had glimpsed on the chef's long table by the tearoom door a little while ago? If she were up in that tearoom now as a shopper selecting her fare from the menu what would she choose? Not lobster! Not codfish! Not even ice cream! She was beyond all that. Just something hot and thin and heartening. The kind of lunch her mother used to bring her when she was a little girl, and sick. Fragrant toast from homemade bread, buttered and salted and wet with boiling water, and then a steaming cup of tea that smelled like roses. That was what she wanted and nothing else. Could a body be sustained by the thought of the right food when one couldn't actually get it?

She smiled to herself at the queer vagaries of her troubled mind. If her customers could read her thoughts they would think she was crazy. If her floor manager could know what was passing through her mind she would lose her job.

But her mind continued to function steadily on, her fingers worked accustomedly, and the buttons were marshaled into ranks and went out into the world to appear on costumes. But Jane was growing fainter and fainter, and the heat grew more and more unbearable to her till it came to seem as if she could not breathe another breath. Yet she went on, answering the questions lifelessly that were put to her.

It was growing late in the afternoon. She could just see the clock from one end of the counter but somehow suddenly its figures did not mean a thing to her when she looked at them. She put a hand dazedly to her forehead and tried to take a deep breath, but something failed within her, and all at once she crumpled into a little heap on the floor behind the counter.

She had just handed a customer a package, and the woman had turned away. The other two girls were busy one at either end of the counter, and did not notice Jane for a full minute after it happened, and she lay there quite still till one of them coming in haste to look for wooden buttons almost fell over her, and gave a quiet alarm to the floor manager.

The wrapper in her little alcove abandoned her wrapping and was down on her knees beside Jane with a glass of water she had slipped into her cage, and a bit of a handkerchief, bathing Jane's face, when Mr. Clark came blustering to see what was the matter, his fault-finding frown upon his face as if he would be ready to blame Jane for not foreseeing this possibility and guarding against it.

But when he saw Jane's white impassive face even his Clark-frown disappeared and he blustered at all the others, giving orders right and left. The few customers left stood around staring and saying what awful weather it was, and stretching their necks to see which girl it was who had fainted. One lady produced a bottle of smelling salts. And after a time, which seemed a long time, Jane vaguely opened her eyes and closed them again with a sorrowful little trembling sigh, and all the ladies on that aisle looked and said "Oh!" in various stages of sympathy and interest and curiosity.

A boy presently brought a wheeled chair, as even Mr. Clark could not seem to induce Jane to take an interest in walking, and they wheeled her off to the freight elevator, Nellie Forsythe walking importantly by her side with her hand on the chair, and Mr. Clark circling around it and giving directions, clearing the way with authoritative gestures.

But the passing of Jane took but a brief instant and then the summer crowds closed in and the aisle was as full as usual, only that the ladies who wanted buttons tapped their impatient toes on the floor and wondered why the button counter was manned by a single girl.

Young Gaylord on the stocking side of the main aisle looked tentatively over to the button counter several times late that afternoon, with a view to dating up Jane, wholly because she had seemed so indifferent, but Jane was not in sight. She had meant to slip out through the counter back of the wrapping desk, and so make her way to a street door without his seeing her, but she had no need for diplomacy. It had all been managed nicely for her instead. Jane was lying in a little white soft bed in the hospital of the store on the ninth floor, with a white garbed nurse watching over her, and an electric fan cooling the air about her.

The nurse was feeling her pulse.

"When was your lunch hour?" she asked crisply.

"Eleven-thirty," murmured Jane, wondering why she cared.

"What did you have for lunch?" asked the nurse in a quiet interested voice as if she were saying to a baby: "See the birdie?"

"Why, I didn't have much. It's in my handbag somewhere," said Jane feeling aimlessly around on the bed with one hand. "I didn't eat but a bite. I wasn't hungry." Her voice was very weak.

"I thought so," said the nurse. She vanished into a tiny kitchen from whence came presently an appetizing odor, and then she was back with a cup of delicious chicken broth which she fed to Jane.

"There!" said the nurse when she had finished feeding her the soup. "Now, shut your eyes and take a good sleep. Then they'll send you home in a taxi, and tomorrow morning if it is still hot I'd stay in bed all day. They won't expect you back. I'll tell them you ought to have three days off at least."

"Oh, I couldn't!" said Jane, roused at last. "I couldn't afford to lose time."

"You have a right to three days' sick leave, you know," said the nurse. "I'll tell them you should."

"Oh, I'll be all right with just a few minutes' rest," said Jane and drifted off into the most restful sleep she had had for months.

The trumpets were sounding the signal for closing when Jane woke up again, and the nurse fed her more soup and took her home in a taxi.

"I hope you have a cool room," she remarked hopefully as she glanced doubtfully up at the dismal looking boarding house.

"I haven't," said Jane decidedly. "You wouldn't expect it in a house like that in this neighborhood, would you?"

"No, I suppose not," said the nurse regretfully, "but why do your people live here when there are so many nice little suburbs where you could live almost as cheaply, I should think? Do they have to be here? Do they own the house?"

"I haven't any people," said Jane trying to speak resignedly. "This is a boarding house. I suppose somebody owns it, but I don't know why."

"Then why do you stay here?" asked the nurse. "I know a peach of a place. It's eleven miles out and it isn't expensive. It's co-operative."

"There'd be the carfare in," said Jane despondently. "It sounds nice but I guess it's not for me, yet. Not till I get a raise."

"Well, I'm sorry," said the nurse. "If I wasn't going away for the week-end I'd invite you out to stay with me over Sunday. You need a change and a rest or you're due for a breakdown."

"Oh, I think I'll be all right tomorrow," said Jane determinedly. "I've got to be. Tomorrow's pay day, and I've got to pay a dollar and a quarter for a crystal clasp a customer broke herself and then charged me with."

"What a shame!" said the nurse indignantly. "I think if you'd go to Mr. Windle he'd do something about that."

"I'd rather pay a dollar and a quarter than go to Mr. Windle. Good-bye. I thank you for all you've done for me! And for that wonderful soup. It seemed like soup my mother used to make!"

"Well, my advice to you is to go home, wherever home is and stay with your mother."

"Yes?" said Jane somewhat bitterly. "Well, perhaps I will. Who knows? She happens to be in heaven though, and one can't just go to heaven when one feels like it. But meantime I wish I had a lovely cool room with palms and ferns around it and a view of the ocean with cool breezes to invite you up to right now. I'd serve you with delectable cakes and ices and make you understand how grateful I am for what you've done for me."

The nurse smiled and squeezed her hand.

"I'm sorry," she said penitently, "I didn't know, of course. Now don't forget to run up to the hospital room and call on me when you get back to the store. Good night. Be careful what you eat for a day or two, and no more starving, understand, or you'll be worse off than you are now."

Jane smiled and went slowly into the house.

How she dreaded to go up all those stairs. And there was ham for dinner. She knew by the smell. Ham and cabbage again! So she decided to subsist on the memory of the chicken soup and go to sleep at once if the heat would let her.

Up in her room she took off her dress and dropped down weakly upon the bed. Oh, if there were only a way to have a pleasant comfortable room and plain decent food! Well, if she lived through this she would try to manage a change as soon as possible.

Then her thoughts reverted to the morning. The interview with the young lawyer. The man with the kind eyes. He would be somewhere now in a cool place she was sure. He would be about to have a good dinner with pleasant people. He had the atmosphere of such a background. Any girl he knew would be well cared for and wouldn't have to worry. He wasn't the kind of young man who drank and was undependable. How she would enjoy it to have a few friends like that who were decent and friendly and good fun. Well, she mustn't expect anything like that, but if ever she got on at all she would have something to call home. A room in a pleasant house in a wide airy street no matter if it wasn't fashionable. Old fashions were best anyway. Brick perhaps, with high ceilings and vines on the house. Wide windows and pretty curtains. Cool in summer and warm in winter. A little fireplace somewhere with the brightness and comfort of firelight! A canary in a pretty gilt cage. But how could she have a canary if she stayed in the store? A canary would have to have someone to care for it.

She would have a pretty rug. Perhaps not an oriental, but one with soft colors. And a bookcase with books she loved. A desk to sit and write letters at, only she knew no one to write to, and a little table to have five o'clock tea on with frosted cakes, when her friends came in! Only she had no friends!

But of course there would be friends if one had a place to invite them to.

There would be deep chairs, too, with soft cushions, and a couch where one could drop down and read and get all the ache out of one's bones. Home! It would be a home! Even if it were but one room it could be home.

Well, if one could make a home out of one room why could she not make a semblance of home here in this third story back?

Here with the smell of cabbage and ancient ham? With the noises of the street, and the thunder of the railroad beyond the back fence? Well, why not? It had four walls. What if they were blackened with smoke, and stained from their years of service? They were clean, for she had washed them down herself when she first moved in. Here with only a box for a wash stand and a tin pitcher and bowl that did not match. There was a calico curtain around it for she had tacked it there herself, and underneath were her other pair of shoes that needed to be half-soled, and her shoe polish and her dust rag. And there was the ugly painted bureau with its paint half gone, and its warped distorted mirror that needed resilvering. It had four drawers where she could keep her simple wardrobe. Some hall bedrooms hadn't even that. And over there in the corner around the nails on which she hung her garments there was another calico curtain. She had bought it and hemmed it and put it up herself. She was thankful for that. It did make her room more like a habitation. Even if it was unbearably hot and smelly in summer and unbearably cold and lonely in winter. It had a touch all her own. But some day she would have a real home that she had made. That is, if she lived long enough to have one. It would take hard work. It would mean that she had to concentrate on a home and nothing else. So far there was no one to make a home for her, and she was sure, sure she would never find a man she was willing to marry who would want to marry her, so why not have a home as a life ambition?

When she dropped down on her hard little bed words came to her mind that she had learned when a child:

"In my Father's house are many mansions. If it were not so I would have told you. I go to prepare a place for you. And if I go and prepare a place for you I will come again and receive you unto myself, that where I am there ye may be also."

And then it came to her that perhaps that was the only home she would ever have. Perhaps the nurse had been right and she was really run down. Perhaps she wasn't going to live very long and was going Home to the many mansions, to where her mother was, to her Father's House!

She closed her eyes and drifted off to sleep, and over and over there rang the words in her ears:

"In my Father's house are many mansions!"

Mansions, not just hall bedrooms!

When she awoke later in the evening she was gasping with the heat, and she stumbled up and dipped a towel in water, hanging it in her window to cool the air a little.

"In my Father's house! My Father's house!"

V

MR. CLARK, the floor manager, was worried at the ghastly
look in Jane's white face. He carried the memory of her
eyes and the look in them with him as he went away from
the freight elevator. Was that girl taking it to heart like
that about the crystal clasp? Perhaps she didn't break it
after all.

He went and hunted up Hilda and made her cry again
asking her questions, till he didn't know but he was about
to precipitate another collapse in the button department.
So in desperation he told her not to worry any more, that
Jane had offered to pay for it, but he would fix it so that
neither of them would have to do it. It was unprecedented,
such generosity from Mr. Clark. Hilda dried her eyes and
beamed out a watery smile at him and to his amazement
he felt a twinge of something new in his experience. Was
it joy? It didn't seem possible. He didn't know joy ever
came from acts that were not done for one's self. Perhaps
he would try it again sometime if he didn't forget it. Well,
anyway he would settle once for all about that clasp. So
he took a dollar and a quarter out of his own pocket and
went up to the credit department and adjusted the matter
so it would never come up again to trouble anybody. Of
course Mrs. LeClaire herself should have paid it, but as it
was he suddenly felt himself rise far above the millionaire
lady in his own esteem. He hadn't suspected himself of
having such generous qualities, and he left the store quite
pleased with himself. He went home and gave his little
three-year-old a whole dime to put in the Sunday School
collection and his wife looked at him in amazement and
asked him if he really felt well.

That night there were other supper tables besides the
Clark one, where Jane's eventful day made a difference.
The nurse had been invited to dine with an old school
friend in a beautiful house where everything was ordered
and cool and delightful. The friend's father and mother
were present and the talk was general.

38

"I had a young patient today who interested me greatly," said the nurse. "She was overcome by the heat and was sent up to me. I found she had had no lunch and I imagine scarcely any breakfast. I fed her soup, and petted her up, and took her home when the store closed. But I found the poor thing lives in the most unspeakable neighborhood. Noisy and dirty and crowded. A boarding house of the worst possible type. How she is going to survive till cool weather I don't see. It's a crime to own a place like that boarding house. It ought to be pulled down, and nice cool livable quarters made for poor folks."

Her friend and her mother expressed sympathy for the poor girl and wished they could do something for her. The head of the house asked a few chary questions, for he had great possessions, mostly in tenement property, and an atrophied conscience got up and stirred within him. He told himself that he didn't know but he would do something about some of his property sometime.

Kent Havenner came home to the seashore and grinning announced to his sister:

"Well, I interviewed your glamorous button-vender today!" He said it in a low tone while the hostile cousin was telling their mother about her experiences that afternoon at the Woman's Club.

"Yes?" said Audrey quickly alert. "How did you find her?"

"Haughty!" said Kent. "She answered my questions as briefly as possible and walked back to her work."

"Kent, you didn't annoy her in any way?" His sister studied him searchingly.

"Well, I'm not sure," twinkled Kent. "I think I got her guessing toward the end."

"Kent, you promised me!"

"Did I? What did I say?"

Then came the cousin:

"What are you two saying? Am I missing something?" she attacked playfully, in a kittenish manner she had.

"Yes, you are," said Kent with a wicked grin. "You always miss something when you fail to hear what I say!" and he sauntered provokingly out of the room.

And the two girls, her fellow workwomen at the button

counter talked her over as they walked part way home
that night.

"Did you know she was called up to the office this
morning?" said Nellie.

"*No!* Was she? Don't you suppose it was about that
silly old crystal clasp?"

"No, it was before that LeClaire woman came in. A
boy from Mr. Windle's office came down to call her. I
heard him. 'Mr. Windle wants to see you in his private
office!' Just like that! And she turned as white as white
—! Who is she anyway? Where did she work before she
came to our store? She's mighty close-mouthed, I think."

"I don't know. Somewhere up in New England, she
said. Maybe Boston. I forget. But if you ask me, *I* think
she's a perfectly grand girl."

"Oh, but they never would send for her to Mr. Windle's
office unless something was wrong. You can better believe
they've found something crooked, or else she's been careless."

"She isn't careless. She's very conscientious."

"Well, say, she didn't faint for nothing this afternoon,
did she? There must have been something pretty awful
or she wouldn't have passed out that easy."

"Say, look here, it's been pretty awfully hot, and she's
been here all summer when you and I were off having a
good time at the shore."

"Well, we didn't any of us pass out for the heat, did
we? It's my opinion she had some good reason for flop-
ping, if you ask me."

"Maybe she did. I'm sure I don't know. But it's none
of our business unless she tells us, and anyhow I like her.
She's a good scout. She sold some buttons to a good
customer of mine who asked for me, and she charged
them up as if *I'd* sold them. I'll say that was pretty white
of her when I was off on vacation."

"Who told you?" said Nellie suspiciously. "Did she
tell you herself? Because I'd check up on it if she did.
That sounds pretty phony to me."

"No, she didn't tell me. Miss Leech at the desk told
me. She said she came and asked her how to give me the
credit, because she knew the woman always bought from
me. But anyhow I like her, and if I were you I wouldn't

be so hard on another girl. You can't tell what kind of a fix you or I might get into, at that."

"I never do anything I'll get caught at!" said the other sullenly.

"Still you might even at that, and then you wouldn't want the rest of us to be hard on you. I think we ought to stick by each other. The work's hard and the pay's small. And anyhow you know Jane Scarlett has always been square."

"Well, yes, she makes it appear that way of course. I'm sure I hope she's all right. But it always makes me jittery to have anything happen like this afternoon. I'd hate to faint. One always looks so washed out and unhealthy. Of course she would anyway without any make-up. I wonder why she doesn't use any?"

"Oh, she hasn't got on to being smart yet, that's all. She'd really be stunning with that dark hair and her big blue eyes if she'd get her hair done now and then. She acts as if she doesn't care how she looks."

The two girls separated at the subway after agreeing that Jane didn't know how to dress, and went on to their separate paths.

But Jane lay in her little hard white bed in her third story back and slept.

And in the night when she stirred and turned over and sighed deeply she kept hearing a voice far away saying:

"In my Father's house are many mansions. I go to prepare a place for you."

VI

THE old Scarlett house was high and wide and comfortable. It was built of brick with a hall through the middle. It had wide low stairs with white spindles and a mahogany rail, the kind of staircase that antique lovers rave over. It curled around at the top and made a lovely line of itself, with a nook beneath where a great old mahogany couch with claw legs and rich upholstery nestled. In front of the stairs there was a rare hall table highly polished, where many notable hats had reposed in time past. And over it hung a handsome mirror.

The front door was one of the finest specimens of the old time doors with fanlights above, and a knocker of brass that would have been a valued museum piece.

On either side of the front door there were rooms, one on the left extending the full depth of the house with a full length mirror at front and back between the windows. There was an old-fashioned square piano with a mother-of-pearl floral design above the keyboard, on which the generations of Scarlett children had learned to play, and there were some fine old portraits in oil of distinguished Scarlett men and women. The furniture was beautiful old wood of satin polish, the work of some of the old masters in design. The fabrics which covered the chairs were well-preserved silk brocades of quaint pattern, and there were charming tables and chairs and sofas scattered about.

Across the hall from the front room was a library, furnished with leather chairs and a sofa, a fine old secretary, and rare prints.

The dining room was back of that, with a sideboard that would make treasure-seekers gasp with joy, and a whole dinner set of willow pattern, not a piece missing. The spacious cupboard contained much fine old glass and other interesting pieces, and the kitchen that was housed in a deep gable at the back spoke of years of plenty, in pleasant working quarters.

Upstairs there were five big bedrooms, and two bathrooms that had been added in later years, with an attic overhead that looked like a fairy tale out of the past. Spinning wheels and old chairs, haircloth trunks and chests of drawers. It would be a joy just to rummage in that attic. And in one corner under the eaves, an old table of the kind known as a "stand" on which reposed an ancient Bible with a full record of all the Scarlett births and marriages and deaths. Someone had covered it with a piece of dark muslin to keep off the dust. But that was all. The years had come and gone, and the precious record of a family that had been honored in its time, lay there carelessly unguarded except by a bit of cheap calico that had once been part of a common kitchen apron!

And in that Bible record there was a name set down:

"Jane Scarlett, born to John Ravenal Scarlett, and Miriam Warrener Scarlett April 17th, 19—"

The old house stood in the shadow of great trees, shrouded in thick ivy, its fireplaces empty and dead, its rooms without inhabitant, save for a temeritous mouse or two that ventured in now and then and finding no food hurried away.

And Jane Scarlett, the last of the Scarletts in direct line, lay sleeping desolately in a hard little bed in the third story hall bedroom of the cheapest boarding house she had been able to find.

There was myrtle growing around the edges of the yard, and lilacs overshadowing the wide back porch. The grass was neatly kept and the hedges trimmed by arrangement with the caretakers of the estate, but the garden had run wild, growing weeds and flowers and vegetables at will in one bewildering mass.

Out under a great elm tree an old swing hung, where all the little Scarletts had swung to their heart's content during the years. It needed only a new rope to make it swingable again. And out at one side of the lawn a rustic summer house still stood, repaired occasionally by the caretaker, where the Scarlett girls used to have afternoon tea with their friends. But there was one Scarlett girl who had never been so privileged. Five o'clock teas had never come her way.

There was a gravel driveway from the old barn where once upon a time high-spirited horses were stabled, and victorias and surreys and phaetons rolled proudly down to the stepping stone in front. Then the family got in and drove away. And of later years various cars used by more modern members of the clan took their place. But now the stable was empty and clean. One or two old harnesses and bridles still hung from hooks in the wall. A collection of whips lay on a high dusty shelf, hard pressed by empty oil cans of a later date. And the tool house, just behind the barn, though it still held hoes and shovels and spades galore, was huddled and disorderly, everything pushed back to make way for a couple of modern lawn mowers. It all reminded of nothing better than a well-kept cemetery, giving respect and honor to the past, but meaning nothing whatever to the present but a memorial.

So it had stood for the past seven or eight years while the last owner, Harold Scarlett, had traveled from place to place abroad, at first seeking pleasure, and finally searching for health.

There had been a caretaker all this time who kept the outside of the place immaculate, and whose wife had gone through the gesture of cleaning the inside of the house after a fashion twice every year. But the house had an unloved look, like a dog whose master was dead. It did not seem to belong any more to the cheerful street of pleasant houses on which it was located.

Once, years ago, Jane Scarlett had been taken to that house when she was a very little girl to visit her grandmother who was very old. She retained only a dim memory of a sweet old lady with a crumpled face, kindly eyes, and hands that were startlingly soft and hot and vivid when they touched her.

But she remembered the big old house among the trees as the grandest mansion she had ever seen. At least the grandest she had ever entered. And when she heard of "In my Father's house" she always pictured the many mansions as looking like the ivy-clad brick Scarlett house, and hoped to see more of it in heaven.

The house was located in a place called "Hawthorne," from the many hawthorne trees in the countryside. It was a suburb of a great city, the name of which the child Jane never heard in connection with the house. The old home was always at Hawthorne. But Hawthorne had since become a part of the city itself, and the name Hawthorne was only commonly known through its broad avenue on which the house was located. Perhaps if Jane had known definitely where this dream-mansion was located she might have started out to find it when she drifted on her own and went to find a home and a job. But being only in a vague place called Hawthorne, with the likelihood that it had long ago been sold and thus obliterated from things belonging to herself and her family, it had never occurred to her as possible to go and see it. Moreover her going had depended largely upon chance. She had started out to get away from the country boarding place in whose kitchen she was no longer needed. Heaven had seemed too far away then to hunt for one of the many mansions for her immediate need. So it had never occurred to her that when she found the job at Windle and Harrower's store, she might not be so far away from the starting place of her family. As she lay in her hot room in her narrow bed and tried to be thankful for such blessings as she had, it never occurred to her that the old house where her grandfather, and her great grandfather Scarlett had lived was not many miles away from the place where she was lying.

But even if she had known it, it would not have made any practical difference in her situation.

She was almost dropping off to sleep when she heard footsteps lagging up the stairs. The strangeness of it startled her awake again. The forlorn woman who helped in the kitchen roomed up there, with her slatternly daughter who waited on table. But neither of them would be coming up to bed now. They hadn't finished the dinner dishes.

But the steps came on and paused at her door, and she held her breath and listened. Then there was a hesitating tap. Then again, more insistent.

"Who is it?" Jane managed to ask.

"It's me," the landlady answered belligerently. "I just wanted to find out what's the idea of your staying away from meals this way? Was you expecting to take it off what you'll owe me at the first of the week? You wasn't down to dinner last night nor tonight, and I can't afford to buy good meat and things and then not get paid for them. Besides, if you're coming down you oughtta come on time, and not expect me to keep vittles hot for ya all night. All the other boarders have et and gone. I thought mebbe you'd got asleep and didn't know you was lettin' the meal hour go by."

"Oh, I'm sorry, Mrs. Hawkins," said Jane wearily. "I should have stopped and told you not to save anything for me. I've not felt so well today. The heat kind of got me, and I don't feel like eating anything."

"Well, that's all right, ef you don't want nothin', but it seems ta me you oughtta eat ta keep up yer strength. Don't come round late at night and ast me fer a piece. I ain't gonta be bothered that way. And by the way, I may's well tell ya, I gotta raise the rent of yer room a buck, beginnin' next week. They've raised the rent of the house, and meat's gettin' awful high, an' I can't make ends meet no way ef I don't raise me own rents. I jes' wanted you ta understand."

"Oh, Mrs. Hawkins!" cried Jane in despair, "but I told you when I came I couldn't pay any more, and you said that would be all right."

"Well, I know I did, but I can't do it, I tell ya! Besides I gotta young couple will be gladta come in here an' pay me a buck an' a half more apiece ef I put in a double bed, an' I guess I'll havta do it. I ain't runnin' a boardin' house fer benevolence ya know. I just thought I'd tell ya. You can think it over an' let me know tamorra mornin'. I gotta give them an answer right away."

With the last word the door closed with finality and the slipshod steps went steadily on down the stairs, the workworn hand of the woman feeling her way on the wall as she went.

Jane lay there filled with dismay. What was she going to do? Here she had just been trying to be thankful for this little smelly old room, and now even it was going to be taken away from her!

It came to her presently to wonder about that nice place the nurse had talked to her about. Why hadn't she asked her where it was? But then of course it would have been too expensive. Any place as cheap as this would be awful, just like this. But she'd got to do something. If she paid a dollar more to stay here that would cut out all her margin for sickness, and it looked now as if she might even be sick pretty soon if this weather kept on and she didn't get some kind of a change.

Well, she'd got to do something. Was there any place she could go tonight hunting a room? No, that was out of the question. She wasn't fit to walk and she couldn't afford carfare. She must husband her strength for tomorrow. She *had* to keep going tomorrow. She *must* get that pay envelope.

It was even thinkable that she might be going to lose her job, dropping down in a little heap that way right in the midst of the afternoon work! Maybe they would think they didn't want salespeople like that who could faint on them in the midst of things.

Well, there wasn't any use fretting. She'd better get some sleep. She wasn't hungry. She couldn't eat cold ham and cabbage even if she went downstairs now. She reviewed what the table would probably be like besides the ham and cabbage—and only the worst of that would be left of course. There would be bread, dry pieces that had been left over from another meal, with the mark of a greasy knife on one side. It wouldn't be the first time that one like that had fallen to her lot. She wondered why she ever ate in that place anyway. The food in the cheap restaurants was so much better. Maybe just a room in some decent rooming house would be better, and she could take a bottle of milk and get her own breakfasts, just dry uncooked cereal and an orange. Why hadn't she thought to try that before? It was all an experiment. But as she thought it over she was almost glad that her landlady had raised her rent, for now she had a real excuse to hunt another place.

Well, she would go to sleep now and get all the rest she could, and in the morning she would try and eat whatever breakfast there was, and tell her landlady she was leaving that night. Then she would go down to the store and pay for that crystal clasp, and take what money was left and find some place to live.

Her decision made she fell asleep again, a restless

burdened sleep, that broke toward morning, and woke her into a frenzy of despair. Suppose she should give up this room and then not be able to find another at any price she could afford? Maybe she was wrong to give it up. And yet she couldn't pay another dollar a week and go on enduring this hot room and the life here. And it would presently be as cold here as it was hot now. There was no chance of comfort here at all.

So she prodded her jaded muscles to get up and dress, though it was a full hour before her usual time for rising. But then she had a great deal to do before she went to the store. And she must keep moving or her resolve would weaken. She must be determined, to face that woman downstairs.

So she dressed carefully, to give the best impression at the store. They mustn't think she was worn out.

Then she smoothed over the bed, and began to take her things down from the hooks in the improvised closet. There weren't many of them, so they wouldn't be hard to carry. She folded them neatly, three or four plain dresses, and a meager pile of underwear. She was glad she hadn't bought that coat yet. Of course it would have had to be bought on credit anyway, but now she didn't have that to worry about, not till she got another home and was sure of things.

The breakfast bell was ringing when at last she had her garments all folded neatly into her suitcase. Then she pulled down the curtain to her closet and folded it smoothly, with the curtain from her wash stand, and put them in a pasteboard suit box she had brought from the store. She tied the box firmly, and put it and her suitcase by the door. Then she put on her hat, took her handbag and was ready to go. Her rent was up that night, all paid in advance. At least she would not have to pay out anything to move. She would take the suitcase and box with her to the store and put them in her locker. At noon she could slip out and look for a place, or maybe there would be a way to get excused early, if Mr. Clark was in a good humor after that clasp was paid for.

She ate her breakfast quietly enough. She was really hungry, though it was none of it appetizing. She found a little white worm in her shredded wheat biscuit, and the cream was sour. At least it was near-cream. But she reflected that white worms were likely not very unhealthy, especially if you didn't eat them, and that sour cream wouldn't kill her. So she fished out the worm and laid it aside, comforting herself that this was the last breakfast she would ever eat in this house. She might even eat in worse places of course, but this was the last here.

There was toast, burned and cold, and muddy coffee. She managed a few mouthfuls and then went upstairs to get her things. When she came downstairs Mrs. Hawkins was dickering with a huckster at the door, so she only said as she went down the steps. "Good-bye, Mrs. Hawkins, I'm going!" and then hurried away before Mrs. Hawkins could rally from the shock of being taken at her word.

But the walk to the trolley seemed longer than usual, burdened with the heavy suitcase and box, and the air was sultry with a coming storm. She looked anxiously up at the sky and made for the subway as rapidly as she could. That would land her almost at the store. It would be nothing short of a calamity if she got wet this morning, and no chance to change her garments before she appeared before the floor manager.

But the rain held off until Jane was safely inside the store, and her luggage put away in her locker. Then she appeared as usual in her place behind the button counter. They all looked surprised to see her back again.

"I don't see why you didn't take a day or two off and rest up," said one girl. "Believe me I'd have stayed away and got a good rest."

"Oh, I'm all right this morning," said Jane trying to appear as usual and not realizing how white she was looking. It quite surprised her that so many people were interested to ask after her. It is true that she found a great weakness upon her, but she did not speak of that. It embarrassed her that they should have seen her when she fainted. She was not a fainting girl.

But when Mr. Clark came solicitously up and asked how she felt she certainly was astonished. It hadn't occurred to her that he really counted her a human being like himself.

And then that stocking manager with his permanent wave beautifully set came smiling up.

"Well, little girl, you staged quite a scene last night, didn't you?" he said gaily, as if she were an old friend.

Jane looked up astonished.

"I'm sorry," she said. "It wasn't premeditated. I'm feeling quite fit this morning. Thank you for asking." And then she gave attention to a casual customer who had just lingered to gaze at a new display of buttons.

But young Gaylord was not to be discouraged. He appeared in the midst of the morning's work with a frosty glass of ice water.

"I thought this might help out a little," he said with a cheerful smile, and he handed the glass to her. Jane couldn't exactly refuse. Besides the water looked good.

It was amazing how the other girls flocked around her after that little attention. If that good-looking young man was going to take her up, they wanted to be in her circle.

Jane thought about it as she put her domain in buttonly order and grinned grimly to herself. What would they all say if they knew she was homeless this morning? Well, they shouldn't find it out! But what was she going to do?

At her lunch hour she went out to a good restaurant and ordered a wholesome lunch. Somehow she had to offset that awful breakfast she had eaten that morning. Somehow she had to get a little strength to go on. Fifty cents for her lunch! But it was worth it. Still she couldn't go on paying fifty cents for every meal. Well, when the day was over she *must* find a room, and then she could rest all day Sunday. She wouldn't even wash out a pair of stockings! She would just rest!

She put her head down on her lifted hand and closed her eyes a moment while she waited for her order to be brought.

"Oh, God," she prayed, "when you've so many mansions, couldn't you help me find a room, just a *little* room, right away?"

Then she lifted her head and looked around her.

Did God really care what became of her? Her mother used to say He did.

And then almost like an answer to that prayer, though she had felt she had no real right to pray for such things for herself, she saw Miss Leech coming toward her smiling.

"Jane," she said hopefully, "are you all tied up for the next two weeks?"

"Tied up?" said Jane, wonderingly.

"Yes, are you somewhere you have to stay and can't get away from, or are you going on a vacation yourself so you couldn't do something for me?"

"Why no," said Jane, "no, I'm not going on a vacation this year. I can't afford it. What can I do for you?"

"Why, you see, I'm taking my vacation beginning tonight, and I've just discovered that the girl I thought I had secured to come and stay in my apartment and look after my canary and my plants and goldfish is going off to Maine herself on a trip, and can't do it. I'm all upset. It isn't everybody I'd be willing to trust with my canary and goldfish. But I thought of you right away when I knew Elinor couldn't stay. Would you be willing to come and live there and look after things? I'd be glad to pay you for it. I feel I could trust you. I've watched how conscientious you are. I would know you wouldn't go off to a dance and let the poor little creatures starve or anything. Can you come?"

"Why, Miss Leech! How wonderful! I'd love to come. But you needn't pay me anything for that. I don't go out to dances and I'd adore having birds and fishes for companions."

"But certainly I'd pay you. I'd feel happier that way. Besides there might be times when you wanted to go back to your own place to stay and it's right you should have something for putting yourself out to stay there."

"But I shouldn't be putting myself out," said Jane. "You see, I'm homeless. I left the room I had this morning. It was unbearable. And I've got to hunt something after the store closes. Your proposition will just give me a chance to look around and try to find something respectable within my means. I'd love to come."

"All right, then, that's settled. You go home with me tonight. We'll have supper together in the restaurant downstairs in my apartment house, and then I can tell you about it. There's a kitchenette and you can get your own breakfasts whenever you feel like it of course."

"It sounds very much like heaven," said Jane with sparkling eyes. "Where do I meet you?"

They arranged the details quickly and Miss Leech went back to her desk, leaving Jane to enjoy her lunch with a lightened heart. Now did ever anyone see a happening like that? And just when she needed it so much. Could it be possible that it had anything to do with her prayer? Well, mother used to believe in prayer that way, but she always said that people who were not abiding in fellowship with Christ had no right to expect such amazing answers to things they asked. She well knew that verse, "If ye abide in me and my words abide in you, ye shall ask what ye will and it shall be done unto you." But she had not been abiding. Neither had His words been abiding in her heart; she hadn't read her Bible for months, and then only a hurried snatch at it. That wasn't abiding. But perhaps the Lord had given her this reply to her request just to call her attention to Himself and let her know He still cared for her. Was that it? She was His. At least she had given herself to Him when she was a child, though since her mother's death she had grown far away from any fellowship. She had almost come to doubt it had ever been anything to her but an idea.

But she couldn't ignore this thing that had happened. God had surely been thinking of her. It was as if a tender hand had touched her, a gentle voice said "I love you, my child!" Well, she would think about all this when she got somewhere and was rested.

The afternoon went better than the morning. The good food helped, and the relief from worry about the morrow. And when it came time to go up to the office for that pay envelope, and to settle about that clasp, she went with almost a cheerful heart. Even if she did lose that clasp money she would have two whole weeks without having to pay rent, and leisure to look for a room. She didn't need to worry. Of course she wouldn't let Miss Leech pay her for living in a perfectly good room. She hadn't seen the room yet, but any room that was good enough for Miss Leech would be a rest and vacation for her. Especially since she didn't have to pay for it.

The storm had cleared away leaving the atmosphere cooler and Jane felt as if life were more bearable. Though she was glad indeed when the signal came for closing, and she could conscientiously put away the last button, spread the covers over her cases and take her way up to the office.

But Mr. Clark stood at the door of the office and as she entered he motioned to her.

"Miss Scarlett," he said, "don't say anything about that broken clasp. It has been paid for, and you can forget it."

"Oh, Mr. Clark, they didn't make Hilda pay, did they?"

"No indeed! We found it was in no way her fault, and it was also proved that it was not your fault. Don't think anything more about it."

Mr. Clark was embarrassed at his unaccustomed task, for this was actually the first time he had ever assumed a debt of that sort for the sake of anyone who worked under him. It sent the color into his cheeks, and gave him a heady feeling as if God might be pleased with him, though he didn't explain it to himself in those words exactly. But he added hastily, "I'm sure I hope you'll be feeling quite well again by Monday, Miss Scarlett," and then he bowed and turned to speak to another man who came by and Jane went on to the pay-envelope window, and saw Hilda just before her. Hilda with a bright face and no trouble in her eyes.

It was good to look into her pay envelope and find her full amount there. Was this another sign that God was thinking of her, caring for her?

So she went downstairs, got her luggage and met Miss Leech by the door which they had agreed upon and they went on their way to the apartment.

It was just about that time that the postoffice car was delivering a special delivery letter for Jane Scarlett at the old boarding house she had left that morning, and Mrs. Hawkins was explaining in a high key that the girl had left and she hadn't the slightest idea where she had gone, and *wouldn't* be responsible for the letter, though Mrs. Hawkins was careful to take the letter in her hand and study the heading in the left hand upper corner before she handed it back to the delivery man. A firm of lawyers! What would they want of Jane Scarlett? Would it be money? She almost wished she hadn't raised the girl's rent.

Well, she was gone and she wouldn't be responsible for holding any letter for her. No, she wouldn't sign for it, either.

So the letter went on its way back to the sender, with "NOT KNOWN AT THAT ADDRESS" written large across its envelope. And Jane had gone into a new world where the message within that envelope could not find her.

VII

THEY had a good supper together downstairs in the restaurant and then Miss Leech took Jane up to the apartment. It seemed to her unaccustomed eyes to be palatial. It consisted of a pleasant little living room, a small bedroom, a bathroom, and a tiny kitchenette not much more than a sink and a stove, but still big enough. What luxury! And she was to be here for two whole weeks! It seemed like heaven. She was sure she wouldn't feel the heat here at all, and anyway there was an electric fan.

She was introduced to the goldfish and the canary, and given full directions how to care for them.

Miss Leech left in a taxi a little before midnight and Jane with awe crept into a big soft bed and lay down in wonder. To think she was in such a lovely place and comparative coolness, for two whole weeks! She meant to lie there awhile and think it all over and enjoy it, but she was asleep before she knew it, and exhausted nature kept her asleep until well into the morning.

When she did waken it was to the voice of a little silver-toned clock across from the bed. Nine o'clock! When had she slept until nine o'clock? But she lay there a few delicious moments longer listening to the new sounds about her. The low rumble of high-powered cars instead of trolleys and freight trains. The deep-throated bell from some steeple not far away, the high fine strains of radio music from an open window. And over it all clear, golden and ecstatic, the sweet flutelike voice of the canary reveling in his morning joy. It was all wonderful, and she found tears burning out from her eyelids. Tears of joy. The pain of having so many things that she had never had before. Would her mother up in heaven know what comfort had suddenly come to her child? Did God plan this for her? She couldn't but feel that He had.

In a little while she got up and reveled in the luxury of a warm bath in a clean tub with all the hot water she wanted to use! Why just that comfort was enough to be thankful for all the rest of her life. How she had hated that tin-lined, roughly painted, light blue bath tub at Mrs. Hawkins', a tub that had to be waited for almost hour after hour on Sunday mornings, and then always had a rim of grease and dirt around its middle.

There were cereals in the minute cupboard which she had been ordered to use up because they would be stale by the time their owner returned. There was a bottle of real cream in the wee refrigerator, and a bottle of milk also. She did not need to make coffee, though she had been instructed in the ways of the percolator. There was bread and butter on hand and some peaches. What a breakfast! And how good everything was!

She fed the canary and the fishes and talked to them as she did it, and the little creatures seemed to be cocking a wise eye at her and recognizing that she was somebody new.

After she had washed her dishes and put things to rights she turned on the radio and came upon some wondrous music, and a message that reached her tired discouraged soul. A message that Jesus Christ not only was the Saviour of all those who accepted His atonement on the cross for their sins, but that He wanted to be more. He wanted to be the guide and daily companion of each one whom He had saved.

That was a new thought to Jane. She had often wondered if God cared for her, but that He should desire her love and companionship, and long to have the confidence of her soul, had never occurred to her. Was that true? She listened to the message to the end, and during the closing prayer she slipped down beside the big chair where she had been sitting and put her heart in the attitude of prayer. There were no words to her petition, just a longing, just apology in the eyes of her soul, just a wistful yearning for something she did not as yet understand.

By and by she found a pleasant book to read, and in the cool of the afternoon she went out and took a walk in the park that was not far away. Then about five o'clock she began to be hungry and went in to the restaurant and got a good dinner. A chicken dinner. It seemed to her a marvelous day, and when she had finished her dinner she went up and read awhile and then went to bed early. This had been like a real vacation. Why this was the greatest thing that had happened to her since her mother died!

The canary welcomed her with soft conversing cheeps, and she did not feel alone. She was almost happy.

She began to calculate. If she got her own breakfast and a very cheap lunch she might be able to take her dinners down at that restaurant every day. She had got to be well fed or she would collapse in the store again and that wouldn't do. She would lose her job if that kept on happening.

She went to bed and to sleep very early that night. The church bell on the tower not far away rang again, and it seemed to keep time to the words: "In my Father's house. Many mansions in my Father's house."

She was up bright and early next morning, her breakfast got and her work done. The housework was like play, a doll's house. Then she was off to the store.

She tried walking to the store. Miss Leech said she did it every day for the exercise unless it was very stormy. But when she was almost there she began to feel weak in the knees and realized she should not have attempted it yet. She probably had been going beyond her strength for a long time, on insufficient food, as that nurse at the store had suggested. She should give herself another day or two to rest before she tried such long walks. Well, she would take things as easy as possible today, and she would eat a good lunch, no saving of food till she was stronger and quite fit for her work.

She was in her place a little before time, getting her stock settled and greeting the other girls pleasantly, and then, just after the opening bugle, Mr. Clark came hurrying up. His very attitude filled her with alarm, though of course it really didn't matter so much now if she did have to pay for that crystal clasp, now that she was getting a room free for two whole weeks.

"Miss Scarlett," he said, "I've just been up talking with Mr. Windle, and he feels quite strongly that in view of your having had such a bad time day before yesterday you should certainly take your vacation. He says that your record has been so good, and you have been so faithful during the hot months, that he feels we should let you have your vacation *with pay!* He doesn't often do that, you know, but he's making an exception of you because you were sick. So if you will go up to the office right away you will receive your pay check at once and then you will have something to make your vacation a little easier. I think you are looking a little better this morning and I hope by the end of your vacation we shall see a decided difference in you. I hope you have a wonderful time. Good-bye and we'll be looking for you back again."

In a daze Jane took the slip he gave her to take to the cashier and went slowly down the aisle and up the stairs to the office.

She was weak with amazement. She wondered when she reached the office whether she had remembered to thank Mr. Clark for telling her, and whether it would be right to interrupt Mr. Windle to thank him. She decided against that. Two whole weeks with money in hand as if she was working, and a lovely place to stay. Not even a grand hotel at the shore could be as good as that. There were all those lovely books to read, and the radio! Why it was wonderful. God surely had been taking thought for her. She could not doubt it.

And she would have time to look about her in a leisurely way for another room. She wouldn't have to take another terrible place because she simply *had* to have some place in which to stay right away.

Gradually she came out of her daze sufficiently to get excited over her good luck. As she came downstairs she met Mr. Clark and she looked at him with shy eagerness.

"I guess I didn't thank you," she said. "I know you used your influence or this wouldn't have happened to me."

"Oh, that's all right," said Mr. Clark with a wide generous gesture. "Take care of yourself. I hope you have a good time!"

So Jane started out to go back to her new quarters. She wouldn't have to save her strength for work today, so perhaps she could manage to walk back. She could stop and rest in the park on the way. How wonderful to be a lady of leisure!

Two days later the letter that the firm of lawyers had sent to Jane Scarlett at Mrs. Hawkins' boarding house came back to the office with the legend stamped on it that one Jane Scarlett was not at the address given below and her present whereabouts was unknown.

In due time the lawyer who received the mail came with it to Kent Havenner.

"How about this, Kent," he said, "didn't you say this Scarlett girl had given you the address where she was living?"

"I did," said Kent Havenner emphatically, "what's the matter?"

"Not there! Address unknown!" announced the other man. "You sure that's the right address?"

Havenner took the envelope and examined it, comparing it carefully with his notebook.

"Yes, that's correct," he said. "I wonder—?"

"Well, it seems we're up a tree still," said the lawyer. "You thought you had such a good lead, and now our bird has flown. We'll have to begin all over again. Probably she wasn't the right Scarlett after all."

"Well, here, give it to me and I think I can find her. She works in a store."

"All right, hunt her up and be quick about it. I'd like to get that Scarlett matter settled up and off the docket. I'm tired of seeing the documents in the safe every time I go there."

So Kent Havenner went out in the middle of the afternoon and made his way to Windle's store, going confidently to the button counter, expecting to be able to pick out his girl at a glance.

But though he walked up and down the aisle three times and watched every girl that was waiting on customers there, there wasn't a single one who looked like Jane. Could it be possible that his eyes deceived him?

Finally he went up to a girl who was idle for the moment:

"Isn't there a Miss Scarlett at this counter?"

"She's not here today. She's out. She's been sick. I guess that's why," explained a girl who wasn't a regular at the button counter. "There's the head of the department, he might know."

So Havenner interviewed Mr. Clark.

"Oh! She's gone on vacation," explained Clark loftily.

"Well, could you tell me where she has gone?" asked the young lawyer. "It's quite important."

"No! I'm sorry! We don't require our salespeople to sign up for vacation absences. Probably if you would enquire at the office they would know her residence."

Clark eyed the man hostilely. He was dressed too well to be a friend or relative of Jane Scarlett. What could he want of her? Perhaps there were drawbacks in Jane's life even worse than hot weather and ill health. At least he was doing nothing to encourage this young man.

Kent Havenner went on his way. He decided to go to Jane's boarding house. Doubtless the wrong person had got hold of the letter.

So he went to Mrs. Hawkins and she dilated irately on how Jane had left her at a moment's notice just because she asked for a little more money. And no, she didn't know where she went!

"She just walked off with her back up!" said Mrs. Hawkins, and went in and shut her door.

Kent Havenner even went to the trouble of interviewing the office at the store, and found that what Mr. Clark had told him was true. Jane was on vacation and nobody—not *any*body—knew where she was. There was nothing he could do about it, and so he went back to the office to confess himself beaten for the time being. And there was nothing anybody could do but wait till Jane Scarlett came back to the store.

But meantime Jane Scarlett was having the grandest time of her life.

She had portioned out her money so that she could have one good square interesting meal a day, and for the other two fruit and cereal and milk. That would leave her a little more than a week's wages to put by. Then she got a map of the city at a newsstand, and studied the region within walking distance, or cheap riding distance, from the store, and regularly every morning she started out hunting a room.

More and more as she hunted she was filled with distress over the places from which she must choose. Not one had a semblance of homelikeness or comfort. Not at the price she should pay. Yet there must be something better somewhere. Perhaps her ideas were too fine. And of course the place where she was now living made the contrast all the more deadly. Yet she did not ask so much. Cleanliness, a reasonable amount of fresh air, and of heat in winter. The room might be bare and guiltless of paint. The bed might be narrow; if it could only be tolerably smooth, she could stand its being hard. Were just these few necessities so expensive? Surely there must be something bearable somewhere.

But so many hall bedrooms were the same. No heat in winter, no air in summer. Few and far bathroom privileges.

So one day she went in to the big city station and hunted up the Travelers Aid woman. Yes, she knew of a few rooms where conditions were more tolerable. She wrote a list of them, but warned Jane that they were usually in great demand.

So Jane started out again, and at last found a room that she thought she could stand. It was bare and desolate in the extreme. A bureau, a sagging woven wire cot, a straight chair, and a wash bowl on a shelf in the corner. It was fifty cents more than Mrs. Hawkins' room, but would be vacant about the time she needed it, so she took it tentatively, and hied her back to Miss Leech's apartment to look disconsolately around its comforts and tell the canary sadly how she was going to miss it when her vacation was over. If she didn't have to have a warm coat this winter she could get a better room, but she must have a coat that was really warm.

So she put the thought of a homelike room out of her mind and sat and read Miss Leech's best books, trying to absorb all the pleasure possible so that it would last through the winter that was to come.

Yet while she sat enjoying herself and trying to forget the time that was swiftly coming when she could no longer sit in comfort and read the best books and listen to a good radio, Kent Havenner was worrying himself greatly about her. As he walked the streets or went about outside the city, his eyes were always alert, thinking perhaps he would come on her. That word that she had been ill troubled him. He didn't understand why it was, but he could not get away from the look in her eyes when she had said that all her family were dead. She had seemed so alone, and so quiet and self-contained as if she expected so little out of life and wasn't even getting as much as she had expected.

He tried to put the thought of her out of his mind. There wasn't anything more he could do about her until her vacation was over, but it kept coming to him what if she didn't come back? What if they never found her? Would he have to go on thinking of her and that sort of resigned unhappy look in her eyes?

His sister Audrey had been away in Maine for a few days, but the day she got back he took her for a walk on the beach, eluding the incessant cousin who would have accompanied them, and when they were a good distance away from the house he began:

"Say, Audrey, are you going up to town some day pretty soon?"

"Why, yes," said Audrey, considering. "I was thinking of going tomorrow unless mother has other plans. Why for?"

"Well, I wish you'd do something for me. Go see if you can find your button girl. She's disappeared!"

"Kent, what do you mean?"

"Jane Scarlett! She's disappeared I tell you, and it's important that she be found."

"Disappeared? What do you mean? On purpose? Kent, she hasn't done anything they want her for, has she? I mean I'm sure she hasn't, and if anybody's hounding her for anything and wants me to help, I won't and that's flat."

"Now look here, Audrey, did I say anybody was hounding her? Did I give you any reason to suppose she was wanted by the police? Well, she isn't at all. She's just wanted. That is, there's a letter for her that she ought to have, and it's been the rounds and got back to the office with an inscription that she's unknown."

Audrey looked up startled.

"You don't mean it, Kent."

"S'the truth, kid. And I went myself to the address she gave me and they said she'd left. And then I went to the store and they told me she was on a vacation."

"You mean you've really seen her and talked with her,

Kent? I thought perhaps you had just been joking. *Did* you talk with her?"

"Sure thing, sister. Had a very dignified interview."

"Was she frightened?"

"Not in the least. What was there to be frightened about? I went to Windle and he sent for her. I told her I was a friend of Windle's collecting statistics about a family and I wanted to ask her some questions."

"How did she take it?"

"Cool as you please. She looked me through and through and then answered everything I asked her as quietly as you please."

"Well, is there any great hurry about it? Why don't you wait till she gets back from that vacation if it's genuine?"

"That's it, sister. I want you to find out for me if it is really genuine. I want you to go to the button counter and ask for her, and if they still say she's on vacation just get friendly with the other girls and find out when she really is coming back, and where they think she went. You could do what I couldn't, you see."

"Yes, I suppose I could," said Audrey. "But I think you'd have to tell me a little more about the affair before I'd be willing to get into this at all. If I thought they were going to get her into any trouble I wouldn't touch it. I liked that girl."

"No trouble at all, kid. It's just an estate being settled up and they are trying to get information about other members of the family that may be living."

"Did you tell her that?"

"No, I told her only that we were getting statistics. I think she gathered that it was for a book, a family tree or something. I was not supposed to tell the nature of the affair. I was only a factotum, you see."

"You're sure she wasn't frightened?"

"I don't think she was. Not after I began to ask her questions."

"What did you ask her?"

"Her name and where she was born and the names of her father and mother and where they were born and married and died, and the names of her grandfather or any cousins etc. she had."

"Well, that oughtn't to have frightened her," said Audrey thoughtfully. "All right, I'll try and find out where she is. But don't tell cousin Evalina, and don't let's talk about her at the table, because I really mean to invite her down here to stay over the week-end, sometime, and I don't want Evalina barging in and making a fool of you and the girl."

"I should hope not," said Kent fervently. "But say, I don't blame you for being enthusiastic. She's some girl. She has an air as if she was to the manner born and then some. Isn't exactly pretty, either, but might be if she had the money or at least I got that impression."

"Well, I should say you're about as quick at judging character as you think I am. But I'm glad you agree with me. Come on, let's get back to the cottage. If I've got to go to town tomorrow I'd better get busy getting ready."

VIII

ONE day in the second week of her vacation Jane turned on the radio and heard a woman's voice speaking. It said:

"If you are sad and weary and questioning what life is all about, if you want to find an answer that will satisfy, and help you to go on amid disappointments and hardships and loneliness, come to Mrs. Brooke's Bible hour at seven o'clock every evening in Bryan Hall, for a time of real help and comfort."

Somehow that little invitation seemed spoken just to Jane. It voiced her own longings and promised something that she did not know where else to find. A great desire came to her to go and see what it was, and if it would indeed bring peace to her troubled soul.

She found out that Bryan Hall was only three blocks away from Miss Leech's apartment and she resolved to go that very night and listen. To that end she ate her dinner earlier than usual and was at the place appointed before seven.

As she entered the hall she was handed a little red book which she found to be a copy of the gospel of John. She turned the pages over interestedly and there was her own fourteenth chapter, "In my Father's house are many mansions—." It made her feel right at home. And then a sweet-faced woman came to the desk and bowed her head in a short tender prayer that made God seem very present.

The leader's voice was brisk and intriguing.

"Please turn to the twentieth chapter of your little red book, and you will find its introduction in the thirtieth and thirty-first verses. Away at the end of the book. Isn't that odd? Let us read:

'And many other signs truly did Jesus in the presence of His disciples, which are not written in this book: but these are written that ye might believe that Jesus is the Christ,

65

the Son of God; and that believing ye might have life through His name.'

"You see John is not a biography of Jesus, like the other gospels. It is a book of signs. Signs that Jesus is the Christ, proofs from an eyewitness. And the purpose of writing them is 'that ye might have life.'

" 'Oh,' you say, 'I want to see life!' And you may have tried this or that pleasure or pursuit, and actually said 'This is the life!' "

She imitated so well the tone of voice peculiar to that phrase that a boy and girl on the back seat nudged each other and giggled, and even a few older, quietly staid women glanced at each other understandingly.

"But," she went on, "what you may have thought was life may have been a very poor imitation. Turn now to the seventeenth chapter of your little books, the third verse, and read:

" 'And this is life eternal, that they might know thee the only true God, and Jesus Christ, whom thou hast sent.'

"Now, I see some of you looking disappointed. You are saying to yourselves, 'That's not the kind of life I want.' But friends, *there is no other kind* of life, not real life. There is no life apart from Christ. Perhaps the reason you are dissatisfied with life is because you've been seeking it apart from Him and all you have been getting is an imitation. Turn to the first chapter, verse four: 'In Him was life; and the life was the light of men.' Now the third chapter, verse thirty-six: 'He that believeth on the Son hath everlasting life: and he that believeth not the Son shall not see life; but the wrath of God abideth on him.' Now the tenth chapter, verse ten: 'I am come that they might have life, and that they might have it more abundantly.' And chapter fourteen, six: 'I am the way, the truth, and the life.' Of course this isn't animal life Christ is talking about. It is eternal life. It is God's life.

"And there are seven signs in this book which prove that Christ is the only life-giver and that the life He gives is real. The first is Jesus turning the water into wine, just by a look. Wine is the symbol of joy, the ecstatic joy of living. Notice that He told the servants to *fill up* the waterpots. You may guess rightly from that, that the kind of life He gives is *full* of joy.

"You may say, 'I never saw a Christian full of joy.' Well I have, and you'll find that the long-faced people, while they may be full of creeds or theories, are not full of Jesus Christ. Those who are have joy.

"In chapter four you find the second sign. Christ heals the son of a nobleman. Here we find that the life He gives is a spiritually healthy life. There is never any fanaticism or lack of balance in it.

"In the third sign you find Him giving power, in the fourth, nourishment, in the fifth, peace. 'My peace I give unto you.' His peace is calm even in the midst of betrayal and a cross in the offing. In the sixth sign He gives light. The healing of the blind man, you know. Watch for that when we come to study it, you who feel you are in the dark now. There is no perplexity in your life that His life cannot make plain.

" 'Death,' you say?

"But the seventh miracle deals with that. That is the crowning sign of all that Jesus is the Christ. He has conquered death itself, and has the authority to say 'I am the resurrection and the life.'

"To whom else shall we go to find life? Joy, health, sustenance, power, peace, light, victory over death itself? If we really have Him, His life, there is nothing, *nothing,* that need dismay us. And we receive that life by believing. Let's read our key verse again: 'These are written that ye might believe.' "

When the lesson was over, all too soon for Jane, she carried away with her the little book and the brief notes she had jotted down, and read them over again in her room, resolving not to miss any of these wonderful lessons. Somehow the few minutes' talk had made life seem a wider thing than just her little environment where her thoughts were all centered on herself and her own perplexities. She had had a glimpse into a vast universe, where she was a child of the Father's love, and she longed inexpressibly for that Life that the teacher had talked about. That Life that was joyful, sane, fruitful, peaceful and unafraid, guided, secure, eternal!

She took the book of John and sat down to study over

the chapters and verses the teacher had used, and let them sink deep into her heart and memory for future use.

For three days Jane enjoyed the evening lessons, and was beginning to plan how she could attend them after Miss Leech came home and she had to vacate her fine quarters, but just as she was about to enter the hall the fourth evening she heard a voice behind her calling:

"Oh, I say, Beautiful! Where have you been all this time?" Looking around in startled annoyance she saw to her dismay the young man Gaylord from the stocking department. Now, what could he possibly want of her? With all the girls he had at his beck and call, why should he bother her?

Other girls were turning and looking at him and at her; she couldn't just walk in and not return his salute. So she managed a nod, and said: "Oh, good evening!"

She was about to turn and go into the hall, but annoyingly the young man sprang up the two steps between them and came to her side.

"Oh, I say, what became of you? I thought we were going to have a date that next night and then you disappeared."

"Oh, I'm on vacation," she said. "I'll be back all too soon next week."

"Oh, well, how about tonight? I have time on my hands and not a thing to do. A friend I expected to date is sick. Can't you and I see a picture?"

"Oh, thank you," said Jane in a panic, "but I'm going in here. There's something I wouldn't miss for anything."

"Oh, I see!" The young man looked perplexedly up at the building and couldn't quite make out from the various signs at the door just what it might be she was interested in.

"All right," he said gaily. "How about my going along? Perhaps that's the best way to find out what your line is anyway."

"Oh, but I'm afraid you wouldn't like it," said Jane startled. "It's just a class. I'm sure it's not in your line. Please excuse me. They always begin on time and I wouldn't like to miss a word."

She turned and sped up the remaining steps and into

the hall breathlessly. But when she went to a seat she found him beside her, curiously studying the little red book someone had given him as he entered.

He sat down grinning.

"You see you didn't get rid of me so easily," he said, staring around the hall alertly. "What is this anyway? A spiritualistic séance?"

"Ssh!" said Jane shaking her head.

He looked up at the teacher and frowned, and then he looked down at Jane's little red book, and suddenly saw that all the people had the same book.

The lesson that night was most interesting to Jane, but somehow it didn't seem to click with the young man. He fumbled the leaves of his book for a minute or two in an attempt to understand what it was about, and then he fidgeted another five minutes. And finally he leaned over and whispered to Jane.

"Say, I'm about fed up on this, aren't you?"

"Ssh!" said Jane shaking her head.

He frowned and tried to listen for another three minutes and then he gave a deep audible sigh.

"Well," he said at last, leaning toward her, his voice by now quite unguarded, and audible to those sitting near, "you win. This is too deep for me. I'm going to the movies. I can't go this any longer. Come on out and find a nice picture!"

Jane was writing down a particularly interesting sentence in her notebook, and looked annoyed.

"Come on, kiddo!"

"No!" she said firmly. "I wouldn't miss this for anything."

"Okay, kiddo. I'm leaving you. See you subse!" and he got up noisily and went out.

Jane was relieved to have him gone. She had been worrying in the back of her mind to know just how she was going to get rid of him after the class was out. She distinctly did not want to go with him to see any moving pictures. She did not want to go with him anywhere. She did not like him. She wondered if that were a wrong attitude. One might suppose she would be grateful for any attention, lonely as she was. Perhaps she was all wrong. But somehow her mother had given her ideals that would not be satisfied by the trifling youth of today. There must be some real people somewhere who looked upon life as more than a good time when work was over. Well, anyway, she didn't have to worry about him any more tonight. And she could get the ending of the lesson without being further distracted.

So she wrote happily on to the end.

She was half fearful as she went out lest she would find him waiting for her outside, insisting upon a picture, and she slid out in the crowd and hurried away, thankful that he was not to be seen.

Those last days of her vacation were very precious. She husbanded each hour. There were certain books in the little bookcase she wanted to be sure and read before she left, and she read three or four hours at a time. Conscientiously she took walks, always choosing the time when she would not be likely to meet anyone from the store. Somehow it seemed more like a vacation than if she came into contact with any of her fellow laborers.

Hungrily she wrote down a list of the books in the little library which she knew she would not have time to read. Sometime perhaps she could find one or another of them in a second-hand store. Or perhaps she could afford a membership in some library. But then when would she have time to read them? Or light and comfort in which to read? She could take a book to a park bench in the early evening and read a few minutes every night, but the daylight would soon be growing shorter, and of course she had her washing to do, and some mending. There wouldn't be much time. Certainly, though, she had a right to a little pleasure. Other people went to the movies, and she could take her amusement by reading, if she only had a good light.

Ah! Here was a thought. It wasn't so many blocks to the big railroad station. Why couldn't she sit in the waiting room for an hour or so now and then and read? Provided she had something to read? Well, she would see when she got settled in her new room.

She wasn't very happy about that room either, but it seemed the best she could find unless she went entirely out of the region near the store, where she could not possibly walk to her work. Perhaps if she got a raise around Christmas she might be able to afford carfare and get a more homelike room. The one she had now was even more bare than Mrs. Hawkins', but it did have a heating pipe running across one end. That might make some difference in the temperature, though she doubted it. However, she couldn't do better just now. And when she got home to the many mansions of course it wouldn't matter what she had gone through down here. *"My* peace I give unto you." His peace would be calm in any kind of environment.

The weather was not so continuously hot now, and when it was intense for a few hours there was always the electric fan to make it tolerable. The respite from the heat had given her a new lease of life, and she had lost the look of strain that had characterized her before she had the collapse in the store. The good food and the rest had given a roundness to her cheeks and a brightness to her eyes, and one morning when she was brushing her hair before the mirror she suddenly stopped and looked at herself.

"Why, I'm not so bad-looking as I used to be," she said to herself. "I guess I was just starved. I'll have to look out for that, even if I don't get a warm coat for winter. I can't afford to look like a ghost or I'll lose my job and then where would I be?"

Carrying out that thought she realized that if she were taken very sick there would be no place for her but a charity hospital, and a charity grave if she died. That was no way for a Scarlett to be, on charity. She must keep well, be self-respecting, and save her money. She had had an honorable father and mother and belonged to a respected family. It was up to her to take care of herself. Or—*was* it? Wasn't it perhaps God's care? If He cared for her that way, the way the book of John seemed to say, then He would provide for her. She must trust and not be afraid. But of course it was up to her not to be careless of her health.

The next day was her last evening in Miss Leech's apartment, and she had tidied it all up. Miss Leech would arrive about ten o'clock that night, and Jane had arranged to go straight to her own new room as soon as she had welcomed her friend home.

The canary's cage was clean, the goldfish had a fresh water, the plants were flourishing, and there wasn't a fleck of dust on anything. Jane had her small belongings packed and ready to go. There were still ten pages in a book she wanted to finish, but there would be plenty of time for that after she got back from the Bible class.

She put on her hat and took her little red book and notebook, and went out. The sky was soft with evening. A red glow hovered over the horizon, as much of it as she could see afar at the end of the street, with a vivid bit of coral, golden streaked, dashed across its corner. There was even a little breeze from the direction of the river. A perfect night for the end of her vacation. How wonderful it had been! And she hadn't expected nor intended to have a vacation at all. It just came to her like a blessing out of heaven!

She would not think that this was the end of her pleasant interval. Rather think of it as a beginning, perhaps, of new things. She had found a hope in those Bible classes, and a peace was beginning to grow in her heart as her faith increased.

She walked slowly for there was plenty of time. She wanted to put away in her memory this night, the light in the sky, the cool breeze on her brow. They would be refreshing things to remember if hot hard days came when it scarcely seemed that she could go on. She would go on remembering that in her Father's house were many mansions, and what He chose for her residence here was His ordering, and it was not for her to demur.

There was still plenty of time as she reached the steps up to the building. She mounted slowly. Only a few of the class were as yet going in. She lingered on each step, looking off to the horizon where a flood of gold was pouring into the clearness of the roseate hues. What a lovely picture, even amidst the noise and grime of a city street!

With a last lingering look she turned to go, glad that she was alone, and no one could question her lingering.

It was just then she heard the sound, a voice vaguely familiar, calling her name:

"Miss Scarlett! Wait! Miss Scarlett!"

Without turning she hastened on, startled, dismayed.

Could that be young Gaylord again? She had thought him cured of coming here for her.

But the voice had called her Miss Scarlett, and she doubted if he knew her name. He had always called her "Beautiful!" Who else could it be? Not Mr. Clark. And he was the only one who called her that.

Or was it all imagination? Just some combination of sounds in the street that seemed like her name? She was too sensitive. No one was calling now. She had just imagined it. No, she would not even turn and look back. If it should be Gaylord, somehow having found out her name, she would not let him know she had heard him. She would go in and take her seat. Get a seat by others, where there was no room for him. Then if he had taken a notion to come after her again she would escape his tormenting chatter. She wanted to get all of this lesson. She would surely need it on the morrow.

So she hurried on and drifted into a seat in the third row with others who were filling up the front rows. Surely no one would come up there to search for her! And after she had sat there a few minutes she would get free from the feeling that someone was following her. It was just nerves anyway. She had had a nice vacation and she mustn't allow nerves to dominate her any more.

So she settled down and gave attention to the lesson which began almost immediately, and took her thoughts from everything else.

IX

KENT HAVENNER had stayed in town that evening to see a girl who had sent him word that she would be at her married sister's overnight.

He had been going with her more or less for some months. She was a girl his mother and sister did not like. She used a great deal of make-up, smoked incessantly, drank on occasion, and was moreover divorced. That the reason for the divorce was the fault mainly of her former husband did not make her any more desirable as a companion for Kent in the eyes of his mother, or according to the traditions under which he had been reared.

The girl's name was Evadne Laverock. She was considered very beautiful in a startling way.

There had been some difference of opinion between them for the past four months and Evadne had taken herself abroad for a time. Now she was back and wished to see Kent. And Kent had so far recovered his sense of the fitness of things as not to be quite sure whether he wanted to see Evadne or not. But he remained in town, and telephoned his sister that he had business that would keep him till the late train, or perhaps he would not come home until tomorrow night.

Nevertheless he had not hastened to meet her. He had taken a leisurely dinner at some distance from the house where the married sister was living, and dallied within his own conscience and his common sense awhile before he went out to take a leisurely way to the rendezvous. He did not intend to give in too easily. He would let Evadne make all the concessions.

As he walked along he noticed a number of young people going his way. A score or more of good-looking young girls, at least they were sensible-looking, and most of them had becoming curly hair and bright faces. Some of them were even noticeably pretty, and there was one who had a sweet charm of bearing that seemed to set her apart from the rest. Where had he seen her before?

There was something familiar about the way she held her head. There were several young fellows among the girls, some in company with them, and some going by themselves. They were all going to the same place. Up the steps to a building, a hall! Who was that girl with the dark hair? Somewhere he had met her, he was sure. She was distinguished-looking. Evadne wouldn't think so, but she was. He had certainly seen her somewhere, talked with her! Where were they all going? Was this a school?

Then the girl with the dark hair mounted the steps slowly, looking óff toward the sunset, and he caught a glimpse of her face. Yes! There she was at last!

It was then he called out! He completely forgot Evadne Laverock, and cried:

"Miss Scarlett! Wait! Miss Scarlett! *Jane!*"

But she went right on up the steps deliberately. Yet she must have heard. If that was her name she would have turned, wouldn't she? He was a fool. Of course it wasn't Jane Scarlett! And yet, if it only was how glad he would be. She was very much wanted at the office, and he certainly would like to be the one to complete the contact and produce her, after the way he seemed to have fumbled the job in the first place.

"Miss Scarlett!"

He was standing at the foot of the steps looking up and other girls turned and looked down at him curiously, but she did not turn. If she had been Jane Scarlett she would surely have heard and turned, wouldn't she?

Of course it was time he went to Evadne Laverock if he was going at all, and yet so strong was his impression as he watched the shoulders and back of this girl disappear into the darkness of the hall above that he seemed compelled to follow her. After all it would take but a minute in a lighted room with a good square look at her to discover his mistake if it was one. So he followed up the steps, and came, after a devious way through a winding hall, to stand in the doorway of the classroom where he saw the lady he was following just sitting down in a seat away at the front. From here he could not be any more definitely sure by the look of her back and shoulders whether she was the girl he sought or not.

So he walked all the way up the middle aisle to the

only vacant seat anywhere near her. It was across the aisle one row ahead of hers, in the middle of the row. Here he might hope to get a good view of her face.

And so, after various twistings and turnings, and trying to appear to be watching for somebody coming in the door at the back, he finally got a full view of her and knew it was none other than Jane Scarlett.

But Jane Scarlett was bending over a little red book, finding the place, and then opening a small notebook and getting out a tiny pencil. She was not noticing in the least the people about her. And though he turned his head and looked full at her as long as his natural courtesy would permit him to do, he could not seem to make her look up and recognize him.

At last he settled back in his chair with folded arms and resigned himself to wait till whatever this was was over and he could speak to her. What had he come in on anyway, and how long was it likely to last? Some sort of class? A business course? Was she trying to get ready to do something more lucrative than sell buttons? That was commendable. She seemed a bright girl. The rounded line of her cheek was really lovely.

He glanced at his watch. It was still early. Evadne would not be expecting him yet. And a class of any sort would likely be out in a half or three quarters of an hour.

So Kent Havenner sat still and waited, studying the faces of the quite large group of young men and maidens who were gathered eagerly, with their attention fixed on the woman who was speaking.

Then suddenly his attention was caught by the speaker.

"If you want God in your life you must be willing to comply with the conditions."

Heavens, what was this, some kind of religious quackery?

Then he gave entire attention to the teacher.

"Life is not a mere matter of seventy or eighty years on this earth. Life is eternity-long. Did it ever occur to you how queer it is that we spend about a quarter of the time we count as life in getting ready for it? Going to school to learn how to live? To learn how to earn money and enjoy ourselves? And never give a thought to getting ready for eternity? Some of us try to persuade ourselves that there is no eternity. That when we die we just pass out and are never conscious any more.

"Yet Jesus invites us to a life that never ends. A life that is full of joy with not a disappointment. A life that need make no mistakes under His guidance. And we take no pains to acquaint ourselves with it, nor even try to find out if it be true. This book gives us unmistakable signs of eternity and shows us how to prepare for it."

Kent looked down at the little book in his hand. It was evidently a portion of the Bible. He was more or less familiar with at least the outside of the Bible, but he had never looked upon it as a book that contained any *proofs* of anything. He had always supposed it mere theories.

He listened to the teacher as she briefly went over the résumé of the past weeks' studies, and he followed her in chapter and verse, surprised at the apt quotations.

Now and then he cast a quick glance at Jane and noted her intent interest, the quick kindling of her eye at a new thought. Then all at once he thought of Evadne, and glanced at his watch. She would be wondering why he did not come. He tried to fancy telling her about this place and explaining to her how he happened to be here. He tried to imagine her here with him, and somehow couldn't do it. If she sat over there where Jane sat she would certainly not be gazing up with that eagerness. She would be uneasily looking at her watch, or openly yawning, or definitely getting up and leaving. Evadne was impatient. She would never sit still and listen to words about eternity. Evadne knew the smartest fashions, she knew the price of jewels and other precious things of earth, fine cars, and mansions, and the latest dances, new shades of lipstick but perhaps she was not figuring on eternity. And if he were to try to tell her about what he had heard tonight while she was awaiting his coming she would but laugh him to scorn.

Was it possibly true as his mother claimed, that Evadne had a vapid mind incapable of serious thought?

And then the old question got the ascendency for the instant, to the exclusion of all that was going on about him. Should he go and see Evadne again at all, or just let the summer's break that had come between them be the end? Did he really want her for the daily companion of his life? Or would he regret it later when he found someone more suited to him?

But the teacher's voice broke upon his consciousness again:

"Did you ever think what it would be in your life to know God intimately and to have Jesus Christ your hourly companion?" she asked. The words fell into his perplexities with almost a shock. It came to him that if that could be true he would have an answer to all his perplexities. He needn't be in danger of making lifelong mistakes. He didn't really want to make mistakes that would affect his whole life, as his family seemed to think he was in danger of doing.

But Evadne was very lovely in her way. He had thought that perhaps his mother was only over-anxious. Also he had hoped that Evadne might change after they were married. But now after the interval of her absence he wondered. Would she? Could she? Did she want to be molded to go his way, or was she determined to go her own?

Looking sharply thus into his inner consciousness he was almost afraid to meet her. He knew her subtleties. She would wind him around her finger again the way she used to do. Just one smile of her red lips, one glance from her topaz eyes and he would be in her toils. Did he want that?

He was practically free from her influence now. They had parted because he had taken a stand against some of her decisions and wishes. He wouldn't go her way in everything.

It had been frightfully hard at first, but he had held out and plunged into his law work, and now he was really interested in it. He wanted to get on and attain great things. And if she came into his life again he knew it would at once mean late hours and gay living, not the steady quiet life to which he had been brought up. She laughed at that. It would mean a constant struggle to hold his own in his work if he were trying to please her. He could not serve two masters.

Well, whatever he was going to do later in the evening, he was working now. He had to contact Jane Scarlett and put her in touch with his law firm. That was his business. And he had been learning these last few months since Evadne went away that business must come first, pleasure afterward. And Evadne had to learn that too if she was going to be around with him. If she did not like it let her go away again. He was getting on well enough without her. Of course he knew that Evadne would not understand why he had to stay in a Bible class and watch one girl, one plain poorly dressed girl who sold buttons in a store, but he was convinced that what he was doing now was his business and it was important. He was quite sure that whatever Evadne was using as an excuse for getting him to come and see her, it could not be important.

How long this session of study would last he couldn't tell, and it was impossible to forecast how long it would take him after this was over, before he was free to go. Better let it rest at that. If he got away from this duty at any reasonable hour he would go to Evadne and have it out with her, find out whether she cared enough for him to go his way or not. If he didn't get away early enough he would just take it that he wasn't meant to contact Evadne tonight, and let it go at that. It was like tossing a penny up, or leaving it to a higher power to choose.

"There is eternal life to be lived here and now. But you will never find it if you try to live for this world also!"

The teacher's words were projected into his thoughts again and seemed almost as if she were answering what he was thinking. " 'And this is life eternal,' went on the sweet strong voice, " 'that they might know thee, the only true God, and Jesus Christ whom thou hast sent.' Do you want to begin to live this eternal life now, tonight?"

Something stirred in Kent Havenner's heart. Impulsively he wanted to accept that invitation. But how?

And then the class was breaking up. They were stirring all about him, rising to go. How short it had been!

He rose and looked toward Jane Scarlett, and she was looking straight at him, but with unseeing eyes alight with earnest thought. There was no recognition in her glance. She was obviously thinking of what she had been hearing.

He came a little nearer and stood at the end of her aisle as she waited for the girl ahead of her to pass out.

Then as she came on he spoke in a low friendly courteous voice.

"Miss Scarlett?"

Jane started and looked up. This was not young Gaylord. Neither was it Mr. Clark. Yet she knew the voice. But she had no acquaintances who came to this class. Because of her extreme shyness the few girls who had spoken to her did not know her name. And none of the young men had so much as looked at her nor she at them.

Then recognition dawned.

"Oh, Mr. Havenner! I did not expect to see you here."

"Well, no, it's scarcely one of my haunts,"—he smiled. "I have you to thank for the discovery. But I think I'll come again. It's very unusual, isn't it?"

A blaze of light suddenly shone in her face, making her almost lovely.

"It is wonderful!" she admitted. "But I don't see how I was the means of bringing you here. I only just found it myself a few days ago."

"Well, you see, it happens that you are very much wanted at our office, and I've been keeping an eye out for you for the past two weeks. I even went to your boarding house to search for you, and when I was told that you had left there I tried the store again, but was told you were on vacation. As nobody knew where you had gone there was nothing else to do but wait. But I've been more or less alert for you ever since, for I knew the office was annoyed about my not being able to produce you after having had an interview with you. So when I spied you entering this hall tonight, and failed to be able to attract your attention, I followed you in. I hope you don't mind."

But a sudden troubled look had come into Jane's face.

"Why of course not," she said, "but I don't understand what anybody would want me for. Is something the matter somewhere?"

The young man smiled disarmingly.

"Nothing to be alarmed about," he said. "It was just that the office wrote you a letter, and it came back to them with a stamp that you were unknown at that address. As I was responsible for the address they used, the matter naturally was brought to my notice."

"A letter?" said Jane. "But what would they be writing to me about?"

"Well, I wasn't shown the letter, but I understood it had to do with the settlement of an estate, some papers that had to be signed. Nothing to worry you, I'm sure."

Jane's brows puckered in perplexity.

"Oh, they surely must have got me mixed with some-one else. I wouldn't be having anything to do with the settlement of an estate. I couldn't even be a witness, I'm sure. I've never really had much to do with any of the relatives." She gave a little nervous laugh.

"Well, you'll soon have opportunity to know exactly what it is, Miss Scarlett, for I am quite sure the letter will be delivered to you tomorrow morning if you will be good enough to tell me where to deliver it."

"Oh!" she said a bit breathlessly, for she could not yet fathom the why of the letter. "Why, my vacation is over tomorrow morning. I shall be back in the store."

"And back at your same boarding house? I understood the lady to say that you were done with her, or she was done with you."

Jane laughed at the twinkle in his eyes.

"No, I shall not be there. I've found a new room."

"Will it be all right to deliver the letter to you at the store?" he asked respectfully. "I want to make sure it reaches its destination this time."

"Oh, yes, quite all right."

"Then I'll be there. Please don't evade me this time."

They had reached the outside door now, and began walking down the steps, Jane evidently expecting him to leave her. She had that attitude. But Kent did not intend to leave her yet.

"You won't mind if I walk with you a little way, will you?" he asked. "I want to ask you a little about that class tonight. What is it? How did you find out about it? I've never heard of a class like that before, that is, outside of a church. I suppose they have such things in churches, though I don't know much about it from ex-perience. Or perhaps this *is* a church affair. Is it? I was very much interested."

"I don't think so," said Jane, instant interest in her face, and a quick light in her fine eyes that made them lovely once more. "It seems to be just a class. I don't know who sponsors it, or even whether it is sponsored. I just happened to hear it announced on the radio the other night in such a unique way that I determined I would go and see what it was all about, and I liked it so much that I kept coming."

"Well, I liked it too," said Kent with surprising candor. "I wouldn't have expected to like it, but now I'm so interested to see if they can bear out what they said that I'm minded to go again myself. It sort of hit me home right where I live."

"Oh, did you feel that way too? That was the way the announcement made me feel. They said 'If you are sad and weary and questioning what life is all about, if you want to find an answer that will satisfy, and help you go on amid hardships and loneliness, come to Mrs. Brooke's class and get help and comfort.' Well, I went and I'm finding it."

He looked down at her questioningly, searched her earnest young face deeply, and said at last:

"Then perhaps I shall find what I need there too. I'm half a mind to try it."

"Well," said Jane with a timid little smile, "you wouldn't of course have the same trials and disappointments that I have, but I believe, or I'm coming to believe, that there is a remedy in that book for any need one could have."

"I wonder!" said the young man, and walked on by her side thoughtfully.

Presently Jane came to the apartment where she had been staying, and hesitated at the door.

"I have to go in here now," she said shyly. "I'll be expecting that letter in the morning."

Kent cast a glance up at the building. Quite a different affair from the place he had gone to seek her two weeks ago.

"Oh," he said looking at her and the opulent entrance again, "are you living here? I don't blame you for leaving that other place."

"No," said Jane with a sad little twist to her voice, "oh no, nothing so nice as this. I've just been staying here with a canary and some goldfish while their owner was away. I made it my vacation. But it's over tonight.

The owner is returning at ten o'clock and I'm leaving for quarters more suited to my pocketbook. I'm sorry of course to go, but it's been a lovely vacation and rested me a lot."

"Oh," said Kent Havenner giving his watch a quick glance, "then you've almost an hour to wait before you move. Have you anything to do in the interval? Because I've been noticing the notebook you are carrying with you and wondering if there isn't some spot where we could sit down for a few minutes and you could tell me about the other lessons in this little red book. I have a great curiosity to know just what the preliminary line of study was. I'm sure I saw you taking notes. Isn't that right? Well, then, would you have time, or are there still some duties awaiting you upstairs?"

Jane hesitated.

"No," she said honestly, "I'm all packed. I've only to go up a minute or two and give an account of my stewardship, and then I'm moving on to my new home. I'll be glad to give you an idea of what I've gleaned from the meetings so far. Or you could take my notebook with you? Though I'm not sure the notes would be very clear. I had to take them down so briefly."

"Thank you," said Kent with alacrity. "Why couldn't we sit down on that bench I see in there across from the elevators? There seems to be a good light. Would you be able to see your friend from there when she arrives, or is there some better place?"

"No, that's fine," said Jane with relief in her voice. She was afraid he might be going to ask her to go to some hotel or place of amusement, and that she was determined not to do. She might be late and then what would Miss Leech think?

So they entered the lobby and sat down. Jane got out her little notebook and Kent opened his book of John and they were soon deep in study.

Kent Havenner had forgotten all about Evadne for the time being. He was studying an entirely different type of girl, and he had no intention whatever of letting her out of his sight until he knew just where she was located. Not that he doubted her genuineness, but she had been lost out of the scheme of things once, and there was no telling

but something might happen again. Besides, he was really
interested to know just what type of girl this was who had
gotten interest and apparently entertainment out of a Bible
class.

Jane opened her notebook at the beginning and made
him turn to the different chapters and verses, and then
went on. With remarkable clearness, in well chosen words,
she spread out the story in John as she had heard it,
coloring it all by what it had done for her own soul,
and incidentally revealing the sadness and desolation of
her own lot. She did not know she was doing this latter.
It would have been the last thing in life she would have
willingly done, to have projected herself into his notice.

He watched her face which had suddenly become vivid
as she detailed the lessons she had got, and now and
then the listener was startled at the applicability of the
truths given.

"You couldn't, if you had tried, have told me anything
that would so have hit my own case," he suddenly confessed, looking into her sweet eyes with a kind of wonder.
His sister had sweetness in her eyes and so had his mother.
But most of the girls he knew had sharp, brilliant un-
sympathetic eyes. He marveled at this girl. This girl who
had been living in the very common walks of life.

But his confession brought a sudden consciousness to
Jane. Before that she had been talking to him much as if
she were talking aloud to herself, going over a lesson that
had helped her. Now suddenly he became a stranger, an
utter stranger, and she felt herself presumptuous to be
talking thus so freely. She was only a button salesgirl.
She had no business to be preaching a sermon to this
stranger.

The color stole up into her pale cheeks and she dropped
her lashes shyly.

"I have talked too much," she said abruptly. "I did not
intend to apply this to anyone but myself."

"Perhaps that is the fineness of your ability, that you
could use a lesson which has touched your soul to touch
mine also. I thank you for it. And is that all?"

"No, there is one more before tonight."

Rapidly she went over the tiny pages, touching upon
the main points, and just as she finished she heard a taxi

drive up in front of the building and glancing up caught a glimpse of Miss Leech getting out and lingering to pay the driver.

"And that brings us up to tonight," finished Jane hastily, "and there comes my lady. I shall have to go now. Take the notebook if you like and copy it. I can get it again when you bring the letter." She smiled at him and rose with a finality that startled him. There was something about it that seemed so self-possessed, so like a woman of the world who was dismissing him. "Good night!" and she walked gracefully over to the door and possessed herself of the suitcase Miss Leech was capably carrying in.

Kent Havenner sat absolutely still where she had left him, glancing up at the newcomer, but not intruding himself upon the scene. He was pleasantly surprised to notice that the elderly woman who came in, greeting Jane with friendly eyes, was neither a snob, nor a woman of the world in appearance, just a quiet self-possessed business woman.

The elevator came down with a slam just then and clattered its door open, and the two walked into it without looking toward him. He had a feeling that Jane Scarlett would prefer it so.

And so Kent Havenner sat and conned the little notebook till he knew its phrases by heart, caught the turn of words and sentences that spoke of the personality of the writer, the lesson coming through her own heart to his.

It is hard to say just what Evadne Laverock would have thought if she had passed that way and looking in had seen her erstwhile lover who she thought was now under discipline, studying a little book like that and sitting there at his ease as if he had all the night before him, while she waited impatiently for his coming. But there he sat, and several miles away across the city Evadne sat and fumed and waited.

X

Miss Leech was delighted with the look of her apartment, especially with the pot of African violets that Jane had bought at a wayside stand as a little expression of her thanks.

Jane insisted on her going around and looking at everything before she took her departure.

"I hate to have you go," said the older woman looking at Jane approvingly. "It's so late wouldn't you like to stay here and sleep on the couch tonight?"

"Thank you, no. I have a room, and I must go to it and get settled for the morning. I'm so glad you are pleased with everything. I've tried to keep it just as you left it."

"Oh, you have! At least I believe it is cleaner than when I left. I'm afraid you haven't done anything but clean house every day."

"Oh yes, I have!" said Jane eagerly, her eyes lighting up. "I've read two whole rows of books, and I've listened to the radio a lot. I've had a wonderful time, and I've gained five pounds. I'm proud of that. I was really getting too thin."

"Yes, you're looking very well. I'm so glad! I was a little worried about you. I thought perhaps I had been the means of keeping you in the hot city when otherwise you might have gone somewhere in the country."

"Oh, no!" said Jane quickly. "I couldn't. I should have stayed right here and worked hard in the store if you hadn't let me keep your house for you. I had no idea of taking a vacation at all till Mr. Clark came and told me the store was giving me a vacation with pay because I had been sick. I thought that was wonderful of them. But I wouldn't have had any place to go if it hadn't been for you. You see my room was perfectly dreadful. It was breathless and the food was something terrible. Some days I could scarcely eat a bite."

"Oh, my dear! That's too bad. But what are you going to do now?"

"Oh I have another room," said Jane lightly, evading the searching glance of the older woman's eyes. "I hope it is going to be much better."

"Well, I hope so," said Miss Leech. "You must keep in touch with me, and come and visit me for a day or two if you have to hunt for another place."

"Oh, thank you!" said Jane. "You've been just wonderful to me. I won't forget it, ever!"

"Well, I hope we'll always be friends. You don't know what a comfort it has been to me to know I could trust you with my room. It being the only real home I have in the world, of course I prize it."

"Oh, of course. It's a beautiful place. If I ever get rich I shall try to have one just like it, only I'm sure I shall never be as prosperous as all that."

"You can never tell, my dear!" said Miss Leech. "I used to be terribly hard up fifteen years ago when I first got a job, and I tell you I've worked hard for every little thing I own. Except of course a few of the old things, furniture and dishes that came from my home after my mother and father died. So I love it all. And now I shall feel that you have a share of interest in it too, and shall want you to come and see me as often as you can spare the time. Of course I'm getting to be an old woman, and I can't be very good company for a young girl like you, but I shall enjoy you whenever you haven't any better company."

"Oh, I'll love to come," said Jane. "You and I have a lot in common for I've read some of your wonderful books, and so I feel as if I knew the same people you know. And now I must run along and let you get to bed, for I know you are tired after that long journey. Goodbye and don't forget there are some cinnamon buns in the tin box for your breakfast, and fresh eggs in the refrigerator."

Jane picked up her suitcase and the suitbox that held her curtains, and started toward the door, but Miss Leech held out an envelope.

"Here, my dear," she said. "Here is your compensation for looking after my place."

"But indeed, *no!*" said Jane drawing away. "I couldn't think of taking anything for that. I've had a wonderful vacation and couldn't have had it if you hadn't loaned me your room."

"Indeed you will take it, little girl," said Miss Leech determinedly. "I always pay something for having my place looked after, only I never had such efficient service before. And you don't want to spoil my vacation, do you? I should feel like a selfish thing if you refused to take this."

"But you needn't at all. I really don't need it. The store gave me my vacation with pay, so I have enough to get a start."

"That makes no difference," said Miss Leech. "I'm giving you this little bit because I want to, and you're going to be a good girl and take it. If you don't want to count that you've earned it, then play it is a present I've brought you, and you go and buy something with it to remember me by."

They argued for two or three minutes more, but finally Jane came away with the money. Ten whole dollars! It seemed a fortune to her. Just for staying in a better place than she could possibly have afforded!

Her face was shining with happiness as she got out of the elevator. And there right before her stood Kent Havenner, her little notebook in his hand, and a smile of welcome on his face.

"I've copied it all," he announced pleasantly, "and I thought you wouldn't mind if I stayed till you came down and gave it to you tonight. Here! Let me have that baggage!"

"Oh, thank you, no," said Jane, her face crimsoning with embarrassment to think how shabby her baggage was, and to remember that she had only a very poor rooming house as destination. He mustn't find out where it was. She would be ashamed!

"But yes," he said possessing himself of the box and suitcase. "I'm going to see you to your apartment. I couldn't think of letting you go alone at this time of night."

"Oh, I'm not afraid," said Jane. "I'm used to it, you see. I have to do it often. You mustn't spoil me. I'm a working girl, you know. Please let me have them."

"Oh, no," he said gaily. "You may be a working girl, but you're in my care tonight, and I have a debt to pay you for introducing me to the book of John. I have a hunch I'm going to be pretty crazy over that before I get through."

She walked perforce by his side to the door and tried to make another stand when she reached the sidewalk, but he only laughed, and gathering the two pieces of luggage under one arm he waved his other hand to a taxi.

The taxi swept up to the curb and he handed the luggage to the driver, as he swung open the door.

"Now," he said as he put her in and got in beside her, "where to? What's the street and number?"

Jane faltered out the address, and added, "But please, I wish you wouldn't feel that you must go out of your way to go with me. I'll be quite all right alone now."

She reflected that after all it wouldn't cost much to pay taxi fare, just this once, and of course it was rather a long way to carry her baggage herself.

But the young man only closed the door of the cab and laughed.

"Sorry my company isn't agreeable to you," he said, "but I've a great desire to see you definitely located for the night so that I shall be reasonably sure to be able to find you in the morning in case you are detained from going to the store. You see I've got to deliver that letter, and I'm taking no chances."

His face was a broad grin, and Jane reflected how pleasant he looked when he grinned, and thought how nice it would be to have a real friend who looked like that and insisted on taking care of her now and then.

"Oh!" she said. And then her face grew troubled as she thought of that letter.

"Is—that letter—so important?" she managed to ask.

"Well, yes, I imagine it's rather important to one member of the Scarlett family, or at least I've been led to suppose that. Anyway it's important that I shall be able to discharge my duty toward the letter, and prove that there *is* a Jane Scarlett, and that I have seen her and talked with her."

"But I can't imagine that I could have anything to do with an important document," mused Jane, the worry stealing into her eyes again. "You see I scarcely know the family at all."

"Well, don't try to imagine, then," said Kent still smiling. "Wait till morning and let the letter settle it. Is this the house?"

He gazed out of the taxi window at the tall bare-looking building before which they had stopped. There was nothing in his facial expression to show what was in his heart about that stark ugly building, nor how unsuited an abode it seemed for that sweet-faced girl, with the delicate features and great serious eyes.

He helped her out and they stood together in the bare uninviting hall while she waited for the landlady or matron or whatever she was to finish talking to a slatternly girl with sly eyes who was trying to get a room for the night without any money to pay for it.

"This is no place for you," said Kent's eyes as he gave a critical glance about and then looked down at Jane's worried eyes. But his lips tried to smile and take it all for granted as if it were an abode of luxury.

"It's—" Jane glanced around her with a disapproving glance, "not so very—grand!" she finished apologetically. "But one can't expect grandeur for a pittance."

"No, I suppose not," said Kent glancing up the straight steep stairway that loomed at the end of the hall, "but it's not very homelike."

"It isn't a home," said Jane with a quick drawn breath of sadness. "One doesn't always have a home. That's why that fourteenth chapter of our little red book of John seems so wonderful to me. 'In my Father's house are many mansions. . . . I go to prepare a place for you.' *They* will be *homes* I'm sure, and there will always be those at the end of the road."

Kent looked down at her in wonder. Such an earnest young face, so sweet and wistful! Audrey had been right. She was unusual. And Audrey had seen that look in her face. She must have. It was a look that once seen was to be remembered.

"I wouldn't know about that," he said seriously. "I've never thought about homes at the end of the road. I'm afraid I've been occupied with thinking of homes along the way, like the teacher said tonight. But perhaps after this I shall think more about it. What chapter was that verse you just quoted about your Father's house?"

"Oh, that's the fourteenth of John. I learned that when I was a little girl. I hadn't thought about it for a long time, until recently, and it came back and—helped me."

She confessed her experience gently with a fleeting smile, as if she scarcely could believe that one like this young man would be interested in such things, or in anything she could say. Yet she was pleased and touched with awe that he really seemed to be.

An unusual conversation to be carried on in, and actually inspired by, that crude rooming house, yet there they stood, he lingering with a strange unexplained reluctance to leave.

Then the matron dismissed the other girl and came forward to Jane. Her eyes narrowed, looking nearsightedly through sparse faded lashes. Suddenly, with a rare smile, Kent lifted his hat, with fine impulse not to embarrass Jane by being a listener to her conversation.

"Well, good night! See you in the morning!" and he was gone.

Jane gave a quick glance out of the door into the warm darkness where he had disappeared, and it suddenly seemed to her that the sun had just been withdrawn from a very bright day.

Afterward when she went up to the fourth floor back room, and discovered its utter desolateness, it did not seem quite so depressing because her mind was on her evening. She discovered that the young man and her talk with him had even superseded and blotted out the coming of her friend Miss Leech. Yes, and the extra money she had not expected to have! Why, there were pleasant things in the world, even though one had no place but this bare room to call home. She had friends, she had more money than she had hoped for, and best of all she had her Heavenly Father's house to look forward to.

But what a pleasant man Mr. Havenner was! How his eyes spoke volumes when he was talking about the class. How he had responded to her own thoughts and feelings. Oh, what would it be to have a real friend like that for her very own!

But of course she mustn't let her mind dwell on him or anything connected with him. He was a great man, that is, he was likely going to be great, a lawyer, and well started on his way toward success from all appearances. And she was only a button salesgirl. She must never forget that. Perhaps sometime in the Father's house

above they would meet and talk over their common interest in the book of John, but down here he was separated
from her by impassable barriers. For of course he had
only been kind and courteous. So she must not dwell on
their conversation, nor make anything of it. He was keeping in touch with her just to be sure to get that letter to
her in the morning. And that he spoke interestedly of the
class and the lesson might only have been an extreme of
courtesy. He might not even have meant any of it. Yet
she couldn't but think it had been real interest in his
eyes, interest for the things of another world.

However, that was not for her to speculate about. She
would just be glad that he was interested, or seemed to
be, because it made her comfortable and happy to have
a bit of fellowship with another one of God's children. Or
was he God's child?

But that letter! What was that going to mean to her?
Constantly the thought of it recurred to her as something
to be dreaded. Of course it might be some mere technicality that had no significance to her personally, though
she couldn't imagine a circumstance that would make that
possible. But she would be glad when it had come and
the dread of it was over. Now, she would do as the
young man had advised, just put it out of her mind and
forget it until it arrived.

So she turned to the quick settling of her room.

She made her bed swiftly with the skimpy bedclothing
the woman downstairs had given her. She got out her little
hammer from the ten cent store and tacked up her closet
curtain, and then hung her meager garments on the few
nails, resolving to purchase a few hooks on her first opportunity and put them up. Then very hurriedly she prepared for bed and was soon discovering what a hard,
hard narrow bed she had tonight in place of the lovely
soft one in Miss Leech's room. But she was very weary,
and it didn't take her long to get to sleep. And it seemed
no time at all until her dependable alarm clock was giving her the signal to rise and remember that she was no
longer a lady of leisure, but was once more a working girl.

XI

WHEN Kent Havenner was out in the narrow street again he walked along briskly, thoughtfully, thinking of the girl he had just left. A most unusual girl!

There were no taxis on this street, and so he must walk until he reached a more frequented district. He was not thinking of where he was going, either, strangely enough. The evening that had begun so definitely as a visit to Evadne, had ended with another girl's wistful face looking at him as she said good night. And he so entirely forgot Evadne that when he reached a street car line that went directly to the railroad station he swung aboard it without thinking. He mind was on the evening's events, trying to think them through to a finish of some sort.

Once he glanced idly at his watch and saw that it was almost time for the last train to the shore, and that if the trolley was not interrupted in any way he ought to be able to make it, but even then he did not remember Evadne.

He made the station just in time to swing himself on the last car of the train, and it was not until he reached into his pocket for his commutation ticket and pulled out inadvertently Evadne's letter that he was reminded of the engagement which he had not kept.

He stared down at the letter in his hand, and finally read it through again. It did not take long. It was just one of her casual scrawls. She never wrote a letter as if she really cared. She always made it appear that it was a privilege to be informed that she was in the vicinity and would deign to receive one.

Old thing:
Am staying over night with Gloria. If you could drop in we could talk.

As ever,
Vad.

Somehow this reading of the letter gave him a distinct shock. It did not sound in the least like a girl who was sorry for her part of their separation. When he had read it the first time he had only seen in it a concession that she should stoop to inform him she was near and willing to talk. Now a careless insolence was uppermost.

"We could talk." She promised nothing. There was no penitence. And why talk more? They had talked hours upon hours and got nowhere. Why should he expect they would get anywhere tonight? And in the light of the evening he had just spent, her letter seemed most vapid and uninteresting. True it was couched in the accepted parlance of the day, that affected indifference. Was it true that he had ever admired that style of address? Why should reasonable human beings affect a disregard of the decencies and refinements of life? Almost he could see from his mother's point of view.

Well, it was too late to do anything about it now. The train was speeding on its way. Even if he could stop it there would be no way station where he could get transportation back to the city.

And besides, did he care? Had he the least desire to talk with Evadne? If she had anything worth while to tell him she would in time write it to him, or even come and see him. He was satisfied of that. She wasn't in the least backward about carrying out any of her own wishes, and she would find a way. It wouldn't hurt her in the least, even if he wanted eventually to bring her back to his wishes, to see that he was not as keen about her as he used to be. And even if she were now ready, after due coaxing, to promise what he had made a condition of their further acquaintance, he wasn't at all sure that he could trust her promises. Why had he ever thought he could? And what had changed him, without seeing her again? How did he now know so well what she must have been going to say?

Was it possible that it had taken that hour with the little clear-eyed girl from the button counter to show him Evadne's irresponsibility? How was it that a girl like Jane Scarlett in a few brief meetings had opened his eyes to this and more?

Or could it be that that quiet time spent in reading

portions of the Bible had somehow toned his spirit to a place where he could discern between real and false?

Well, all this argument with himself was nonsense of course, and why waste the time? Jane Scarlett was only a working girl, with a courageous and a brave outlook, but he mustn't let his thoughts get tangled up with different points of view, and lives. He had enjoyed the evening, of course, and he had to own that he was glad he had got free from the talk with Evadne, but he mustn't get the "Cousin Evalina attitude" as Audrey called it. He probably would seldom see Jane Scarlett again, but he was sure that her genuineness and sweet character had helped him to see the false in Evadne. Maybe it wasn't being half fair to Evadne, but he didn't care. He was going home to bed, and he wasn't sorry. If he had gone to Evadne he would have had to take her to a night club, maybe two or three of them, and how would he have felt tomorrow after that? No, he was glad he had been so absorbed in thinking about what Jane had said that he had forgotten to go in the other direction. Probably tomorrow morning he would have to call Evadne up and explain and apologize, but anyhow he would have a good night's sleep. That was better than going to a hotel bed at five in the morning.

So he settled back and closed his eyes and thought of all he had heard that evening. And without his voluntary bidding Jane Scarlett's face in its wistful eagerness kept coming to his mind.

About the time that Kent Havenner boarded the train to the shore, the telephone in the Havenner cottage by the sea rang insistently, and Audrey answered it.

"Is this Havenner's?" a languid voice asked sharply.

An old familiar fury rose in Audrey's soul, at the sound of that voice. Insolent, that was what the voice was, and her heart sank with apprehension.

"Yes?" she said with crisp dignity.

"I want to speak with Kent," the voice drawled, ignoring the one who had answered, though she must have known who it was.

"He is not here at present." More dignity.

"Oh! When will he be in?"

"I'm not sure. He said he might be late."

"Well, tell him to call me up at once when he gets

in." The words were a command, as if they were being given to a servant. "This is Vad Laverock speaking," the voice went on. "Tell him to call Maurice 1011-J."

"Very well!" said Audrey without a shade of recognition in her voice, and immediately there was a quick click. Evadne had hung up.

Audrey stood there with her soul boiling within her. Was this what had made Kent stay in town tonight? Had he somehow found out that Evadne was in the vicinity again? Poor fool of a boy!

So that creature was back!

And now would Kent go into a slump again and be worthless as far as business or anything sensible was concerned? Just when he had been doing so well, and was getting interested, really interested in his work! Oh, why did Kent admire her anyway? Painted, artificial, unnatural creature! How terrible it would be if Kent should marry her! Mother and father would feel it so. And as for herself she would be entirely separated from her beloved brother!

Not that Evadne was one who would long endure any yoke like marriage. And that again would bring about another intolerable situation. Divorce was utter disgrace in the eyes of their parents. In fact both Audrey and her brother had been brought up to feel that way about it. Oh, if there was only something she could do to save Kent!

So, instead of going to bed early as she had planned, Audrey took a book and sat up and pretended to read. Though if the truth were known she did very little reading, for she kept continually thrashing over the problem in her mind, hearing again the insolent accents of that hateful voice.

Also she had a situation of her own to ponder. A situation not quite as obnoxious perhaps to the family, but almost as perplexing to herself. Ballard Bainbridge was a scholar of parts. He was so brilliant that some who knew him regarded him almost as highly as he regarded himself. He was handsome withal, and weathy, a pleasant playmate when he chose to play. But did she want him in any closer relationship than as a playmate?

The trouble with him was he was a cynic and a scorner.

He had an innate conviction that nobody knew as much as he did. Not even God, or the president, or the Bible.

Now Mr. and Mrs. Havenner were not distinguished church people, nor noted religious workers, but they went to church at least once a Sunday whenever it was convenient, and they did not like to hear even a scholar criticize churches and ministers and religious beliefs. It did not seem well-bred to them. They liked the manners and customs of an older day, and thought it poor taste for youth to presume to depart from them. Audrey well knew that it would be a sore trial to have their daughter marry a man of that type. And then to have their son marry an Evadne, linking them up with a world which they felt had gone mad, and was no longer safe and sane and conservatively respectable, would be the final blow. Audrey was dealing with the family problem for really the first time, and seeing her own part in it as she had never seen it before.

Now after considering her brother and the terrible mistake he seemed about to make, she came at last to face the facts in her own life. What was it she saw in Ballard Bainbridge anyway? Did she really think she was in love with him or hadn't the affair progressed that far yet? Perhaps it was time she looked things in the face and settled that before things went any further between them. Could she ever really love Ballard? She admired him immensely. His brain fairly scintillated with brillancy. His clever sayings were a joy, even if most of them did end in a sneer at somebody. And sometimes even a sneer at some pet idea of her own? Could she possibly fancy herself as going through life continuing to admire him, and to love him the way father and mother admired and loved one another? Listening to his everlasting cynicism day after day? Fighting the depression that came over her sometimes when he laid low some time-honored custom or faith? Not that she had any very strong religious convictions herself, or wanted to have, but her own nature was sunny and sweet and it depressed her terribly to hear constant criticism and sneers. His nature was wild and turbulent. Everybody wrong but himself, and he set to tell them where they made all their mistakes. Would he ever get over it? Would the time come when he grew a little older and still wiser, that he would realize that he wasn't the only wise one in the whole world? As she looked at the matter honestly, without bias now, she found herself wondering if a woman could really go on loving a man, or even love him enough in the first place to marry him, when she saw his glaring faults as plainly as she did Ballard's. And was it conceivable that if she should ever get up the courage to talk with him about it frankly, that he would consider what she said seriously, and try to look into himself and mend his ways? Would he not rather tell her she was a mere woman, and had no brain or she would know that her criticism of him was all wrong?

Distantly amid her thoughts Audrey heard the late train coming in and suddenly her mind reverted to her brother. Would he be on that train? Or would he stay in town all night as he had suggested he might and go even yet to see Evadne? She knew enough about that girl to realize that the night for her had just begun.

More and more as she considered this her soul rebelled at this possibility for her brother. She couldn't bear to have her precious brother spoil his life. Oh, how did he get in with such a girl anyway? Did he really think he cared for that worthless selfish bit of froth? She had driven him once to take a stand, and then had sulkily gone away to Europe, and apparently not even written to him all this time. Now she was back and was endeavoring to order him around as if he were an old possession of hers. After all this interval would he go back to her? What a sorrowful outlook for the family if he did! Would Kent stand for her high-handedness? He had always been so independent, so decided and self-assured! Would he let this girl wind him around any way she pleased? It didn't seem possible.

Then suddenly she heard Kent's quick step on the path outside. He had *come!*

But her heart went down as suddenly, as she remembered that she must give him Evadne's message. Probably he hadn't known she was in town after all or he would not have come home. Perhaps now he would take mother's car and drive back. There was no telling. She began to wish she had gone to bed and not waited up to tell him.

"Hello!" his voice came cheerfully. "You up yet? What's the idea?"

Then he gave a quick look around.

"Not expecting company at this time of night, are you? Or has that walking encyclopedia of yours just gone? Honestly Audrey, I can't see what you see in that conceited ape of a Bainbridge. I thought you had better sense! If you attach that baboon you and I'll be two people. I can't see him for a brother-in-law, ever. And you won't ever be happy, either, with his exclusive company, for I warn you dad and mother won't be likely to come and see you very often. Maybe you didn't hear him correcting dad the other day, telling him how to run his business on more up-to-date lines. If you had been watching dad and mother then you'd have known about what the atmosphere is going to be if you ever marry that bag of wind."

Audrey's face flushed angrily, and then she laughed.

"You're a pretty one to talk. How about the girl you've picked out? What do you think mother will look like if you ever bring that common painted Evadne home as your wife?" She looked at him with flashing eyes, and for an instant his own dropped. Then he looked up again, and laughed half shamedly.

"Now Audrey, that's not a parallel case. I haven't seen Evadne Laverock for six whole months. She's been in Europe. We haven't even written."

"Yes?" said Audrey raising her eyebrows questioningly at her brother, and lifting her chin a bit haughtily.

"Well, she isn't in Europe any more," she said, studying his face as she spoke to see if he had known this, "and she's waiting right now for you to call her up. The number is Maurice 1011-J."

Kent took on an annoyed look immediately.

"What do you mean? Did she call up?"

"She did!" said Audrey, "which is the reason for my staying up, to give you the message, in spite of my good advice. You'd better call her at once. It's getting fairly late."

"Thanks a lot, sister," said Kent in a dignified carelessness, "but morning will be plenty of time. I'm dropping over with sleep, and I'm not keen to call anybody up."

"Well, but really, she was quite insistent."

"I have no doubt of it, but will you kindly let me manage my own affairs?"

"Oh, certainly," said his sister, rising, "with the condition that I may have the same privilege."

"Okay with me!" said the young man yawning. "I wasn't managing. I was just telling you what possibilities were ahead for you if you continued in the way you seem to be going. However, of course, it's your privilege to choose between that know-it-all and your humble family. Good night, kid, I'm turning in. I'm frightfully sleepy!" and he turned and flung up the stairs.

Audrey turned out the lights and went up to her room, but she lay awake for sometime listening. She wanted to make sure that Kent didn't go downstairs afterward and telephone Evadne. It was so inexplicable that he had taken her message so casually. It wasn't like Kent's former way at all.

But though she lay awake for a long time, considering not only the possibilities connected with her brother, but her own as well, Kent did not go downstairs, and presently she heard his regular breathing down the hall, and knew that he was asleep. Well, it was most extraordinary! That he would get a message like that from Evadne and not even bother to call up! Well, if he was really going to be sensible and give up Evadne perhaps she ought to look into her own case and see whether what he had said about Ballard was really true, or just a bit of foolish prejudice. She wouldn't of course want to marry a man who would antagonize her own brother. He might get over it, but then perhaps he was counting on her getting over her feeling about Evadne sometime, and she never would! Never!

At last she went to sleep, her mind more than troubled over her own problem.

She was awakened earlier than usual the next morning by hearing Kent go whistling downstairs. He stopped at the telephone. She sprang up and threw her kimono about her, listening at the door. Was he going to make an appointment for the day with that girl after all?

Then she heard her brother's voice clear and cool.

"Is Miss Laverock there? Oh, sorry! No don't disturb her if she is still asleep. Just give her a message. This is

Kent Havenner. Tell Miss Laverock that I couldn't possibly make it last night and I got her message very late, too late to call her. That's all. She'll understand. Thank you. Good-bye!"

Just that. Then Kent went whistling out on the front porch and presently Audrey glanced out the window and saw him walking briskly down the beach in the morning sunshine and gazing off at a white sail on the sea.

Now what did that mean? Was Kent off the girl for life, or just still angry at whatever she had done?

So presently, when Bainbridge called up and wanted Audrey to go sailing that morning she considered seriously before she answered. Should she go and study the young man from her brother's point of view, or should she decline and stay at home?

She finally decided on staying at home. Why should she go when she had no particular desire to do so? Especially as she was not at all sure what her future attitude was to be toward this young man? Why go on any longer until she knew her own mind or heart in the matter! And why force a situation until it came naturally? Didn't the very fact that she was not keen to go with him show that she did not care for him very much? Had she ever thought that she did? There were at least a dozen other young men who came to see her often, whom she would have liked as well. This one had simply come oftener, asked her to go places before anybody else had a chance. Would she really care if she never saw him again? Would she be hurt or sad, except as it might be a matter of pride, if some other girl won him away from her? She had to own honestly that she would not.

So she settled it with her heart that all was well so far. At least she would have a respite for one day and get calm enough to know what she was about. For truly, it did not seem to her that any young man she knew, so far, had stirred her heart to its depths. She could not think of any one whose words of love would set her senses going with delight. Maybe she wasn't the kind of girl who would ever fall in love deeply anyway. Why worry? Why go after love till it came after you? Life was sweet and pleasant enough without it. Why did every woman think that of course she had to get married or her life would spell disaster? There were lots of nice things to do without that.

So she set herself to do some of the things she had put by for a time of leisure, and a happy little peace filled her heart and made her feel that this day was a nice restful interval.

XII

JANE awoke the next morning not quite as refreshed from her night's sleep on the new bed as she had been in Miss Leech's lovely apartment, but she got up with interest in the new day. She was going back to work at the button counter and she felt so much better than when she had left for her vacation that she was almost thrilled at the prospect of returning. After all it was so nice that she had a job, and was feeling better and able to get back. It was so nice that she had pleasant things to remember, the books and the canary, and the goldfishes, and the delightful bed, and then most of all that wonderful Bible class.

Memory of Kent Havenner's appearance last night and the pleasant time they had had together talking over the lesson came like a dash of bright color into the picture and made her smile to herself into the scrap of a mirror that hung over her bureau. He had been nice, and he had said he would come again this morning with that letter. However portentous the letter might be, at least it was interesting to have a courteous gentleman bringing it. She would be able to ask his advice or explanation in case the letter was not a pleasant one or involved some sort of action on her part.

So she hurried with her dressing, and went down to the unpretentious cafeteria downstairs, where oatmeal and weak cream featured prominently with orange juice at a premium and not so good at that. She got a simple breakfast. She was rather too excited to eat much. And then she went on her way to the store.

They greeted her quite gaily, those other girls with whom she worked. They told her the latest news of the store.

"And you know that Mr. Gaylord over at the stockings? They say he's married! Can you believe it? And after the way he's been carrying on with all the girls! Why he's made love to half a dozen at least, and Marianne

Featherton went around all day today after she heard it, crying her eyes out for him. Isn't she a fool? She says he proposed to her Saturday night! Isn't that the limit? And they say his wife left him six months ago. I don't blame her, do you? Of course Adele Burridge says she doesn't believe a word of it. That she usedta live in the same town where he came from and if he'd ever have been married she'd have heard of it. She's got an aunt living there yet that always writes her all the news, and she says he isn't that kind of a fella at all. But my eye, you don't havta watch him but halfa day ta tell what he is, the way he carries on with all the girls."

"Yes?" said Jane looking at the girl with a quiet calm in her eyes. "Well it's likely he knows the truth himself, and it isn't our business, of course."

"Yeah, course, but I think we should let it be known what kinda fella he is, don't you? How's a right-minded girl ta know? Why, he even came 'n ast me would I go to a dance with him, an' o' course I said yes, a nice lookin' fella like that, an' now here I find he's married, has been all the time. At least they say he is, so what is a girl to do ef she wants ta be half decent?"

"Well," said Jane with an amused smile on her lips, "I should think a girl would have to go a little slow with any stranger and not accept an invitation until she is really well acquainted. A right-minded man wouldn't ask a girl he scarcely knew at all to go out with him, either, until he had a chance to know what kind of girl he was asking. You can't judge either a man or a girl just by appearances, you know, not in these days anyway. Don't you think so?"

The girl shrugged her shoulders.

"Oh, I don't believe men are so particular these days, do you?"

"Well, I wouldn't care for the man who wasn't, would you?"

"Oh, I dunno. It doesn't do to be too particular or you get left outside of everything."

"Not anything worth while."

"Well, I guess you're pretty straight-laced, aren't you? You don't get much fun that way."

"There are plenty of ways to have fun without that,"

said Jane. "And even if you didn't there's a lot more peace and security."

"Oh rats!" said the other girl. "I should worry about peace and security. You get plenty of that when you're dead!"

"Oh, do you?" said Jane. "I wonder!"

Then a customer came along and she turned away from the conversation, wondering what this girl would say if she were introduced to the Bible classes she had been attending.

It was almost twelve o'clock when Kent Havenner arrived.

He had taken the precaution to cut off a button from one of his partly worn coats, and he had it ready in his hand along with the letter when he arrived in the store. He lingered long enough to get Jane's attention.

"Can you match this for me?" he asked quietly as she handed a package to a lady.

She looked up a bit startled, but controlled the flash in her eyes and smiled casually enough, her salesgirl smile that she turned on all customers, and then glanced at the button.

"Oh yes, I think so," she said pleasantly and taking the button she turned back to the tiers of button drawers. She soon returned with an open box in her hand.

"Yes, I think these are an exact match," she said and held them out to him.

He scrutinized them amusedly.

"Yes, those are the ones. Charge and send a dozen, please, and here is the address."

He handed out the letter with his card slipped over the address. Not the closest observer could see anything unusual in that transaction. He wasn't embarrassing her among her co-laborers in the least.

She gave a quick look at the letter, took her order book and slipped the letter inside, put a rubber band firmly and deftly about it and wrote the address into her order book from the card.

"It's a pleasant day," Kent remarked pleasantly. "I could be at the door when you go out in case there are any questions about the letter you would like to ask. What time are you usually free?"

She gave him a swift comprehending look that carried gratitude.

"That is kind of you. I'm free at five, or three or four minutes later, unless there is a late customer."

"And what door would be most convenient?"

"The Thirteenth Street door."

"I'll be there at five," he said, and turned swiftly away, as Jane gave her attention to another customer.

There was a faint tinge of pink in her cheeks as she stooped to one of the lower drawers to search for a certain kind of buckle the lady wanted, but no one was noticing her. The whole thing had been so swiftly done that even Mr. Clark if he had been watching, would scarcely have noticed the transaction. But Jane's heart was beating wildly, and the next half hour before she was due to go to her lunch seemed long indeed. She had time enough to think of all the wild possibilities that letter might contain, and to draw a cloak of dignity about her in preparation for the afternoon closing time when she would have to meet that kind young lawyer, and perhaps ask him troublous questions. But she went steadily on with her work, trying to remember the verses she had been reading that morning: "Peace I leave with you. *My* peace I give unto you. Not as the world giveth, give I unto you. Let not your heart be troubled, neither let it be afraid."

But at last the time of anxiety was over, and she could escape to the cloak room, and read her letter in peace.

It was not long, that important letter with the name of important lawyers in its upper left hand corner. With trembling fingers she opened the envelope and read, the letters dancing menacingly before her eyes as she tried to take in their meaning.

My dear Miss Scarlett:

As a result of the death of Mr. Harold Scarlett, his will must be probated as soon as it can be conveniently done. As there is a possibility that you may be somewhat benefited by this, we are asking you kindly to call at our office at your earliest convenience and bring with you your birth certificate if possible, or any proofs you may happen to have that will prove your identity.

The property has greatly depreciated during the years of

depression, and is not the opulent estate that it was in former days. But if you can prove your identity satisfactorily it may be that you are one of those mentioned in the will and will therefore have a voice in whether a modest property belonging to the estate shall be sold, or remain within the Scarlett estate. As there is a possible purchaser in view who is anxious to settle the matter at once, it would be a favor if you could come to the office within a short time.

Very truly,

J. Waltham Sanderson

Jane felt her knees weaken under her and suddenly dropped down on a bench, the letter trembling in her hands. What did it mean anyway? What did she have to do with it all? Did it mean that her name had been mentioned in Uncle Harold's will?

She read the letter over again, trying to fathom the exact meaning of each phrase.

How strange if she were mentioned in the will! Why, she didn't even know that Uncle Harold knew her name! Mother always said that he was very different from her father, he was much younger, he was proud of his wealth and family, haughty and disagreeable. He had made a great fuss when he heard her father was to marry her mother. He had said her mother was not good enough to marry his scholarly brother.

The only time that Jane had been at the old homestead, when she was still a little child, Uncle Harold had been abroad. So he had never meant anything but a name to her, and a very vague one at that, whose life would probably never touch hers. She had understood that he traveled a great deal, and spent his money freely in whims of his own.

So now to have him suddenly speaking to her as from beyond the grave filled her with a strange awe.

She tried to recall all her mother had told her about him. He had married, she knew, and his wife had died a few years ago, just before her own mother died. She could not remember whether there had been children or not. Well, probably if there weren't, or even perhaps if there were, there was some technicality of the law whereby it was necessary for all possible heirs to sign off or some-

thing, to make everything legal. Law was a queer thing
that she did not understand. It might be of course that
there was some clause in the grandfather's will that would
take in his other heirs. It must be something like that. It
didn't really make sense to her mind, but it was the only
explanation she could think of, so she had to let it go
at that. At least the letter relieved her anxiety lest someone
were trying to involve her in some crooked business,
stealing or something like that. She didn't just know what.
Anyhow she could do nothing but just wait and trust.

And now she must get a bite of lunch, or she would
be collapsing again. She mustn't run the risk of that.

She folded her letter safely into her handbag and hurried to the dairy lunch in the basement where she could get
a glass of milk and a sandwich quickly. But all the time
her mind was going over this strange new thing that
had come to her, trying to figure out what was its portent.

Suppose Uncle Harold had had no children, what would
he have done with his property? Suppose there had been
fifty or a hundred dollars or perhaps a little more than
that left over after his funeral expenses were paid. To
whom would he have been likely to leave it? Did his
wife have any relatives? She didn't know. Perhaps he
would leave it to a hospital that took care of him in his
last illness, or a nurse, or some club, or maybe even a
church. And perhaps it was necessary in law to have any
relatives sign, to make sure that no possible heirs could
make trouble afterwards. No, that didn't sound very likely.
Law was law, and didn't need possible heirs to agree
to what the dead man had willed, surely. Well, it was
all right, whatever way it was. She still had her job with
a little money ahead, and a Bible class to look forward
to one evening a week all winter, for there had been a
notice given to that effect just last night at the class.
Why should she worry?

Then it suddenly came to her remembrance that the
nice young lawyer was going to meet her at the door at
closing time, ready to answer any questions she had. She
could find out what was closing time in the lawyers' office,
whether they kept open Saturday afternoons, or whether
there would be a time in the evening when she could go
without having to ask off at the store. She really ought

not to run any risks at the store of course. Or maybe she could run over at lunch hour, and just eat a cracker on the way in the street instead of lunch.

Then she was back behind the counter and the day swung into a busy afternoon. She tried to forget all about her personal problems and do her work conscientiously, but all the time in the back of her mind was the exciting consciousness that something was going to happen to her, even if it was only a dull visit to a lawyer's office to sign a prosy paper that meant nothing in the world but a formality. Also she was going to meet young Mr. Havenner again after closing time. It would probably be the last time she would ever see him, but he was someone she would enjoy remembering when days were lonely and time seemed long and weary. He was a gentleman. Perhaps a Christian, she wasn't sure. He had really looked as if he meant it when he said he was going to look farther into the book of John and perhaps turn up at the class again.

And yet Jane did not hasten when the bugle blew. She finished putting away her buttons carefully, and took out her purse in a deliberate way. She waited until Hilda and Louise were gone, and took her time getting her hat, and when she finally reached the Thirteenth Street door they were all out of sight. But there stood Kent Havenner leaning against the wall quite casually and not even facing toward the door. He had a folded newspaper in his hand as if he were perusing it. Nobody could suspect, even if there had been anybody watching, that he was waiting for someone to come out of that door. Yet she had a feeling that he saw her instantly when she appeared. He waited until she stepped out to the pavement, and then he fell into step beside her and walked along smiling as if he belonged there, as if she had left him only a few minutes before.

After he had helped her across the street he said casually:

"Well, was your letter all right?"

"Oh!" she said excitedly. "What is it all about? Do you know? And when do I go to the office? They'll be closed after five, won't they? And I *mustn't* risk losing my job!"

He looked at her with an amused wondering glance. Didn't she really understand?

"I suppose that *would* be important," he said.

"Oh, very!" said Jane tensely, and had a secret feeling that he wouldn't in the least understand how important her job was to her very life.

"Well," he said, still amusedly, "you can go to the office right now if you will." There was a twinkle in his eyes as he said it. "Mr. Sanderson is waiting there now for you, on the chance that I might be able to persuade you to come at once."

"Oh!" she gasped amazed, and then her heart suddenly contracted in a panic. Then it must be more important than she had thought! "Yes, I could go now. I don't suppose it will take long to sign a paper, but I'm sorry if I have inconvenienced him to wait longer than usual."

"Oh, that's nothing for him," said Kent. "He often stays late in the evening when he has extra work to do."

Then suddenly he signaled a taxi and put her in, whirling her away to a great high building, and she was soon shooting up to the fifteenth floor in an elevator, her heart beating excitedly. She was glad that the uncertainty at least would soon be over.

"You don't need to be frightened," said Kent gently, looking down at her anxious young face as they got out of the elevator. "You know there is nothing to be afraid of."

She looked up gratefully.

"You are very kind," she said with a faint smile on her pale lips.

And then suddenly they were in the office and a tall elderly man with gray hair and bushy eyebrows stood looking down at her and she felt a great trembling come upon her.

Kent was introducing her now. This was Mr. Sanderson, and he was offering her a chair.

XIII

JANE dropped down upon the edge of the chair, and her face was very white. Somehow more than ever the business upon which she had come seemed so frightening. If she could only have run out the door and down the stairs and got away she would have done it, and she couldn't just tell why she was so frightened. Somehow the shades of all the things and people that had ever frightened her, seemed to cluster around her and focus in that stern-looking Mr. Sanderson.

"You are Miss Jane Scarlett?" he said, and gave her one of his searching glances. "Did you bring a birth certificate?"

"No," said Jane taking a deep breath and trying to speak steadily. "My birth certificate and the few other things I have of that sort I left in a house where I worked for awhile before I came to this city. It would be several days before I could get them. At least I hope it wouldn't be any longer than that."

Mr. Sanderson drew his brows frowning.

"Are you sure you could get them then?"

"Oh, I think so," said Jane. "I couldn't bring a trunk with me when I came away. I didn't know just where I was going, and the people said I might leave it in their attic."

"Didn't it occur to you that something might happen to that house? A fire or something? Didn't you know that papers like that were very important indeed? Such papers should have been put in a safe-deposit box in a bank for safekeeping."

Jane suddenly smiled. His frowning disapproval, and the utter impossibility of safe-deposit boxes in her life heretofore, made the whole thing seem a farce.

"Why," she laughed, "I didn't have any safe-deposit boxes. I had only the trunk, and no place else to leave it. I couldn't carry it with me, it was too heavy, and I had a long way to walk, at first anyway, and no money to pay for a drayman. But really, I didn't know those papers were worth anything to anyone but myself. And they were only precious to me because they reminded me of my family who were all gone."

The tears all at once welled into her eyes and she winked them away. Just one slipped down and splashed on her white young hand. And there was a mistiness in Mr. Sanderson's eyes, too. An unaccustomed one. Kent flashed a look at him, and then his eyes went back to the girl, the little girl who was facing an unknown dread all alone, and with all his heart he knew he wanted to help her.

"Well," said Mr. Sanderson, clearing his throat, "well, doubtless you did the best you could. And don't worry. Of course there will be some way, either to get the proofs, or to get along without them. Though I understand that there is a relative by marriage who is endeavoring to find out all about this, and try to prove himself an heir. However, we shall find a way, I'm sure. Suppose you tell me exactly what papers you have that show who your father and mother were, and when and where you were born. Can you remember exactly what you have?"

"Oh, yes," said Jane in a clear voice, "there is an old Bible. I think it belonged to grandmother and grandfather Scarlett. It has the dates of all births and marriages and deaths. And there is my mother's marriage certificate, and the certificate when I was baptized, and a little certificate of membership in a Sunday School class when I was very young. And then I have an old photograph album with the pictures of my father and mother and my grandparents on both sides, and a number of the other relatives. Their names are there, written by my father. I think there is a picture of the old home in that album too. A snapshot somebody took."

"Well, that ought to be pretty good proof, if you could produce it," said Mr. Sanderson brightening up a bit.

"Proof of what, Mr. Sanderson?" Jane's voice was very low, but there was a hint of the anxiety in it that she was feeling.

"Why, proof that you are who you claim to be."

"But I haven't claimed anything," said Jane, bewildered. "I just answered the questions that were asked me, and I don't understand yet why I should have been asked.

I don't see how I could really prove anything, because you see I have not had anything to do with any of the family at all since I was a very small child, except just after my mother died, when a great aunt seemed to feel a little responsibility for me for awhile, and put me in a school where I could work for my board and tuition. But then she got married again and didn't want to bother about me any more, so she got me a place to work where they kept summer boarders. You see I couldn't really testify anything that would be worth your bothering with me."

"See here, young woman," said Mr. Sanderson getting on his professional roar, "is it possible you don't understand that we are seeking the heir of Mr. Harold Scarlett, and that if you should turn out to be that heir you would benefit by it?"

Jane sat staring at him in wonder.

"Oh!" she said in wonder, "why, I wouldn't be an heir of course, that is, not to any extent, I'm sure. Uncle Harold never saw me in his life, and I doubt if he remembered I was alive. I'm sure he wouldn't leave anything to me. I didn't even know where he was, and he wouldn't know where I was unless great aunt Sybil Anthony told him, and if there was any question of my being an heir she wouldn't have let him know. She would have thought her daughters would come first."

"No!" said Mr. Sanderson sharply, "they would not come first. She was only a half sister of Mr. Scarlett, the daughter of a second wife married late in life. If you were the daughter of Harold Scarlett's older brother, as you state, you would be next in line. You see it is the husband of one of these daughters of this great aunt who is contesting the will, and it is important that your proofs be found as quickly as possible. These more distant relatives will not delay to file their claims, and the man who wants to buy this property must have an answer soon. Would it be at all possible for you to get in touch with this person who cares for your trunk by telephone?"

"Oh! I don't know," said Jane with a startled look. "I have not heard from her for almost a year. I don't even know whether they are living in the same place now."

"Well, if they aren't what will have become of your trunk?"

"Well, I don't know that, either. I never realized it was important to anybody but myself, and I wasn't in a position to do anything about it."

Mr. Sanderson uttered a sound almost like a growl.

"Well, look here, young lady, we've got to get to work on this thing right away. What was the name of this person who has your trunk? And did she have a telephone when you lived with her?"

"Her name was Janet Forbes. Yes, they had a telephone when I was there. But they went to Florida for the winter. I suppose they were coming back if everything went well with them. The trunk was left in their attic. The telephone would be in her husband's name, Aleck Forbes. Blairstown—"

Mr. Sanderson glared over at Kent Havenner.

"See if you can get that phone, long distance, Havenner!" he commanded.

Kent Havenner sat down at a desk and took up the telephone. His quiet business-like voice calmed Jane's frightened heart. She hadn't yet taken in the likelihood of any advantage coming to herself through all this trouble. It all seemed just another bothersome thing she had to do and get through with to satisfy somebody who wasn't anything to her.

But as Kent Havenner talked with the operator, and was at last given someone in Blairstown, Jane's eyes grew wide. This thing they had fantastically called forth out of the air was actually materializing into something genuine.

"Is this Mrs. Janet Forbes?" he asked quietly. "Yes, please, I would like to speak with Mrs. Forbes herself. You say Mrs. Forbes is serving dinner? Well, this is a very important matter. I must speak with Mrs. Forbes for just a moment. I won't keep her long. Yes, please call her to the phone at once."

There was a brief wait and then a sharp voice answered.

"Mrs. Forbes," said Kent, "Miss Jane Scarlett is calling about a trunk that she left with you. Just a moment."

Jane went forward excitedly as he held the phone out to her.

"Yes, Mrs. Forbes. This is Jane. Jane Scarlett. Yes, I'm well, thank you, and I have a good job in a store. No, I haven't written you before because I wanted to get ahead enough to send you the money for the trunk. But now I want it in a hurry, and if I send you money by telegraph would you see that it starts in the morning? Yes, Mrs. Forbes, I want it very much. No, I'm not getting married. I haven't time for such things. But there are some things of my mother's in that trunk that I want to use. Yes, surely, I'll write to you right away, but I'd like the trunk to start in the morning if you can possibly get it off, and by express so it will come quickly. It's really very important."

When Jane finally turned from the telephone she felt as if she had suddenly entered her former life again. How queer things were!

"She is going to send it in the morning!" she announced to the two who had heard all the transaction. And then a radiant expression came into her face. "I am glad!" she said musingly. "There are things in that trunk that I really needed."

Grim Mr. Sanderson grinned wryly at Kent.

"Yes," he said, "if all you say is true I think that you will find that there are things there that you need very much indeed. And now, young woman, when can I see you again? You know we haven't any time to waste. You don't seem to take it in that you are a very important factor in a matter of really important business."

"It doesn't seem at all real to me," said Jane with a wide smile.

"Well, it had better seem so," said the lawyer.

"But," said Jane with a sudden startled look in her eyes, "how much is it going to cost to get this trunk here, and how do I go about it to send that money? Mrs. Forbes said she couldn't afford to send it herself. Her husband has died, and she's had a hard summer. But how much will it cost? I might not have enough."

"Don't worry about that, young lady. We'll attend to that from the office. Havenner, get on the wire and fix that up right away. You got the address and the phone number, didn't you? All right, get that over with, and arrange about the arrival of the trunk, where it's to be sent."

"You want it at your room, where you went last evening?" asked Kent courteously.

Jane nodded, half frightened at the thought of taking her precious belongings out of the past into her forlorn little room. But of course it would have to go there. She had nowhere else to take it.

Kent Havenner went to a telephone in an adjoining room, and while he talked Mr. Sanderson asked Jane more questions about her father and mother, her visit to the old home, and where she had lived since. Incidentally he brought out the fact that since her parents' death she had been for a time in a New England school, the very school where the lawyers had been searching for a trace of her.

Then Kent came back to report.

"It's all fixed," he said. "I wired the money, and then I called up Miss Scarlett's present apartment and arranged with the landlady to have the trunk put at once in her room when it arrives. Is that all right, Miss Scarlett?"

"Oh yes," said Jane looking at him with startled eyes. She hadn't yet got so far as to plan about that trunk in relation to her present lodgings. But this young man seemed to think of everything and know just what to do about it at once. She was deeply grateful.

"Thank you," she said with a shy smile. "And now, is there anything else? When do I come again?"

"Just as soon as you get entrance to that trunk and can bring me your evidence. Have you the key?"

Sanderson's voice was sharp as he asked the question, as if it were a matter that had almost escaped him.

"Oh, yes," said Jane. "I carry it in a little bag around my neck. I was so afraid I might lose it."

Her hand went instinctively to her breast, and then suddenly she exclaimed:

"Oh, I forgot. I have one bit of evidence with me! I just remembered. My mother's wedding ring! It has initials and a date! Would that help any?"

"It certainly would!" said Mr. Sanderson excitedly.

They gathered around her as she drew a fine gold chain from around her neck, and brought out a tiny bag of firm white kid, that might have been cut from a glove.

Jane bent toward the light and unfastened two little

snap catches that held its top firmly together, and took out a plain old fashioned gold ring.

There it was, the initials, "J.R.S. to M.W." and the date.

Mr. Sanderson examined the letters carefully under a tiny glass, and at last straightened up.

"Well, I should say you had pretty conclusive evidence there," he said as he handed the ring back to Jane. "So run along, and don't fail to let me know by telephone just as soon as your trunk arrives."

"Oh, I will," said Jane earnestly. And still she was not quite sure what it was going to mean to herself, even when the papers should arrive. It all seemed too fantastic to be true.

"And now," said Kent Havenner, smiling and looking toward his chief, "I guess that's about all for tonight, isn't it? So, Miss Scarlett, you and I will slip out and get a bite of dinner. Good night, Mr. Sanderson!"

When they were down on the street again Kent hailed another taxi.

"Oh, but you mustn't!" protested Jane. "I can perfectly well find my way back to my—" she hesitated for a word—"home!" she finished with a laugh. "It isn't much of a home, I know, but it's all I have so I have to call it that."

"Yes, well—but we're going to have dinner together first," said the young man, putting her into the taxi, and stepping in after her. "You won't mind going with me for once, will you? I'm tremendously hungry and I know you must be too, and besides isn't the last daily class tonight, and don't we go to it?"

Her heart gave a sudden little leap of pleasure! The class! She had forgotten it entirely in her absorption in this strange new matter that had been thrust upon her. The class! Yes, of course! And he was really going again himself!

"Oh! Yes!" she said. "Of course I'm going to the class. And I'm glad you're going too. But you didn't need to bother about taking me, or getting me dinner. I'm not lost any more, and I'll be sure to let the office know when that trunk comes. I'm all excited about it myself."

"I'm not worrying about that," said Kent, "but don't

you realize that I'm sort of your lawyer, and I have a right
to take you to dinner once in awhile? I know a nice
pleasant place where my sister likes to go. I'll take you
there. And it isn't far to the class after that. We'll have
a little over an hour to eat. I guess that will do. Here we
are!" and the taxi slowed down and stopped before a
dignified quiet-looking building, and he helped her out.

"But, this is a grand place," said Jane taking in the
inevitable signs of affluence about the building.

"Not so grand as some," said Kent in his easy way.

"But I'm only a working girl, and I'm not dressed up.
People don't go into these places wearing their working
clothes."

"Oh, yes, they do. I go, and I'm wearing my working
clothes. Come on. You'll find it very unobserving."

And so he led her to a table and Jane in a panic of
embarrassment entered, looking about, half frightened to
death over the quiet unostentatious grandeur.

"This is just a good home place," said Kent as he sat
down opposite her and smiled.

"A very magnificent home," murmured Jane in a low
voice, and cast shy glances all about her.

"Now," said Kent, "may I order for you? I'm pretty
well acquainted with some of the nice dishes they serve
here."

"Oh, please," said Jane with relief. "But just get something very simple for me. I'm not used to fancy meals."

And so Jane was launched on a new experience, going
out to dinner with a young gentleman, a real gentleman
such as her father had been.

XIV

IT all moved off so very smoothly and pleasantly Jane wasn't embarrassed at all after the first minute or two. Afterward she thought it over and wondered at herself. How at home she had felt there in that new environment! But after all, she reflected, her father had been a gentleman and her mother a lady, even if she herself did sell buttons and live in a little hall bedroom at the top of the house.

Kent quietly took charge of things, talking with the waiter as if he were an old family servant, ordering nice unusual things, thoughtfully giving her a choice between this and that.

And they did not have to wait long. The delicious dinner was set before them in almost no time at all, it seemed, and they were talking.

"You weren't really frightened, were you?" Kent asked when they settled down to eating.

Jane smiled ruefully.

"I'm afraid I was, quite a little," she admitted shamedly. "You see I didn't really know what it was all about, and I'm not sure that I do yet."

"Well, I'm sure I hope you will be quite happy in the outcome, even though it does seem like a fairy tale to you now. It's nice to get real surprises sometimes, and life isn't always all disappointments, you know. Now, tell me about this class. Did I understand aright that it is only to be held once a week after this?"

"Yes, it's only in the summer they hold it every evening. I think they said it is to take a whole hour after this instead of half an hour. But they are going to have a new teacher, you know. Mrs. Brooke is going out west, I think."

"That's too bad!" said Kent. "I had it in mind to attend that class right along, but I don't know that I should care for a new teacher. I thought she was most unusual. Everything she said seemed to have a greater significance than any preacher I ever heard. Who is the new teacher? But then I wouldn't be likely to know one from another. Such teachers are not in my line. I don't remember ever to have had even a Sunday School teacher who interested me."

"I never heard anybody teach as Mrs. Brooke does. But she has told us several times that we will like the new teacher better. She says he is wonderful."

"A man?"

"Yes. I was sorry for that. It didn't seem to me as if a man teacher would understand us quite so well. Mrs. Brooke talked like a mother, right into your heart."

"Yes, she did," agreed Kent, watching the lovely light of interest in the girl's face, and being glad he had brought her to dinner. "Well, if she likes him perhaps he'll pass. We can give him a try anyway. I somehow don't feel like dropping it entirely. So this is Mrs. Brooke's last night! Well, I'm really sorry. Although I haven't heard her but a couple of times, she really opened up new vistas and possibilities in life to me. I almost feel as if I'd like to tell her 'thank you.' "

"Oh, and so would I, if I dared. It does seem strange how I happened on that class from a radio notice. I think really God must have seen my need and sent it."

Kent grinned.

"Perhaps you weren't the only one," he said. "After all, there's the Bible and anybody could have had it and read it without a class of course, only we wouldn't and didn't until she brought it to our notice. But really it was you that brought her to my notice. I'm quite sure I would never have gone into a Bible class of my own accord for anything in the world. So I've you to thank for my interest in this." Then he got out his little red gospel of John and called her attention to a verse that had been given in the last lesson, and asked if she had the reference in connection with it. Then she pulled out her little book, and they conned it all over, like two university students going over their studies together.

Some people came in and took the table a little way from them, looking over and speaking to Kent interestedly. Kent nodded to them but went on turning the pages of John and pointing out something he had read on the train the other night.

After the dessert arrived Kent looked up suddenly and asked:

"Have you thought anything about that property? Are you likely to sell it in case you prove to be the heir?"

"I?" said Jane with a startled look. "Why, no, I don't really believe I'll have anything to say about it. Somebody else will turn up that will take the right, I'm sure, even if it were left to me. I can't think of either my great aunt or her daughters ever giving up any family property to me." She laughed ruefully. "You see they think the earth was especially made for their benefit."

"Well," said Kent, "but if it turned out that it was in your hands to say, would you want to sell it?"

"How could I tell?" said Jane sadly. "I've never seen it. I don't know what it is. If it were really something associated with my people of course it would be wonderful to keep it, but how could a poor salesgirl keep property? It costs money to keep property, even very plain property, doesn't it? There would be taxes and repairs. Oh, no, of course I couldn't keep it, but I'd love to if I could. I've often thought about the beautiful old home where my grandfather lived, and where I was taken as a child, and wished that it might have been kept and I could have lived there. But it takes money to live in dear old homes. I can remember the walls, beautiful wide walls with ivy on them, and there was a swing—"

Kent couldn't help thinking how very sweet her eyes were as she talked about the old days she seemed to love.

"Where was that old home? Do you remember?"

"It was in a place called Hawthorne, not far from a big city. I don't remember the name of the city. That is, it never made any impression on me. Of course it's all written down in my father's diary, and I can look it up when my trunk comes. I'll have to brush up my knowledge of my father's house. Why, it's a good deal like what we're doing in the class, isn't it, brushing up knowledge about our Father's house in Heaven! It's queer how we get interested in this world and drift away from the other life, isn't it? Even when I was very forlorn and unhappy and hadn't a job, and was afraid of what would happen next, I scarcely ever thought to go to God for help. I had no realization that He cared to have me come and talk to Him and ask His help."

"Yes, well, I've done that a lot too, but since I've been reading this Book I've almost come to the conclusion there is another life, and it's worth a lot more than this one down here. I guess I'm glad you led me where I heard about it. Of course dad and mother and my sister go to church, and likely they know all this lingo, only I never hear them talk about it. Maybe they never heard it our way. But I guess it's worth a try. But say, it's time we got going or we'll be late to the class!"

Kent paid the check and they hurried away to the class, Jane suddenly wondering again to find herself escorted as she had seen other girls, and a sudden pang came to her heart. Pretty soon this business about the property would be over and settled one way or the other, and her young lawyer would go his way. He would have no occasion to hover about her and see her here and there and take her to dinner in grand places. When his business no longer linked itself to her, of course he would drift back into his own world. He would probably forget the Bible class too. Or was that quite fair to him to doubt the interest he had acknowledged? Well, she would at least have this pleasant evening to remember, so that when she saw other girls going about with their young men friends she would understand their happy times a little better, and think how she had had at least a little taste of young companionship.

At the class they sat up near the front together, and it was so nice not to be all alone as she had been heretofore.

The lesson that night was beautiful. The two as they listened seemed to be closely bound by their interest, and now and again they would look at each other in mutual recognition of a truth that struck home more deeply than another. If Evadne could have watched her former lover's face that night she certainly would have been filled with scorn and wonder, for never had she seen such a look of awakening on his face, the look of a soul just seeing the light.

At the close of the lesson Mrs. Brooke introduced a young man, their new teacher. They saw to their amazement that he was virile and attractive with a face of radiant happiness. He didn't make a speech, just nodded to them all informally and told them how he loved God's word and that he hoped they were to have many happy hours of study together, beginning next Thursday evening. Then Mrs. Brooke asked him to sing them a song that she might remember as she went away, and sitting down at the piano he sang, a simple rhythmic melody, with the words that wrote themselves in their hearts, and could not easily be forgotten:

> "Oh Lord, you know,
>   I have no friend like you,
> If Heaven is not my Home
>   Oh Lord, what shall I do?
> The angels beckon me
>   To heaven's open door,
> I can't feel at home
>   In this world any more."

He sang it so tenderly, so longingly that it sank deep into the soul life of them all. And then he made them sing it once or twice till they caught it, and went out humming it. It was obvious that the whole group would go home singing that song. The new teacher had won his class. They would all be there next week if at all possible.

Jane and Kent went up and spoke to Mrs. Brooke and said good-bye.

"You've done great things for us both," said Kent, because he was the bolder of the two, and really felt gratitude for what he had received. She introduced them to the new teacher, and they liked his personality at the nearer view. They went out pledged to come again, and perhaps to try and bring others.

"Oh Lord, you know," Jane sank softly, almost inaudibly, as they left the hall and fell into step on the street, "I have no friend like you——" Her voice was very sweet and Kent drew her arm within his own, and looked down at her, and never knew that Evadne had crossed their path on her way to the theater, and was looking back, staring unbelievingly at Kent Havenner walking along with a very simply dressed girl and looking very happy indeed. It really was quite time that she did something about this. She had not counted on such extreme indifference as this.

> "If Heaven is not my Home
> Oh Lord, what shall I do?"

"You have a really lovely voice!" said the young man. "It is unusual. I like to hear you sing that."

"It is a lovely song," said Jane. "I never heard it before. It seems as if it was made just for me. As if God sent it to show me something. Here I've been mourning all my life that I never had a real home, and perhaps God allowed it just to remind me that Heaven is my home and I mustn't put my hopes on earth. I think that is going to make a great difference in my way of looking at life. I'm not going to fret any more that I've only a hall bedroom to call home. My Father is getting ready my home up there!"

Kent looked down into the loveliness of her exalted face, as if Heaven had opened and given her a quick vision, and a mistiness came over his own eyes. Something contracted in his heart. This was a wonderful girl, and she had hold of something that was worth more than all the nonsense of the smart set with whom he had been trying to enjoy himself for the last two or three years.

Suddenly a vision of Evadne's selfish, hard young face came beside Jane's illuminated one, and he knew all at once that he had been a fool ever to think Evadne was interesting. But he answered Jane thoughtfully enough:

"I guess you're right. But I never thought about these things before. This life has always been enough for me. I've been fairly satisfied with my earthly home, and I never thought of the time that might come when it wouldn't be enough any more. I've got to get busy and grow Heaven-wise, for I don't believe I'm going to feel satisfied down here any more either. That's a great song. I wish you kept a piano in your reception room. I'd suggest that we step in and try singing it together. I mean to try the tune out the minute I get home tonight."

They were happy eyes that met at the door of the rooming house as they said good-bye.

"I shan't be seeing you till Monday," he said as he

paused at her door, his hat lifted. "The firm is sending me out of the city for a couple of days, and I don't suppose I shall be back before late Saturday night. But by Monday that trunk ought to be here, and I'll be stopping around to hear your report. Good night!"

He was gone and Jane was conscious of a sudden blank. But what were his comings or goings to her anyway? She had no right to be disturbed of course. She wouldn't likely have seen him at all even if he hadn't been going out of town. Only going out of town was so definite, and as he was really her only friend, it did make a difference to know that she wouldn't even meet him by chance somewhere.

But she ought not to call him her friend. A friend implied a closer relationship than just a business contact, and that was all there had been between them, or likely ever would be. She must jack herself up in this matter. It was unwise to admire or become interested in anybody who was so utterly out of the range of any possible idea of companionship. He had been nice to her, yes, and she was so lonely and forlorn that she had just enjoyed this contact as much as possible, but she must not let herself be lonely when the contact ceased. That was the way fool girls got their hearts broken, and she certainly did not want to be a fool girl. Her mother had always warned her about counting too much on friendships with men. Even the fact that he was interested in that Bible class did not make any difference. It was wonderful to think he might be a Christian. That would always make a little bond of friendliness. Just to know she knew one of God's children, even if she didn't see him any more was nice. But she must get to work somehow and do something to occupy her mind, and not think about this matter of Uncle Harold's will. Perhaps after hours tomorrow she would go and take a long walk in the park, and bring up at a new place for dinner. That would be a change and give her some other interests.

So she hurried up to her room and got busy putting her things in better order, washing out stockings, and finally writing a letter to the Scotch woman who had been taking care of her trunk. Poor thing, she must be lonely now that her husband was gone! And she was such a kindly soul, and such a wonderful cook. What would she do now, all alone in the world? Would she try to carry on a boarding house alone?

She wrote her kindly letter, tucking in a dollar bill as thanks for the care of her trunk, and saying she liked her job and hoped some day to be making a good salary, although it wasn't very large yet.

Then she hurried to bed and congratulated herself as she lay down that she hadn't thought about that troublesome property nor her young lawyer once since she came upstairs.

XV

EVADNE LAVEROCK bided her time for two days, thinking that perhaps her letter had miscarried and would at length reach Kent Havenner and would bring her lover in apology to her feet. She loved so much better to put a man in the wrong, than to seem to be running after him. But the two days went slowly by and he came not.

The stay in the city at that season of the year was an utter bore. The house was in a semi-closed state, and her sister was away at the mountains. Moreover there were few of her old acquaintances about at this time of year, and absolutely nothing going on. She must do something. She could not let Kent drift through her fingers this way.

She would not call up at his seashore home, because she simply detested his sister, and she didn't want to encounter her again even incognito. So she decided on calling the office.

But all the satisfaction she got from the office was the information that Mr. Havenner wasn't in at present, and they did not know how soon he would be in. After an exasperated attempt to get more information from a higher source, she arrayed herself for battle and went forth. It was her experience that she could accomplish a great deal more with a man if he could see her. So she put on her most alluring summer street garments, and arrived at the office about eleven o'clock Friday morning.

She asked for Mr. Havenner and was told as before that he was not in at present. Then she asked for Mr. Edsel and was informed that he was engaged with a client, and not to be disturbed. Finally she asked to see Mr. Sanderson. She did not like Mr. Sanderson but she had to get some action quickly, and he was the only one left.

Now it happened that Mr. Sanderson did not like Miss Laverock even as well as she liked him, and he had hoped that she was permanently out of the picture, for he had said to his partner more than once that if ever Kent

127

married that flibberty-jib he personally was going to find some good excuse to get Kent out of the firm, for he would be absolutely worthless if he married that piece of selfishness.

So when Evadne came languidly into his austere private office where he sat frowning at the interruption, and settled her delicate attire in one of his great masculine leather chairs, he almost growled at her as a lion might have done, as if she were too trifling an object to make it worth his while to pause long enough to make even one bite of her.

"Hello, Sandy," she addressed him gaily, "I'm trying to find Kennie and I can't get any service out of your minions. I thought I'd be bold and come to headquarters. What have you done with my Kennie?"

"Your Kennie!" Mr. Sanderson snorted contemptuously. "I wasn't aware you had left any of your property about our offices. To whom were you referring? Could you by any means mean our Mr. Havenner? I have never heard him called Kennie, but possibly his name might be tortured into that. However, I was not aware that he was your property."

"Now, Sandy!" reproached the girl with a languid giggle, "don't be dense with your Vad! Of course I mean Kent Havenner."

"Kindly omit the 'Sandy,' if you please, and I'm quite sure I never called you Vad, or even thought of you in that way. You are not mine in any sense of the word. If it's Mr. Havenner you're in search of you won't find him here. He's out of town for a few days. He won't be back until late Saturday night if he is then. You'll have to search elsewhere for him."

"Well, but Mister Sanderson, surely you can tell me where to locate him on the telephone? It's very important!"

"No, I can't!" snapped Sanderson. "And I wouldn't if I could. Mr. Havenner went away on business for the firm, with several destinations in view, and he has no time for frills and follies."

He picked up the telephone.

"Miss Worth, is Mr. Hawkins there yet? Well, send him right in. I'm waiting for him."

Then with a stiff bow toward Evadne:

"Good afternoon, Miss Laverock. I haven't any more time to discuss this matter with you. Ah! Mr. Hawkins!" as the door opened to let in a client, "be seated, won't you? Miss Worth, kindly escort Miss Laverock to the elevator." And Evadne found herself summarily dismissed. With head up and angry mien she followed the secretary down the hall without a word, her eyes flashing fire. She went back to her sister's lonely house to plan revenge and meanwhile solace herself with the best a city in summer provides for its worldlings.

Friday was an unusually busy day at the button counter. There were bargains in clasps and buttons and buckles, odd lots and broken numbers, closing out the summer's novelties, and getting ready for fall. There was after-hours work, too, which kept Jane until nearly seven, marking the prices on the bargain sales, getting them ready for morning as advertised.

Feverishly Jane worked to get done as soon as possible. She had a strong hope that her trunk would be at the boarding house when she got back, and she was eager to unpack it and look once more upon the beloved possessions. Strangely enough the articles which might prove her identity in connection with the will of her uncle, took second place in her mind now. Her great longing was to touch and see once more the possessions that were connected with her dear mother. It was a great overwhelming longing, and now she began to wonder how she had gotten along so long without them.

But when the work at last was finished and she went to what she now considered "home" there was no trunk awaiting her in the hall as she had hoped, and there was no letter or explanation of any sort. Well, perhaps it would come tomorrow.

She went to bed early so that the morrow would come that much the sooner.

Audrey Havenner had had time on her hands for the last three days. Ballard Bainbridge had been away on a yachting trip with some friends, and while she had not realized how dependent on him she had become for companionship, she found that the days were twice as long when there were no telephone calls suggesting golf, sailing, or swimming. It was not that she was not self-sufficient on occasion, and she had been wanting to do some special reading for a long time, but now that her usual program had failed and she was thrown on her own resources, she discovered that there was altogether too much time for debating with herself whether or no she wanted to let this intimacy with Bainbridge go on to its logical conclusion, or whether she wanted to put a stop to it right here and now, and have her days fully planned by the time Bainbridge came back, *if* he came back, so that there would remain no part for him.

Having looked the facts of the case straight in the face and owned to herself what was the matter, she went and got the books she had been intending to read and settled herself in a breezy hammock on the porch, with a broad stretch of beach and a wider view of the ocean ahead of her. Deliberately she put her mind to the task in hand. She had promised to write a paper for a club meeting in the city which was to be held early in the fall, and this reading was in preparation for that paper. This was a grand time, just made for this preparation. She would work it to the last minute!

But when she got through the first paragraph, some turn of a phrase recalled to her a remark of Bainbridge's, and her mind was off on a tangent at once, arguing the subject from every angle.

In vain she jerked herself back to the duty in hand and tried to go on, but phrase after phrase reminded her of Ballard's line of argument, and now she recalled that he had been the one who had suggested these books for her to read. And his conversation was so like the author that she began to wonder whether he was an original thinker, or was just echoing authors he had read and admired.

She put down the first book, finally, and turned to another, but here again she was reminded of another conversation they had had, and after reading a few minutes she threw the book aside and stared off to sea, her problem all written before her again, the pros and cons, about Ballard Bainbridge. And the more she thought about it the more sick of the whole thing she grew. The facts had grown clearer since his absence, and she began to see how her own natural conclusions and actually her own wishes and tendencies had been deliberately set aside, and his own substituted, until she was getting into the habit of no longer asking herself what she wanted to do, but trying to seek out what Ballard wanted and liked, so that he wouldn't turn that vitriolic scorn of his toward her. She began to wonder if he hadn't just decided to take her over and mold her until she suited his desires, and then take possession of her. Then suddenly her naturally sweet nature, and her love for things beautiful and wholesome rose up in protest and cried out for the happy normal life she had lived before she knew him.

The morning train from the city shrilled along the distant tracks, and all at once a great longing came over her to get away from all these thoughts, and the inevitable decision that was going to be demanded of her by her conscience presently, and just do as she pleased for a while. Just have an old-fashioned good time, doing any pleasant little crazy thing that came into her head.

There was that girl at the button counter whom she had wanted to bring home for the week-end. This was a good time to do it. Kent was away in New England, and not likely to return till early next week. Evalina had gone down the coast to stay with a friend over a few days. She hoped she would not be returning till after Sunday. Why not take the up-train which left for the city in about a half hour, and find that girl and persuade her to come home with her for over Sunday?

She was the more persuaded that this was the thing she wanted to do because when she had spoken of the matter to Ballard a few days ago he had laughed her to scorn. He had called her an emotional philanthropist, and had given her a string of stories about Russia and how the working people were developing there, and how things ought to be that way in this country, and would be presently when the new order of things was thoroughly established. He said that individuals were not responsible for one another. That under a truly modern regime the worth-while people would rise and develop without assistance and those who were not worth while would slough off like scum from a boiling caldron. He told her that she belonged to a higher order of being and should not waste her time and thoughts on girls who were mere button sellers. They wouldn't be that if they were capable of being something better.

Always as he had talked she had felt in her soul that these things he was saying were not true, but it had seemed so much trouble to try to answer him. And really she hadn't given much thought to the subject. Perhaps there was some subtle truth in all he had been saying that made it necessary for her to do some deep thinking and definite studying before she attempted an answer. Well, anyway, she would invite that girl down and get close to her if she could; try to find out just what kind of mind and soul was behind her tensely quiet personality that she had taken such a liking to. And then if Ballard should turn up before the visit was over he would see that she had a mind of her own, and was not trying to follow the almost commands which he had put upon her concerning this desire of hers to know the button girl.

So she sprang up suddenly and sought out her mother who was sitting in the house putting delicate stitches into the hems of some exquisite organdie curtains for the cottage.

"Mother, I'm going to town. Is there anything you want?"

Her mother looked up interested.

"Why, yes," she said. "I was just wishing I had bought more ribbon for those tiebacks. Could you match it? I need five more yards of the pink, and seven of the blue."

"Delighted, mother. Cut off a snip of each and I'll bring it back with me. And mother, may I bring a friend home with me for over Sunday? Do you mind?"

"Of course not. Bring anybody you like. We're having steak for dinner tonight, and chickens tomorrow. Who are you bringing?"

"Well, I'm not sure. Anybody I take a notion. Will that be all right?"

"Quite all right, dear."

So Audrey got herself into a thin smart dark blue frock and caught the up-train to the city.

She matched the ribbon first so she wouldn't forget.

Then she walked around the store trying to decide what to do. Finally she marched slowly past the button counter to see if Jane Scarlett was still there, and if she looked as interesting as the first time she had seen her.

Jane was hard at work, flying about, waiting on two people at once, and being very cool and businesslike about it. Audrey stood leaning against the opposite counter and watched her for a few minutes. Then when the two customers departed with their little packages and Jane was for the moment free, she saw her draw a deep tired breath, and mop her face with her handkerchief, as if she were very hot and weary. Her resolve was taken at once.

"You are entirely too impulsive!" Ballard had told her. "You fly off the tangent on an idea. You should cultivate calmness. You should deliberate before you act."

The counsel came to her now as she started across the aisle straight toward Jane Scarlett, and she smiled at herself. She was not following Ballard Bainbridge's advice now and she was glad she wasn't.

"I want a dozen of those lovely filigree buttons down there in the front of the case," she said in a clear voice.

Jane smiled and gave her a quick look. Where had she heard that voice before? And of whom did it remind her?

But she didn't stop to answer those questions. She reached down and took out the buttons.

"They are pretty, aren't they?" she said pleasantly.

When Jane brought back the package and handed it to her, Audrey looked her straight in the eyes.

"You don't remember me, do you?" she said, laughing up at Jane.

Jane gave her a quick startled look and then a sunny smile lit up her face.

"Oh yes," she said. "You invited me to go home with you to your seaside cottage. You didn't think I'd forget a person like that, did you? I had many a pleasant moment, thinking about that, imagining what it would have been like if I felt I should go. I couldn't forget your face. I thought that was the loveliest impulsive thing anybody ever did."

"Thank you," said Audrey. "I'll treasure that. But now

I've come again, and it isn't impulse this time, for I came to town just on purpose. You see I've been thinking about you ever since, and I really want to get to know you. Will you go down to the shore with me this afternoon when the store closes, and stay over Sunday? We can get you off on the early train Monday morning so you will be here in plenty of time for the store opening. And this time my mother is expecting you. I told her I hoped I was bringing someone back with me."

A soft pink color stole up into Jane's white face, and her eyes glowed with appreciation.

"Oh, that would be wonderful!" she said wistfully. "I wonder if I should go! I never heard of anybody doing a beautiful thing like that for an entire stranger."

"Well, we're strangers to you, too," laughed Audrey. "You might not like us at all, in which case you can take the next train back to the city, of course. But maybe you could stand us over Sunday even if you didn't like us, because there is always the sea to look at and a nice breeze to cool you off. Come on, do! I really want you, and I'm sure we can have a nice time together. Do you have to go home first, or could you go right from here? I can lend you a nightie and a hairbrush, or do you have to let someone know you are not coming back till Monday?"

Jane gave a quick thought to the trunk that might arrive.

"I can telephone," she said thoughtfully.

"Well, anyway, I'll be back here and meet you right here at five. Is that all right? Then we can catch the five-thirteen train. However, if you find you can't go at once, why there are two later trains. Now don't you fail me. I'm looking forward to this. Good-bye till five!" and with a bright smile she walked away and was lost in the crowd of shoppers.

Jane, watching her away, was again dimly reminded of someone. Who was it? Just a trick of her walk, the turn of her head. Ah, now she knew. It was Kent Havenner. She was dismayed at the idea. Was she going to be obsessed by the thought of him? How ridiculous. She must remember that he was only her lawyer. She must not be so conscious of his appearance and attraction. Well, anyway, she had enough else to think about now. Was she really going to the shore for two whole days? Ought she to have allowed that nice girl to persuade her? Of course she could still tell her at five o'clock that she had found she couldn't make it, but she didn't believe that she was going to. She was simply longing for a breath of sea air and a real change, and why not take it? This was a lovely girl. They must be nice people. What would her own mother have said if she were here now?

Customers were coming in now. It was the late morning rush hour. She must forget all this and work, or she would make some foolish blunder and maybe lose her job in her childish excitement. And there was that trunk to think about, too. Perhaps she ought not to go. If the trunk came tonight she ought to be there to attend to it at once. But it would be put in her room and she couldn't do anything about the contents for those lawyers until Monday, anyway. Their office was closed Saturday afternoon.

So an underdrift of thought pursued her as she went on with her work. But there was a light in her eyes, a snap to every movement as the morning progressed, that made people look twice at her and say to themselves "What an attractive girl that is!"

XVI

GRADUALLY Jane's thoughts grew steadier. They centered on her clothes. She looked down at herself, glad that she had put on her dark blue linen that morning, because the brown dress she had been wearing all the week had developed a small hole in the elbow and she hadn't had time to mend it. The dark blue was clean, and neat. But she did wish she had something to change into for Sunday. Just a simple cotton dress such as other girls would have had for over a Sunday. She didn't want this new friend of hers to be ashamed of her. Well, it couldn't be helped on such short notice. But at lunch time perhaps she could find some cheap little garments that she could carry in a paper parcel. She needed several new things badly, anyway.

She hurried away to the telephone as soon as she was free for her lunch hour and called up the landlady of her rooming house. She was told that her trunk had not come yet but it would be kept safely for her if it arrived while she was away. That off her mind she took a hasty glass of milk at the soda fountain, and purchased a small package of cracker sandwiches which she slipped in the top of her handbag where she could pinch off a small bit now and then and slide it into her mouth without being noticed. She simply didn't dare attempt going without food for even one meal. She mustn't run risks of fainting.

She hurried to the bargain counters and looked them over with a glance. Yes, there was a sweet little nightie at a very low price, and not so coarse that she would be ashamed to have it seen. Just white muslin with a facing of scalloped pink. It wasn't pretentious at all, either, and she did need one badly. Her only two were so worn that they were constantly needing slits sewed up.

As she turned away from the salesgirl with her package in her hand she saw a counter piled high with light summer dresses. There was such a pretty one of pink dimity with a lovely white collar, and a wisp of black

136

velvet ribbon making a tiny dash of smartness at the throat! But the material was very fine, it couldn't be that the price was that advertised on the card over the table. Or perhaps there was something the matter with it. It looked like a dress from the French department.

She stepped near and began to examine it. No, there did not seem to be any defect in it, except that it was very much mussed. And of course she would have no chance to get it ironed. Or stay! Could she possibly get the woman up in the alteration department to iron it for her in exchange for something she could do for her? The dress was really lovely. Simple and unostentatious. Could she smooth it out a little with dampened hands after she reached the shore?

A glance at the clock showed her time was almost up. Well, she would risk it somehow. There wasn't time to go up to the alteration room and ask, and then come down and go up again. So she bought the dress, and then wondered, while it was being wrapped, whether she had done a silly thing. Just to think of her being so proud that she had to have a new dress! Well, it was bought now, and it was too late to change her mind.

She received her box with a trembling hand, and hurried upstairs.

"Why, sure I'll iron that out for you," said the girl. "Madame isn't ready with the work I have to press, and there isn't a thing for me to do till she is. No, she won't make any trouble for me. How much time you got? Five minutes? Sure, I can make a lotta difference in a cotton dress in that time."

Her skilled fingers were unwrapping the box.

"Say, ain't that a pretty one! And only a dollar ninety-eight! I believe I'll run down to the basement and see if I can't find me one as good. You got a bargain and no mistake."

Jane stood watching the pretty little dress widen out into smoothness, and tried to realize it was her own. Maybe she had been crazy to buy it, just for one day, when she might not have another place to wear it this summer. And yet, it was simple enough to be in style another year. Well, it was hers! And she was glad!

The girl folded the dress carefully and laid it back in

the box. Jane put the other package inside and tied the box up. That was a perfectly respectable package to carry, even if she didn't have an overnight bag. She wouldn't look peculiar carrying a suitbox from a store

She put the suitbox in her locker and hurried back to her button counter, a delicate pink flush on her cheeks. Mr. Clark noticed it as he passed down the aisle.

"You're looking better, Miss Scarlett," he said pleasantly as he signed a return slip for a customer of hers, and it warmed Jane's heart to think of the friendliness in his tone, so different from the severe tone he used to use toward her before she was sick that day.

Then five o'clock came rushing along, and she was so excited she could scarcely get the last things done.

She had managed to slip away long enough to buy a toothbrush and a five cent comb, and now she felt she was thoroughly equipped for her wonderful week-end. Would it be as wonderful as she was hoping?

Just then she caught sight of her hostess standing across the aisle, looking at her with a bright smile, and Jane nodded and smiled toward her.

Briskly she finished with her last customer and came across the aisle.

"I have to go up to the cloak room for my hat," she said. "It won't take me but a minute. There's a chair over there by the glove counter."

She hurried away and was back before Audrey had expected, for she was deeply interested watching the details of closing, and noticing how many salespeople were hindered by customers who came late as she had done not so long ago. They were not all as nice about it, either, as Jane had been.

Jane had found a wooden handle and fitted it to the string around her suitbox, and it looked very neat and trim. They were like two shoppers going on their way to the station. Jane had a sudden overwhelming shyness upon her. It seemed somehow a great presumption to have taken this stranger girl at her word and accepted the invitation. But Audrey was overjoyed.

"It's going to be fun!" she said exultantly. "I was so afraid you were going to get up some excuse and back out of coming, and I had quite set my heart upon it. I want to show you all my pet views, and pleasant spots that I have loved since I was a child. I have a hunch you'll understand why and enjoy them too."

"Of course I shall," said Jane. "I shall just revel in them. Do you know, I haven't been to the seashore since I was three years old and my father took me on his shoulder and walked away out into the water and let the spray dash up around my feet. I loved it. I had a little red bathing suit and I made houses and pies in the sand and built a wall with pebbles and shells. I can't really believe I'm going to see the ocean again."

"Oh, that's just the way I wanted you to feel, and I'm going to enjoy my ocean all over again with you," said Audrey. "We'll go in bathing, too. I think we'll get out in time for a dip before dinner."

"I couldn't," said Jane wistfully. "I haven't any bathing suit."

"Oh, we've loads of bathing suits of all sorts," said Audrey happily. "People are always coming down without any, and mother keeps them on hand, all sizes. It spoils the fun to have somebody left out. Listen! That's our train he's calling. I believe we've caught the earlier train. That means we'll have ten minutes more to go in bathing. Come on, quick! If we run we can get there before it starts!"

Breathless they were seated in the train at last, and there were real roses in Jane's cheeks now.

The two girls sat talking, having a nice time getting acquainted, Audrey pointing out the simple landmarks along the way, and Jane exclaiming over every new sight.

"Such sweet quiet little village streets!" she said wistfully. "I do get so tired of the everlasting pavements in the city, especially on a hot day. I've never really lived in a city before, and sometimes I just long for some green grass, and a cow or two in the distance along a country road."

Audrey looked at her appreciatively.

"I just knew you'd be like that!" she said. "I'm so glad you came."

"Oh, so am I!" said Jane. "But I'm afraid you're going to be ashamed of me in my plain clothes. I didn't have anything grand to bring along, even if I had had time to go to my room and get it. I just have a simple dimity dress I bought at lunch time on the bargain counter."

"We don't wear grand clothes down here," said Audrey. "Nobody minds what we wear. We're down here to get away from that sort of thing. Now, here is our station. Watch and you'll be able to see the ocean in a minute. We pass quite near the beach. There! There it is! Come on, we get out here. It's just three blocks to our cottage on the beach. It will be more fun to walk than wait for the bus. That box isn't heavy to carry, is it?"

"Oh, no. Of course, let's walk!" said Jane, feeling new life in the very air as she trod the platform, and followed Audrey down the sidewalk to the street.

"Oh, isn't it wonderful here! It doesn't seem like the same world we were in a little while ago!"

And then they were facing the sea, and a lovely breeze was blowing into their faces. Jane could think of nothing but "heavenly breezes" to express it.

Mrs. Havenner came to meet them as they ran up on the porch. She was a sweet-faced woman, but, Jane thought suddenly, another woman who had something familiar about her!

"This is my mother, Jane," said Audrey. "Mother, this is my friend Jane Scarlett. Have we time for a little dip before dinner?"

"Oh yes, plenty, dear," said the mother. "Your father telephoned that he couldn't be out till seven-thirty, so we'll have dinner late. We're very glad to welcome you, Jane, and I hope you'll have a pleasant time with us. Audrey, I mended your bathing suit and it's hanging in the bath house as usual. There's one there for Jane, too, if she hasn't brought hers."

So the girls were soon down on the beach running along like children, and laughing together as if they had known each other always. And strangely enough, Jane didn't even know her hostess' full name yet.

Jane couldn't swim of course. She had never had opportunity to learn, but she stepped into the water like a thoroughbred and thrilled to think she was in the great ocean again after all these years.

At last Audrey announced it was time to go in and dress, and they ran dripping up the beach.

"Goodness! Can you beat it?" exclaimed Audrey. "Mother has a caller on the side porch! Let's go around this side of the house so we won't have to converse. I can't seem to recognize her. A blue dress. It doesn't seem to be any of the natives. I hope she's not staying to supper. I want to have you all to myself tonight. We've a lot of getting acquainted yet to do. We have to find out what we each like, and where we've been, and what we've read, and all that, so if she should be staying I'll just give you the high-sign after supper and we'll slip away and walk down the beach in the moonlight!"

"Lovely!" said Jane appreciatively.

A moment under the shower, a quick rub, a hasty slipping into attire and then sliding up the back stairs to complete their toilets.

Jane had a cosy room next to Audrey's where she could watch the sea from her window. There were crisp new curtains blowing in the breeze tied with braids of the lovely pink ribbons that Audrey had brought home. Audrey noticed that her mother had taken time to finish these for the stranger guest. Mother never forgot little dainty touches.

Jane looked about on the sweet guest chamber with awe. It seemed to her that she was in a marvelous dream, and must be going to wake up pretty soon and discover that it was all a dream. But she reflected that if there was a possibility of company perhaps she had better put on her new dress and look her best.

So with a hope that the dress would fit, after all her trouble, she put it on, and was astonished that she looked so well in it. It fitted as if it had been made for her. With a great sigh of relief she got out her little new comb and attacked her hair. It was nearly dry and the dampness had left it softly billowed into loose natural waves. She had always known it was somewhat curly but it had never seemed worth while to take any pains with it. Now, however, she realized how much better it looked in loose waves, rather than brushed sternly back as she had been wearing it.

"How lovely you look!" exclaimed Audrey as she tapped at the door to know if Jane was ready to go downstairs. "I'm sorry you felt you had to buy a new dress

to come here, but it certainly is becoming. You look like
a young rose about to bloom."

"Oh, if you get poetic about me," said Jane slightly
breathless with pleasure, "I'll not be fit for the button
counter Monday morning."

"You're too nice anyway for the button counter, you
know," said Audrey. "But I'm certainly glad you were
there or perhaps I would never have known you."

They went slowly downstairs hand in hand just as a
little silver bell was ringing for supper, and Audrey's mother was coming in from the porch with the lady in blue.

It had all happened while the girls were in the water.
The next city train had come in and brought the blue
lady, and she had arrived at the cottage via the bus from
the station, wearing a small blue hat and veil, and carrying a brief coat, and a diminutive overnight bag. The
bag and the hat were both still reposing on the porch
table outside, so that the lady in blue appeared to be a
member of the household as she came in.

Jane heard Audrey utter a soft dismal exclamation
as she caught sight of the visitor's face, and she felt that
the guest was not as welcome as she might have been.
Anyway, she was glad she had worn the pink dimity
tonight if there were to be other guests.

Evadne Laverock had stood Kent's silence as long, if
not longer, than she ever stood indifference and silence
on the part of any of her intimates. She had arisen in her
might that morning and determined to do something about
it at once. She would find him in one of his haunts and
demand immediate attention, and she flattered herself
that she knew how to do that effectively. The only trouble
was that she knew of but two haunts in which to search
for him, his home and his office. He really was most unsophisticated in spite of all she had tried to teach him.

So she arrayed herself in a charming blue costume that
her mirror told her was most fetching, and betook herself to the office, very near to noon, which she argued, by
all laws of any business she knew, ought to be closing
time on Saturday afternoon. She paused an instant at the
door before she went in to take in the additional name to
the sign on the glass, "Sanderson, Edsel *and Havenner*."
So! They had taken him into the firm! That was what he

had been doing while she was away then, getting on in his business! Well, that wasn't so bad! Money was a great necessity, and she could use plenty! So all the more she wished to find Kent.

But when she entered and succeeded in getting belated attention from a very busy secretary long enough to ask for Kent, she was again informed that he was out of the city on business, and would probably not be back to the office until Monday, or later.

Baffled for the present Evadne walked out of the office with a high head, puckering her brows and trying to decide what to do next. She wondered, should she go to his home? She found a telephone downstairs and called up the railroad station, discovering that the train she should have taken had left five minutes before. That was annoying. However, if Kent really was in New England he would scarcely get back before late in the afternoon, and maybe it was just as well. She certainly did not wish to spend the afternoon conversing with his mother, whom she had always felt was a stuffy old woman with terribly victorian ideas. If she should decide to marry Kent she didn't want to raise any false hopes in the old lady's mind about being a companion of hers. They would never in the world hit it off together. So she decided on the five-thirty train. That was an express, and she could fill in the time shopping. Of course she would need a few things if she were going down to the shore, and she'd been meaning to get one of the new blue leather overnight bags. Her own was getting shabby.

So Evadne filled the intervening hours before her train with agreeable shopping, lunching about two o'clock with a young artist whom she'd dug out by telephone from his natural environment. Their choice was a modern little joint that went under the title of a tavern. After lunch she possessed herself of the overnight bag, with its elaborate fittings of crystal and turquoise enamel, and went searching for a luxurious set of pajamas in pale blue satin with real lace edges. Then she added a few other expensive trifles, including a Japanese hand-embroidered kimono—apple blossoms on black satin with a pale blue satin lining. The price of all these things was simply staggering, but as she had found the charge coin belonging to her sister, it was easy enough to charge them all on her sister's account and trust to the future for settling the bill with her when she should discover it. Evadne was clever about things of this sort. Of course she counted herself honest in the long run, but what was a bill among sisters? Gloria would have done the same by her under like circumstances.

So Evadne had taken the train following the one Audrey and Jane had traveled on, and reached the Havenner cottage just after the two had gone down to swim.

When Kent's mother told her that Kent might be back that evening, though she wasn't sure, Evadne, without waiting for an invitation, exclaimed with an annoyed air:

"Oh, what a bore! And I wanted him to take me somewhere this evening. Well, I suppose I'd better wait. He'll probably come."

Mrs. Havenner with a troubled look in her eyes took the unexpected and utterly unwelcome guest up to Cousin Evalina's room, breathing a relieved sigh that Evalina was away, and not likely to return until the first of the week.

Evadne made herself at home in the room, hung up a gorgeous backless evening dress she had purchased at the last minute, fluffed up her hair, and descended to the porch to watch for Kent, hoping his family would not disturb her.

But Mrs. Havenner, reflecting that this was a Heaven-sent opportunity for finding out whether she had been right in her worried estimate of this girl's character, came out at once and settled down with a bit of sewing in her hand, to talk. So Evadne, realizing that it might be a good stunt to be in loving converse with his mother when Kent arrived, searched her idle brain for topics that might offer possible contact with this antiquated woman, and succeeded in bringing forth some in which they had not a thought in common.

They were laboring through a forced conversation when the dinner bell summoned them, and they arrived in the wide cool sitting room from which the stairs ascended, just as Audrey and Jane came down.

XVII

EVADNE eyed Jane. Who now was this little unsophisticated child with a face like a seraph, and a bearing like one to the manner born? Hadn't she seen her before somewhere? Or had she? Was she a sister, or a cousin? No, she was sure Kent had no other sister than Audrey. It must be a cousin. Or perhaps just a neighbor.

But though Evadne thought she had never seen Jane before, Jane knew suddenly that she had seen Evadne. She had seen her across the aisle in the store, charging the saleswoman of the trimmings-counter with having picked up her purse and secreted it. The saleswoman was weeping and protesting her innocence, and Mr. Clark was doing his best to alternately soothe her, and calm the customer's fears, promising that a thorough search would be made, and sending for Mr. Windle himself— who happened to be out of town at the time. But Evadne had raved on, denouncing the whole store for her loss. Until suddenly the salesgirl from costume jewelry came rushing over excitedly with Evadne's purse in her hand, asking: "Is this yours, madam? You laid it down under a box of clips and I just found it."

Jane could not forget that selfish empty little face as it had been wreathed in anger. Perhaps this very memory served to give that haughty little lift to her chin, and that steady unsmiling look to her eyes as she acknowledged the introduction that the other girl didn't even take the trouble to acknowledge. Evadne was trusting to her intuition that this girl wasn't of any account whatever.

Mr. Havenner came in as they were sitting down and was duly introduced to the two girls as "my father," by Audrey. And so far Jane had not yet heard the family name.

Mr. Havenner gave Jane a swift appraising look and then his glance rested on Evadne with a scrutiny that few guests at his table received. And it was noticeable that his face did not light up as he studied the indifference of the girl. His wife could see that his former opinion of her remained, and she gave a little sad suppressed breath of a sigh as if it coincided with her own opinion.

Jane felt all this, almost as if another language were flashing these things around the table, though it was invisible to the guest herself. She wondered not a little who she was. It was evident that Audrey did not know her very well, and that she was an almost stranger to them all. Yet it was also evident that the girl herself did not care in the least what they thought of her. She was only killing time, waiting for—what?—to happen.

The answer came very soon. There were sounds of footsteps at the front door, and the new girl sprang into action.

"Oh, would that be Kent?" she said. "Let me go to the door and surprise him. He'll be so delighted to find me here!" and she jumped up from her chair and dashed into the living room without waiting for permission.

Kent!

But there must be other Kents in the world beside the one she knew, Jane reflected. She recalled the startled look that she had shot at Evadne without knowing she had done so. She sent a swift furtive glance about the table. The family were sitting perfectly still, not even looking at one another, each one engrossed in his plate. There was disapproval in their very attitude, but it was evident they were trying to be very discreet and not show their annoyance. There was an utter silence in the room, and the chirpy murmurs of the guest and the rumble of the man at the front door could be distinctly heard.

Suddenly the mother roused to consciousness of the other guest.

"I think it's getting a little cooler, don't you?" she asked of Jane, with a charming smile, that somehow made Jane feel as if she were not classed with that other forward guest in the living room.

"Well, it certainly is cooler than where I've been all day," said Jane with a lovely smile in answer to the mother's smile.

And then they could hear Evadne coming slowly back. "It's a man for you, Audrey," she said, dropping lazily into her chair again. "And he seems to be terribly possessive. He wants you at once!"

"Oh?" said Audrey indifferently. "Did he happen to say what his name was?"

Evadne looked a little surprised.

"Oh, yes, something that began with a B. I forget what it was. It doesn't matter. I was convinced that he knows you well, and wants to see you at once."

Audrey laughed lightly.

"How amusing!"

And then without the slightest sign that she was answering the man's demand she looked toward the waitress.

"Molly, please find out who is at the door, and give him a chair. Say I am engaged at present, but will be out in a little while."

Evadne watched her in amazement.

"I don't think he'll stand for that treatment," she remarked amusedly. "He seemed to me to be the touch-and-go kind."

"Yes," said Audrey, still amusedly. "Well, it's a matter of indifference to me whether he touches or goes. I've sent him a chair however."

Mr. Havenner barely suppressed a chuckle, and Jane kept her eyes upon her plate, struggling with her sense of humor.

"You're foolish," advised Evadne. "He's stunningly handsome."

"Really?" said Audrey. "Oh, but you know I see so many like that!"

Then Molly appeared in the doorway.

"It's Mr. Bainbridge, Miss Audrey. He says he hasn't a minute to spare and he wants to see you right away. He says it's very important."

Audrey fixed a level gaze on the worried maid.

"Tell Mr. Bainbridge I have a guest at dinner and I cannot come at present. Tell him not to wait if he is in a hurry."

"You must be pretty sure of him," remarked Evadne.

Audrey smiled sweetly.

"Is that the way you treat the ones you're pretty sure

of?" she asked with a pleasant lifting of her lashes. And then she turned to Jane.

"Are you going up to New England next week to the regatta?" she asked innocently.

Jane stared at her an instant and then her face broke into a wreath of impish smiles and she answered:

"Well, I haven't quite decided. Perhaps if you would be willing to go with me I might go. We could have fun, couldn't we?"

"We certainly could. I know some of the men who own those yachts, and no end of people who are going."

"Let me see, what date is that?" asked Jane demurely.

"The eighteenth," said Mr. Havenner unexpectedly. There was a sedate twinkle in his eyes that his daughter knew was a sign that he was extremely pleased at something.

"Oh," said Jane, "that might be all right. But I can't say definitely until I get home to my calendar."

"Well I certainly do hope you can go. I think it would be swell, and if you decide you can, I'll switch all my dates and go along."

"Well, I'll do my best," said Jane with a bright little air as if she had been used to making dates like this all her life.

Audrey looked at her in wonder. What a clever girl she was to be able to put over a thing like this without even a hint. She felt a thrill of pleasure to think that the girl she had picked at sight was turning out to be even more than she had hoped.

"All right," she said, fairly sparkling with eagerness. "That settles it. If there's the least possibility of this being pulled off I shall go down the first thing Monday morning and buy that perfectly darling dress I saw in the store today. It was in the French room and I know it must have been a scandalous price, but I'm determined to have it. Mother, it was one of those perfectly tailored smart things that look so simple it seems as if a three-year-old child could make them. But it is made of the most gorgeous material you just know it must cost all kinds of prices."

The mother gave a little gasp as she looked up, and then swallowed her surprise and managed a smile.

"That sounds wonderful, Audrey. I'd get a couple of them if I were you, dear. You don't come on a thing like that often, you know."

Suddenly the father looked up with a very wicked twinkle in his eye.

"Hop to it, Audrey girl!" he said pompously. "My entire bank account is at your disposal."

Jane almost lost her composure then. The look on Evadne's face was so full of so many things. Astonishment, incredulity, wonder. For the first time that evening she seemed to be really interested in them all. "They are just taking her for a ride," giggled Jane to herself, "and she doesn't seem to know it. Well, they probably have some reason, and it certainly is wonderful to see a girl like that getting razzed."

But these dear people, the father and mother, and Audrey, were kindly, and not naturally sharp-minded. What reason could there be for their animosity? Was it their son? Were they afraid for him? For surely this girl would not be good for any young man, a girl with a cruel twist to her character!

"Thanks, dad," said Audrey. "Come on, Jane, if you have finished your lemon pie. Let's take a run on the beach and work off some of our extra spirits. May we be excused, please? We have a date with the moonlight!"

Audrey arose as her mother nodded assent, and catching Jane's willing hand led her out of the room by a side door, out of the house, and down onto the broad stretch of smooth white beach, with the shimmering opal-tinted expanse of sea stretching as far as eye could reach.

"Weren't you great!" said Audrey. "You certainly played up to my lead in fine shape. I nearly ruined it all by laughing, you did it so well."

"Well, I wasn't quite sure I *should*," said Jane. "It didn't seem quite true. Of course I couldn't go to a regatta, and I never expect to see one, but I couldn't resist the temptation to answer like that. I don't suppose I'll ever see her again, but it was fun."

"Yes. Wasn't it? Isn't she the worst ever? I can't stand her. She's waiting on the chance of seeing my brother tonight, and he may not come home till next week. He's off on a business trip. I wanted you to meet him. He's a dear! But some other time perhaps! Now, we came out to run, let's run!"

So they dropped hands and flew down the beach till they were entirely out of breath. At last they slowed down and walked more quietly together.

"I'm afraid you will think we are terribly rude, the whole family, I mean. We don't usually ride our guests that way. But it happens that this particular one has been most obnoxious to us all in more ways than one, and I think dad especially was trying her out on one or two points and studying her."

"Yes," said Jane, "I thought it must be something like that. Has she any right,—that is,—is she—engaged to your brother, or anything?"

Jane could not shake off a certain sense of embarrassment as she spoke of the brother. How silly, just because his name was Kent! It couldn't be her Kent, it just couldn't! Things didn't happen that way. Even if it were, he wasn't hers. Why should she care? But she must remember to ask Audrey her last name at the next lull in conversation. It was absurd to be visiting here and not know it.

"Engaged? Goodness, I hope not!" said Audrey vehemently. "Still, you never can tell. A girl like that has ways of getting around a man that are inexplicable. Oh, it would break our hearts if my brother should marry her, or even be engaged to her."

"There are a lot of couples who must have been deceived in each other," said Jane. "I don't see what some of them see in each other. Of course we see a good deal of that in the store, and it makes me disgusted. There are some really good-looking young men there that act the fool with every girl they meet. A girl can scarcely know whom she can trust. So many men are all for themselves!"

"Oh gracious!" said Audrey. "That makes me think of the man who came to the door while we were at dinner. And we slipped out the side door and ran away! Now I suppose he is sitting there yet, waiting for me, or else he is very angry and has gone away forever! Well, I really don't care. He was getting to be a nuisance. But I don't want to be rude. Would you mind running back with me part way? I don't like to leave you away off here alone, but if you don't want to come in right away you could linger down by the lifeboat where we were this afternoon till I can get rid of him and come to you."

"All right," said Jane. "I'd love sitting in that boat and just looking out to sea. I wish you wouldn't hurry. Stay as long as you want to. I'll be quite all right. Don't come back unless you want to use me for an excuse to get away from something."

"Ah! It's rare to have a friend who understands!" said Audrey, catching Jane's hand and squeezing it. "Now, let's go!" and they were off again down the beach.

Jane climbed into the stranded lifeboat and settled herself, gazing off into the silver sea, across the molten stretch of sand. She spread her rosy dress about her and could scarcely believe it was herself sitting there by the sea. So much sea, so much moon, so much silver and gold, and not a rift of a cloud in the sky!

Presently her thoughts went back to the dinner, and the strange girl, and the young man named Kent who was supposed to have come to the door and didn't. Oh, could it be her Kent, her lawyer? Of course not. That would be too fantastic.

But if it should be, and he came home while she was here, what would he think of her? Wouldn't she appear to be just in a class with that Laverock woman at dinner? How dreadful!

It seemed awful to think of him as interested in such a girl—if it should really be the same man. She couldn't believe it. She just wouldn't. And she wouldn't think about it nor him any more. She would just enjoy this wonderful silver vision. Why, this was as near as an earthly mind could ever vision the heavenly shore! Would it look like that when she died and was nearing the shore of heaven? She could almost see the towers of a Heavenly mansion, off there in the silver-blue sea.

"Oh God! Keep me from getting mixed up with this earth so that I shall forget that this world is not my home!"

Then as her thoughts sped back into the past week she began to hum softly and then to sing louder:

"Oh Lord, you know
I have no friend like you,
If Heaven is not my Home
Oh Lord, what shall I do?"

Her voice rolled out sweetly in the wide silver night. She felt as if she were talking to God. She had a strong consciousness that she was all alone with God, that no one else could hear her. It had been literally years since she had been as much alone as this. She always felt that she would be overheard if she sang. She had never dared even in church or the Bible class to let her voice out to its fullest. But now she felt that the soft murmur of the sea would drown any sound she made, so that it could not possibly reach up to the house, and there was not a creature in sight either way.

She leaned back against the tiller of the boat and sang on. When she had finished the simple song she sang others, some which she had heard recently at the Bible class, and more from the store in her memory, until the past came trooping about her and peopled the lovely silver world with those she had loved and lost. There were tears in her eyes now, and her voice broke occasionally, but she sang on with that full-throated beauty that she scarcely had known she possessed. She was just singing to the Lord. At last she paused and it was as if all the sacred truth she had been taught by her parents, all the wonderful new Bible truths that she had been learning the past few days, blended together and thrilled her young soul till it wanted to speak aloud to God. Instinctively she went back to the new song which had been ringing in her heart more or less ever since she had first heard it. She sang it as if she were singing to God from the depths of her being; slowly, soulfully, beautifully, through to the end:

"Oh Lord, you know,
I have no friend like you—!"

and coming out of the silver night it sped up the beach and down the beach like the cry of a saved soul suddenly learning its isolation from all around it. The wistful longing of her desolate young heart rang out hopefully with the final lines:

> "I can't feel at home
> In this world any more!"

And suddenly, as she ended, the melody rang on from the beginning again, with other voices like an echo taking up the strain:

> "Oh Lord, you know,"

Startled, yet still feeling herself alone, and as if angels, or some trick of her own imagination, had supplied the harmony, her voice took up the air again and she sang as if inspired.

It was only an instant before she realized that they were real voices, those voices, and not a figment of her imagination, not angels, like those that came to the shepherds of old, not supernatural as for a minute it had seemed, but human. They were live real voices singing with her. Tenor, bass, and now Audrey was humming an alto with them also!

She sprang up and looked around, but kept right on singing. She dared not stop. There they were, standing just a little back of her boat on the sand. She couldn't see their faces enough to distinguish who they were, till they drew nearer, singing as they came.

It was then that she saw Kent, and a great gladness filled her heart. She didn't stop to realize how astonishing the situation was, nor what he might think of her to find her here. She was just glad, and a flood of light filled her face and lit her eyes as she looked toward him with instant welcome, answering the radiance of welcome already in his own face for her. It was only a moment that they turned the glory light upon each other. Then Jane came to herself and began to take account of other factors in the situation. Who was this man with Kent? Could it be the man who had come to the door while they were at dinner? No, for she had seen this man before. Who was he? Ah! She knew now. It was the new teacher of the Bible class, Mr. Whitney! And no wonder he could sing like that, his own song that he had sung for them!

Oh, and they had all heard her sing alone, and maybe she had made mistakes! But how grand it was for them all to be there singing it together! And no wonder Audrey and her parents seemed familiar to her! She could see now, even in the moonlight, how very much the brother and sister resembled each other. Strange that she had not recognized that at once! She certainly would not have come here if she had! What should she do? Disappear?

"Sing it again," exclaimed Audrey, as the last notes died away on the brilliant night. "I'm just getting on to that alto. It's lovely. What tender beautiful words!"

So they sang it again, and it seemed even more exquisite yet.

Jane was standing down on the sand now with Audrey's arm around her lovingly, looking off to the edges of the silver sea where little golden lapping wavelets caressed the silver sand. And suddenly she was aware that two other figures were coming slowly toward them down the beach, a woman and a man.

XVIII

THE woman was dressed in blue, with golden hair that gleamed in the moonlight, and all at once something clutched at Jane's throat with cold frightening fingers, and drove the gladness away from her heart. What impossible situation was this anyway?

Here she had been rejoicing that Kent Havenner had come, when she had no possible right to rejoice. He belonged definitely to this other girl in blue! This insolent girl. No wonder Audrey didn't like her. But it didn't make any difference that she was a disagreeable girl. She evidently had a right to him. She had made it plain that she came down here to see him, had planned to surprise him at the door as if they had an understanding between them. And of course she, Jane, had no claim whatever upon Mr. Havenner, except in a business way, and possibly as a member of the Bible class. She never had had any claim, social or even religious, which should give her a right to such a tumult of joy as had come to her when she recognized him behind her singing. The blood burned hotly in her cheeks and she was glad that moonlight would somewhat camouflage her face and hide her confusion. For she was ashamed. Almost as if her joy had been written flamingly across her face, she was ashamed! A nice girl did not admire a man so much as that at first. A man who was really nothing to her, a man she did not know except as an honorable respectable business man. It was all wrong that it set her heart to singing. She had no right. Even if he did not definitely belong to any other girl yet, she had no right to be so happy about his approach. It was probably because she had had so little really enjoyable companionship, that she had idealized him. And she must snap out of it! Right here and now she must get wise to herself, and take this all in a matter-of-fact way. He was nice of course. But she would miss even the nice time she might have for a couple of hours tonight if she got silly about this thing.

She would just act to him exactly as she had always acted since she knew him,—after all the acquaintance was so very brief—and then when she got by herself she would read herself such a lecture as she never had before, and try to get some sense into her head. Meanwhile this was a nice time that God had sent her, and she must not spoil it. This teacher and Mr. Havenner, and Audrey! How nice that she was his sister! Still, of course she mustn't count on coming down here again. But while she was here she would enjoy everything, and not make them ashamed of her before these strangers, whoever they were.

The last notes of the quartette died away and there were the other two, standing a few yards away from the boat!

It was Evadne's voice that broke the sweet silence, trilling out an empty little laugh.

"My word!" she said lightly, "what a lugubrious song! It sounds as if you all were about to pass out! Why can't you sing something cheerful?"

"I should say!" echoed Ballard Bainbridge. "Where did you rake up a deadly song like that? It sounds as if you were on a sit-down strike in a mine or something. You should sing something cheerful on a gorgeous night like this. How about this?" and he struck into the most modern air he knew, with a pompous voice so filled with pride of itself that it sounded as if it were stuffed with Indian meal, or dry mashed potatoes.

There was utter silence while he sang, and Evadne stood beside him posed in the moonlight, wishing that it were the fashion to take pictures by moonlight and that someone had a candid camera. She knew she must be rather stunning with that light on her gold hair, and that handsome man beside her. So Audrey thought he was hers, did she? She'd better look out or she would lose him. Evadne had ways with her that could ensnare any number of men at once, no matter how impervious they thought they were to charms. She was glad that Kent was there where he could watch her. She had had no words with him as yet, for he had come in by the back door with his friend, and gone out again with Audrey by that same door. Evadne was not sure whether he had known she was there, for she had been sitting on the end porch, facing the other view of the beach, when he came in. But he knew she was here now, and she exulted in the thought that he would see her for the first time under such favorable circumstances. It had been a good hunch that had led her down here to his home. She was triumphant also that she had a good-looking man by her side. That was always an asset. Of course she did not know how he despised that particular young man.

But Kent did not seem to be attending to the solo that was being rendered so affectedly. He was stepping quietly over to that Scarlett girl's side, and taking her hand, smiling down into her face. Evadne darted a lightning glance at him. Was this only a gesture to show her that he had friends also? He was talking earnestly to Jane, as if he knew her well, smiling at her, and she at him. They were not disturbing the singer. They did not make a noise. But they were carrying on a silent little aside and enjoying it. She set her stubborn lips hatefully, and flashed her jealous eyes, boding no good for any who displeased her.

Then the song was ended, and the singer beamed about waiting to be commended, but Evadne was busy and no one else cared to commend him.

"Let me introduce my friend Mr. Whitney," spoke up Kent eagerly. "This is Miss Scarlett, Pat. And over here, Miss Laverock and Mr. Bainbridge. My sister Audrey you have met."

The stranger acknowledged the introductions courteously, and then Kent, still at Jane's side, said:

"Now, how about a walk on the beach while the tide's out?" and possessing himself of Jane's arm he whirled her about and started briskly up the beach, she falling quickly into step beside him.

"Shall we follow?" asked young Whitney of Audrey, and they started on a few paces behind the others.

There was nothing left for the other two guests but to follow. Ballard Bainbridge strolled lazily along, mortified that his song had made so little impression. He considered himself a fine singer.

"I'm afraid our efforts were scarcely appreciated," he

said loftily. "That is the trouble when one tries to uplift depression of any kind, it is so seldom understood."

"Well, I thought your singing was swanky!" declared Evadne, lapsing into her lingo. "I never come out here but I'm depressed. It is a great pity that these young people have been brought up by such antiquated parents. I thought Kent had gone out into the world enough to get over his early training, but he seems to have lapsed badly since I went abroad."

"Yes, I suppose that is what's the matter with them," agreed Ballard, drawing Evadne's arm into his and settling it comfortably close, their shoulders touching. "They are so bound by laws and customs and rules! It will be great when a new order of things is finally established in our country. Children will be no longer parent-ridden, they will be brought up by the state, and able to express themselves as their wills prompt."

"Do you really think we are coming to that, Ballard?" asked Evadne, leaning a little closer to him and looking up into his face. "Oh, you do encourage me so! When I look about upon the people who are so tied down by the wishes of others, by old customs, by what is so mistakenly called courtesy, it is so pitiful, and seems so hopeless."

"Yes, it is pitiful," said Ballard Bainbridge, looking down into Evadne's vapidly pretty face, and laying a possessive hand over her small one that lay relaxed upon his arm, "certainly pitiful, but not hopeless, my dear Miss Laverock."

"Oh, call me Vad, won't you?" said Evadne in a wheedling tone. "I shall think you don't love me if you call me Miss Laverock so formally."

"Oh, but I do love you," said Ballard with a fulsome smile. "I find you are the answer to my heart's desire. Even in the little time I had with you up on the porch I found myself wondering how I have lived so long without you," and he slid his arm about her and drew her closer, stooping and laying his hot lips upon hers. This was what Audrey never would let him do.

Slower and slower their footsteps lagged as they exchanged vague views about the world today and what was coming in the future, a future wherein one's passions and desires should be the only criterion, and there should be no more thou-shalt-nots.

Now and again Evadne, clinging to this new-found man, a lover after her own heart, glanced up occasionally to see if Kent were observing her, for she had acquired so cunning a skill in dealing with men, that one never fully absorbed her whole consciousness. But Kent was far out of sight, and the other two were just vanishing around the curve of what was called "the Point."

Jane's heart was fluttering happily. She told herself she was having a nice time, just like other girls. A young man who was a real gentleman was walking on the beach with her, just as he might walk with any girl. He knew she was only a button girl, and yet he was treating her like a lady, just as if she were any nice girl out for the evening. There wasn't a tinge of condescension in his manner. He was acting as if she was his equal in every way. And that was the height of courtesy, to forget social separations and just be friendly.

He was holding her arm and guiding her to the firm smooth places on the beach, walking briskly and calling her attention to the lovely lights on the ocean, to the pathway of moonlight that trailed out across the waves, telling her about a little ship that went curtseying over the billow, explaining what it was, whence it came and whither bound.

"It certainly looks like the way to the heavenly city out there, doesn't it?" he said suddenly, stopping for a moment and gazing across the water over the bright path.

"Oh, it does!" said Jane wistfully. "My, if it really was, I would certainly start walking!"

He was looking down at her, watching the expression on her face there in the moonlight.

"Yes?" he said sympathetically, but suddenly drawing her arm a little closer within his own. "Not just yet, please!" he added. "We—don't want to spare you so soon. We're just getting to know you."

She looked up startled, almost thrilled at the friendliness in his tone.

"Oh! that's nice!" she said with a faint little smile on her lips. "I—was afraid—perhaps you wouldn't like it that you had found me here, just a client from your business life. You know I hadn't an idea this was your home I was coming to, or I never would have come. Your sister just picked me up out of the blue and brought me. I never even knew her name till we got here, and even then only her first name. But if I had found out before you came I should have tried to make some excuse to get right up and run away. Especially when I knew there was company."

"But why, pray? Do you dislike me so?" asked Kent, smiling down into her eyes.

"Oh, no!" disclaimed Jane fervently. "It was just that I thought it might mortify you to find a button girl in your home. It was all very well to be kind to a stranger, a working girl, when it was a part of your business, but you can surely understand why I would not have wanted to force myself upon you socially if I had known. I would have felt it was a discourtesy to you."

There was something lovely in Kent's eyes as he met her earnest upturned ones.

"Yes, I understand," he said gravely, and then slipping the hand that held her arm down to her own hand he gave it a quick warm pressure like a clasp. "Yes, I understand you, but—I do not feel that way in the least. I look up to you almost reverently, because you were the one who led me to the way of Truth. And I think maybe you will be glad to know that today I've made an important decision. You see I came down from Boston on the train with our new teacher, Pat Whitney, and we talked a lot on the way. He made me see what it is I've needed all my life, and gave me a vision of my own heart that was full of sin. I never called it sin before. I thought it was only youth, and good spirits, and a desire to do as others did. But now I think I understand it better. I see all these wild impulses to have my own way, and work out my life for my own glory, and my own pleasure, were really a turning away from God, and what He had planned for my life. And I realize now that that is not the way of happiness. For a long time I've been unhappy, and dissatisfied, and I didn't know what was the matter. When I would get what I went after for a time, it didn't satisfy, and I was restless and full of longing. But tonight

I saw what the great trouble was. I needed my Saviour. I've taken it in at last that it was my sins that made Him have to suffer on the cross." Kent spoke slowly in a low tone, and as if he had almost forgotten Jane was there, as if for the moment he were in a world apart. Then he drew a deep satisfied breath. "But now I've accepted Him, and a great burden of uneasiness has rolled away from me. My whole outlook on life seems changed. I want Him to have His way with me from now on. Do you know Him this way? Have you ever taken Him as your Saviour?"

"Oh, yes," said Jane softly. "Once a long time ago when I was a little girl my Sunday School teacher talked with me, and I accepted Christ. But that was long ago, and during the years I drifted very far away from Him. My mother was a Christian, but after she died I felt bitter toward God for having taken her away from me. I stopped praying, stopped reading my Bible, until I heard that announcement over the radio and went to see what it was about. But—now—I've come back. I told Him so a few nights ago. I think He accepted me and forgave me. I don't know a whole lot about it all yet. But I want to learn."

"Then that's a tie between us that is greater than any social differences," said Kent gently. "Besides, there aren't any of those differences either. Your Scarlett family is just as good as any socialite living. But when one is related to the Lord Jesus Christ, in a tie of blood, it counts far more than mere human rating."

"Oh! I'm so glad about you! I wanted you to know Him!" said Jane ecstatically.

"Did you—dear!" The last word was breathed so softly it was scarcely audible. Afterwards Jane was sure she had only thought it, or perhaps only wished it, and she chided herself for the thought, yet it had seemed so reverent, like a blessing, that she could not feel about it as she would if it had been upon another's lips.

Kent reached out and caught both her hands and pressed them warmly and close, and then drawing her arm within his own again they walked on together in silence for a few seconds, a brief sweet silence.

It was the sound of other voices that broke the holy quiet between them.

"Did you know that Pat Whitney is preaching near here tomorrow? About two miles above our cottage at a little shore church. Would like to go and hear him in the morning?"

"Could I?" she asked eagerly. "Oh, I would love to. Will your sister think it is all right for me to go?"

"I'm sure she will," said Kent. "I'll see that she does,— if she doesn't," he added grinning. And then his face grew sober again.

"Do you know who the others are?" he asked with a nod backwards and a little anxious pucker to his brow.

"I know their names."

"Yes, well, their names are enough. They won't be in sympathy. Not either of them."

"I—thought so—! That is, I don't know the man at all. I hadn't even met him till you introduced him. The lady was at dinner. She didn't sound as if she would be."

"No!" he said thoughtfully.

And then they could hear the others coming nearer, and they swung around to take the homeward way. Arm in arm, talking earnestly, they passed Pat and Audrey, and then a little later Evadne and Ballard.

Evadne waved a hand of greeting and called out to Kent:

"How about changing partners, Kennie?"

But Kent merely waved a casual hand in acknowledgment and passed on with Jane, scarcely looking up.

Evadne walked on greatly dismayed and deeply angry. She had not counted on a rebuff like that! She would certainly pay Kent well for his action. Kent belonged to her, body and soul, or so she had for a long time supposed. This had started out as a much-needed discipline for him; she had had no idea he would turn her sword upon herself. Yet with Evadne, a man looked never so interesting as when he was hard to get.

However, the man with whom she was walking now was not to be sneered at. He was far more congenial than Kent ever had been.

And because Ballard saw that his new companion was ready to go to Kent whom he despised, he roused himself to challenge her interest. And Ballard was attractive. He reflected that this girl was far more to his liking in her ways than Audrey. At least he would enjoy her for the evening, and probably give a salutary lesson to Audrey, who was getting too much out of hand.

So he walked Evadne far down the coast, put her on a local ferry, and carried her to another resort where a noted hotel offered a ballroom and plenty to eat and drink. Evadne danced far into the night, dined and wined to her heart's content, and was brought back in the wee small hours of the morning, desposited at the door of the cottage, and met by Audrey's mother, though she had hoped to have been met by a repentant Kent. She had planned to shock Kent by her own condition of intoxication, though to tell the truth it took a great deal to put her beyond her own control. But to meet Kent's mother at that hour, with a thickened speech and the breath of liquor heavy upon her lips was another matter. Mrs. Havenner escorted her to Cousin Evalina's room, thankful that she had not as yet returned, and then herself lay down, but slept no more that night. Was this the girl who intended to marry her son?

XIX

MEANTIME Audrey had been walking in a new world, listening to an evangel.

Pat Whitney was fresh from extensive study in a seminary where the gospel of the Bible was taught in its purity, by lips of holy men as noted for their scholarship as for their spirtuality. He had been for four years in close companionship with a body of young men who lived in the consciousness of the constant presence of Jesus Christ, and to whom the Holy Spirit was a real Person of the Godhead. The study of God's word had been a delight, and he had no joy greater than to talk about it and impart its meaning to others who did not know all its wonders. Yet he spoke so simply, so humbly withal, that he gave no sense of being dictatorial.

Audrey had been attracted by him the minute she saw him, and wondered if his attraction was all in his looks, or if in reality here was another Ballard who thought he knew it all and wanted to make everybody bow to his knowledge.

But before they had talked many minutes she was sure he was not conceited, and she had also decided that he had a fine sense of humor, a quality in which young Bainbridge was greatly lacking. When she reached that point she forgot to try to card-index him. She only knew that he was delightful and not the least bit of a pedant.

But they had not gone far before they were talking on the subject that was ever uppermost in his mind, the great wonder and glory of salvation for a lost world. And it was Audrey herself who introduced it, all unaware.

"And you," she said, "what *are* you? A business man? No. I'm sure not! A lawyer? Somehow you don't look it. A professor? An astronomer? An archaeologist? Not a minister! *I* have it, a writer! Is that right?"

He smiled.

"You're wrong," he said. "I'm not a writer, though there may come a day when I shall want to set down some of the wonderful things I have learned, after I have had more time to put them into practice. No, I'm not any of those great things you have mentioned. I'm just a plain servant."

She turned an astonished gaze at him, trying to fathom what he could possibly mean.

"A servant of the Lord Jesus Christ," he said with a ring of pride in his voice, "Whose I am and Whom I serve!" he added reverently. "He loved me and gave Himself for me, and now I live to give the good news of Him to others."

She looked still more puzzled.

"You mean you're some kind of missionary?" she asked. "Surely not! You don't look like any missionary I ever saw."

He laughed.

"Perhaps you've been unfortunate in your missionaries. But no, listen! I'm just a plain teacher of the Bible. You may call me by whatever title you choose. It doesn't matter. I like to tell people that there is a Saviour who will save from sin, and give life and joy and peace and brightness in this dark world."

"That sounds wonderful!" said Audrey. "Tell me right away how to get that."

And there, walking by the summer sea in the moonlight, he told her how he had found the Lord, and what He had been to him, and before their walk was ended he had made Audrey long inexpressibly for the peace which he himself had.

It was a bright talk, interspersed by laughter now and then. Audrey soon recognized that here was a strong man going a hard way, and *liking* it. Happy he was in an eternal joy, and with the constant consciousness of his Lord walking with him! It was the most amazing thing that Audrey had ever heard, and she kept him talking about it by asking many questions, unwilling to pass to other topics.

They came back at last to the wide inviting porch and found Kent and Jane talking and looking off to sea. They grouped themselves on the steps and lingered, waiting for the other two who had been in their party at the start. Mrs. Havenner brought out lemonade and tiny frosted cakes. They had a little party, and kept wondering why the others did not return.

The mother had lingered watching her own two, and studying the two strangers, approvingly. She thought of the two who were out and away somewhere, with relief that they were not here.

At last Kent said:

"Well, Pat, if you're going to preach tomorrow it seems to me you ought to have a little sleep. How about it if we turn in now?"

"Preach?" said Audrey opening her eyes wide. "You didn't tell me that about yourself!" she accused.

"But did I have to tell everything, lady?" he grinned. "I only tried to answer what you asked. It didn't really matter, did it?"

"He's preaching over at Silver Beach Chapel," explained Kent, "and you won't get much information about himself out of that baby, sister. He's got too many other important things to tell."

"Yes, I found that out," said Audrey. "But I'm going, of course. What time?"

"Well, Jane and I are walking by way of the beach," said Kent. "We thought we would start about ten-of-ten in the morning and take our time. I imagine Pat won't mind our tagging along. If he does, the beach is wide."

"Delighted to have the company of *all* of you," said Pat happily, his tone including them all, but his eyes smiling down into Audrey's.

Perhaps if Mrs. Havenner had happened to be out there just then and heard what they said, it might have saved her lying awake and worrying about her son, after she had escorted the disheveled Evadne to her room.

But in the morning at breakfast she found out what was going on, and watched the four start out for their walk with relief in her eyes. Later she told her husband and they drove over also to hear the young man preach. But they had not been gone long before things began to happen at home.

Evadne had of course not come down to breakfast, and nothing had been heard from her before the family left for church. Mrs. Havenner instructed her maid to give the lady a cup of good strong coffee if she should appear before they reached home, and she went off thankful that none of the family knew what time this unwelcome guest had come in.

But they had scarcely been gone from the cottage half an hour before a car drew up at the door and deposited Cousin Evalina there, and then drove off again.

Evalina gathered up her bags and essayed to go up to her room, but when she entered she was amazed to see a handsome dress of sheer blue stuff lying in a heap on the floor, and a number of other articles of apparel scattered about.

Indignantly she turned toward the bed and there lay the golden-haired Evadne in a drunken sleep. Evalina had had little experience with drunkenness, but she did know enough to recognize the heavy stupor that enveloped the sleeper, and the strong odor of liquor on her breath. She was indignant beyond words that her room, *her* room, had been commandeered for such a purpose as this. For any purpose in her absence! Evalina considered that as long as a few of her garments were left behind her, the room was occupied by herself, and belonged to her, and never considered that she was not even an invited guest, but had come unannounced and taken possession.

But when Evalina drew nearer to the bed, and studied the face of the interloper, she recognized who this girl was. This was Evadne, Kent's girl, who had run away to Europe and left him.

She had always thought it was somehow Kent's fault that he had allowed a girl as sophisticated and beautiful as this one to get away from him, after he was practically engaged to her, and everybody was expecting an announcement. So her first reaction when she recognized Evadne was triumph, pleasure. So, the girl had come back!

Did Kent know it? Where was Kent? Had he taken her to a dance or a night club or something last night and got in late? She cast her eyes about and took in every evidence that could possibly tell her anything. Then she laid aside her own wraps, put her suitcases in the closet out of sight, and tiptoed softly out of the room. She must find the family and get an idea of how the land lay. Perhaps they were wanting her to take the other guest room and let this guest have the one where she lay asleep.

But Mrs. Havenner was not in her room. Audrey was not in her room. Nobody seemed to be anywhere. Further investigation showed evidence of a second guest in the other guest room. Her anger rose. What did they think they were going to do with her? Of course they hadn't expected her back until tomorrow or next day, but it seemed a strange performance. She hadn't said definitely she was going to stay all the week!

She went downstairs but none of the family were there. She looked up and down the beach, and even traveled out to the bath houses, but there was no sign of anybody, and only dry bathing suits greeted her eye as she swung back the doors of the bath houses.

Well, of all things! What had the family gone and done? Leaving Evadne alone asleep! And perhaps Kent was upstairs in his room asleep also. She would go and find out!

So she climbed the stairs again and swung Kent's door open. No, no one was there. Well, this was extraordinary. She decided reluctantly to interview the maids. She hesitated to do this because neither of them had what she considered a proper respect for her. They resented her suggestions, and served her most reluctantly. But this was a case where it was most necessary to find out the exact situation. So she raided the kitchen.

"Molly, where are the family?" she demanded of that worthy as she came into the dining room to set the table.

"Oh, they've all gone to church!" said Molly with a toss of her head and a kind of triumph in her voice, as if going to church were a regular habit of the Havenners.

"To church?" asked Evalina with a lifting of the eyebrows. "What do you mean, to church?"

"Why, they've gone to church to hear the young preacher," she related with evident relish, drawing out her tale to its utmost possibility.

"The young preacher! What young preacher?"

"Why the young preacher Mr. Kent brought back with him from Boston or somewhere. His name is Whitney!"

"But I never heard of him!" said Evalina indignantly. "Where is he preaching?"

"I heard them say he was preaching down to Silver Beach Chapel!"

"Silver Beach Chapel! That little dinky place! Why, nobody that was worth anything would preach there. You must have heard wrong, Molly. They couldn't have gone there!"

"Yes, ma'am, that's what they said. The young folks walked down the beach, but Mr. and Mrs. Havenner went in the car later."

"Young folks! What young folks?"

"Why, Miss Audrey and the young preacher, and Mr. Kent and that other girl that's staying here, Miss Scarlett. Miss Jane Scarlett, that's her name!"

"Jane Scarlett! You don't mean *that* girl is here, Molly?"

"That's what they call her, Miss Evalina."

"Mercy!" said Evalina. She turned as if to leave the room and then she remembered and turned back.

"But Molly, what about this young woman who is in my room? How did she get there? Who put her there?"

"I donno, Miss Evalina. She was at dinner last night, and then she didn't come down to breakfast with the rest. Mis' Havenner said I was to give her strong coffee when she comes down."

"But why was she put in my room?"

"I donno, Miss Evalina, deed I don't! She come along before dinner, and Mis' Havenner took her up there to take off her hat, and then after dinner they all went out somewheres. Mr. Bainbridge was over too, an' the young folks all went out on the beach, but I went out when I got my dishes done, and I don't know nothing more."

Evalina looked thoughtful an instant and then she said, as if in explanation to herself:

"So Mr. Bainbridge was here, was he? To dinner?"

"Oh, no'm! He come askin' after Miss Audrey, and she sent word for him to wait, but she didn't go out for a long while and then she just walks down to the beach with Miss Scarlett."

"Where were the young men? Where was Kent?"

"Oh, he and the preacher-man hadn't come yet. They come afterwhile. I heard them singin' hymns down on the beach. The preacher has an awful pretty voice."

"Singing *hymns?*"

"Yes, singin' hymns. Some awful pretty ones!"

"Well, but what became of Mr. Bainbridge?"

"Oh, he was out on the front porch talkin' to the lady with yella hair that's upstairs asleep. You gonta be here ta dinner, Miss Evalina? Shall I put on a place for you?"

"Certainly!" said Evalina, and swept upstairs severely.

Evalina went into her bedroom with a very firm expression on her face. She glanced at the clock, and saw that it could not be long before the church-goers arrived at home.

She closed her door with decision and stood gazing for a minute at the sleeper who seemed not to have stirred since she left her. Then she walked firmly and heavily over to her washstand, and taking a large clean washcloth from the drawer, wet it thoroughly in the coldest water she could get from the faucet, and going determinedly over to the bed she sloshed that wet cloth swiftly over the face of Evadne until she gasped, and let out a scream.

"There! That's all right!" said Evalina. "Nobody's going to kill you. I'm only doing this for your own good. It's high time you were awake and dressed. I know you'll be glad I did it pretty soon."

Thus she instructed the invincible Evadne until amid much groaning and struggling and protest she had her thoroughly awake. Evadne's first rational act was to fling the wet cloth which had just been freshly soused at the faucet, straight into Evalina's face, and thus, caught by her own weapon, hoisted with her own petard as it were, Evalina was forced for the moment to retire from action and rescue her best dress from water stains. But she did it with set lips, uttering no sound.

Evadne sat up and blinked at her, using language that was not in the usual Havenner vocabulary. But Evalina merely gave her a withering glance and went on rubbing the front of her skirt dry. At last Evadne reached the end of her repertoire and stared at Evalina.

"Who in heck are you anyway?" she stormed.

"I'm part of the family," said Evalina complacently, "and you happen to be occupying my bed."

"Oh!" said Evadne contemptuously, stared back at it, and laughed. "So what?"

"Nothing, only it's almost time the family came home from church, and I thought it was time you got into some clothes and were ready to meet them. Dinner will be served in about three-quarters of an hour."

"What in heck do I care?" said Evadne insolently. "Who do you mean will be back from church? Where are all the folks anyway?"

"Why, Kent, and Audrey and the preacher and that Scarlett girl they tell me was here all night."

"Oh!" said Evadne, startled really awake now. "Say, who *is* that Scarlett girl? Where have I seen her before? She just simply walked off with Kent all the evening and I never did see him at all."

"She's nothing in the world but a button salesperson from Windle's store. What did you let her walk off with Kent for? She's nothing but a *working* girl."

"A *working girl?*" Evadne's eyes were wide with anger. "Do you mean to tell me that Kent Havenner would go off with a working girl when *I* was here?"

"Well, I expect Kent has been pretty angry at what you did. You can't expect to have him smile right off the bat when you come back after a silent six months in Europe."

Evadne stared at her.

"Do you mean to tell me that Kent Havenner has no better sense than to use a little baby-faced working girl dressed in pink dimity to make me jealous? *Me?* Well, if that's all it won't take long to bring him back to his senses!"

Evadne flung herself out of bed and began to dress swiftly. But she went on asking questions.

"What's Audrey trying to do to his royal highness, Prince Bainbridge?"

"She? Oh, I'm sure I don't know. They've been pretty thick all summer. He brings her quantities of books to read, and they quarrel a lot, but I think she's about engaged to him now."

"Well, you'd better think again," said Evadne. "I'm thinking of taking him over myself if I need an understudy for Kent. He's a looker and presentable. He dances well, too, which is what Kent never did."

"You were out dancing last night!" charged Evalina. "What's that to you?"

"I had to wash your face to get you awake," remarked Evalina significantly. "I wouldn't advise you to play that act of getting half-stewed around here very often. Kent's father and mother are very old-fashioned."

"Don't I know that? I can get along without your advice, thank you. But say, can't you take your glad rags out of here, and let me have this room to myself? For I'm thinking of staying here several days. This is going to be some campaign!"

"I'll say it is," said Evalina, "and you'd better keep in with me if you want to win, for there isn't anybody else you can depend upon, I'm afraid. They're all a narrow lot here!"

"You're telling me!" said Evadne.

"There! They're coming now!" said Evalina. "See! They're *walking* back! I thought they'd come in the car, but I think I heard that come in some time ago. See! There they are up by the pavilion."

Evadne went to the window and looked up the beach.

"Yes," she said sourly, "and that Scarlett girl is walking with Kent again! The insolent thing! I know her by that pink dress! Little bold thing!"

Evadne turned and went on rapidly with her dressing. Not that she had so much to put on for her garments were few and scanty, but there was her make-up to repair, without its usual nightly anointing.

Nevertheless Evalina was surprised that she was ready so soon, calm and cool and haughty, a beauty crowned with golden curls walking lazily down the stairs.

"Good morning, folks," she called noisily as the churchgoers came in. "Been out boating or swimming already?"

Nobody answered her. They were talking to one another.

Then Evadne marched straight up to Jane and addressed her.

"What are you doing here, anyway?" she asked, as a prince might have addressed a cur. "I wonder, do they know who you are? How did you steal in here unaware?"

Jane turned a bewildered look at the woman of the world.

"*Evadne!*" said Kent in a shocked voice. But she paid no heed to him. She only raised her voice a little higher so that even the servants in the dining room could hear.

"Haven't I seen you selling goods in Windle's store? Answer me! Don't you sell buttons at Windle's?"

And then Jane's careful training by her mother stood her in good stead.

"Why, yes," she said with a nonchalant smile. "Certainly. Ask Audrey, she has bought buttons of me. Why? Did you want me to use my influence to get you a job?" She gave a little twinkling look at the astonished Evadne.

From the back door that led to the garage Mr. Havenner had entered unseen a moment or two before this conversation began, and now there came a chuckle, appreciative and hearty. Mr. Havenner had a great sense of humor, and Mrs. Havenner, her face full of worry, slid over by his side. It always relieved the tension when her husband laughed.

Pat Whitney, too, had a twinkle in his eyes, and let them dance at the angry lights in Audrey's eyes, as if to say, "Why worry? It isn't worth all that, is it?"

Kent, furious, opened his mouth as if to speak, and just then the dinner bell rang, and instead he closed it and turned to Jane.

"Well, I guess that means we won't read that article till after dinner, doesn't it, Jane?" he said, and taking her arm led her out to the table.

Jane was tremendously embarrassed, now that she had met her crisis and said her little say. She was afraid perhaps she had overdone it, and was too rude. Yet what else could she have done? Burst into tears and left the room? Taken the next train home? Wouldn't that have embarrassed her hostess more than this?

So quietly she walked out to the table, thankful for the courtesy which was placed at her disposal, as if the whole family were doing their utmost to offset the insult that had been offered her.

Evalina had been on her way downstairs just as Evadne began her attack, and Evalina had stepped back to await developments. What a brave girl to go to the root of the matter right at the start! Surely they would all see now what the world thought of people who took up with poor working girls! This was going to be rare!

But a moment later when Jane gave her gay little answer Evalina drew back farther into the upper hall. How did the girl dare to speak that way? It showed what a bold thing she was.

Her cousin's chuckle from the doorway did not fail to reach her ears, and an angry look crossed her face. Then with set lips she went down the stairs in a stately way, and marched over to Evadne effusively. That poor girl should see that she was not alone.

"My dear!" she purred as she came on, "was that the dinner bell I heard? How welcome. I'm simply starved! Aren't you? I don't believe a soul offered you even so much as a cup of coffee this morning."

Together they sailed out into the dining room and took the seats Mrs. Havenner indicated, each inwardly indignant that the little button girl was given the place of honor at Mr. Havenner's right hand. They sat and stared at the circle of bowed heads while Pat asked a blessing on the food.

The dinner was a very quiet one. Evadne scarcely opened her lips. She had the air of one who had been outrageously insulted.

The talk was mostly of the service that morning, grave, sweet talk in which neither Evadne nor Evalina had any part. They simply stared at each one who spoke in inexpressible astonishment. Now and then Evalina broke out with some bubbling remark irrelevantly, concerning something nobody cared anything about. Frequently Kent would recall some interesting phrase or sentence from one of their Bible classes and ask Jane if she remembered what Mrs. Brooke had said about that, and Jane, doing her best to overcome her shyness, answered well, so that the young minister asked her several questions.

"You know I'm to have that class now," he explained to Mr. Havenner, "and I really feel very reluctant to follow such a wonderful teacher as Mrs. Brooke. It seems too bad they have to lose her."

Somehow they got through that dinner, got out of the dining room, and then Kent and Jane took themselves out of the way, with Audrey and Pat following not far behind, and no one said a word to Evadne about going along. No one paid any attention to Evadne, except Evalina. She felt the poor child was being treated abominably. She went upstairs, rooted out a pack of cards from her trunk and

brought them down to the porch, setting up a card table
in a conspicuous place where everybody who went by
on the beach could see them. There they sat and played
cards all the afternoon, though she well knew it would
annoy her cousins beyond expression. They were not very
spiritually inclined it is true, and did not hesitate to play
cards on occasion themselves, but they did not think it
looked well to have it going on in their house *on Sunday*.
They were quite good religionists.

Evadne played with sullen eyes looking off down the
beach watching for the wanderers to return. What she
would have said, how she would have looked, it is hard
to say, could she have seen the four, ensconced in a comfortable group around an old wreck of a dory, Pat with
his Bible out, Audrey looking over his shoulder, and Kent
and Jane each with a little red book, while Pat unfolded
the meaning of the wonderful words.

"Well, I never knew the Bible was a wonder-book
like that!" said Audrey as she arose at last and shook off
the sand to start for home. It was almost time for the
young people's meeting when they reached the house.
They rushed in and took a bite from the buffet lunch that
was set forth, cold chicken, biscuits and jelly, cake, and
little raspberry tarts, fruit and milk and iced tea.

Evadne had counted on the evening and the moonlight
to make up for a lost day. She had counted on a chance
to lure Kent out onto the beach and feed him a large
piece of humble pie. Make him eat it and like it, and
apologize!

But lo and behold the whole crowd of them were going
to church again! Even the father and mother!

"We don't hear a preacher like that very often," father
Havenner said. "Better hear him when we get the chance."

So Evalina and Evadne were left disconsolate. Had it
not been that Ballard Bainbridge arrived a few minutes
after the departure of the church-goers, Evadne would
have been desolate indeed.

Of course Ballard did ask for Audrey first, but he
seemed content to substitute Evadne, and they sauntered
away together into the moonlight. There were places, it
appeared, where they could get plenty to eat and drink,
especially drink, even on Sunday.

And so Evalina was left alone, with no apologies whatever.

What she did was to sit on the porch and turn things over in her mind until she came to the conclusion that this cottage by the sea was no longer going to be a pleasant refuge for her, not for the present anyway. The Havenners had let her see by their manner ever since dinner that she had done an unspeakable thing by taking up for Evadne, and she felt that life was not going to be pleasant there the rest of the summer. So, as the dusk drew on and the sea grew silver and beautiful, she withdrew to her room, and proceeded to repack her things. She had decided to leave early in the morning. There was an old aunt who spent her summers in the mountains who might be persuaded to welcome her for a time, now that many of the summer people were leaving, and the bridge players were not so numerous. At any rate she was going. She had outstayed her welcome here. It was better to go before they asked her to. So she folded her things and laid them neatly in suitcases, and was safely and soundly in bed and asleep when the family got home from church and sat in peace on the porch to talk for a little while. But she was not so sound that she did not hear much that was said by the young people. One thing she heard definitely enough, and that was Kent's plan to take Jane in on the first early train that she might be in plenty of time to get to the store. She resolved when she heard that, that she would not go to sleep until Evadne came back, and that she would tell her at once. Perhaps Evadne would go on that same train with them, and spoil their plans. It was terrible for Kent to get so interested in this working girl!

But Evalina was very weary. The excitement of the day, added to her early trip, had utterly worn her out, and she fell asleep and never knew when Evadne came in, never heard her creep into bed, and didn't even waken very early in the morning.

When she did wake up and looked at her clock she saw it was too late. Kent and Jane would be gone. Her plans were all awry.

When the two finally did get up and go downstairs to a very late breakfast, they found themselves the sole inhabitants of the cottage except for the servants. The Havenners had gone up the coast in their car to visit some friends, and all the young people had gone to town! Kent, Molly said, would not return for several days perhaps. Evalina and Evadne were left in state to enjoy themselves.

Evadne had promised already to go sailing with Ballard Bainbridge at eleven o'clock, and as she had no relish for staying at the Havenner cottage, she packed her effects and took them with her, knowing she could get Ballard to drop her at some livelier resort. Not that she was going to abandon her fight for Kent. No indeed! Not for a little working girl, even if she was smart and saucy! But there were other ways of working that Evadne knew and she would go to more promising fields for the present, eventually getting Kent by himself where she knew she could use her keenest charms upon him.

After Evadne was gone Evalina lost no time in taking the next train, and she could almost hear the maids in the kitchen as her taxi drew away from the house exclaiming:

"Well, thank goodness, she's gone! And good riddance to her! May she never come back!"

XX

BACK in the store again selling buttons, Jane felt as if she had been in a glorious dream and was suddenly let down to earth again. She was almost dazed with the shock of it.

There had been no time for her to go to her rooming house. She had called up before Kent left her, to know whether the trunk had arrived yet, but could get no satisfaction from the girl who answered the phone. The girl didn't know, and the landlady had gone out to market. So they had to wait.

"It wouldn't likely have come on Sunday, anyway," said Kent. "Never mind. But you'll call me up just as soon as you hear, won't you?"

Jane promised with a wistful smile. Too well she realized that the little chance of a telephone call would probably be the last she would see of Kent. Pretty soon this business about the Scarlett will would be settled one way or the other, and that would be the end.

All day she worked fiercely to keep the ache of loneliness out of her heart, trying to make herself see how foolish she had been to let herself get interested in Kent. Of course there was excuse. She was lonely, and had no friends who were congenial. She ought to have been willing to take up with anybody who offered a passing friendliness, like that young Gaylord. But how could she? If what the girls said about him was true it was just what she had surmised. Her feeling about him wasn't merely her prejudice. And she would rather go alone all the days of her life than take trivial favors from a trifler.

Well, she had had one good time anyway, and she must not let this ghastly feeling that it was all over and she was back in loneliness overcome her. It must not. What was her new found faith worth if it could not sustain her even through loneliness? Perhaps she would go and see Miss Leech a little while after hours. But no, she couldn't do that, for the trunk was her first concern. If it didn't come tonight she would have to do something about it.

Perhaps she ought to call up Mrs. Forbes again and see if it had started yet.

So the day wore on to its close and Jane went back to her desolate little bare room. But there was no trunk there.

After a poor Monday-dinner she went out to a telephone pay station and called up the railroad express office, but they said they had received no such trunk. Then alarmed she called Mrs. Forbes again, but Mrs. Forbes was sick in bed. A strange voice answered. She couldn't come to the phone. Jane sent a message to her. Had the trunk gone yet? But after a long wait the girl came back and said no, she didn't think it had. She said Mrs. Forbes had fallen downstairs and struck her head, and she wasn't quite "all there." They had asked her about the trunk but she didn't seem to know. Sometimes she said it had gone, and sometimes she said it hadn't, and finally when they pressed her to think hard and tell what had happened, she had roused to say pitifully: "Tell her she'd better come and get it herself. The man won't know which one it is."

It was all very bewildering, and Jane's heart sank. What should she do? She couldn't get away from the store. And Kent would be expecting those papers to come soon. Mr. Sanderson had had his secretary telephone the store just before four o'clock to tell her to bring them up tonight if they arrived after she got back to her boarding place. He would be very much annoyed if they hadn't come yet. Should she telephone Kent? She shrank exceedingly from doing so. Now that she was away the shame of her having appeared at his home in his absence had come over her with renewed power. He must not, *must not* think that she was running after him. At the same time if this matter was really as important to somebody as they seemed to think, had she any right to wait longer?

Of course it might be true that the trunk had started before Mrs. Forbes was hurt, and it might arrive all right tomorrow. But if it did not, and the lawyers questioned her, she would have to tell about her telephone conversation. So, it was better to let Kent know at once.

But what would the Havenners think of her? Oh, she *couldn't!*

So she debated the matter over and over, and finally with fear and trembling called the Havenner cottage. At least if her courage failed her she could say she called up to thank them for the nice time they had given her, although of course she had done that most thoroughly before she left that morning. And suppose Mr. Havenner, or Mrs. Havenner should answer the call. Would she have the nerve to ask for Kent, or should she just leave a message? It would have been so much easier if she could have called him at the office. Then no explanations would have been needed.

Then suddenly Kent's voice answered her:

"Yes?"

"Oh, Kent!" she began. "I thought I ought to let you know—"

"Oh, Jane! I was wondering if you had any news. Has the trunk come yet?"

"No, it hasn't," she answered in a worried tone. "And I was so troubled about it I telephoned again, and I find that Mrs. Forbes fell downstairs and had a concussion of the brain. They don't know whether she had sent the trunk or not, and they can't seem to find out from her. She is still in a state of delirium, or daze. When they asked her about it again she answered that I'd better come and get it myself, that nobody else would know where it was. Now, what do you think I ought to do? I could go, of course, but I might lose my job, and I really can't afford to do that. I thought perhaps you might be able to find out from the express company whether the trunk ever started or not. Could you?"

"Why, of course. I'll phone right away, and I'll call you back. Where are you? At a pay station? Can you stay there half an hour if it takes me that long? All right, I'll call you back. But say, in case you should have to go —yes, I really do think it is important enough to you to risk asking for a day or two off. But—I'll call you back in a few minutes."

Jane sat down, her heart in a tumult, her mind in a turmoil. If she was going to tremble and get all stirred up every time she heard his voice over the telphone it was just too bad. She never supposed she would be like that, and she had got to snap out of it mighty quick.

"Oh God my Father, Oh Jesus Christ my Saviour, deliver me from this foolishness, and make me a right-minded person!" she prayed quietly in her heart.

Then she turned her mind to the possibility of that journey. If she had to go, had she money enough? How much would it cost? More than ten dollars? She couldn't afford it of course, but it seemed as if she must anyway. Why, here she was planning to use the little pittance she had put away with a hope toward that lovely winter coat! When would she ever get any more?

Well, she would get the cheapest ticket possible. Maybe she could travel at night and save one day away from the store. She wouldn't need to take a Pullman. She could sleep curled up in a day coach.

Then she thought of her clothes. If she only hadn't bought that sweet little pink dimity and that new nightie she would have had almost enough to cover the ticket! But she was glad she had bought them. Somehow the memory of that blessed time beside the sea, those heavenly talks, those Sunday services, those moonlit walks, had cheered her soul and made her stronger for whatever hard things there were ahead of her now. But what should she wear on the train? This blue linen would be the right thing, but it was mussed now, and perhaps they would expect her to go at once. There would be no chance to get anything new, even if she had the money. And of course the pink dimity wouldn't do. Perhaps she would have to wear the brown dress. It was clean, but she would have to mend the rip in her sleeve that had kept her from wearing it last week. She could wash out a collar and iron it dry. No, it would take less time to press the dress she had on. Well, it wasn't as if she were going to a grand place. These people back at Mrs. Forbes' house would remember her, if they remembered her at all, as merely a girl who helped with the dining room and kitchen work a year ago. If she was clean and neat it wouldn't matter.

So she let her mind settle everything, while her heart waited for marching orders.

Then suddenly into her thoughts shrilled the telephone bell. She went to it at once.

"Jane? You there? No, they haven't sent that trunk

yet. They say that they went to the house but the woman who knew about the trunk had met with an accident, and they were told they would have to wait till she was better. No one else could identify the trunk. Now, you poor child! I'm afraid you'll have to go. I've telephoned Mr. Sanderson, and he thinks it's quite important that you have those papers tomorrow. He says to make your claim legal you should have your proof in at once. There are only two more days before the time will be up, and the property can go to other claimants. That would make a great deal of trouble getting it back."

"Well, why not let it go, then?" said Jane wearily. "Why should I bother? It won't be very much anyway, will it?"

"More than you think, little girl. And anyway, it isn't right not to get this thing done as it should be done. There is no point in letting other people get things that were legally left to you."

"But you know I haven't asked permission to leave the store. I might have trouble about that. You know I've just had a vacation."

"Oh, yes. I thought of that, and I took the liberty of telephoning Mr. Windle, and he said that it was quite all right for you to go, and he would personally explain your absence in the morning to the head of your department. I hope you didn't mind my doing that. I thought it might save you a little anxiety, and I know you won't have much time, if you leave tonight as I think you should. Could you leave tonight?"

"Oh, I guess I could," said Jane, half frightened. "But I certainly thank you for asking Mr. Windle. That is wonderful. I did dread asking to be let off."

"Well, that's all right. I'm glad you're not sore at me. Now, I've looked up your train and it leaves the main station just five blocks from where you live, at eleven-forty-five. Can you be ready by that time? That's good. Well, then, meet me down at the front door of your rooming house. I have to go back to town on an errand and I'll be glad to put you on your train. Now, take it easy and I'll see you at eleven-fifteen at your own door. It's lucky you phoned just when you did or I might have been gone. Good-bye. I have to run for my train."

She hung up the receiver and caught her breath in amazement. What a wonderful man he was! How he had taken her little affairs and put them through in the face of all odds! Ought she to let him do this? But how could she help it? He had taken it all right out of her hands as if it was his right.

Well, perhaps as her lawyer it was, who knew? She hadn't of course chosen him for her lawyer, but so all the more she must do as he said. But why was all this so important? Was it really true that she would get some money? Was this property they talked about that somebody wanted to buy, worth enough to pay her railroad fare to get the trunk? Well, perhaps she was just silly and ignorant, but why was it so vital that these people be kept from getting something they wanted? She had no faith whatever that there would be much. But of course, if there was a hundred dollars or more, it would be wonderfully nice to have it.

So she hurried to her rooming house, thrilling as she entered to think that Kent would be there pretty soon waiting for her.

She went up to her room and got together a respectable costume for her journey. And then money occurred to her again. Would she have enough for that ticket? She counted it out. How lucky she had not yet put it in the bank. She couldn't have cashed a check tonight! There would have been nobody who knew her well enough to do that. She took out the little cotton bag she had made to pin her valuables into her dress, and counted out the cash. Two ten dollar bills, two fives and three ones! She handled it wistfully. It had made her feel so safe and happy to have all that to fall back upon if she should be sick. And now this would likely take every cent and she would have to begin to save all over again. That would be the end of the lovely green coat with the dear brown fur. Well, never mind. What was it Mrs. Brooke had said? "Nothing can come to you, that is not permitted by your Father." Therefore this must be all for the best, somehow.

Well, it was good to have something like that to trust in when you couldn't understand.

So Jane hunted through her small store of garments till she found those she needed, rejoicing that there was a clean collar after all that she had forgotten. And at last she was ready as she could be. Then she turned and knelt down by her hard little bed and asked God to go with her, and guide her, and help her to find her trunk, and get safely back again. And then while she still knelt it came to her, what if something had happened to that trunk? What if it was lost or stolen or strayed? Nobody would steal it intentionally of course for there wasn't anything in it that would be valuable to anyone but herself. Oh, if those false heirs knew about it, and knew what was in it, they might have connived to get hold of it and destroy her evidence. But they didn't. At least she didn't see how they possibly could. But she added to her prayer: "Dear Father, please take care of that trunk. I wouldn't like to lose mother's pictures and things! It's all I have left of home!"

Then she rose and glanced at her cheap little watch. In ten minutes she would go downstairs and Kent would be there, and she would enter upon a new experience in her life. It had been a long long time since she had taken a journey on a train. And oh, if she didn't have money enough what should she do? Would she have to be subjected to the humiliation of having to borrow from Kent?

She lay down for five minutes and closed her eyes, trying to quiet her excited nerves.

And then at last it was time to go downstairs. At least, it was almost time, and she would rather be early than late.

But when she reached the lower floor there was Kent sitting on the hard little bench that served for visitors, smiling and watching her with relief in his eyes.

"You're all ready?" he asked. "I'm glad. I came over a little early, thinking there might be something I could do for you."

"Oh, thank you. You're so kind!" she faltered. "I think there's nothing left to be done but to get my ticket. Do you have any idea how much that would be likely to be? I wonder if I have enough."

He smiled and held out an envelope.

"Here are your tickets, lady. All paid for. The firm looks out for this. It's part of the expense of probating the will. Keep your money for a better purpose. Now, shall we go? I think there might be more restful places for you to pass these few minutes than sitting on this hard bench, though I suppose we should be thankful for even this."

He grinned and picked up the brief case he had with him, and then possessed himself of the package from Jane's hand.

"Come, let's go! Do you have to tell your landlady you are leaving for a few hours, or not?"

"No," said Jane, "I told her I was spending the night away, but if the trunk should arrive during my absence would she please look out for it. She doesn't care whether I go or stay. It's odd to feel that no one cares. You know I think that must be pretty bad for some young girls that haven't had any bringing up."

"I should say!" said Kent. "But you're not that. Plenty of people care for you!"

"For me?" said Jane with unbelieving eyes lifted, "I'm afraid you're mistaken."

"No, I'm not," said Kent assuredly. "Mr. Windle told me not two hours ago that he valued you very highly, and he was glad to give you as many days as you needed. That he felt you were a very lovely girl."

"Oh," laughed Jane, "Mr. Windle wouldn't know me from a fly on the wall if he should meet me in the store. But just the same I value his appreciation."

"And my mother thinks you are a wonderful little girl!" went on Kent. "She thinks you are charming, and very pretty, and smart as a whip. She especially appreciated some of the bright things you said, and the way you met trying situations."

"Oh, I really do love to know that," said Jane. "She is dear! I fell in love with her the first minute I saw her."

"That's nice," said Kent with satisfaction. "And my sister thinks you are the nicest girl she ever knew, and a lot more expletives I haven't time to repeat. Here's our taxi."

"Oh, but we could walk," said Jane. "You are being much too nice to me. You will spoil me, you know, and then all these nice things won't be true."

"Oh, but that's not all of them," he said, as he got in beside her and closed the door. "Molly and the cook think you're the grandest thing that ever walked the earth, and dad said he was glad to see I'd been able to look at the right kind of girl at last! And that's not all either. Pat thinks you're a marvelous singer, and a real Christian, and he's so glad we're both going to be in his class this winter. There! If that isn't enough I could tell you what *I* think, but I'm afraid that might take too long, and we don't want to miss your train."

He helped her out and they walked through the big bright station.

"How about a spot of ice cream?" he said as they came to the station restaurant. "I think we've plenty of time, and I'm hungry, aren't you? I didn't half eat my supper tonight I was in such a hurry."

"That would be lovely," said Jane, "but I'm afraid it was my fault you didn't have time for your supper."

"No, it wasn't. That was before I had heard from you. I missed my usual train out and took a bite in town before the next train left."

Such a pleasant little time they had together, talking of the sea and the moonlight, and what a wonderful preacher Pat was.

"Audrey thinks he's swell," mused Kent, "and I'm glad she does. I can't abide that egg of a Bainbridge she's been affecting. I was afraid she would lose all ability to judge character if she kept on companioning with him. I certainly was pleased she liked Pat, and so was dad. You know, that's another thing we have to thank you for! If you hadn't gone to Mrs. Brooke's class I never would have heard Pat, and known him in Boston, and brought him home with me. Oh, all things are working together for us with a vengeance these last few days. I'm going to have all kinds of a good time with Pat. He was just what I needed."

Soon they went down the long steps to the train, and Kent led her to her car and introduced her to her seat.

"I got you a whole section," he said. "Then you don't have to worry about anybody getting up above you. I'll tell the porter not to make up the upper berth, so that you can have all the air there is."

"Oh," said Jane, "you shouldn't have got me a berth at all. I could just as well have sat up. I can sleep anywhere."

"Oh, yes?" he said grinning. "And look like a little washed-out lamb in the morning, too, I'll bet. Well, you've got a berth. And now, I guess I'd better be going. Good night, and I wish you success. I'll be praying!" That last was in a soft voice just for her ear. Then he gave her hand a quick warm clasp and was gone, down a little narrow alley at the end of the car. Jane felt suddenly all alone and very small and inefficient. What a difference it made to have someone look after you!

Well, there she was again, harping on Kent Havenner. After all it was God, not Kent Havenner. If Kent had been just a nice pleasant man, without some consciousness of God, he probably wouldn't have looked at her, even for the sake of his business. He probably would have been going after girls like Evadne Laverock.

But Jane had little time for meditation. The porter asked her if she would like her berth made up at once, and told her she could sit on the other side of the aisle while he did it. So it was not long before she was getting ready for her night's rest behind heavy green curtains. But it wasn't hot there. There seemed to be clean breezes in every corner. Probably it was all air-conditioned. Well, she would be thankful for every bit of rest and comfort that came her way. The memory of it would help her sometimes when the days were hot and unbearable in the store, or when she lay on her hard little bed in that hall bedroom and wished for morning because she could not bear the heat of her room.

So she folded her cotton kimono about her and snapping off her light lay down on the incredibly soft bed, resting her head on pillows such as she had never owned.

She fully intended to stay awake awhile and enjoy this luxury, not waste her time in sleep, but before she knew it she had drifted away into unconsciousness, her last thought the words of Kent as he said: "I might tell you what I think of you myself, but it would take too long—" She wished she might have heard what he thought. But no, that remark was probably just a polite nothing. He knew so well how to say such things gracefully. It was an art to say pleasant things as if you really meant them. Perhaps he did mean them in a way, only she must be very, very careful never to think of them as if they were anything special for herself. He would have said the same to anybody.

And then oblivion came down with a vision of Kent's kindly smile lighting her path through the unknown way of tomorrow.

XXI

MEANTIME Audrey was having troubles of her own. Ballard Bainbridge was on the warpath.

Audrey had just settled herself with a new Bible she had gone in town that day especially to buy, and with a list of notes Pat had given her propped up on the table beside her, and a brand new pencil with a lovely green handle, she was about to begin a new and fascinating bit of education which she had come to feel in the last twenty-four hours that she sadly needed. Then Molly came up to her room to say that there was a caller downstairs.

Audrey arose with a sigh when she heard the name Bainbridge. Now it had come, what she dreaded. She would hear plenty of comment upon the new people, she would be lectured severely for her behavior Saturday and Sunday, and urged to amend her ways. She would hear that detestable Evadne held up as a model. Audrey could see in her suitor's eye Saturday night the retribution that would be coming to her.

Almost she was tempted to send down word she had retired and couldn't see him tonight, and then it occurred to her that that would only be putting off the evil day. She would have this to meet eventually, why not get it over with once and for all and be done with him? She needed no further time to think. She knew now she would never marry him, nor even care to hold him for a playtime friend.

So she slipped on a plain little dress and went downstairs as quickly as she could, anxious to get it over with and get back to her study. There were certain verses she had promised Pat she would look up and memorize before the class Thursday night. She had no more time to waste.

She appeared suddenly before the prancing impatient young man, and his expression grew blank as he looked at her.

"Oh," he said, "I hoped you'd be dressed. There isn't

overmuch time. I'm taking you across the point to the
hotel where Vad and I found a marvelous dance floor
Saturday night. Champ is taking us in his car and he'll be
here inside of ten minutes. Hustle up and change as quick
as you can. Put on the gaudiest thing you have. They
certainly are swell dressers over there."

Audrey held her head high. It happened that she had
heard from her mother the condition of Evadne when she
came back Saturday night.

"Thank you, Ballard," she said firmly, "I can't go anywhere tonight, and I certainly wouldn't care to go over
there, of all places."

He frowned.

"Don't waste time!" he said. "Go and get ready and
talk on the way!"

But Audrey did not stir.

"I'm not going out tonight, Ballard. That's final. I am
exceedingly busy. And I'm saying again, I do not wish
to go over to that hotel. Its reputation is anything but
savory. And I wouldn't care to have anyone know I went
there. I *wouldn't* go. I guess perhaps you don't know in
what condition you brought home Miss Laverock Saturday night."

"Oh, what utter nonsense!" raved the young autocrat.
"It's time you got over such archaic notions. Certainly I
know. Vad wouldn't have got into that condition if she
hadn't wanted to, would she? She had a reason all righty."

"Yes?" said Audrey. "Well, I have a reason for not
wishing to go out with you tonight, or any other night.
I am done! Please consider that final!"

"Aw now, Audrey, I didn't think you'd be jealous!
You've always seemed bigger than that. Just because I
went out a night or two with Vad, do you have to act
like a child? In fact it was you started the whole thing
if you'll remember. I called for you to take you out for a
plane ride, and you refused to come to the door to speak
to me. In fact you simply ran off with another man and
left me. Could I be blamed for taking the lady you handed
over to me?"

"I'm not blaming you, Ballard. I simply say I do not
wish to go anywhere with you tonight, and especially not
to the place you have selected. In fact I may as well

tell you that I have been discovering lately that you and I haven't even two ideas in common. I know you expected to change me, to mold me to suit your own ideas, but I have just come to realize that I don't wish to be molded. Not by you anyway. I don't agree with your ideas about modern life and the new order of things that you are always talking about. And I don't wish to discuss them any more. I'm done! I'm sorry if I seem to be unpleasant, but I felt it was best to be frank."

"Now, Audrey, don't be a simp! Go and get your best togs on and we'll talk on the way."

"No." said Audrey. "Positively *no!* You'll have to excuse me from now on. I'm really sorry that I've let you waste so much of your valuable time on me. But you see I never quite understood until a few days ago just how I felt about the matter. I kept putting off thinking about it, hoping, perhaps, that you might change. I don't know just what it was I thought. I guess I was too lazy to think. But now I know what I think, and I'm telling you."

"But Audrey, I'm really very fond of you."

"Is that so?" said Audrey wearily. "That's a nice way to part, I'm sure. But I guess it was because I found out that I wasn't really very fond of you, that made me come to this decision. You know two people who are not of one mind about things in general couldn't possibly go on together very long without a clash, and I had reached a clash, Ballard. I really had. I couldn't go on and hear you denounce the things my father and mother count precious, even if I didn't always myself. I couldn't go on and hear you talk about morals and laws being all nonsense, and the Bible untrue, and God a fake. It was getting on my nerves. So, Ballard, go and find Evadne Laverock and take her with you to the places you both like. Or find somebody else like-minded—"

"But see here, Audrey, that's it. I told Vad I was coming to get you to go with us, and she's got a man for you she's sure you will enjoy. He's a man who has never gone in for sophistication before, and he wants to step out. We thought you would be just the one to induct him into a delightful evening. Now, Audrey, be a good pal and help us out. I can't go back to Vad and tell her I failed. I never fail, you know."

"Don't you?" smiled Audrey. "Well, this time you have! But I suspect you needed that to teach you that you aren't as wise as you think you are."

"What do you mean by that?"

"I mean that I've found something vaster and more exciting than all your theories and all the books you loaned me. I've found the Book of books and it's fascinating. I wouldn't give it up for all the pleasures of the world. I've found a friend and a Saviour, and I'm happier than I ever was in my life before."

"You talk like a fanatic! Don't tell me you've got religion, Audrey, after all the trouble I've spent upon you!"

"Well, I don't know whether I've got religion or not yet, but if I haven't I soon will have, for I'm going after it with all my heart. Only I don't call it religion, I call it Christianity. I understand there are a great many fallacies masquerading under the name of religion, and I want something real. If you'll excuse me now I'm going back to what I was doing. I really haven't any more time to waste in talking about nothings. I'm only sorry I ever wasted any that way. And now I bid you good night!" And Audrey swept up the stairs and left her erstwhile lover alone, staring after her. Did she really have that much spirit? What a pity it wasn't active in something worth while instead of chasing after outworn dogmas! Well, let her go awhile! Doubtless she would tire of religion and return to her natural world. Young people didn't live like ascetics the way they used to do in bygone ages!

But what was he going to do now? This was going to be awkward. He had wagered a goodly sum on the expectation of bringing Audrey to prove his power over her. And incidentally to get rid of the young man whom Evadne had attached for the evening.

Slowly he walked out of the house and down the steps, greatly to Audrey's relief as she listened. She even hurried downstairs to lock the doors so that he could not return and call her back to conflict. She was most eager this time to dip into her new Bible. Would she really be able to find all those wonderful things that Pat had showed her yesterday? Or were they all in his own fertile brain?

So Audrey settled down again to her study, and her

mother coming anxiously in an hour later found her hard at work.

"Oh, I'm so glad you're here, and alone!" she said with a relieved sigh. "I thought I heard Ballard Bainbridge come in, and yet it was so still here I couldn't think what had happened."

"He did come in, mother. He wanted me to go to a dance over at that awful Red Lion Hotel with Evadne and some strange man who needed lessons in sophistication. Imagine it! I think I told him pretty clearly where to get off, and I hope you won't be troubled with him around here any more. I'm about fed up on him."

"Oh, my dear!" said her mother, dropping down in a chair and bowing her head in her hands, the tears running down freely. "I'm so relieved! I was so afraid you were getting fond of him, and I didn't know what to do, with both of my dear children running right into danger that way. Oh, I'm so glad you're done with Ballard."

"So am I!" said Audrey impetuously. "I was getting more and more involved and didn't know how to get out. It took a fool girl like Evadne, and a little button salesgirl, and a real man who teaches the Bible to show me the false from the true, but now I guess I'm wise to my follies. Mums, why didn't you ever make us learn the Bible and know what it means when we were kids? It's simply great! It would have done more to keep us straight than anything else you could have done. Why didn't you?"

"Oh, my dear, I don't know," wailed her mother. "I guess I never knew much about it myself, but I've always respected it. My own father used to read it for hours, and seemed to love it. Is that a Bible you have?"

"Yes, I bought it in town today, and I'm going to study it regularly. Pat Whitney is helping me. I'm going to his class Thursday evenings. I think it's great. Why don't you and dad take it up? I believe you'd like it better than bridge. I really do. Neither of you ever cared much for cards. And this would be something unique. Not just like what everybody else is doing."

"Why, I wonder if your father would like it. I'll talk to him about it. I always thought it was hard to understand, and maybe it was better to let ministers interpret it for us."

"Oh, but it's not hard the way Pat teaches it!" exclaimed Audrey. "If I'd known it was like that I'd have studied it long ago. He makes it very interesting."

Her mother sat watching her wistfully.

"You like Mr. Whitney pretty well, don't you?"

"I think he's simply swell, mother. Only I feel so awfully ignorant when I'm with him, more ignorant than I did even with Ballard. You know he always took it for granted you were ignorant anyway, even when you knew a thing pretty well. But Pat is so humble he never assumes that he is dead right. He just tells what the Bible says and I think he must know it all by heart. Whereas Ballard didn't believe the Bible was anything but a bunch of lies. Now go to bed, mother. You're all shivery and shaky and you need a good night's sleep. You don't need to worry any more about me. I'm cured. No more Bainbridge for me. And as for Kent, I shouldn't wonder if he had had almost enough of Evadne too. He seems to like Jane a lot, doesn't he? You liked Jane too, didn't you? I thought you would. I think she's sweet. So lay down your burdens and get a good night's rest, and let's do something nice, make plans and things in the morning."

Mrs. Havenner kissed her daughter and went away with a smile on her face, and Audrey plunged into her study again. She didn't want to stop until she had looked up all the references that Pat had given her, and proved that everything he had told her was true.

XXII

WHEN Jane awoke the next morning she did not know where she was for a moment, and then the motion of the train and the softness of the bed on which she lay recalled her to the present, and she realized that she was on her way to get her trunk. What a lot of changes had come into her life lately! A vacation and a week-end at the shore, and now this wonderful trip in a Pullman train!

Then she realized that it must be near morning and she pulled up her shade and looked at her watch. Yes, it was late. The train would be at her destination in half an hour! She must get dressed at once!

She hadn't really undressed fully, so it did not take her long to be in neat array and ready to get out. Then she went to the washroom and washed and made her hair tidy. Everything she had to do, even the washing of her face, seemed a part of a play in this complete little dressing room, and she longed to linger and enjoy it. But she knew she must have her hat on and everything ready to get out at once when the train reached her station. It did not stop long at small stations. She mustn't run the risk of being carried on to Boston!

So in a very short time she was ready, hat on, little box packed and watching each station. As she drew nearer to the well-remembered locality, things began to seem familiar to her. She watched the farms she knew slip by. The Gilmans had painted their house by the lake. The Fosters had built a garage. How interesting it was to see changes in the places she knew so well.

And then they reached her stopping place and she got out and walked slowly down the long platform to the station, noticing the line of new busses that were drawn up on the side next the street. The whole place looked pleasant to her just because it was familiar.

"Good morning! Did you have a comfortable sleep?"

said Kent suddenly, getting up from behind a pile of baggage and coming forward to greet her.

"Oh!" she said blinking at him, half frightened lest she was losing her mind. How could he be here?

"You didn't expect to see me here, did you? I'm real, indeed I am. I traveled on the second car ahead of yours and that's how I happened to be out ahead of you. You see, I wanted to surprise you. I thought it would be fun to greet you and see how surprised you would be." He ended with one of his pleasant grins.

"But how, why—?" she began, and looked almost as if she were going to cry. "Did you have to travel all this way and lose all this time from your work? Couldn't you trust me to come back?"

"Oh, Jane! Of course! Yes! But you see I had some business up the road a little farther which I can transact while you are repacking your trunk and saying hello to your friends. I thought it would be nice for me to be here and make arrangements for that trunk to be sent. Mr. Sanderson thought so too. He said there was no telling what contingencies might arise about that trunk, and I ought to be here to help you out with it. You see it is quite important that we get those proofs on file. There is only one day left now, and we don't want to run any risks. Incidentally, too, I'm to wipe out another errand that has been troubling the office for a week. It's only thirty miles above here, and ought not to take long, a mere formality, but had to be attended to by one of the firm, so they wished it on me, besides the job of personally conducting you on this treasure hunt. Now, young lady, the next act is to get some breakfast. Do you suppose this restaurant is any good, or should we go to a hotel?"

"I'm afraid this is rather expensive," said Jane shyly. "It used to have that name."

"Then let's go in. It ought to be good. I'm hungry as a bear, aren't you?"

"Why, I wasn't going to bother to get any breakfast," Jane grinned back. "I was too excited about being off traveling alone."

"But you aren't off traveling alone any more, lady, so what? Do I get any breakfast or not?"

He seated her at the table and started in with orange

juice, oatmeal and cream, beefsteak and flannel cakes and coffee.

"Don't forget the maple syrup," he said as he handed the order to the waiter.

"Now, Jane, what is the order of the day?" he said, leaning back and looking at her with satisfaction. "Do we take a taxi to the residence of Mrs. Forbes at once, or are there preliminaries?"

"Why, I was going to walk," said Jane thoughtfully. "I don't know that they would know me if I came in a taxi."

"It could be done I suppose, if time is not too much of a factor. How far is it?"

"About two miles."

"Oh! In that case I think we'd better take the taxi. It seems a good thing that I came after all in spite of the rather cool welcome you gave me, if you were going to economize at that rate. We've got to get back to the city tonight, lady, if possible!"

"Oh! Of course! I didn't realize!" said Jane. "But listen. I didn't give you a cool welcome. I was just surprised. I just didn't understand it."

"You weren't very glad to see me, were you? Honest?"

Jane's cheeks suddenly got very red.

"Yes, I was," she owned, with her eyes down half shamedly. "I was a great deal gladder than I wanted you to see!"

"But why?"

"Well, I thought this was a matter of business, and I had no right to just friendly gladness. Besides I was a little scared."

She lifted her eyes with a swift glance and downed them again, quickly.

"Why you everlasting little fraud, you!" laughed Kent. "You weren't willing I should get any satisfaction out of coming. I see. Well, I'll take pains to rub that in on you some day and make you bitterly repent. Now, tell me the rest of your plan. Should we arrange with a truck to follow us at a reasonable distance to get the trunk, or arrange with him to come at telephone call?"

"Maybe that," said Jane. "I was beginning to be afraid there might be something queer about their not being able to find that trunk. It might take time to find it, you know. Oh, I'm so glad you came along!"

"Thanks! So am I. Now, shall we go, or will you have another batch of griddle cakes?"

"Oh no, thank you. Let's go!"

So they went.

While Jane went up to see Mrs. Forbes, Kent sat on the porch of the Forbes residence and visioned Jane going about there as a little serving maid, a little lonely girl with only an old Scotch woman for a friend, and a lot of hard work to do.

The old Scotch woman lifted a frail hand in greeting, and smiled a faint smile.

"I'm sorry—" she faltered, "couldn't get it—off."

The sullen maid who had let her in explained to Jane that Mrs. Forbes' accident had happened the same evening she had telephoned for the trunk. She had been coming downstairs with some blankets that she had brought from a room she had been cleaning for a new boarder. The blankets needed mending and she was going to do it that evening. She caught her foot in a torn blanket, and fell the full flight, rolling down to the foot and striking her head on the railing several times.

"No ma'am. She hadn't been up to the attic yet to look for the trunk. She was awful busy and she thought it would be time enough to do that when the man came for it in the morning. But when he came she didn't know nothing at all, and couldn't answer a question, so we couldn't give him no trunk, and she didn't never get so she could show us, so the man stopped comin'. Yes ma'am, you could go up an' find it if you know where you left it."

Jane was greatly relieved that Mrs. Forbes had not fallen going after her trunk, and she tried to talk cheerily to the sick woman.

"Never mind, Mrs. Forbes," she said gently, "I'll find the trunk, I'm sure. Is it just where I put it before I went away?"

The sick woman looked dazed.

"I think it is. Though mebbe my husband—he mighta moved things around—a bit—afore we went south."

She closed her eyes as if it had been an effort to say so much, and Jane arose.

"Don't you worry," she said, "I'll go up. I'm sure I can find it. I have a friend downstairs who will help me. He's strong and can help me bring it down."

"All right! You go find it!" said Mrs. Forbes, and shut her eyes again.

Jane called Kent and together they went upstairs to the attic.

At first, when they got up to the attic, Jane's heart sank as she looked toward the corner where she knew she had left her trunk, for there wasn't any trunk there. Only a pile of old broken chairs and an old-fashioned bedstead and bureau. The whole arrangement of the attic seemed to be changed, and it was crowded full of things, furniture piled up to the ceiling. Cards tacked on the backs of several boxes with a name and address showed that the Forbeses must have allowed somebody to store all their furniture there.

In despair Jane walked around, poking into corners. Kent followed her, suddenly realizing that this expedition might not turn out to be as successful as he had hoped after all.

"If it wasn't so dark here!" said Jane desperately. "I'll run down and see if I can't borrow a flashlight."

Presently she came back with a candle, and holding it aloft Kent finally discovered several trunks back under the eaves behind a lot more furniture. He flung off his coat and got to work, and presently cleared a path to the trunks.

"There it is!" cried Jane in a relieved tone. "Oh, I'm so glad!"

Kent hauled it out and brushed the dust off his hands.

"I certainly am glad I came along," he remarked, "even if you're not!"

"Oh, but I am!" said Jane. "I never said I wasn't! What would I have done without you?"

"That's the talk. Now, lady, here's a bit of advice. Don't you think it would be wise in you to open this trunk right here and now and make sure that nobody else has done so in the interval and removed any of the contents? We don't want to have to return again tomorrow if we can help it."

"Oh, I never thought of that!" said Jane aghast.

"Have you the key?" asked Kent anxiously.

"Oh, yes." Jane produced it promptly.

There followed another anxious moment while Kent wrestled with the lock, and then the ancient hinges groaned as he flung back the top.

"Full to the brim!" said Kent as he arose and brushed the dust from his knees. "But are they yours? Make sure of that. Are the special things there that we need?"

He took the candle from Jane and held it high while she knelt before the trunk and laid out pile after pile of folded garments, touching them tenderly because they reminded her of her beloved mother.

"There's mother's wedding dress!" she said softly as she laid out a long white box.

"That's nice!" said Kent in a voice that was soft with sympathy.

"Yes. And here is the Bible!" said Jane, feeling deep into the trunk. "And the photograph album!"

"That's good!" Kent's voice rang with satisfaction.

"And here's the box with the papers, birth and wedding certificates. I don't believe a thing has been touched!" cried Jane in excitement.

"That's grand!" said Kent. "Now, the next thing is to get back home as fast as we can. Had you planned to take this trunk to the office or to your rooming house? Because if you want to take it straight to the rooming house we'd better take out these things that are important and carry them by hand, hadn't we? We could get a box or a suitcase in this town somewhere, I suppose. But why don't you just take the trunk along to the office and unpack it there. You know it might turn out that there was something else in it we needed."

"Oh! Could I? Wouldn't it be dreadfully in the way?"

"No indeed. We have an extra room, and nobody would need to see it. We could pack it right up again after Sanderson has all he needs out of it, and take it in the taxi with us back to your rooming house tonight. Let's see. It is nine-thirty now. If I remember aright there is a return train leaving here about eleven. If we can get that we'd be home around seven. I'll telephone Sanderson and get him to wait. We'll keep track of the trunk and have it right with us. It isn't large and I can have it checked on our train. How's that?"

"Wonderful!" said Jane. "Oh, I'm glad you are here. I wouldn't have known what to do next."

"All right! Let's get to work."

"But you have to do something else for the office," reminded Jane.

"Yes, well, that's secondary. I'll talk to Sanderson first."

"I suppose I could take the trunk to the office myself if you would tell me how to manage, and then you could stay and do your work," suggested Jane dubiously.

"Yes, you could," said Kent, "but I'm not going to let you. You see there are so many things that men can do in the way of dealing with railroad men and taxi drivers that women wouldn't be able to work, at least not quiet inexperienced girls like yourself, and I'm not taking any chances."

Jane's heart sang a little song of joy, though she tried to still it, making out to herself that she was only frightened lest she would somehow bungle this and disappoint the office. But the song sang steadily on, and its reflection shone in the look on Jane's face.

Kent put the things back in the trunk and locked it. Then he turned around to Jane.

"Now, you are a little glad I came along, for some other reason than just to help you do this work, aren't you? I see it in your face. I hear it in your voice. And how about letting me kiss you? Just once, anyway. You know I love you, Jane. And this looks to me like the quietest place we'll have for several hours for me to show you how I love you. May I?"

Jane's face flamed a joyous rosy tint. She looked up and her eyes were alight with beauty.

"Oh!" she said. "Oh!"

But she did not draw away. She did not say no.

And then he folded her in his arms and laid his lips tenderly on hers, holding her close for a long moment.

"But—I'm only—a poor—working—girl!" gasped Jane with glory in her face. "And you are—"

"Go on," he said, looking adoringly down at her and

holding her closer, "what am I? I've been wanting to know what you thought I was and I couldn't find out."

"You are—" Jane started again shyly, "a gentleman!"

"Oh, is that all?" said Kent looking disappointed.

"Well, that is—a great deal," went on Jane, "but—besides that—you are—" She paused and looked up into his eyes adoringly, "you are *dear!*" she added softly.

Then he grasped her closer and laid his face down to hers.

"You are *precious!*" he breathed. "You are the dearest thing that ever came into my life!"

A little after, when she could get her breath to speak again she said:

"And yet, I am a working girl and you are a gentleman! Why, I worked in the kitchen in this very house. I used sometimes to scrub this attic floor when we were housecleaning."

"Yes," said Kent, smiling down into her face just below his own, "that is the reason why I wanted to kiss you here, right here where you did humble work. It is beautiful to me. It reminds me of the lowly way your Lord and mine came to earth for us. It helped to make you what you are, a fine, strong, all-around womanly girl. Not a little fool like most of the girls I know. I've tried to think I loved some of them and I couldn't. Beloved, I love you!"

And then he kissed her again.

Suddenly he drew back.

"But I haven't time now to tell you all the reasons why I love you. We've got to get to work and catch that train. Do you suppose they will let us telephone here? I'll get an expressman right away. If you've anything more to say to your old lady, go say it and we'll get off as soon as our truck goes. I'll phone Sanderson from the station."

It was astonishing how quickly things got moving, once they were downstairs. The expressman arrived hot haste. Jane said good-bye to Mrs. Forbes and left a crisp five dollar bill in her hand in sympathy for her in her illness, received a shower of blessings from the poor paralyzed tongue, and they were away to the station.

Kent talked with his chief, agreed to telephone to the

nearby town instead of going there, and was able to arrange the business satisfactorily.

Then suddenly the train came, and Kent saw the trunk on to the baggage car, came back and got Jane just in time to swing on to the Pullman with her, and they were embarked on a blissful journey, which seemed all too short to them both when it was over.

Later that evening they arrived at the office with the trunk on the taxi with them, and a porter whom Sanderson had bribed to stay late helped Kent take the trunk in.

It was almost like a sacred rite as the two men stood by watching the girl unpack her treasures. Sanderson found a mist in his eyes more than once, as one and another trifle full of memories was brought to light. For Jane had forgotten their presence, at least the presence of Sanderson, and was talking now and then to herself, evidently recalling dearest memories.

"And there is my first little dress, and my baby bonnet!" she would say, almost in a whisper. "And mother's wedding gown!"

She lifted the cover of the box for a brief second and disclosed a satin dress of other days, its modest train and high puffed sleeves carefully folded back with tissue paper, its wreath of orange blossoms lying on the top. And where the satin had slipped back a little, soft folds of malines, the wedding veil, were disclosed, bordered with a dainty edge of real lace.

Sanderson stood with his hands clasped behind him, and blinked away the tears, thinking of another bride who had been his, and of the dreary years that had come between that vision and now, ever since another scene with a casket had taken her away from him forever.

At last he received the big Bible and handled it almost as if it had been a sacred vessel of some sort. And when Jane brought forth the pictures and the important papers they all sat down at a long polished table and laid them forth. Sanderson was very much impressed. The pictures brought out a good many facts.

There was Harold Scarlett when he was only a baby, and Harold Sacarlett when he was a boy in school, and again when he was in college, and then as best man at his brother's wedding. The wedding picture, too, was a proof in itself. For there stood Jane's sweet mother in her bridal array, looking almost like Jane today, and there was Harold Scarlett standing in the group, smiling a gay irresponsible smile at the world.

There were later pictures. A couple he had sent from Europe, one taken at Monte Carlo, another at some famous resort in the south of France. And then a few clippings and a newspaper picture carefully pasted in and labeled by the hand of Jane's mother. It was all most convincing. And then there was a photograph of the old Scarlett home.

Jane looked at it lovingly.

"I was there once," she said ruminatively.

"Why!" said Sanderson looking at it sharply, and then turning to Kent Havenner he said in an undertone, "Identical! That settles it!"

But Jane was too busy with the dear old pictures and did not notice.

"Well, now, young lady, I'll see that your claim goes through quickly," Sanderson said in a kindly tone. "You can leave these things here with me for a few days, and when all is settled up I'll return them to you. No, I don't need the wedding dress. But yes, the marriage certificate, and the other papers. Now, Kent, help Miss Scarlett pack up, and you can take the trunk with you. I've all that we shall need. You've done good work and done it expeditiously. Good night! I'll let you know, Miss Scarlett, as soon as all is completed."

So Jane packed her trunk again and Kent took her home.

"I'm not going to let you stay long in this dump!" said Kent as they neared the rooming house.

"Oh, it's all right," laughed Jane. "I've so much other joy I'm sure I shan't mind any more."

"Darling!" he murmured and held her hand close. And then the taxi stopped and he had his hands full getting someone to take that trunk up to Jane's room.

"Remember, it won't be for long," he murmured in her ear as he said a staid good night.

XXIII

It was the very next afternoon that Evadne put herself in her grandest battle array and started out to get her revenge. She began by trying to call up Kent for she had intended to ring him in on it too, but Kent was not in his office. He was out on business for the afternoon they said. That was the same answer they had given her for the last two days, and she felt there was intention in it, which made her all the more wrathful.

She arrived at the button counter while Jane was waiting on two very nice ladies who were buying buttons and clasps for their fall outfits, and she stormed up to the counter and interrupted.

"I want to speak to you, Miss Scarlett!" she demanded.

Jane glanced up at sound of the voice and gave her a startled glance.

"Just a moment," she answered.

Evadne waited impatiently for as much as a full minute, then she repeated her request.

"I'm busy just now," Jane said quietly.

"Well, that doesn't make any difference," said Evadne, raising her voice still higher, "I'm not going to wait on you all day. I've important things to do. I've something to say to you that won't wait, and if you can't stop what you're doing and listen to me, I'll say it now where everybody can hear. I've just come to tell you you can lay off my fiancé, that's all! He belongs to me, and you've no right to try to take him over."

The button customers looked at her curiously, and gave a startled glance at Jane whose cheeks were rosy red, but whose demeanor was still quiet and controlled. Save for the color in her cheeks she paid no heed whatever to the tirade that was going on, but other people were giving plenty of attention and Evadne had known they would.

"Some people might not pay any attention to such actions on the part of a mere working girl, but I don't feel that way. Such carryings on as there were last Saturday night and Sunday are not to be endured. I intend to see that there isn't any more of it. I just thought it was fair to warn you that if you have anything whatever to do with him any more, I shall go the limit in having you punished. You're a menace to the public and it is a benevolence to others to put you where you can't do any more of it. A life sentence wouldn't be too long for such as you!"

By this time Mr. Clark had heard the loud voice from afar and had arrived on the scene. Ladies were rushing from this aisle and that to peer above one another's heads and see what was happening now. Evadne was looking straight at Jane, for all the other salesgirls at that counter had hastily gone as far away as the limits of the counter would allow. Everybody else, too, was looking straight at Jane, whose face was calm and restrained, but turning very white now. Mr. Clark's eyes upon her, his lifted eyebrows almost demanded some explanation from Jane.

But Jane only finished writing her slip for the buttons she had sold to the two ladies who had charged their purchases and gone. Then she looked up straight at Evadne.

"I don't understand you," she said coldly.

"Oh, yes, you do!" taunted the angry girl, well knowing that she had the upper hand. "You understand me well enough. You know who it was you went walking off up the beach with Saturday night, and took to church all day Sunday. You knew perfectly well he was my fiancé and you just exulted in taking him away from me and making me a laughing stock. And I'll have my revenge, I swear I will!"

Suddenly Mr. Clark stepped up to Evadne.

"Excuse me, madam," he said, "but wouldn't it be better to wait until closing time and talk quietly with this girl, if you have to talk? You'll be making *yourself* a laughing stock, doing it so publicly. And we really can't allow this to go on in the store, you know."

"Very well, then, make this girl answer me. I told her I wished to speak with her privately and she was insolent. She said she was busy."

"That was her privilege of course when she was working."

"Oh, indeed! Well, if you are going to be insolent too I shall have to demand to see the owners of this store. For I intend to have an answer from this girl before I leave."

"Have you anything to say, Miss Scarlett?" asked Mr. Clark, with an almost pleading expression in his eyes.

Jane swept him a grateful glance.

"Yes," said Jane, still quietly, and not looking in the least frightened. "I would just like to say this. If the gentleman to whom you refer as your fiancé is really so, surely you could trust a man such as he is! If you know him as well as you seem to think you do, you would know that he would never do anything unbecoming to the man who was your fiancé. That's all, Mr. Clark. Would you like me to go off the floor?"

"No, Miss Scarlett, stay where you are and go on with your work. Madam, I shall be glad to take you up to Mr. Windle if he is not too busy at present to see customers of the house."

Mr. Clark led the angry Evadne away, into another aisle, and the customers closed in around the button counter, stretching their necks to see who this girl was, but Jane had disappeared into the tiny wrapping cubbyhole behind Hilda, with her hands on her hot cheeks, taking deep breaths and praying in her heart for help.

She got it too, and presently came out calmly and went to work again.

"My, but you were swell!" whispered Louise, fluttering up to her between sales. "I wish I could be cool like that and carry off a situation. I would have gone all to pieces and got furious. I would have slapped her old painted face for her. That's what she oughtta have got. Say, did you really snitch her man from her?"

Jane laughed.

"Of course not," she said. "What an idea! Forget it, Louise. I'm sorry I had to be the cause of a disturbance in the store, that's all. Say, are there any more of those blue enamel buttons with the rhinestones in them?" and Louise was turned aside and went hunting blue enamel buttons. But Jane had come to the place where she had begun to tremble and wanted to sit down and cry. However, she remembered that she had a stronghold that would not fail her and went on to the end of the day.

That night when Jane came out of the store she found Kent waiting for her, and her heart forgot its worries and joy flooded her face.

But a few minutes later he looked at her keenly.

"What has happened today?" he asked. "You look pale. Are you not feeling well?"

"Oh, I'm perfectly all right," smiled Jane.

"No, something is the matter! Now tell me everything. Anything disagreeable happen in the store?"

She looked at him startled and then grinned.

"Yes," she said, "I've been accused of carrying off a girl's sweetheart! What do you think of that? Perhaps you won't want to have anything to do with me any more."

"Darling!" he murmured in a low tone. "Tell me. What was it?"

"I've told you. Just that. A girl came into the store and openly accused me before everybody of stealing her fiancé."

"Who was it?" There was a hard set look about Kent's mouth.

"I'd rather not tell you, if you don't mind."

"But I must know. Was I that fiancé?"

"Yes."

"I thought so. And the girl was Evadne Laverock?"

"How did you know?"

"Because that's just the kind of thing she would do. Oh, if only I had never seen her! It's my foolishness that brought this on you. I should have the public shame, not you. Anyway, I should have guarded you against this, by telling you all about her, in the first place, though I didn't realize there was anything much to tell. Not yet, anyway. We had more important things to say. Well, here's the truth in a nutshell. I pretty well lost my head over her last summer, and thought I was in love for a few weeks, though we were never engaged. She had too many lovers, and when I protested she only laughed, and we had a disagreement. When I told her I wished she would stop drinking and swearing and smoking and live a quiet respectable life she got very angry and ran off to Europe for six months with never a word to me, thank God, all that time. By the time she came back I had begun to get my eyes open, and I knew I did not love her and never would. So that's the story. I am not her fiancé and never was, though one night when she looked particularly charming I almost told her I loved her. *Almost,* not quite, for somebody else came along and interrupted, and was I glad afterwards that they did? But oh, I'm ashamed that I ever had anything to do with her. You should have known it at once when I told you of my love, only it didn't seem at all important to me then. I know I never really loved her at all, and I thank God that she's out of my life forever!"

Jane smiled at him.

"Thank you for telling me. I knew it must be something like that or you never would have told me you loved me," she said, giving him a trusting look.

He crushed her hand softly in his.

"I knew you'd be like that," he said. "That's one of the reasons why I love you so. And now, let's forget her for awhile, and then by and by I want you to tell me all about it, where I can be sorry and comfort you in a proper way. I have my car near here and I thought maybe you'd like to take a ride, then we'll have dinner together somewhere. Will you go?"

"Oh, yes!" said Jane. "How lovely!"

So he put her into his car, and they drove out along a sunlit way into the near country, where the long shadows were beginning to fall across road and grass, and the night seemed wide in its preparation for the sunset which was coming soon. At last they drew up before the old Scarlett mansion!

Jane who had been watching the houses along the other side of the road suddenly looked up and saw it, recognized its likeness at once and exclaimed in wonder:

"Why, there is a house just like my grandfather's old home! Isn't that wonderful? And why are we stopping here? Do you know the owner?"

"Yes, I know the owner fairly well," said Kent, "though I haven't known her long. But I thought perhaps you would like to look at the house, it seemed so lovely, and so like the picture you showed us of your grandfather's.",

"Yes indeed!" said Jane eagerly, not suspecting in the

least. "How very nice of her to let us see it. Do you mean we may go inside?"

"Oh, yes. That's what she said."

"But I've just my working clothes on!" protested Jane looking down at herself.

"Oh, that won't matter," said Kent. "She won't be noticing your clothes."

They started up the brick walk and suddenly Jane stopped abruptly, looking off at the little rustic teahouse on the far side of the lawn.

"Oh!" she said excitedly, "it *is* my grandfather's house! It must be! There is the teahouse I remember, and isn't that a swing beyond it? But how could it be? Grandfather's house wasn't anywhere near here, was it? It was in a town called Hawthorne, near some city, I can't remember the name."

Kent was smiling and watching her with delight.

"This is Hawthorne," he said, "or used to be called that until it was incorporated into the city. And this was your grandfather's house, but isn't any more, because now it is yours! That is, if you want to keep it. It was not sold as you supposed. It passed to your Uncle Harold, and he in turn left it to his brother's child, evidently not knowing exactly where you were. The man who wants to buy it has friends living out here and he wants to pull it down and build it over into a modern house. He wants to begin at once!"

"How dreadful!" said Jane. "May I go inside?"

"That is what we came for," said Kent, slipping his arm inside hers and falling into step by her side.

He took out a key and unlocked the door and Jane stepped within the wide beautiful hall of her ancestral home.

An hour later they came slowly down the stairs after having gone from room to room examining everything, and arrived back in the big living room, Jane sitting down in an old handsome chair opposite an oil painting of her grandmother when she was a bride.

"Oh, it is all so lovely!" she said plaintively. "I wish I could keep it. It is just as it used to be when I was little, and it would be wonderful to have it. But of course I never could."

"But why not?" asked Kent tenderly. "There seems to be no reason in the world why you shouldn't. Just because a man wants to buy it is no reason why you should sell something you want to keep."

"But," she said sadly, her eyes wide and earnest, "it costs a lot of money to keep a house, I've always heard. Just taxes are a big item, I know. I've heard people talk about them. Mrs. Forbes is worried now about the taxes on her little house, and what would this be? Something awful! I could never hope to make money enough to pay even a tithe of the taxes. And there would likely be repairs some day! No, it wouldn't be right for me to keep it!"

"Young lady, have you forgotten," said Kent watching her amusedly, "that you've taken me on for life? Do you count it nothing that I would be your husband, and as that I might naturally be counted on to help you out with your taxes now and then if it ever became necessary?"

"Oh!" she gasped, her cheeks turning pink. "I hadn't thought that far. But, of course, you are a young man and just beginning. It wouldn't be right for you to be hampered by a burden of debt and taxes and things. No, I'm sure it wouldn't be right. I must not be so selfish!"

"Well, bless your heart, you darling unselfish child! There's nothing like that to be in your scheme of things. The inheritance will carry the house many times over. Neither you nor I will have a cent to pay. The house was not all that was left to you in the will. There is quite a large fortune that was left you besides. There will be plenty to cover all expenses the house could make, and not be noticed out of what is left. I did not know until this morning how much it would be. I thought perhaps there was only a few thousands beside the house. But now I know, I am ashamed that I am daring to marry a rich wife. Of course I have a nice little sum put away myself, enough to start on, but not as much as you have. And so, in the face of this knowledge I could not do less than offer to let you off if you want to be let."

Jane looked at him aghast. Then suddenly when she saw the look in his own eyes, the hunger, the longing, the delight in her, she sprang from her chair and dashed across the room.

"Kent!" she cried as her arms went around his neck

and she laid her lips on his lips, his forehead, his eyes. "This from you! To think I should have to endure such a ghastly thought twice in one day. First from that Laverock woman demanding that I give you up, and next from you, suggesting that you don't want me!"

"Jane! Did I say that? Oh Jane, can I ever forgive myself that I let you in for such an awful experience!" His arms were around her now, and his head bowed with shame. But Jane was at peace, with her face nestled in his breast, and his lips on her hair.

"Oh, joy, joy, joy!" she breathed at last when they finally went reluctantly toward the door, in the gathering dusk, his arm still about her. "I never dreamed that there was joy in the world like this! Much less that I should ever have it!"

"Nor I either!" he said tenderly. "I never dreamed there was such a girl in this world as you, not in these days! Oh what a fool I was ever to think I could be satisfied with anything less!"

"And now," said Kent as they started back to the city, "will you go to a nice quiet hotel somewhere and stay till we get married? Or do you want to go back to that pestiferous rooming house tonight?"

Jane thought for a minute and then she shook her head.

"No. No hotel!" she said decidedly. "I'll go back to the rooming house, for now anyway. I want to lie on the hard little bed and think there is a softer one coming. I want to look around that bare little room and know I've a whole home all beautiful and ready! I've been so used to telling myself my home was over in another world, in my Father's house, that I didn't think I'd ever have any other nice one down here. I thought maybe I could some day get a more comfortable room, when I was older and needed to save myself, but I didn't see how I could get it for a long, long time, if ever. So I'll enjoy anticipating it for a little while before I go anywhere, and get used to the idea before I change. It's been rather a long hard way, and I might not bear such a sudden change."

She laughed as she said it, but Kent looked at her tenderly and said, "You dear!"

Yet as they drew nearer the rooming house he looked up at its looming gloomy windows and sighed.

"I can't bear to think of you in that gloomy place, even for a night. I wish you'd let me take you home to the shore, to mother."

Jane shook her head decidedly.

"Not tonight!" she said. "And not to your mother, yet, either! Oh, I haven't had a chance yet to stop and think what your mother will say, or what your sister will think! I'm not the kind of girl they would want for you!"

"They'll be happy as two clams!" said Kent. "Trust me. Don't I know? And so will dad! I could see he liked you wonderfully well. They'll all be so glad I'm off Evadne for life they won't know how to stop rejoicing. They hated her. But that brings back my shame. I should never have gone with a girl like that, even for a day, and somehow back in my mind, I knew it all the time. I'm so glad God took hold of me and opened my eyes in time. But don't you worry about my family. They like you all right already, and wait till they really know you. They'll take you right into their hearts."

"I don't know," said Jane a little sadly, shaking her head. "They may not have liked Miss Laverock, but you know I'm a still different kind of a girl. You should have a well-educated girl who is used to the ways of the world. Your mother will feel so, I'm sure."

"No, she won't!" said Kent vehemently. "She recognizes your exquisite culture. As for the ways of the world, have you forgotten that you and I are not of this world any more?"

She gave him a sudden bright smile and nestled her hand in his, and he stooped over and kissed her tenderly.

"All right," he said resignedly, "go on up to your desolate little cubby hole if you must for tonight, but believe me I'm going to take you home to mother just as soon as possible. And I'm going right home and tell the folks now so that bugaboo will be out of the way forever, and you won't need to worry any more about your position with them. Good night. I'll see you tomorrow!"

XXIV

"But I thought she told me she had no home and never had had one," said Audrey as they were discussing plans for the wedding.

Kent had come home and gathered his family together and broken the news to them that night, his face shining, his eyes full of a glad humility.

"Dad, mother, Audrey," he said standing in their midst and looking around on them, "I'm going to marry Jane, do you mind? I've been an awful fool and driven you nearly crazy, I know, going after the wrong girl, and I'm ashamed as I can be about it. I wish I could go back and wipe it all out somehow, out of your memories and mine, and out of Jane's. But she's terribly sweet and she's forgiven me, and I hope you'll love her. She's worried sick because she's afraid you're going to hate having a button salesgirl for a daughter. But I told her you had lots more sense than she thought you had and I'd tell you about it right away tonight. What do you say, folks, do you like my choice or not?"

"Like it fine, son," said his father heartily. "Ask mother. I guess you'll find she agrees with me."

"I'm sure I shall love her, my dear boy!" said Mrs. Havenner.

"Cheerio!" shouted Audrey gaily. "Hallelujah! I think it's the grandest thing you ever did. And I claim the honor of having discovered her."

"Yes, sister, and that was the grandest thing you ever did! But don't you dare take anyone less fine for yourself."

"All right with me, brother!" grinned Audrey. "I get you. I won't. And maybe I'll let you be a picker for me. You noticed I began to take your advice several days ago!"

And by such devious means had the family come to an early discussion of the wedding, which had scarcely

214

been much discussed between the principle participants, save that Kent had urged that it be soon.

"Because I want to begin to take care of her," he explained to his family when they came to broach the question.

It was then that Kent's mother suggested in her large-heartedness that perhaps Jane would like to be married at their home, or perhaps quietly down at the shore. And Kent had explained that Jane had another plan, she had a place of her own where she thought it was most fitting she should be married, which brought about Audrey's astonished exclamation.

"Well, she hasn't ever had a home, Audrey," explained Kent as if he'd known her history always. "Her father and mother died sometime ago. But this is a place that belonged to her grandfather. It is very old. It has just come into her hands. She has a fancy she would like to be married from it! I think it's right she should have things as she wants them."

"Why, yes, of course," said Kent's mother thoughtfully. "But have you seen it? Is it all right? Of course I don't suppose you'll want a very large assembly, but then we have friends who would be hurt if they weren't invited. You could have the ceremony at our church, I suppose, and then have a little private reception at our house or hers."

"Yes, I've seen it, mother, and it's quite all right. You won't be ashamed. I think we'd better let Jane manage the way she wants to. You can offer anything you wish of course, but don't urge."

Dubiously the mother and daughter turned the matter over together and tried to plan ways they could help Jane out, but Kent went on his way rejoicing.

"We'll want to see her right away, of course," said Kent's mother. "Shall I call her up in the morning and get her to come right down to us?"

"She can't," said Kent grinning. "She can't leave the store right away. She insists she must stay through the month. It's one of the rules of the store that an employee does not leave without at least two weeks' notice, and she's going right on working till we're married."

"Why, how will she have any time to get ready?"

"Oh, she'll get ready afterward," laughed Kent. "You watch."

"But, my dear, of course we'll help her out. I wonder where we ought to begin?"

"Begin by loving her, mother, that's the most important thing. When she's convinced of that everything else will fall into line."

"Why, of course we'll love her! If she only knew how I looked at her in longing that first night she came here, and especially after that other painted girl came, if she could have known how I wished in my heart that it was Jane instead of the other that my boy fancied! Oh, we'll love her all right, Kent. She's our kind."

"Okay, mother, then everything else is all right!" and Kent went off to his bed well satisfied.

Jane went to work blithely all those days between.

Especially was she light-hearted after receiving the two lovely notes of welcome into the family, that Kent brought her the next morning after his talk with them all. He passed through the store quietly like any customer and merely stopped to hand them to her unobtrusively with a low-spoken promise: "See you at the door at five."

Not even sharp-eyed Nellie had noticed, for he had chosen the right moment, when all the others were busy and Jane's customer had just left.

And that night he told her all about the family conclave, and the hearty words of his father.

"But they can't understand why I won't let them give you a wedding at our house," he said with a grin.

"Oh," said Jane, looking troubled, "Why, I wouldn't want to disappoint them, they've been so lovely!" And then she added wistfully, "but it did seem nice to have a house that belonged. It's sort of like having a real family of my own, you know."

"Yes, of course," said Kent with quick sympathy, "I understand. And so will they after they have time to think it over."

"Why can't we take them out to the house pretty soon?" suggested Jane. "If they see it perhaps they will understand why I love it so."

"Of course," said Kent, "only I didn't know but you might want to surprise them at the wedding."

added: "It will always make me think of my Heavenly mansion. It seems just as if it was sent me at a time when I had nothing, as a sort of picture-promise of our home in Heaven. It's just a place where God wants us to be happy and work for Him while we are waiting for the Heavenly home."

Then softly she began to sing, and Kent chanted with her, as they drove out into their new life:

> "Oh Lord, you know,
>   We have no friend like you,
> If Heaven is not our Home,
>   Oh Lord, what shall we do?
> The angels beckon us
>   To Heaven's open door,
> We can't feel at home
>   In this world any more."

"No," said Jane, "they are family. They have a right to know. And then if they still think it would be better for me to go to them why—it will be all right! They are *my* family now, you know!"

"You dear!" breathed Kent softly. "Well, all right. Suppose we make it tomorrow after closing?"

"Lovely!" said Jane, her eyes sparkling. "I told the gardener's wife to wash the windows, and dust and take off the chair covers. Maybe Audrey would like to help us put up the curtains. Then it will look really livable."

"Of course she will, dear little housewife! I didn't know you were wise to those things."

But Jane only laughed.

"Perhaps you'd better get wise too," she said. "You might do something about getting the gas and electricity turned on."

"I'll attend to that, lady, right away today," he said humbly.

So the Havenner family, including the father, because he utterly refused to be left out of such an important occasion, arrived at the old Scarlett home in state, a few minutes after Jane and Kent got there, on Saturday afternoon.

They stared in wide-eyed amazement at the beautiful old house and grounds, and there was utmost approval and wonder in their eyes as they came up the brick walk to the porch.

"Why, Jane, dear!" said mother Havenner. "Such a wonderful old place! Of course you would want to be married here! How marvelous that you have it!"

Then they went inside.

Jane had had time to put flowers from the garden in most of the rooms, and it looked so homey they all exclaimed.

It was almost like a gathering of the two families, as they sat down in the big living room and looked up at the great oil-paintings while Jane explained who they all were, and then got out the old album which included her mother's wedding pictures.

And while they put up the living room curtains of delicate old yellowed lace, and admired everything, they settled all the plans for the wedding.

It was agreed that it should be a quiet wedding, no fuss and show. Just the dearest, most intimate friends, invited by note or called up on the telephone, and then the Havenners would give a small reception in their city house afterward to introduce their new daughter a trifle more formally to their acquaintances.

"Oh, it's lovely, *lovely,* Jane!" said Audrey, patting the filmy folds of the last curtain. "And how I do *love* my new sister!" and she caught Jane in a warm embrace and whirled her around the room gaily. "What a grand time you and I are going to have! I never supposed my brother would have the sense to pick out such a wonderful girl as you are!"

They would all have spoiled her if Jane hadn't been through so many hard things that she was impervious to spoiling.

And just before they turned out the lights and left for the night Audrey looked around the lovely room and said:

"Say, Jane, this would be a grand place to have a Bible class sometime! I just know Pat would enjoy teaching in a place like this!"

"Wouldn't it?" said Jane with a sparkle in her eyes. Audrey had been to the Thursday night Bible class with them this week and Jane had been longing to know how she liked it. "I have been thinking about that. When we get acquainted with the people around here perhaps we can get a group together. Wouldn't that be wonderful?"

"It certainly would," said Audrey.

As the days went by Jane flitted here and there in the store, picking out a few pretty clothes. The green coat she had wanted so long she could now buy outright, and not have to arrange for it by installments. She made it the basis of her fall outfit. A lovely green wool dress, and another of crepe. A brown wool, a lighter brown silk, some bright blouses, and then a couple of gay prints for morning around the house. How she enjoyed getting them together, and all the little accessories of her modest trousseau, and realizing that she could pay for them and not need to worry lest there wouldn't be enough over to pay her board for another week. Her heart was continually singing at the great things the Lord had done for her.

It was a pretty wedding, no ostentation, no fuss.

There were about fifty guests present, most of them relatives and intimate friends of the Havenner family. A few from the store, Miss Leech, Mr. Windle, Mr. Clark and his little girl, Hilda and the two other girls from the button counter.

Pat Whitney married them, and Audrey was the maid of honor. The rest of the wedding procession they skipped.

Jane wore her mother's wedding dress and veil and looked very sweet and quaint in the rich satin and real lace, a trifle yellowed from the years.

As the bride stood beneath her grandmother's portrait, some people thought they saw a resemblance between the two.

Mr. Havenner went about beaming, almost as if he were getting married himself. Hilda and the two girls from the button counter sat around adoringly and watched their erstwhile co-laborer going about these sweet old rooms mistress of it all, wife of that "perfectly swell" looking young lawyer. They thought of Jane going untiringly at her work behind the counter, and wondered wistfully if a like change could ever come to them.

And when it was all over, and the wedding supper eaten, the bridal cake cut and distributed, Jane went upstairs throwing down her bouquet straight into the arms of her new sister-in-law, who stood at the foot of the stairs with Pat looking up.

Jane went into the room where she had stayed when she was a little girl visiting in that house so long ago, and changed to her new lovely green suit. Then she and Kent slipped down the back stairs and out through the basement door to Kent's car, which was hidden in the side street. The wedding guests, waiting to see them off with old shoes and rice in the decked-up car that stood before the door, were unaware that they were gone.

As they rounded the corner and caught another glimpse of the lighted windows Jane turned to look.

"It's a dear house," she breathed.

"Yes!" said Kent. "I love it too, you know."

She nestled toward him and slipped her hand in his.

"I'm glad!" she said softly. And then

joined him in New Orleans. "I think we're done for," the captain said. "I don't dare go back to the ship. We lost nearly the entire crew when those shanghaied men got loose. They're going to be after us, and I'm sure by now the authorities are swarming about my abandoned ship."

Taking out a cigar and lighting it, Kellerman listened quietly, managing to appear calm, though inside he was agitated. Perhaps his luck was turning for the worse after all. With the damned Englishman Edward Blackstone now on the loose again, Kellerman was not going to have an easy time of it. Could it have even been Blackstone who had attempted to waylay him with the blonde in her apartment?

Kellerman at last replied. "Well, now. This certainly calls for a change in plans. I suggest the first thing we do is get out of here before we're found."

Suddenly Kayross heard something. Reaching out, he grasped the other man's arm. "What's that?" he demanded roughly.

Kellerman had heard the same sound. His cigar forgotten in a saucer, he was already on his feet, beckoning sharply. Together, they moved the short distance to the back of the establishment, where Kellerman swiftly and silently opened a window, then climbed through it and dropped to an alleyway outside. Kayross and his men were on his heels.

At the front of the saloon, Edward Blackstone and Wallace Dugald, accompanied by the other men who had been shanghaied, halted while Wallace lighted the gas jets that ordinarily illuminated the bar. Dugald wondered why the sign said Closed and yet the door was unlocked. They searched the empty place quickly as they made their way to the rear.

"Look yonder," Dugald muttered as he waved his pistol at Kellerman's still burning cigar.

Edward saw the open window, raced to it, and peered out into the dark night. The alleyway was empty. "Our bird," he said, "has flown."

Wallace raised a fist, brandished it in the air, and brought it down on the table with a crash. "I swear to you in the name of all that's holy," he cried, "that I'm going to find Karl Kellerman if it's the last thing I do on this earth! And when I get my hands on him, I'm going to repay him in full for the misery he's caused me, so help me God!"

Domino disliked the taste of rice and wasn't fond of boiled chicken either, but the doctor had ordered him to continue eating bland foods, and his discipline was so great that he did precisely what he was told. He discovered that by waiting until late evening, when his resistance was lowered, it was far easier for him to down an unpalatable meal, so he rarely ate supper before midnight.

He sat now in solitary splendor, eating the foods that he disliked so intensely, shoveling them into his mouth, then chewing them rapidly and swallowing them. He was lost in thought, his one purpose that of finishing the unappetizing meal as rapidly as possible.

A bodyguard came into the dining room. "Excuse

me for interrupting," he said, "but some of the boys have come back from the Kellerman job."

Domino brightened immediately, and even the unflavored boiled chicken and rice dish tasted much better to him. "What are you waiting for?" he demanded jovially. "Send them right in!" He sat back in his chair and grinned expectantly.

Two burly young men in their late twenties, both of them heavily armed, entered the room.

"Don't keep me in suspense," Domino said and chuckled. "Tell me you nailed his hide to the wall and slowly tortured him to death."

The pair exchanged a quick glance, and then the shorter of them spoke. "The girl is dead," he said. "Everything went off fine until the very end, and then when we broke into the bedroom, we found that Kellerman had cut her throat from ear to ear."

"She was still bleeding," his companion said, "so it had just happened."

"We ran out to the balcony," the first thug went on, "but by then it was too late. We could tell from the way the bushes down below were squashed that Kellerman had jumped from the balcony, and by the time we got outside, he was gone. We scoured the neighborhood, but it was like looking for a needle in a haystack. We even went to that bar you told us he owns, but the place was empty. It looked like someone had been there earlier, but we couldn't find any sign of Kellerman."

As always, Domino exerted great willpower in an emergency. The color drained from his face, but sitting unmoving, he asked quietly, "How did he discover that we'd set an ambush for him?"

The pair shrugged. "Damned if we know," the taller of the thugs declared. "But whatever it was that happened, it must have been awful sudden. The girl died without putting up a struggle."

"What's happened to her body?" Domino demanded.

"The other boys were going to dispose of it after they got the apartment cleaned up. Everything happened so quietly that the neighbors were left undisturbed, and there's no danger of the constabulary being called in."

"It's a shame we lost the girl," Domino said. "She seemed smarter than most, and we could have used her on all sorts of jobs. Oh, well." He sat in silence for a moment. "What are you doing about trying to locate Kellerman?"

"All the boys have been alerted," the shorter of the pair replied, "and they're searching the whole town for him. Eventually they'll catch up with him."

"And then what?" Domino asked sarcastically. "Are they going to shoot him on sight so that he dies without suffering, without being in agony? That's not the way I want to pay him back. What's more, your little posse is sure to bring the constabulary down on our necks. This is a civilized community, you know, and there's a law here against wanton killing. No. I want strict orders issued to every member of the organization. I am to be notified the moment Karl Kellerman is located, but under no circumstances is any member of the organization to lift a finger against him without getting specific orders from me first. Kellerman is too clever, and he's done us quite enough damage. When we find out where he's staying, I'll have to devote some serious thought to finding a foolproof method of eliminating him once and for all, and doing it so that he feels the pain and agony he caused me to suffer."

After much hesitation and self-doubt, Kale Martin finally concluded that the time was right for her to enter Oregon's state politics. Thus she announced her candidacy for the board of trustees of Oregon State College, a position that required a majority vote throughout the state. Newspapers everywhere printed the story.

That same night, Kale and her husband Rob were entertaining Cindy Holt and Clarissa, whose husband had not yet returned from the assignment that took him to San Francisco. As Rob carved the roast, Kale added vegetables to the plates and passed them around the table.

"You certainly touched a nerve when you decided to run for office, Kale," Clarissa said. "I've never read such an excited stir in all the papers."

Rob grinned at her, feeling enormous pride in his wife. "That's because, as luck would have it, Kale's going up against Frank Colwyn, who's running for reelection as a trustee."

"I read about this Colwyn in the paper," Clarissa

said, "but I don't see anything particularly significant in the fact that Kale's running against him."

"It's very significant, I'm afraid," Kale said. "It's rumored that Colwyn has been pocketing money that has been appropriated for the college's use by the state legislature. If so, he and the people he's paying off will fight like fury to get him reelected and keep the cash flowing into their pockets." Kale noticeably stiffened. "So that gives me all the more reason," she continued, "to try to win the election myself!"

"Good for you," Cindy told her. "It makes me furious when I think of the men who are ready to take advantage of a new state and trade on the political inexperience of that state's people. What's more, a woman has every bit as much right as a man to be elected to a position of trust in Oregon. According to the stories I've heard from my mother—and from my father, too—women contributed as much as men to the founding of this state. They suffered equally on the first wagon train that crossed North America, and they fought just as hard against the elements and savages and all the other dangers of travel in those days. I'll work hard for your election, Kale!"

"So will I," Clarissa said. "What's more, I know at least a dozen women who will gladly go from door to door persuading people to vote for you."

"I don't care what kind of pressure Frank Colwyn uses!" Cindy cried. "You're going to win this election!"

Rob exchanged a quick glance with Kale. Both of them knew the difficulties she faced, but at the same time they also believed that there was at least a

chance that Kale would succeed in bringing off the
unexpected and winning the election.

Over the next few days, Kale and Cindy worked
out the schedules for the women who were volunteer-
ing in large numbers to help Kale in the coming
election. Clarissa was busily engaged drumming up
the support of still more women.

"The response has been marvelous," Kale said.
"I've heard from women all over Oregon—hundreds
of them. There are more of them who want to help
than there are jobs to be done."

"Don't you believe it," Cindy told her. "We face
an uphill struggle all the way. The men who have
been obtaining graft at the taxpayers' expense aren't
going to give up without putting up a tremendous
fight, and we'll need all the help we can get!"

There was a tap at the front door, and Kale
admitted two well-dressed men of early middle age,
who introduced themselves as Jeremiah Bates and
Tod Caspar. She politely invited them to come in
and sit down and presented them to Cindy.

"I'm glad you're here with Mrs. Martin, Miss
Holt," Bates said. "This simplifies our task, so to
speak."

"We represent a bipartisan group," Caspar said,
"that's been formed to ensure the reelection of Frank
Colwyn as a trustee of the college. We're calling on
you, Mrs. Martin, in the hope that we can persuade
you to withdraw as a candidate for the board."

"We realize, Mrs. Martin," his companion said,
"that you regard the election as something of a lark,

but we're here to assure you that Mr. Colwyn thinks of his reelection in the most solemn manner and that he's deeply concerned about the issues that the board faces."

A flintlike quality crept into Kale's voice. "What gives you the impression that I regard the election as a lark, gentlemen?" she asked softly.

Bates shrugged and grinned. "Well, you know how it is, Mrs. Martin," he said with a slight laugh. "After all, you're a married woman, and you have a child now. I assume that there'll be others on the way to join it. All of these interests take precedence over the affairs of the college."

"They're personal interests as opposed to business interests," Kale said succinctly, "but I wouldn't say they take precedence. Quite the contrary. As it happens, Miss Holt is an undergraduate at the college, and the education she receives is of very great interest to me. So are the business affairs of the school that she attends."

"As a student at the college," Cindy interjected, "I know that Mrs. Martin has my best interests at heart. Furthermore, my classmates and colleagues feel exactly as I do." Not mentioning the rumor that Kale's opponent was pilfering state funds, Cindy went on, "We have nothing against Frank Colwyn, but we have no idea where he stands on the subject of education, even though he's been a trustee for several years."

There was a moment's pause, and Caspar turned

back to Kale. "You're the daughter-in-law of Dr. Robert Martin, if my information is correct."

"It's correct," Kale said flatly.

The man smiled. "He's practiced medicine here since he arrived as a member of the first wagon train, and he's achieved enormous popularity in the state. We'd hate to think of anyone trading on his standing in order to win the election."

"I make no mention in my campaign of my relationship to Dr. Martin, and I have no intention of bringing it up," Kale said tartly. "I believe in standing on my own feet. What's more, sir, I resent your innuendo that I intend to rely on my father-in-law's name to help me win an election."

Caspar chuckled softly, but Bates, a big man with heavy jowls, bristled and glowered at the young woman. "We know how to take a hint," he said, "and how to deal with those who are stubborn. Frank Colwyn is going to be reelected, and anyone who stands in his path will be trampled. We've gone to some pains to look up your background, Mrs. Martin, and I wonder if the voters of Oregon will approve of your past."

"I'm not ashamed of my background, Mr. Bates," Kale said in a tense voice. "I've traveled a long path in my lifetime, and I've made many mistakes, but I've overcome them, and I haven't repeated them. So you can do your damnedest, sir, and both you and your candidate have my permission to go straight to hell!" She rose to her feet, went to the door, and opened it. "I'll bid you good day, gentlemen. You've outstayed your welcome."

The pair looked at each other, then rose.

"You're making a serious mistake, Mrs. Martin," Caspar said in the doorway. "We don't want to be unpleasant, and we have no desire to drag you through the mud, but if you force our hand, we'll have to act accordingly. We'll just have to see whether the voters of Oregon will elect a retired prostitute as a trustee of their state college!"

Kale continued to face them defiantly, her back straight, her chin outthrust as they climbed into their carriage and drove off. Then suddenly she crumpled. "They weren't making idle talk when they threatened me," she said, her eyes filling with tears. "They meant every word!"

"Don't give in to them, Kale," Cindy said fiercely. "We'll beat them yet! They've declared open war on us, and we're going to fight them with their own weapons!"

Kale usually followed the same routine in her public appearances for her campaign to win a seat on the board of the state college. She accepted all offers of speaking engagements and was always accompanied by Rob, who was present to act as a buffer between her and any in her audience who might cause trouble. Kale had told her husband all about her meeting with Jeremiah Bates and Tod Caspar, and Rob had successfully consoled her, telling her he would let nothing harm her or get in her way as she ran for office.

So Kale went about her business, and in the main, she found that most audiences were sympathetic and friendly. To be sure, some people came to hear her only because they were curious about a woman's running for public office, but it was unusual when anyone was actually hostile.

The crowd that gathered to hear her on Sunday afternoon in a large church located in an as yet unnamed, growing suburb of Portland was bigger than usual. The audience was friendly, applauding her warmly, and the questions they asked were sufficiently sympathetic that she had no trouble in answering them.

The meeting ended at dusk, and as always, Kale's departure was delayed by several members of the audience, who stayed behind to speak to her. Night was falling by the time that she and Rob followed the last of the crowd out to the hitching post in front of the church, where their horses awaited them.

Standing outside the entrance were two men who were handing out leaflets to those who were emerging from the church. They didn't see Kale until she gasped, and then they turned away hurriedly.

Kale caught hold of her husband's arm and clutched it so hard that her nails dug through the fabric of his coat. "Rob," she murmured in alarm, "those two are Bates and Caspar, the pair from Frank Colwyn's headquarters who called on me and threatened me!"

Rob responded instantly. Stepping forward, he called out, "Not so fast, you two. You're handing out some papers there. Let me have one."

Jeremiah Bates reluctantly handed him a single sheet of paper.

Rob glanced at it in the light of the nearest street lamp, and a headline in heavy black type immediately caught his attention: "DO YOU WANT A WHORE IN CHARGE OF YOUR CHILDREN'S EDUCATION?"

Rob instantly crumpled the paper and threw it away, hoping that his wife had not seen it. But Kale's gasp of dismay and anger told him otherwise. She was standing beside him, staring down at the ground, her whole body trembling, and her eyes filled with tears.

Rob saw red, and before he quite realized it, he had drawn his Colt six-shooter and cocked the hammer with his thumb.

"We didn't start anything," Caspar complained in a high, whining voice. "We were just following Frank Colwyn's orders." His partner, too frightened to speak, could only nod his head in vigorous assent.

"Save your breath!" Rob told them, his tone savage. "I don't care to hear your flimsy excuses."

Both of them, staring into the muzzle of the gun, started to speak simultaneously. Rob gestured, and they fell silent.

"I'm only going to say this once," he told them harshly, "so listen carefully. If I ever catch you passing out such filth about my wife again, I'll terminate your miserable lives instantly by putting bullets into your hearts. I'm not joking, so I warn you—don't tempt me! As for your employer, that rotten worm Colwyn, tell him from me that he'd better keep out of my sight. If I ever set eyes on him, his wife will become a widow in a hurry!"

Badly frightened, the pair could only nod.

"My trigger finger is beginning to itch," Rob went on, "so you'd better get out of my sight fast, before I relieve it by pulling the trigger. Get moving!"

Bates and Caspar raced to their waiting mounts, vaulted into their saddles, and spurring the unfortunate beasts, went galloping off down the road at breakneck speed, both crouched low in the saddle to avoid being hit if Martin changed his mind and decided to fire at them.

His narrowed eyes cold, Rob watched them as they raced off. "Scum!" he said, pronouncing final sentence on them. Then, all at once, his manner changed. He put his arm around the still-trembling Kale and said softly, "Put them out of your mind, honey. I give you my word, this incident won't be repeated."

"Frank Colwyn and his cronies made good their threat against me," she said miserably. "Somehow I thought they were bluffing, that they wouldn't have the audacity to attack below the belt like this." Suddenly all her self-control snapped, and the tears flowed freely.

"Colwyn has a rude shock waiting for him," Rob replied, holding her tightly. "He's going to find that vicious personal attacks are counterproductive and create sympathy for you."

She looked up at him, shaking her head and starting to protest.

"Hear me out," Rob said, "and heed what I say. I know what I'm talking about. Every dirty trick like this that Colwyn tries to pull creates that many more votes for you. Don't give him another thought. Just keep on running your own campaign in your own way."

Looking into her husband's eyes, Kale felt great reassurance. They had both known that it was going to be difficult for Kale to be the first woman in Oregon to run for a statewide office, but Rob had never waivered in his support of his wife, and Kale was damned if she was going to let him—or herself— down now. She would fight to the bitter end!

Willie Rowe, generally acknowledged as the best newspaper reporter on the Pacific Coast, sat in his shirt-sleeves in the cavernous city room of the *Oregon News.* Stocky, with tousled, dirty-blond hair and an open, friendly face, the newspaperman studied his guest. It was his business to know something about prominent people in the state, so it came as no surprise to him that the young woman opposite him was the daughter of the fabled Whip Holt and the stepdaughter of Major General Leland Blake. What he found completely unexpected was her intensity, which crackled like lightning in a storm, and her remarkably attractive appearance. It seemed to him that her natural beauty would rival that of the actresses from New York who appeared on the stage of the Portland Theater.

"Give me the facts once more, Miss Holt," Willie said. "I want to be sure that I have them straight."

"It's been rumored," Cindy said patiently, "that Frank Colwyn has been stealing state funds intended for the college. I've tried to find out more on the subject, but I can't get a thing on him."

"Why have you come to me?" Willie Rowe asked.

"If anyone can prove that Frank Colwyn is dipping his hand into public funds, you're the fellow who can do it," Cindy said. "Your record has been marvelous, and you've proved you're not afraid of anyone."

"Thanks very much," he said modestly. "It's nice to be appreciated."

"It'll be nicer still to get a headline story on Colwyn," Cindy said.

"Why are you so eager to expose him?" Willie asked, looking at her intently.

"Because I hate to see Kale Martin deliberately smeared with filth. Her background is no secret. She's never tried to hide the fact that she was once a prostitute, but to have Colwyn's supporters threaten to expose her past and to make an issue of it is quite another matter."

His interest was aroused. "Who threatened her?"

"Two men named Jeremiah Bates and Tod Caspar. I was right there and heard them myself. And their threats weren't idle. A few days later they went out and started distributing handbills full of filth about Kale. Her husband, Rob Martin, had a little run-in with Bates and Caspar, but I don't think they're through playing dirty politics."

"This becomes more involved and still more fascinating," Willie said. "Caspar and Bates are fellow trustees at the state college. Apparently they're afraid their own power will diminish if Colwyn loses the election to Mrs. Martin."

"Apparently so."

"You're sure that everything you've said to me is true?"

She met his gaze without flinching. "Dead sure."

"Are you willing to take a risk that'll mean serious trouble for you if you're caught?" he asked.

"I'm willing to do anything that's necessary to expose Frank Colwyn as a crook and to keep him from winning the election," Cindy said.

Willie Rowe snapped the pencil into two parts, threw the broken halves into a wicker wastebasket, and grinned at her. "That's what I like to hear! You have the soul of a true reporter. Have supper with me at a place I know that serves the best salmon in Oregon, and then we'll drop in on Frank Colwyn's office after hours and snoop around until we find something. This promises to be an evening that neither of us is going to forget quickly!"

A few hours later, the young couple finished dinner, arose from the table, and strolled through the Portland business district, pausing occasionally to window shop. They looked like any young man and woman enjoying a walk on a balmy evening, with nothing in their manner revealing their mounting anxiety.

When they came to Frank Colwyn's office building, they ducked inside, and Willie produced a ring of skeleton keys. He found one that opened the inner door, and they quietly made their way up to the second story, then crept toward the rear, where Colwyn's office was located.

"Keep away from the windows," Willie warned, "just in case somebody down below should be looking up. Fortunately, there's enough of a moon tonight that we can see well enough without being forced to light a lamp." He sighed. "There's only one way to do this. You take the two filing cases over yonder, and I'll start going through these two. If you run across anything that you think might give us a lead, let me know."

Cindy's heart hammered in her ears, and her breath was short as she opened the top drawer of the nearer filing cabinet. She realized she was engaged in an enterprise that was illegal, and if she should be apprehended, the fact that she was Whip Holt's daughter and General Blake's stepdaughter would not save her from a prison term.

She fully intended to go through the files in an orderly way, but she couldn't resist the temptation to glance first through a thick folder marked *Finances, Oregon State College*.

Within moments, she was utterly absorbed in what she was reading and forgot her sense of danger.

"Willie," she called softly, "I think I may have found something."

The reporter joined her and looked at some documents still in the folder. "My God!" he said in tense excitement. "You've stumbled onto a gold mine! These are figures for three years ago. Now we have to find similar forms for last year and this year."

They searched frantically, and within a short time, they found what they were seeking.

Willie was satisfied. "We'll just help ourselves to these papers," he said, "which will be enough to convince any judge in the state, and then we'll get out of here. Make certain you leave everything else exactly as you found it."

They hurriedly straightened the file folder before they departed, taking the telltale documents with them.

Once they reached the street, they abandoned their pose of being a young couple out for a stroll, and they hurried back to the offices of the *News*. There, Willie examined the papers with greater care, shaking his head and whistling softly under his breath as he inspected them. As Cindy continued to wait, he hurried up to the desk of his editor in the center of the room and conferred at length with him. He was smiling broadly when he came back to his own desk.

"I have a go-ahead sign," he said. "We're going to explode a bomb under Frank Colwyn in tomorrow's *News*." He sat down and began to scribble rapidly on sheet after sheet of foolscap. As he finished each page, Cindy barely had time to read it before someone whisked it away for editing and delivery to the printer downstairs. She lost all sense of time and was surprised when Willie sat back in his chair and lighted a cigar. "We don't have long to wait," he told her.

As he had predicted, his article soon was in print. For the first time since the *News* had announced the election of U. S. Grant as the President of the United States, a full banner headline ran across all eight columns of the paper. Frank Colwyn and two of his fellow trustees were flatly accused of stealing state funds that had been granted to the college.

Looking at the article again, Cindy was stunned. It was far more authoritative in print than it had been when handwritten, and the columns of figures beside it taken direct from Colwyn's own files told the story themselves. He and his two fellow trustees had stolen many thousands of dollars in state funds. There was no doubt in her mind that charges would be filed against Colwyn.

"I'll get you a cup of coffee," Willie told her, "and then I'll ride you out to your brother's ranch for what's left of the night. All I ask in return is that when you wake, you set up an early appointment with Mrs. Kale Martin for me. Our readers will want to know all about her, now that her election as a trustee seems to be assured."

The United States Military Academy cadets spent Saturday morning drilling on the parade ground overlooking the Hudson River at West Point, New York.

Prizes were awarded at the conclusion of the exercise, and as always, the first place in close-order drill was won by the squad commanded by Cadet Sergeant Henry Blake, the adopted son of Eulalia Holt Blake and Major General Leland Blake.

Hank Blake and his subordinates, all of them underclassmen, took no undue pride in their achievements. There was a task to be accomplished, and they performed it to the very best of their joint ability. The squad members took their cue from Hank, who was a perfectionist. Never totally satisfied with what they did, they kept pushing themselves to their limits. It was predicted in the corps of cadets that someday all sixteen members of the squad would wear the stars of generals on their shoulders.

The weekends for cadets normally began at noon on Saturdays, but there was no way Hank could take off any time for pleasurable pursuits. He had to practice sprints with the track team for an hour, and after noon dinner he would be required to put on an exhibition of rifle shooting for parents and other visitors. The rifle team was scheduled to hold a contest with Yale University in midafternoon, and everyone was rooting for Hank, who was just beginning his junior year, to lead the army to another victory. He had never suffered a defeat in two years of contests, and there was no reason he should lose today.

Other cadets would attend a dance on campus that night, but Hank had decided to spend the evening in the West Point library. Not that he was behind in his subjects. Indeed, he consistently won high honors in all of his classes, and there was no need for him to spend a Saturday night at his books. He intended, however, to devote the better part of the evening to the luxury of writing a letter.

Academy rules made it impossible for Cindy Holt and Hank to announce their engagement before his senior year, but that did not prevent them from having a private understanding. After Hank was graduated and had won his commission as a lieutenant, they intended to be married. Separated from Cindy by three thousand miles, Hank preferred sending her a letter to spending an evening with some other girl. He had tried to date other girls, but had found them poor substitutes. If the truth be known—and Hank didn't care who knew it—his love for Cindy was the most important factor in his life.

He walked alone to the mess hall, where relatively few cadets were on hand for Saturday night supper. After finishing his meal, he strolled to the library, passing en route the hall in which the dance was being held. The strains of a Viennese waltz, currently the most popular music with the younger generation, drifted out to him but in no way tempted him. If he could not spend the evening with Cindy, he would devote the time to her in another way.

Reaching the nearly empty library building, he sat down at one of the desks and began his letter to her, first rereading her last communication to him. The coming of the transcontinental railroad had made a significant difference in the delivery time of mail; a letter between the Atlantic and Pacific coasts was now delivered within the remarkable time of ten days. Thus he was able to read all about her recent campaign to elect Kale Martin to public office and how she had joined a young newspaper reporter, invading the offices of the incumbent, with startling results.

The incident was typical of Cindy, Hank reflected. Once again, she had demonstrated courage, unflagging determination, and bulldoglike tenacity in the pursuit of her goal.

Ordinarily shy and somewhat inhibited, Hank poured out his love for Cindy onto paper. He told her he would not be fulfilled or become a whole person until they were married. For her sake, as well as his own, he was working hard, and so far he continued to rank first in his class. He wanted General and Mrs. Blake to be proud of him, and above all, he wanted Cindy to take pride in his accomplishments. General William T. Sherman, the army chief of staff, had indicated to General Blake that if Hank ranked high enough in his class, he would win a special assignment with the cavalry when he became a second lieutenant. He had no idea of the nature of that assignment, but for Cindy's sake, he was determined to win it.

He confessed to her that he was counting the days until the time when they could make their engagement public.

The letter flowed easily, filling page after page, and when he finished it, Hank was tired but satisfied.

He had occupied himself in the next best way to spending the evening with his beloved Cindy.

Despite his inability so far to apprehend either Karl Kellerman or Captain Kayross, Edward was determined to find his missing cousin, and he called on the New Orleans constabulary to perform the painstaking task of checking the registration ledgers of every major hotel and lodging house in the city. At last Edward learned that a woman who called herself Millicent Kellerman was a guest at the Louisiana House.

Edward and Jim went there immediately, accompanied by Tommie and Randy, and discovered that although the rent had been paid in advance until the first of the month, Kellerman had already checked out. Gaining admission to the suite, the quartet discovered that the wardrobe closets were filled with a woman's clothing, but that Kellerman had taken all his belongings. They gathered in the parlor of the suite to discuss the problem.

"It's as though she disappeared from the face of the earth," said Tommie, shaking her head.

"All we know for certain," Jim said, "is that Kellerman has cleared out of this suite. By the same token, we can assume that Millicent is still here, although there's no way of knowing where she may be at the moment."

They were interrupted by the unexpected arrival of Jean-Pierre Gautier. After he introduced himself, he explained, "I must ask you to pardon this intrusion, but I will be blunt with you. I've had the pleasure of meeting Miss Randall several times, and I have fallen head over heels in love with her. I am exerting every possible effort to locate her."

Tommie recognized Jean-Pierre's name and identified him as a member of one of the wealthy, old French families of New Orleans. She went out of her way to welcome him and was so cordial that her male companions were equally pleasant to him. After bringing Jean-Pierre up to date on what little they knew of Millicent's whereabouts, they became involved in a long, complex discussion of the best way to proceed to find her.

While they were weighing various proposals, the front door of the suite slowly opened, and Millicent staggered into the room. Everyone present jumped up and began talking simultaneously.

Jean-Pierre, however, had the presence of mind to put a supporting arm around Millicent and lead her to the divan. Her makeshift dress still covered her body, but her feet were cut, bruised, and bleeding, swollen to almost double their normal size. Giving a deep, tremulous sigh, she collapsed onto the divan.

Edward ordered tea and toast sent up to the suite, and all the men left the room while Tommie removed the woman's filthy garment, helped her bathe, and clothed her in a nightgown and dressing robe. At the same time, Jean-Pierre sent a messenger to his family doctor, asking the physician to come to the hotel at his earliest convenience.

Only then was it possible for Millicent to relate what had happened to her. She told her story between bites of buttered toast and sips of tea, and her listeners were horrified as she recounted her incarceration on the *Diana*, the escape from the Malay woman who had tortured her, and the grueling four-day walk back to New Orleans through the Louisiana bayous, during which time she had repeatedly gotten lost.

"This is all Kellerman's doing," Tommie exclaimed. "He must be mad!"

"I thought this was a matter to be handled privately," Edward said, "and I tried. But all of you know the results. I succeeded only in making matters worse for everyone concerned. I'm going to the constabulary and swear out a warrant for Karl Kellerman's arrest."

Jean-Pierre was equally realistic. "I have no intention of leaving Millicent here, where Kellerman could return at any time and do her harm." Turning to Millicent, he said, "As soon as the doctor has been here, I'm going to have you moved to my parents' house. You'll be safe there."

Millicent tried to protest, but Jean-Pierre refused to listen. "I'm running no risks with your safety," he went on. "I almost lost you once, and I'm not going to take that chance again."

The physician soon arrived and subjected Millicent to a thorough examination. He applied an ointment to her feet and gave her an extra supply in a small tin to be rubbed in twice a day. The bruises on

her backside would soon disappear, he said. She was
in good enough condition to make the move to the
Gautier house as soon as she wanted. After the
physician's departure, Jean-Pierre busied himself ar-
ranging Millicent's immediate transfer to his parents'
home, while she hastily dressed and made up her
face.

Before the afternoon ended, she was carried on
a litter to the house in the old French Quarter, and
all of her belongings were moved with her. Her stay
with Karl Kellerman at the Louisiana Hotel became
a memory buried in her past, and as she began to
recover, she was able to look forward with confidence toward her future for the first time since she
had impulsively left Idaho.

VII

Shortly after his arrival in San Francisco, Toby had received an invitation to dine at the home of Chet and Clara Lou Harris. He accepted with pleasure, and when he arrived at the big granite mansion on Nob Hill, he was delighted to find Wong Ke and his wife, Mei-lo, also present.

After Toby told them about his earlier meeting with Kung Lee, the Chinese couple expressed their deep gratitude to him for trying to help. "All the same," the diminutive, black-haired Mei-lo said, "I'm worried for you, Toby. The tong is vicious and cruel toward anyone it considers an enemy, and I'm afraid they have you on the list now."

"That's good," Toby replied, "because I've become their enemy, and I don't care who knows it."

Ke shook his head. "I urge you to tread softly, Toby," he said. "My wife is right when she talks about the viciousness of these people. There's literally no controlling them, and they're always out for blood. Please watch your step."

Chet grinned. "I don't think we need to worry overly much about Toby," he said. "He's Whip Holt's son, so you can be sure he can take care of himself."

"I've heard countless stories of your father's exploits," Clara Lou said, "just as I've heard nothing but good about you in more recent years. All the same, Toby, be careful!"

They dined on clam chowder, sauteed abalone, and the steamed hard-shelled crabs that were a San Francisco delicacy. The talk flowed freely, and not until they were enjoying an after-dinner drink in the library of the Harris mansion did Toby become aware of the time. "I'd better get back to my hotel," he said, "before I overstay my welcome."

Wong Ke and Mei-lo left when he did, and the weather was so balmy and the view from the crest of Nob Hill was so spectacular in the moonlight that Toby decided to walk back to the hotel, first escorting the Chinese couple to their own house a short distance down Nob Hill.

"Remember—take care, Toby," Mei-lo said as they parted.

He assured her that he would, and after they had gone into the house, he stood for a time looking down at the waters of San Francisco Bay and at the islands in the water. The view, he thought, was unparalleled in any American city.

Suddenly he froze. Turning the corner less than a block away and coming toward him in single file were six men, all of them wearing the black costumes of the Chinese tong. In the lead was a squat, ferocious-looking man carrying a throwing knife in each hand. It was Ho Tai.

Toby realized at once that having seen them clearly in the moonlight meant that they had been able to see him, too. It was obvious that they had been waiting for him outside the Harris house and had followed him to the Wong house. The tong proposed to even the score with Toby Holt.

Toby thought for a moment of asking Wong Ke and his wife to give him refuge, but he discarded the thought as soon as it crossed his mind. They had been made to suffer enough, and he did not want to involve them with the murderous tong again.

Walking briskly, but not allowing himself to break into a run, Toby turned the next corner and resolutely headed back toward the peak of Nob Hill. The area was made up of private homes, many of them surrounded by brick walls, and no one else was abroad at this hour. In fact, he saw no lights burning anywhere.

He went no farther than a half-block, when he halted and stepped into the deep shadows cast by a large shade tree. From this vantage point, he saw his pursuers clearly, when they, too, rounded the corner. Ho Tai was still in the lead, gripping his knives as he moved swiftly up the steep incline. The expression in his dark eyes was grim and in spite of Toby's courage, it sent chills up his spine.

As Ho Tai and his companions drew nearer,

Toby glanced over his shoulder and saw a brick wall about five feet high that stood at the edge of the sidewalk, marking the boundaries of the property on the far side of the wall.

Giving himself no opportunity to weigh the consequences, he suddenly leaped up onto the crest of the wall and dropped down into the garden within. He was just in time. As he landed, he distinctly heard the soft patter of rushing footsteps on the far side of the wall as Ho Tai and his companions continued their pursuit.

But Toby was not yet out of danger. He felt rather than saw a dark shape materialize nearby and heard a low, deep, menacing growl.

His eyes adjusting to the darkness, he soon made out a large dog—obviously a watchdog—cautiously approaching him. Fortunately it had not yet started barking.

Toby had no intention of doing anything that would cause the animal to attack him or to bark. Standing very still, he waited for a time until the footsteps outside the wall began to fade. Then he started to speak soothingly to the dog, keeping his voice pitched very low. For what felt like an eternity, the dog continued to growl softly, but eventually the stranger's lack of hostility caused the animal to stop. It continued to hold its head cocked to one side, however, with its ears erect.

Toby knew he couldn't delay indefinitely, that one false move and the dog would attack as it had been trained to do. Continuing to address the animal quietly, the young man measured his distance from the wall and, gathering himself together, suddenly leaped toward it and managed to scramble to the top.

The dog, its fangs bared, hurled itself at the retreating target. However, it succeeded only in crashing into the wall, leaving the man unscathed.

From the relative safety of the parapet, Toby saw that Ho Tai and his associates had vanished. He dropped down into the street and started downhill at full speed, running as he had never before raced.

On the far side of the thick wall, the dog began to bark, but its quarry was gone.

Slowing his pace momentarily at every street intersection to see if Ho Tai and the other tong members were anywhere within sight, Toby ran on, heading downhill for two blocks, then crossing over a side street and heading upward again for a block before crossing another side street and resuming his downward journey. Even though he was in superb physical condition, he soon was gasping for breath, and his legs felt like lead.

Finally he found a coach for hire, and hailing the driver, he climbed into the backseat and fell onto the seat in exhaustion. But he did not feel truly safe until he reached his hotel room and bolted the door behind him.

Looking back on the encounter as he relaxed, Toby had no reason to take any pride in the evening's incident. At the very least, the hatchet man for the tong had forced him to flee for his life, and he knew this had been an inauspicious beginning for a venture that required boldness as well as courage.

For the next few days, Toby spent most of his time in his hotel, thinking about the situation with the tong. He realized he was no closer now to the achievement of his goal than he had been when he accepted the assignment of breaking up the tong.

After piecing together everything he had learned about the tong, Toby concluded that the key figure was not Kung Lee, the executive, but Ho Tai, his bodyguard and strongman. Ho Tai was the symbol of the brute strength that characterized the tong, of the terror that the organization generated in the hearts and minds of the residents of San Francisco's Chinatown and other cities. It was Ho Tai's wanton cruelty that enabled the tong to flourish and to flout the law as it chose. Those who were persecuted and intimidated by the tong were afraid to bring legal charges against the organization and, instead, preferred to suffer in silence. Immigrants from China were so frightened they bowed to the will of the tong, as did those who had been in the United States for as long as two or three generations.

Kung Lee might be the brains of the tong, but few American Chinese would recognize his name or his portrait. Ho Tai, however, would be immediately familiar to them. The ruthless strongman, who carried out the will of his superiors, was the symbol of tong rule in America.

It occurred to Toby that if he bested Kung Lee

legally, few Chinese would hear of his victory and
fewer still would applaud. His triumph in that respect would be met with indifference. But if he
scored a victory over Ho Tai, it would be celebrated
wildly in every Chinatown in the United States.
Since the tong's hatchet man was regarded as the
embodiment of evil, his defeat would be an achievement that no one would forget. The tongs would lose
stature, ordinary men would be heartened and would
rebel against them, and the power of the secret
societies would be vastly reduced.

Therefore, Toby reasoned, the best way to attack the tongs would be to launch an assault on Ho
Tai, no matter how great the risks.

Realizing that he would be exposing himself to
grave dangers, he told none of his friends in San
Francisco about his specific plans. Visiting innumer-
able restaurants, curio shops, silk stores, and other
retail establishments in Chinatown, he carefully spread
disparaging remarks about Ho Tai, declaring that he
was dishonorable and a coward and deserved to be
whipped out of the community.

Some of those to whom Toby spoke pretended
not to hear him, but others listened avidly, and a
number of them made notes of his remarks, so he
was fairly certain that word of his insults was getting
back to Ho Tai.

Three or four days after Toby launched his
campaign, a stranger approached him in the hotel
dining room while he was eating his noon dinner.
The man came up to his table, asked his identity,

and after learning that he was indeed Toby Holt, thrust a small scroll into his hand.

The message was crudely printed in English and bore no signature. It said: *Meet me at three hours past midnight tonight at the offices of the tong. Then we will see who has courage.*

Convinced that the Chinese bodyguard had taken the bait, Toby was satisfied. In the confrontation that was certain to take place, Toby had certain natural advantages, and he intended to exploit them to the fullest. As his father before him, he was endowed with extraordinary eyesight and hearing, qualities that would stand him in good stead in a middle-of-the-night battle with a wily foe. He also knew he was second to none as a marksman, a fact that had been highly publicized. Equally expert with throwing knives, Toby would carry a full set of those weapons with him, too.

Early that evening, Toby ate a light meal, then forced himself to go to bed, where he dropped off to sleep for several hours of necessary rest before he faced the challenge of his life.

Awakening after midnight, he dressed carefully in black boots and trousers, a dark shirt, and a dark, broad-brimmed western hat. As he strapped on his repeating pistols and placed his throwing knives in his belt, he vividly remembered advice that his father had given him years earlier: "Whenever you're involved in a close fight, where the outcome is in doubt, never lose sight of the fact that your most important asset is your attitude. If you're convinced that you're going to win, you will win. Doubt your own abilities, and the outcome of the fight will be in doubt."

It was easy to understand why Whip Holt had never lost a battle, Toby thought and smiled. All he had to remember was that he was Whip's son, and everything would fall into place.

Feeling the need for physical exercise, he walked to Chinatown, stretching his legs and pumping his arms in order to limber them.

When he reached the tong headquarters, he stood in the shadows of the doorway across the street and examined the building with care. The curio shop that occupied the better part of the ground floor was dark, and the second story, where the headquarters of the tong was located, seemed equally deserted, with no lights burning anywhere in the building.

Looking at his pocket watch, Toby saw that he was only five minutes early for his appointment. Rather than wait for the short time to elapse, he would act immediately.

Deliberately crossing the street some distance up the block where he knew he could not be seen from the tong headquarters, he retraced his steps until he reached the front door. The latch responded instantly to his touch, and the door opened silently. Toby quickly stepped inside and found himself in a narrow hallway adjacent to the curio shop. Directly ahead the staircase to the upper story loomed in the dark, and as he approached it, he stopped and smiled ironically.

Directly in front of the bottom stair stood two tin buckets, each of them with several metal kitchen utensils protruding from their tops. Clearly, Ho Tai had placed the crude obstacle in his path as a means of warning that Toby was approaching.

Toby made a detour around the pails and silently began to mount the stairs, one hand on the hilt of a throwing knife. Common sense told him that the knives were preferable to pistols as weapons because the latter would reveal his whereabouts with a flash when ever one of them was fired.

Another obstacle had been set as a trap for him just before he reached the top of the stairs. The top of one step below the landing had been removed, which meant that someone unwary would trip, stumble, or fall into the hole. But Toby's excellent vision came to his rescue for the second time, and he carefully avoided the hole in the step as he moved up to the landing.

Cautioning himself to take his time, he moved slowly down the corridor toward the offices of the tong. He had succeeded in avoiding two crude traps that had been set, and he was inclined to believe that still others awaited him.

The entrance to the tong's suite of offices was wide open, and Toby stopped short, peering hard at the open doorway. At first he saw nothing, but at last he thought that he caught sight of a thin string that was stretched across the opening at waist level. He moved closer to it and saw that it was indeed a trap. One end was tacked to the wall, and the other was attached to the open door itself. Against the door, a number of tin cans had been placed so that a mere touch of the string would cause the door to move and make the cans rattle, alerting someone hiding in the offices beyond the door.

Exerting still greater caution, Toby bent almost double as he advanced under the trap without setting it off.

Taking care to station himself near a wall rather than be exposed by standing completely in the open, he peered hard around the office in which he found himself.

Dividing the room into rough segments, he studied each section separately as he searched for Ho Tai. But his efforts were in vain. He finally had to satisfy himself that his foe had chosen to await his coming somewhere else.

Toby was forced to advance still farther into the suite. Again he came to an open doorway that separated two offices, and he hesitated before he stepped over the threshold. He saw no semblance of any obstacle, no hint of any trick, yet he was convinced that Ho Tai would not miss this opportunity to try to get rid of him.

Then he looked down at the carpet, and for an instant he froze.

Something was inching toward him on the floor. On close examination, it proved to be a snake about a half-inch in diameter and two feet in length. It was impossible to distinguish any of the snake's markings in the dark, but Toby assumed that it was poisonous.

The snake raised its head to strike. Toby was ready for it. Grasping a throwing knife by the hilt, he threw it at the serpent. The snake's head was severed from its body, which thrashed violently on the floor and then continued to writhe feebly.

Knowing he had been spared another time, Toby retrieved his knife and crossed the threshold, where he scrutinized the room with infinite care. As his eyes adjusted further to the light, he saw that the richly furnished room was much as he remembered it. The thick Oriental rug had been changed, but the porcelain jars and the magnificent wall hangings were the same, as was the delicate tea service of porcelain that graced a low table.

On the far side of the room, beyond the tea set, a dark shadow loomed.

Making no move, scarcely daring to breathe, Toby studied the shape intently and finally made out that it was indeed a person. Ho Tai was crouching on the floor, poised for action, ready to attack the moment Toby drew nearer.

Toby realized luck was with him. Ho Tai hadn't counted on his foe's extraordinary eyesight and no doubt believed he remained undetected in his hiding place. Slowly drawing one of his throwing knives, hoping the darkness concealed what he was doing, Toby raised his arm inch by inch until it was in position to release the blade. He had only one chance to hit his target before Ho Tai would launch his own attack.

All at once, Toby realized with chagrin that Ho

Tai had indeed detected his foe's movements and
was about to throw his own knife at the newcomer.
There was only one way Toby could protect himself.
He realized he had to unleash his throwing knife
before his foe could let fly with his own knife. If his
aim was less than perfect, he might be unable to
avoid Ho Tai's blade and would be killed.

Reacting instinctively, Toby threw his knife. The
blade was a dark blur as it sped across the room. All
the years of Toby's rigorous training proved effective:
The blade found its target, and Ho Tai grunted as
the steel sank into his flesh, killing him before he
had an opportunity to release his own knife.

Toby strode across the room and stood above his
fallen foe. Ho Tai stared with sightless eyes at the
ceiling, his knife wound spewing blood on the precious Oriental rug.

Rather than retrieve his blade, Toby preferred
to let it continue to protrude from Ho Tai's body,
where it would serve as a warning to the leaders of
the tong. Realizing that the tong could say that Ho
Tai was sent back to China to perform some duty,
and then replace him with another hatchet man who
would continue the tong's reign of terror, Toby carried an Oriental armchair to the busiest street in
Chinatown. Then he went back for the body of Ho
Tai, which he dragged through the streets, then sat
upright on the chair, the blade still protruding from
his heart. Toby assumed that in the morning when
people started on their daily rounds, everybody in
Chinatown would get the message.

Toby promptly took his leave and went to the nearest police station, where he reported on the incident in full.

"You're one in a million, Mr. Holt," the sergeant in charge of the night shift said. "You have no idea how many men have sought vengeance against Ho Tai and how many of them have died for their pains. I don't know what will happen next: Either the tong will send a whole squad of assassins after you now, or they'll decide to leave you alone."

"I have an idea," Toby replied, "that Kung Lee's reign of terror will come to an end now that his henchman has been killed and disgraced. But if I'm wrong, he'll find out soon enough that I have more knives and that I haven't lost the knack of throwing them!"

Jean-Pierre Gautier held the chair for his mother, Helene, as she seated herself at the table in the opulently furnished dining room. Then the handsome, brown-haired young man seated himself and bowed his head as his father, Josef, said grace. According to family tradition, conversation was permitted only after grace was said, but Josef Gautier waited until the serving maid had brought steaming dishes of large, delicately flavored Gulf shrimp to the table and retreated to the kitchen.

"I think it's only fair to tell you, Jean-Pierre," he said, "that I'm investigating your upstairs guest."

His son registered alarm. "What do you mean, Papa?" he demanded.

Helene Gautier intervened smoothly. "You brought this young woman to us when she was too ill to walk," she said. "We've given her our hospitality freely, and we've had our own physician taking care of her. It seems to your father and me that the least we can ask in return is some information on the girl's background and standing."

Jean-Pierre bristled. "Isn't it enough," he demanded, "that I've fallen in love with her?"

"To be sure," his father replied, "if you should marry her, that will more than suffice for everyone in town whom we know. A Gautier writes his own rules in New Orleans society. All the same, your mother and I have a right to want something substantial in the way of the girl's background."

"You sound," Jean-Pierre said accusingly, "as though you're dubious about Millicent."

His parents exchanged a quick glance. "To tell you the truth," Josef said, "we do have a number of questions about her."

"I'll grant you that she was exhausted and helpless when you brought her here," Helene said, "but, nevertheless, you must admit her face was plastered with far heavier makeup than any New Orleans lady has ever worn, and her dress was extraordinary, to say the least."

"She was lucky to escape with her life and to be able to make her way back to the city from the bayous," Jean-Pierre said indignantly. "When she dressed and made herself up before coming here with me, I doubt if she was giving much thought to her appearance."

"We aren't necessarily being critical," his mother assured him. "On the other hand, if you're as serious about her as you appear to be, I think we have a right to inquire into her background."

"Regardless of what your investigation may disclose," Jean-Pierre said, "I intend to do my very best to persuade Millicent to marry me."

His parents sighed, and his mother deliberately changed the subject. She knew from long experience that Jean-Pierre was stubborn, single-minded, and utterly determined to have his way once he was sure of his course.

Helene talked about the New Orleans Symphony Orchestra, of which she was a patron, then father and son, being in business together, talked briefly about various contractual matters that were pending at the office. Conversation flagged somewhat as they ate their roast, and they paid no attention when they heard the doorbell ring. A few minutes later one of the maids came into the dining room with a yellow envelope resting on a silver tray.

"Pardon me," the maid said, "but this telegram has just arrived for monsieur."

Josef excused himself, opened the envelope, and took quite a long time reading and digesting the message that had been sent to him.

"This," he said, "is a telegram from the banker in Baltimore from whom I made inquiries about Millicent Randall. He begins by assuring me there's no need for him to hire Mr. Pinkerton's agency to look into the young lady's background. He assures me that her social and financial standings are impeccable and that she comes from one of the oldest families in Baltimore. In addition, she has acquired a considerable reputation as a flutist, and she has also composed music for the flute at the Baltimore Conservatory."

Helene stared down at her plate in silence, then raised her head and looked at her son. "We owe you an apology for doubting your taste and your judgment, Jean-Pierre," she said, "and we owe an apology to Millicent as well."

"She's suffered quite enough," Jean-Pierre replied. "If you don't mind, Maman, I much prefer that you make no mention of having doubted her."

"Of course," Helene said. "Rest assured that she'll be accorded every courtesy."

After supper Jean-Pierre went up to the room that Millicent was occupying and found her in bed eating a small portion of chicken cooked in wine on a bed of mushrooms and rice. "How do you feel this evening?" he asked her.

"I'm much better," she replied, sighing contentedly. "The ointment the doctor prescribed for my feet is doing wonders for them, and they should be fine in another day or two."

"What about the rest of you?" he asked.

Millicent smiled. "I haven't felt this free of care and worry for a long time. I'll soon be back to normal, too."

"That's good news," he declared.

"Now it's my turn to ask the questions," she said. "Whose bedroom am I using? From the way it's furnished, it looks like it's a young girl's room."

"So it is," Jean-Pierre said. "This was the room of my little sister, Marie. She died of the plague that broke out in the city during the last year of the war, and my parents were so heartbroken they've left her room exactly as it was when she was still alive."

"I didn't know," she murmured. "I'm sorry."

"This will interest you," he said, and standing, he went to a bookcase, where he picked up an oblong case. He brought it to the bed and handed it to her.

Millicent opened the case and was delighted when she saw a flute resting on a bed of satin. Removing the flute from the case, she fingered it experimentally. "This appears to be a very good instrument," she said.

"I'm sure my parents bought Marie the best that's made," Jean-Pierre told her. "She had a great deal of promise as a flutist, and the music world suffered a loss when she died."

Millicent put the flute into its case, which she placed on the bedside table beside her. "I've got to hurry my convalescence," she said. "I'm afraid I'm taking unfair advantage of you and your family."

"You're not imposing on my parents or on me," Jean-Pierre said flatly. "The least we can do is to take care of you after all that you've suffered."

"I have no right to expect such kindness from strangers," she said.

He looked at her, common sense warning him not to press too hard or too fast. He needed to become better acquainted with her before he revealed his true feelings, and he didn't want to frighten her after her terrifying experience with Karl Kellerman.

"We look forward to a relationship where we'll no longer be regarded as strangers," he said, and felt himself growing red in the face.

Millicent instantly understood what he was trying to say, and he was so ill at ease that she became embarrassed, too. The atmosphere changed suddenly, and they had such difficulty in communicating that Jean-Pierre finally was compelled to cut short his visit. He took his leave, promising that he would see her in the morning after breakfast, before he went off to his office.

Alone now, Millicent thought about him at length. Jean-Pierre was a member of her own class, and she understood him completely, just as he appeared to understand her. She recognized his thoughtfulness and generosity, and she knew that there was no way she could measure his kindness to her.

She doubted if she loved Jean-Pierre and could not pretend otherwise to herself. After her recent experience with Kellerman, she was incapable of loving any man. But the potential for a deeper relationship with Jean-Pierre certainly existed, and she was content at the moment just to wait and see what happened. She felt peaceful and serene in his presence, and she suspected that given sufficient time, love would grow.

Millicent glanced at the flute lying in its case, and gradually a yearning to play the instrument crept over her. She had not really thought about the flute since her days in Idaho, but now the need to express herself through music grew in her until it became an overwhelming force.

Scarcely realizing what she was doing, she lifted the flute to her lips and found herself playing a sonata by Handel, the music soon filling the house.

Every note was clear in the private sitting room located at the far end of the second floor. Josef Gautier put down the commodities report that he was reading and listened intently, his eyes staring off into space. Helene, who was knitting an antimacassar for the back of a chair, stopped her efforts, her needles poised in midair. "Listen, Josef!" she whispered fiercely.

"I am listening," he replied in a barely audible voice.

By now tears were streaming down Helene's face, and she took a handkerchief from her pocket and wiped her eyes. "I can't explain it," she said, "but I know now that our Marie has been restored to us! In a way that defies all reason and logic!"

Josef was weeping openly, too. He removed his spectacles and carefully wiped his eyes. "Our Marie has come to life again in the person of Millicent Randall," he said. "No one else has ever played the flute in that loving, special way."

*   *   *

Edward Blackstone and Jim Randall decided to stay in New Orleans until they finished the business that had brought them there. Millicent had been found and was safe, but there was still the matter of bringing Karl Kellerman and Captain Kayross to justice. For his part, Wallace Dugald, who had re-opened the bar bearing his name, had not let up in his desire to repay Kellerman for the abuses he had made the Scotsman suffer. Patrons of his bar were invariably treated to one of Wallace's tirades about his need for revenge, and the fact was, business at Dugald's fell off greatly, no one wanting to go there and be lectured to. As for the other men who had been shanghaied, having no personal knowledge of their abductors, they were now glad just to have the nightmare over with, to be able to resume their normal daily lives.

Meanwhile, Edward and Tommie, certain they were meant for each other, wrote to Tommie's father, announcing their desire to be married. Captain Harding wired back, giving them his blessing and saying that he would join his daughter and her fiancé in New Orleans so they could plan to be married there.

Randy Savage, Jim Randall's foreman, returned home to Boise in Idaho. Jim had asked Randy to take a letter to his wife, Pamela, at their ranch. He wrote to say that Millicent was safe at last, and although she had made no specific plans as yet, he suspected that before long, she would agree to marry Jean-Pierre Gautier. In addition, Edward and Tommie were also intending to be wed, and Jim told his wife to be prepared to come to New Orleans in order to attend the weddings.

As Millicent convalesced, Josef and Helene Gautier used their considerable influence on the young woman's behalf, and, as a result, every door in New Orleans opened magically to her. She met the conductor of the New Orleans Symphony Orchestra at a dinner party they gave at their house, and she and the orchestra leader discovered they had a number of friends in common in the musical world. After supper, Millicent entertained the guests by playing several pieces on her flute, with the orchestra leader accompanying her on the piano, and the result was an invitation to appear as a soloist the following month with the orchestra. Excited by the challenge, she gladly accepted.

Millicent was thrown into frenzied activity that allowed her no time to brood on the mistakes she had made and on the suffering she had undergone. She spent several hours each day practicing the flute, and for the two weeks prior to the concert, she rehearsed daily with the orchestra.

Dressing and making up—and, above all, thinking and acting—as a lady, Millicent experienced a transformation that was so gradual she had no idea it was even taking place. Totally absorbed in her music, which meant everything to her, she became what she once had been—a lady—and the reversal was permanent.

She was busy, too, with fittings for the new

gown that Josef and Helene Gautier were having made for her to wear to the concert, and there were parties given in her honor almost every night by leaders of New Orleans society. Millicent had returned to her own milieu, the world she knew best, and she flourished happily there.

Jean-Pierre was her constant companion, escorting her to social events, taking her to and from rehearsals in his carriage, and appearing constantly at her side. It was assumed by everyone in New Orleans society that she and the young widower had arrived at an understanding, but the truth of the matter was that Jean-Pierre had carefully refrained from mentioning marriage to her.

"I love her, and I want to marry her," he told his parents when they questioned him, "but I don't want to rush her. She's had some dreadful experiences that would have ruined a lesser person, and I want to give her the time to regain her bearings and stand on her own feet again."

Helene Gautier was both amused and somewhat nettled by her son's attitude. "When do you intend to propose to her?"

Jean-Pierre shrugged. "I can't say for certain, Maman," he replied, "but I'll know when the time is right, and I'll act accordingly."

His mother sighed, shook her head, and kept her own counsel. She thought it ironic that there had been a time when she had been afraid her son would ask Millicent Randall to marry him, and now that Millicent had proved more than socially acceptable,

Helene Gautier was afraid that he would propose too late or otherwise bungle matters.

While Millicent was leading a life of activity and excitement, Karl Kellerman was forced to lead a far different existence. By making discreet inquiries of various small-time underworld figures, he had learned that Domino was still alive and that the powerful gang leader sought vengeance against him. It was Domino's men, no doubt, who had tried to waylay him in the blonde's apartment, he thought. Kellerman knew, too, that Wallace Dugald would not rest until he evened the score with his former partner, and he also realized that Edward Blackstone and Jim Randall were on his trail and would not relax until they obtained justice for his misdeeds in his relationship with Millicent.

So Kellerman was in hiding. He grew a beard and a long, drooping mustache, which he dyed brown along with his hair, and he took up permanent residence in the slum quarters of the city. He took care to avoid saloons, restaurants, and gaming houses where he might be recognized, and he avoided the company of the beautiful women he had made a practice of squiring around town. Buying his food from local greengrocers, he was even reduced to cooking his own meals. He became something of a recluse and spent hours each day railing against fate and building up his hatred for Millicent, whom he regarded as responsible for all his troubles. And the longer he remained mired in the depths to which he had descended, the greater his anger became.

He had no one to whom he could turn for assistance. Captain Robin Kayross, his natural ally, was also in hiding, his ship having been impounded by the New Orleans authorities. There was obviously no reason for Kayross to pay Kellerman the money for the two shanghaied men who had gotten loose and set the others free, and so at the moment, at least, there was nothing that he and Kellerman wanted from each other.

Common sense told Kellerman to get out of New Orleans, but he knew that if he left the city behind him, admitting defeat, he would find it exceptionally difficult to start anew somewhere else. Word of success or failure spread as rapidly in the underworld as it did in the realm of legitimate enterprise, and he would be disgraced for all time if he fled from New Orleans now.

The greatest irony of all—and the thing that caused Kellerman the most dismay—was that he was wealthy beyond his wildest dreams, having in his possession the money from the robbery of the gaming house, the profits from Dugald's Bar, and the sum he had earned shanghaiing the first four men for Kayross. But as financially well-off as he was, he could do nothing about it and was forced to live as if he were in dire poverty.

With time hanging heavily on his hands, Kellerman determined to learn all he could about Millicent's life and movements. On two occasions he saw photo-

graphs of her printed in local newspapers. He read
with interest that she was escorted everywhere by
Jean-Pierre Gautier, and he devoured the news that
she would appear as a guest soloist at a special performance of the New Orleans Symphony Orchestra.

On several occasions Kellerman concealed himself in the underbrush outside the Gautier mansion
and observed Millicent's comings and goings. Her
appearance was no less striking than it had been at
the height of her affair with him, but it was far more
subtle now. Her cosmetics enhanced her natural
beauty rather than called attention to their use. Her
new gowns emphasized her superb figure but were
also discreet, those of a lady.

The realization slowly dawned on Kellerman that
Millicent bore only a slight resemblance to the woman
with whom he had lived. When he had first met her,
she had been under the influence of Luis de Cordova,
and he himself had seen to it that she continued to
dress and act like a trollop. Now she was reverting to
her normal, well-bred state, and he found that she
was even more attractive to him than she had ever
been.

The more he wanted her, however, the more he
sought revenge against her, and his waking hours
were filled with mental pictures of destroying her.
He decided that her forthcoming concert would give
him the opportunity for which he yearned.

The concert would be held in a large auditorium
that he had visited on other occasions with his various lady friends, even Millicent. They had always

had seats in one of the boxes high up on each side of the auditorium, and it was the boxes that captured Kellerman's imagination. Each of these upper boxes had two seats, and the sight lines to the stage were excellent. He knew he would have no trouble in shooting at his target when she appeared on the podium at center stage, next to the grand piano.

Best of all, there was an exit adjacent to each box. By moving only a few steps, he would be able to reach the exit and descend stairs that would deposit him on the street outside the theater.

Now that his plan was gelling, Kellerman proceeded with care. First, he insured himself of privacy by buying both seats in the box for the concert. Next, he enhanced his disguise by buying a pair of spectacles with plain glass in them, and he also purchased a dark, inconspicuous suit and cloak for the occasion. Paying special attention to the weapon he would use, he cleaned and oiled his pistol. He would keep the pistol concealed beneath his cloak and would fire it at Millicent at an appropriate moment.

Rehearsing the scene repeatedly in his mind, Kellerman could find no fault with it. He would be able to obtain his revenge and to get away afterward without any problems.

On the day of the concert, Millicent slept late and ate a breakfast in her bedchamber, Helene Gautier thoughtfully sending the meal to her room. She dressed quickly, then settled down to an hour of practicing scales and doing fingering exercises on the flute. This accomplished, she firmly put the instrument aside and refused to allow herself to dwell on the coming concert.

It was now early afternoon. Jean-Pierre appeared, and when he suggested a carriage drive, Millicent eagerly accepted. She was in the mood for such a drive.

The couple went driving in a phaeton, an open carriage that was pulled by a team of matched grays. Jean-Pierre handled the reins himself. He drove north of the city on a plantation-lined road that followed the Mississippi River. Traffic was light, and he and Millicent engaged only in desultory conversation.

Jean-Pierre let Millicent take the lead, and when she said nothing, he, too, remained silent. Eventually he pulled off the road onto a little spur that led toward the river, and they sat for a time watching the waters of the Mississippi swirling and racing toward the sea.

"I've given great thought to the subject I'm now bringing up," Jean-Pierre said. "I'll be frank with you because I feel that I must." He paused and looked out across the water. "When my late wife passed away, I thought my life would come to an end, too, and for many months, I felt dead inside. Then I saw you, and even before we met, I fell deeply in love with you. From that time until the present, my love has grown with each passing day, until now it has become the core of my very being. I've chosen this particular time deliberately. The concert tonight represents a big event in your life, and I want to share it with you. I want you as my wife."

Millicent was not surprised by his proposal of marriage. In recent days he had approached the subject on numerous occasions, only to hesitate and then back off again. She had thought about their relationship at length, and she knew fairly well where she stood. His kindness to her had been overwhelming, he was generous and gentle as well, and she had grown very attached to him.

Although she had spent countless hours on the subject, she had pondered in vain and was no closer now than she had been at any time to answering the question of whether or not she loved him. If love included the wild, pulsating sense of excitement that Luis de Cordova had generated, that she had felt so strongly for Karl Kellerman, then to her infinite sorrow, she did not love Jean-Pierre Gautier. That animallike feeling was not present in their relationship.

She suspected, however, that such a desire might not be good for her. Certainly, it had brought her nothing but grief whenever she had felt it. Thus she was prepared to accept Jean-Pierre's marriage proposal. He offered her fidelity, and she would give him fidelity in return. He offered her loyalty, and she would be loyal to him beyond all else.

She was encumbered by no lingering shreds of affection for Karl Kellerman or for the late Luis de Cordova. They were a part of her past, a past that she viewed with shame. The woman who had associated with them was far different from the Millicent

Randall who sat now in the phaeton with Jean-Pierre
Gautier looking out at the rapidly moving waters of
the Mississippi River.

Millicent folded her white-gloved hands in her
lap and peered at him from beneath the broad brim
of her black straw hat. "I won't abide by the rules of
the courting game and pretend I'm surprised, Jean-
Pierre," she said. "I've known for some time that you
were going to propose, and I've thought a great deal
about it."

"I hope your thoughts have been favorable," he
said with a slight smile.

"What bothers me is that there are periods in
my past about which you know nothing."

He shook his head. "I don't care to know about
them," he said.

She reached out gently and placed a hand on his
arm. "Say what you will. I've done things that have
caused me great mortification and shame. I can't
excuse myself for having behaved as I did, and I'm
afraid that my past conduct will haunt me for the rest
of my days."

"Forget the past," Jean-Pierre told her. "We
live in the present, and I love you for what you are.
Your past means nothing to me, and I want to know
nothing about it. All that interests me is your future,
and I demand the right to look after you from this
time forward, as long as we both live."

Millicent extended a hand to him and said timidly,
"With your help, I'll do my very best to live only in
the present—for the future. Our future. Together."

"You won't regret this," he told her huskily.

She removed her hat and lifted her face for his kiss. Their lips met, and Millicent pressed closer to Jean-Pierre.

Something stirred deep within her, and Millicent was first astonished, then elated as she recognized the familiar signs of physical arousal. She had been mistaken; there was a physical aspect to her relationship with Jean-Pierre after all. The future was even brighter and more promising than she had imagined it could be.

Their kiss grew more passionate, and when they moved apart, they looked long and hard at each other. Jean-Pierre reached into the pocket of his cutaway coat and brought out a small box, which he opened. Millicent saw a large, perfect diamond gleaming in the sunlight. She removed her glove from her left hand, he placed the ring on her third finger, and they kissed once again.

Later, when they parted, Jean-Pierre laughed shakily. "I guess there won't be any need to announce our betrothal," he said. "That ring will blind everyone in the audience when you're playing the flute tonight."

She joined rather tremulously in the laugh. "I think," she said, "my finger work with my left hand is going to be busier tonight than it's ever been before!"

The auditorium was filling rapidly a half-hour before the concert began, and a large crowd was gathered outside the stage door to await the arrival of the soloist.

Millicent did not disappoint her many admirers. She appeared wearing a bare-shouldered black evening gown trimmed with white feathers, and over her long, thick brown hair she had thrown a Spanish scarf as a protection from the rain that had been threatening to fall the past few hours.

The audience was in a festive mood. Word of Millicent's betrothal had leaked out that evening, and when Jean-Pierre appeared and joined his parents and Millicent's cousins, Edward Blackstone and Jim Randall, as well as Tommie Harding, in the front lower box on the right side of the theater, the audience warmly applauded him. The embarrassed young man became flustered, and his face turned crimson as he acknowledged the applause.

Millicent's performance followed the intermission. When she accompanied the conductor to the podium, the applause of the audience was tumultuous. She curtsied deeply, then gave a special smile to Jean-Pierre.

The audience became silent as she took her stance and began her first piece, Bach's Suite in B Minor, in which the flute was accompanied by the string section of the orchestra. The audience was enchanted by her spirited playing, and the applause that greeted her at the end of the piece echoed and reechoed throughout the auditorium.

Sitting alone in the box at the rear of the tier at the right, Karl Kellerman was bathed in perspiration.

A cape lay folded in his lap and concealed the loaded pistol that he held there, ready to fire at the opportune moment. His disguise was better than he had expected it to be: Certainly no one who knew him would recognize the bearded, bespectacled man with a scholarly air. He had tried the exit door adjacent to his box when he first entered the theater and to his relief found the door unlocked. Everything was working in his favor. He had seen no one he knew, no one who might recognize him. After he shot and killed Millicent, he could escape easily and the police would have a difficult time identifying her killer.

She looked lovelier than he had ever seen her, and he stared at her openmouthed as she began to play. It was difficult to imagine that this austere, talented woman and the abandoned creature who had been his mistress were the same person.

Her black dress fitted her snugly and reminded him that her figure was magnificent, far better than those of the women with whom he had associated since he had abandoned Millicent. Her cosmetics had been utilized with such subtlety that they brought out her rare beauty.

Above all, she carried herself with a confident air, a sense of sureness of who she was and of what she was doing. She gave no sign of the hesitation, the almost apologetic air that had marked her whole approach to other people. She seemed to be saying that she was a professional flutist who played with great skill. The audience recognized this quality in her and responded in kind to it.

What astonished Kellerman beyond all else as he sat in the dark of the box fingering his pistol beneath the cape was the effect that Millicent's music-making was having on him.

Crude, unprincipled, and totally lacking in morality, Kellerman was motivated by his self-interest and never, he thought, by his feelings. But that was not the case at the moment. He was aware that Millicent was casting a deep spell on her audience and over him. Every note played on his emotions.

He was totally ignorant about classical music and consequently had no idea what she was playing. All he realized was that her second number was so sad, so melancholy that it threatened the very roots of his being. He felt a deep, shattering loneliness, a sense of despair that brought tears to his eyes. He had no idea why he was weeping, but he realized that his vision was being affected: He could no longer see Millicent clearly enough to aim his pistol at her accurately.

When she finished playing the piece, it was so deathly quiet in the auditorium that the sound of rain falling on the roof and on the street outside could be heard. Then the audience reacted with a storm of applause that shook the inside of the theater.

Millicent consented to play an encore, and Kellerman was greatly relieved. He hoped he could use the respite to calm down. But to his astonishment, he found that his hands were trembling violently. He realized that he would never be able to hit a target with a pistol until the tremors ceased.

Millicent's playing continued to affect him, however, making it impossible for him to regain his equilibrium. She submerged him in the depths of melancholy, making it impossible for him to react, and he sat very still, transfixed by the sounds of her flute, unable to move a muscle.

Her solo ended. Again the theater rocked with applause, and Millicent graciously consented to play one more encore. She changed her whole approach, and this time she launched into a lively piece that lifted the spirits of the entire audience. People smiled broadly, their feet tapping in time to the music, and Kellerman told himself, "Now! I've got to shoot her now!"

In spite of his urgent desire to right the wrongs for which he imagined Millicent to be responsible, he could not move. He felt as though his wrist were being held in a giant vise, and he could neither raise it nor wrench free long enough to aim at the slender woman in the black dress standing on the stage.

The music ended, and Millicent curtsied low, acknowledging the enthusiastic applause of the audience.

Kellerman realized he had only seconds in which to carry out his plan, but he still could not move. Try as he might, something restrained him and made it impossible for him to aim his pistol and squeeze the trigger. Rivulets of sweat poured down his face and soaked his collar.

Millicent curtsied again, then left the stage with the conductor. The lights were lowered, and the

concert was over. As the members of the orchestra
filed off the stage, the audience rose and began to
leave the theater.

Kellerman had lost his chance. A feeling of great
weariness crept over him as he dropped the pistol
into his pocket, threw his cape over his shoulders,
and slowly followed the crowd out of the theater. He
felt very dispirited, very tired. He had fought the
hardest of battles within himself and, in his own
opinion at least, had lost it. All he wanted to do now
was to return to his quarters, fall into bed, and sleep.

The rain had stopped, leaving puddles on the
sidewalk and on the cobblestone road beyond it.
The air was fresh and clear, and the audience, invig-
orated by Millicent's performance, chatted happily.
Then the crowd parted, and Millicent herself, holding the arm of Jean-Pierre Gautier, moved from the
theater entrance to the curb, where a carriage awaited
them.

Tugging his hat lower over his eyes, Kellerman
huddled beneath his cloak as he stood almost within
reach of Millicent. She had come to life since the
days they had been together, and he had never seen
her more animated or lovelier. He studied her as
Jean-Pierre handed her into the carriage, and somehow he knew that he had suffered an irrevocable
loss. The woman could have been his for all time had
he treated her honorably and with love, but he had
abused her trust and instead had turned her against
him. No matter how many beautiful women to whom

he might pay court in the future, none could be like Millicent. She was unique.

As the carriage pulled away from the curb, the wheels rolled through a puddle and splashed mud on Kellerman's trousers and shoes. But Millicent, unaware of his proximity, leaned back in the carriage and exchanged a look of pure love with Jean-Pierre. "This," she told him, "is the happiest night of my life."

VIII

Kung Lee had been badly disturbed since the morning when Ho Tai's body had been found sitting in an armchair on the busiest street in Chinatown. He knew his luck had changed when his path had crossed that of Toby Holt, and now the recent news from New Orleans was the latest blow. He had received word from a tong member in that city that one of the oceangoing ships owned by the American tong had recently been impounded, the authorities charging that the vessel had been used illegally to smuggle Chinese aliens into the United States. What was more, the captain of the *Diana*, Robin Kayross, was accused along with a man named Karl Kellerman of shanghaiing several men and even abducting a young woman, a prominent socialite named Millicent Randall. The ship's captain and the man named Kellerman had seemingly disappeared from New Orleans, but there were warrants out for their arrest, and the police were determined to find them.

Kellerman, Kung Lee learned, was also wanted by members of the organized crime unit headed by the gang leader Domino.

So Kung Lee found himself in an extremely unpleasant situation, and he pondered on his next course of action. Deciding to kill two birds with one stone, Kung wired tong members in New Orleans, telling them he was coming to that city and that they should spread the word that Kung wanted to see Robin Kayross.

Traveling with a bodyguard, Kung took a train from San Francisco to St. Louis and then transferred to a Mississippi River steamer that brought him to New Orleans within the time that he had specified. He took quarters in a private dwelling that the tong had long owned, a place where a full domestic staff was already on duty. He was no sooner ensconced in the house than a trembling, nervous Robin Kayross was brought to him.

Kung Lee immediately put the Greek ship's master at his ease, serving him tea and smiling benevolently at him. The fact was, Kung had no rancor for Kayross and did not blame him for the loss of the *Diana*. Those things happened, and now the ship's captain could be of use to him again.

Kung read the copy of the court order confiscating the ship, which one of his underlings handed him, then he looked up at Kayross and said gently, "We'll forget all about matters with regard to the ship. We'll make no effort to recover possession of her."

Kayross was surprised. "Why is that?"

The tong leader shook his head. "The reason should be fairly obvious. If I were to step forward and claim ownership of the vessel on behalf of the tong, the federal government would order my arrest. I'd be charged with the illegal importation of Chinese immigrants, and in addition, they'd bring a civil suit against me for the importation of opium. The lack of such charges appears to be an oversight on the part of the federal authorities, but I'm sure it isn't. It's a deliberate trap, and they're waiting for me to step into it. Frankly, I prefer to suffer the loss of the ship rather than run the risk of being sent to a federal penitentiary. We owe ourselves a more modern ship, although I hate to undergo the expense of purchasing one. I don't suppose you happen to know anyone who might be interested in sharing the cost with us?"

Kayross was lost in thought for some moments and then grinned wryly. "There's one possibility," he said. "Karl Kellerman."

"Ah, yes—Kellerman. I learned about him in San Francisco. Is he still hiding from Domino?"

"Indeed he is," the Greek ship's master replied. "As if it's not enough that he has to hide from the police, he also has to worry about being seen by Domino or some of his people."

"Kellerman must be exceptionally foolish," Kung said, "to incur the enmity of a man like Domino."

"In my judgment," the Greek said, "he is not as

foolish as he is impetuous. He often acts without thinking of all the consequences."

"Be that as it may," Kung replied thoughtfully, "he might be useful to us, and he might welcome the opportunity to travel to far places on board a comfortable, safe ship. Invite Kellerman here to dine at your earliest opportunity, and let me look him over."

Karl Kellerman, who was bored almost senseless by his life in hiding, accepted Captain Kayross's invitation to dinner with alacrity. He was somewhat surprised when he was taken to a private home in New Orleans and was introduced to Kung Lee, but he soon learned that the cultured Chinese gentleman was the employer of Robin Kayross and owner of any number of cargo ships. Knowing he had been invited for business rather than social reasons, Kellerman bided his time, spoke only in generalities, and waited for his host to reveal the reason for the invitation.

Kung Lee was a gracious host and talked about sights of interest in both San Francisco and New Orleans as they ate a dinner of dishes that were completely strange to Kellerman. Not until they had finished their soup, the last course served to them, did Kung reveal his hand.

"I have learned from Robin Kayross," he said, "that your movements are somewhat circumscribed these days, Mr. Kellerman. Therefore, the thought has crossed my mind that you might be interested in a deal that would offer you constant changes of scene."

"I might be very much interested," was the

cautious reply. "It depends on the nature of the deal."

"My associates and I," the tong leader said, "are planning to invest in a new ship to replace the *Diana*, which we inadvertently lost. We intend to engage in the Pacific trade with China."

"Will this be the same type of trade in which you had the *Diana* engaged in?" Kellerman asked politely.

Kung smiled and nodded. "There's a steady demand here—a demand that pays very high prices—for merchandise from China, and we would be negligent if we failed to take advantage of that natural phenomenon. So you might say that we plan to be in the same business that we were in previously."

"May I ask what this has to do with me?" Kellerman demanded bluntly.

Kung studied him for a moment and then was equally blunt. "Those who find themselves in special circumstances," he said, "often make unorthodox investments."

"So they do," Kellerman replied politely, "provided they're not too exorbitant."

"What is exorbitant?" Kung asked rhetorically. "That which John Jacob Aster finds to be a reasonable price well might be regarded as exorbitant by one who is poverty-stricken."

Kellerman knew he could not engage in a battle of words with such a man. "Quite so," he murmured.

"My associates and I," Kung said, "are searching for someone who will invest perhaps one-third of the sum necessary to purchase a new trading vessel, a ship that burns wood or coal and that does not take months to cross the Pacific."

"What are you thinking of spending for such a ship?"

"Somewhere in the neighborhood of one hundred thousand dollars," Kung said. "Your share would amount to approximately thirty-five thousand."

"I'm not sure I could afford that much," Kellerman replied.

Kung lifted an eyebrow. "You took away almost that amount on the night that Domino was injured," he said, "and you much more than made up the difference with your profits from Dugald's Bar. Even allowing for all the money you spent on women, you should have more than thirty-five thousand left."

Kellerman looked at him in anger and astonishment. "It seems to me," he said, "that you know one hell of a lot about my business."

"To be sure," Kung said pleasantly. "My associates and I make it a standard practice to learn everything useful there is to know about those with whom we do business. But your private life, I assure you, is quite safe with me. I have no intention of revealing your finances to anyone, and certainly I'm not going to tell Domino your whereabouts. I'm not in business with him, and my associates and I mind our own affairs, just as we expect him and his associates to mind their own and to stay out of our business."

Kellerman was somewhat mollified. "I see," he said in a more normal tone of voice.

"As one of the owners of the vessel," Kung continued, sweetening the pot still more, "you'd be free to conduct such negotiations as you wished in China and elsewhere in the Orient. You would represent all the owners in a sense, and therefore, you would speak for all of us whenever you felt inclined to do so."

"How soon will this voyage take place?" Kellerman asked, and in his voice was the longing of one for the liberty he was currently being denied.

The tong chieftain continued to spread the bait. "You'll depart very soon," he said, "as soon as we purchase the ship and Captain Kayross makes her ready for sea and finishes hiring his crew." He refrained from adding that such activities could take many months, although he, too, preferred to see Kayross depart on his voyage as soon as possible.

He was pleasantly surprised, therefore, when Kayross reported the next day that he had found their ship. It was the *Neptune*, an all-metal cargo steamship with screw propellers, which had been built in New England yards at the end of the Civil War; for all practical purposes, the *Neptune* was virtually a new vessel. Her overly ambitious owners were on the verge of bankruptcy and eagerly accepted Kung Lee's offer of cash for the freighter, so the tong acquired the ship it needed at a bargain price, and Kayross immediately went to work hiring a full crew.

Kellerman was forced to pay the full price to which he had agreed in return for a one-third inter-

est in the freighter. He knew he had no choice, so he
made no complaint. He was quietly determined,
however, to take over the vessel whenever the opportunity presented itself and to leave the tong with
nothing. That desire was sharpened by the knowledge that Kung Lee fully intended to squeeze him
out of his partial proprietorship whenever he had the
chance. When dealing with persons whose motives
were highly questionable, Kellerman knew it was
always wise to strike first and to strike hard, and he
was confident of his own ability to get in the first
blow.

His investment provided him with certain short-
range benefits, and he lost no time taking full advantage of them. Primary among these was the offer of a
guest cabin on the *Neptune*, which was preferable
to the squalid apartment in which he was living near
the waterfront. Giving up his apartment, he moved
to the *Neptune*, and there he felt fairly safe. Certainly it would be difficult for any of his pursuers to
surprise him and to capture him while he was on
board.

In the meantime, on the Pacific Coast, a new
foe, far more dangerous than all the others, was
about to be added to those who were already searching for Karl Kellerman.

Toby Holt, following his battle to the death with
Ho Tai, went to the tong headquarters to request a
meeting with Kung Lee and demand that the tong
cease once and for all their criminal activities in

America. With the death of Ho Tai, the tong had lost much prestige and power and had no choice but to desist. When Toby found out that the tong leader was out of the city, however, he repaired at once to the offices of his business counselors, Chet Harris and Wong Ke. Ke immediately launched his own investigation, and in a surprisingly short time, he reported back to Toby.

"I've learned," he said, "that Kung Lee has gone to New Orleans on urgent tong business. It must be urgent because he almost never leaves San Francisco."

Thus matters were left at a standstill. At least, Toby reasoned, Ho Tai was out of the picture, and the tong would never be able to operate in the same way again.

Wasting no more time, Toby immediately returned to his ranch on the Columbia River in Oregon. He was glad to be home at last, and all he truly wanted to do now was settle down and be with his family and continue building his ranch the way he—and his father before him—had dreamed. But there was one more duty to perform, and before even seeing his wife and son—who were out riding—he quickly crossed the river in order to confer at Fort Vancouver in Washington with his stepfather, Major General Leland Blake. The general had been back at Fort Vancouver only a few days after his tour of army bases, and he was going to have to leave once again the next morning, having been called East to meet with President Grant, about a matter that was still unknown to him.

The generals words came as a shock. "Are you free to follow Kung to New Orleans, Toby?" he asked at once. "If so, I'll give you a warrant for his arrest, together with some blank warrants for any associates you might pick up as well. You see, we now have a crime we can pin specifically on him—namely, the shanghaiing of crew members onto a ship registered in his name."

Toby was stunned. He had thought he was coming back to start a new life at home with his family and instead found he was being sent far away. But he felt he was in no position to refuse the request. "I'm at your service, sir," he replied crisply.

"Thank you," the general said. "I know we keep talking about your desire to stay on the ranch and run it the way your father would have wanted, but this is a job that only you can perform well. I'll telegraph the army garrison at New Orleans and request them to cooperate with you in every possible way. I'll also activate your commission as a major, so you'll be on duty and will be authorized to act with the full force of the army behind you. I realize you've been deputized by the Portland authorities, but the justice department believes that only the army has the strength and the manpower to capture a criminal of Kung's stature. Kung has a start of only a few days, so if you move quickly, you should reach New Orleans soon after he gets there. I'll have the navy meet you with a motor launch in St. Louis to take you down the Mississippi quickly."

The words came at Toby like a torrent. For a moment he wished there was someone else who could do the job, someone who didn't have a home and a family he loved. But he would not shirk his duty, and he replied simply, "I'll be ready to leave first thing tomorrow morning."

At the ranch that evening, when Toby broke the news to his wife, Clarissa showed her own courage and understanding. "I've known from the start that this trip of yours to San Francisco was only the beginning," she said with a sigh. "The fact that you were called away for only a few weeks was too good to be true."

"I have no choice but to make this trip," Toby said. "My country needs me."

"I know," she replied. "Still, these separations become harder for me as time goes on."

"There's no reason for you to worry," Toby told her. "You know I can look after myself."

"Yes," she said. "All the same, the law of averages is bound to come into play sooner or later, and your luck will give out. You've had more near escapes than I care to remember or count, and what makes me afraid is the realization that one of these days you're going to face a situation in which even your talents won't help you."

"I see no point in anticipating trouble," Toby told her. "Besides, this is a clear-cut case. I'm going to New Orleans to locate Kung Lee, place him under arrest, and with the aid of the entire U.S. Army garrison there if need be, haul him back to face a trial."

Clarissa merely nodded and made no reply. It would serve no purpose to tell him her premonition that he was going to be in the greatest danger he had ever faced and that she was worried he might not survive it.

The U.S. Navy cutter that awaited Toby in St. Louis was a vessel about thirty-five feet in length, the main portion of its single deck being occupied by the boiler used to provide steam, along with the pile of coal that was fed into it at regular intervals. The crew consisted of a boatswain and two mates. The noncommissioned officer acted as the little ship's captain and pilot, and his two crew members' principal duty was keeping the boiler fed.

Toby had literally nothing to do except sit on deck and watch the passing scenery. As the vessel moved swiftly down the Mississippi, he had time to think. It was unfair, he once again reflected, that he should be summoned so frequently to serve his government, when others could follow their normal civilian pursuits. He was required to make constant sacrifices, to place his life in jeopardy, and to be separated for long periods from his wife and son.

His mood did not improve as the cutter continued its southward journey. Each night the vessel halted, and the passenger and crew went ashore at some town for overnight accommodations. The boat-

swain and his men were not communicative, and
Toby was left to his own devices for the better part of
each day and night.

As the cutter moved down the Mississippi River
from Memphis, the scars of Civil War fighting became more evident. They passed many buildings
that had been shelled but had not been repaired.
There were graveyards everywhere filled with both
Union and Confederate dead.

The war had come to an end for the people of
these communities, however, and the three sailors
and Toby were greeted warmly everywhere. Nowhere was this friendly attitude more evident than it
was in Magnolia, Mississippi, a tiny river town of
several hundred inhabitants located on a slight bend
in the great river. Leaving their cutter tied up at the
dock, the quartet rented rooms in a boardinghouse.
There they were served a sumptuous southern meal
by their hosts, the McAdams. Early the next morning as they were eating a breakfast of eggs, hominy
grits, bacon, and biscuits with butter and honey,
they were interrupted by Bud McAdam, the teenage
son of the proprietor.

"I—I don't rightly know how to tell you this," the
boy stammered, "but your boat sure is an almighty
mess!"

The quartet raced down to the waterfront, where
they stared in astonishment at the boat. Axes had
been taken to the hull of the cutter, and not only was
the boiler damaged, but the railing and deck had
been severely gashed.

The boatswain hastily inspected the damage, then ran a hand helplessly through his thinning hair. "This is a pretty kettle of fish," he roared. "We gotta get Major Holt to New Orleans fast, but this here cutter ain't fit to be rowed down the river!"

Trying in vain to mollify him, several people in the crowd that had gathered said that Mr. Legett had been notified and was on his way into Magnolia at this very moment. It seemed that Mr. Legett was the wealthiest and most prominent citizen in the community, a plantation owner whose mansion could be seen on the hill behind the town.

Fortunately for the blood pressure of the boatswain, the plantation owner soon arrived and made a careful inspection of the vessel. Then he hurried ashore and approached the three sailors and Toby.

"Gentlemen," he said in a thick southern drawl, "I can't begin to tell you how sorry I am, not only for the damage to government property but also to the good name of Magnolia. There are a couple of stupid gangs hereabouts who won't admit the war is over, and they're probably responsible for this outrage."

At his shoulder stood a slender, almost painfully thin girl in her early teens, with masses of black hair and enormous dark eyes that seemed to take in every detail of what was happening around her.

"We'll delay your voyage no longer than is absolutely necessary," Legett continued, "but you must give us the opportunity to make amends."

He turned to the crowd and began to give rapid-fire orders, pointing a bony forefinger first at one onlooker and then another. To Toby's astonishment, everyone in Magnolia appeared to be a carpenter or a metal worker.

Legett turned suddenly to the girl, his daughter. "You've got some work ahead of you, too, honey," he said. "You get your friends together, and as soon as the boys are finished fixing the decks, you scrub them clean. Get them so clean they shine!"

The girl hitched up her voluminous skirts and raced off.

"It won't do you much good to loiter here at the docks," Legett told Toby and the trio from the navy. "There's no place for you to rest your feet, and that sun gets mighty hot as it climbs up in the sky. I suggest you all come up to my house with me, where you can be comfortable." Without further ado, he led them up a hill.

The house proved to be magnificently furnished, and their host and his wife insisted that the visitors sit on a shaded porch, where they were served tall glasses of iced tea. They remained at the house as the guests of the Legetts until afternoon, and they were given a superb dinner at noon. The soup, which was called a gumbo, was unique in Toby's experience, and the smoked ham was one of the best-tasting delicacies he had ever eaten.

After the meal, the party returned to the porch, where the visitors were regaled with stories about Legett's ancestors, who had owned this same property for almost a century and a half. While he was finishing a story, his daughter approached, considerably the worse for wear. Her gown, which had been prim and pristine, was bedraggled. Wisps of her dark hair straggled down her face, and one cheek was badly smudged with dirt. But her expressive eyes were shining.

"We're through, Papa," she said. "Fact is, every-body's done work, and I swear, the new deck is so clean you could eat off it!"

Legett led the little procession downhill to the dock, and Toby marveled when he saw the refur-bished cutter. The boiler looked new, and the deck and railing were as sturdy as they were spotless.

The boatswain tried to stammer his thanks, but Legett held up a hand, silencing him. "Those idiots damaged United States property," he said, "and tried to make it impossible for you to carry out your mission. Well, Magnolia is pleased and proud to have been of service. We don't rightly know why it's important that Major Holt get to New Orleans quickly, and we have no need to know. All that matters is that it's important to the government that he get there fast, and that's good enough for us. In spite of the damage that was done to your boat, we're all Americans in this town, and we share in the future of this country. If there's one thing we learned in the war, it's the fact that we're all Americans. We all have the same goal, and we're heading toward it together."

Thanking his host and the people of Magnolia, Toby went on board, and a short time later, the cutter was again under way, heading down the river at a rapid clip, making up for the time that had been lost.

Standing on deck and leaning against the rail, Toby looked out at the flat, green land on both sides of the Mississippi. The incident in Magnolia had taught him a lesson he would never forget, and the enthusiasm of the volunteers who had repaired the cutter would remain fresh in his mind as long as he lived.

He no longer felt he was being singled out to make sacrifices for his country. As his host in Magnolia had put it so succinctly, all Americans were marching in step together toward the same goal. If he had talents that could aid the United States, it was only right that he should be summoned and that he should give freely and unstintingly.

Straightening his shoulders, Toby looked out across the land at the distant horizon. This was America, his country, and he was pleased and proud that he had the opportunity to serve her and her citizens.

Edward Blackstone, Tommie Harding, and Jim Randall had just sat down to supper in their hotel when they were electrified by the sight of Toby Holt crossing the dining room to their table. Warm greetings were exchanged, and Toby was introduced to Tommie. Everyone talked at once, and some minutes elapsed before a semblance of order was created. Then, after Toby sat down with his friends and ordered his meal, Edward brought him up to date.

"If you're going to be here for the next couple of weeks, Toby," he said, "you're just in time for Millicent's wedding. She's marrying a local man, son of one of New Orleans's best families, and I've never seen her so happy."

"You well might have come to New Orleans in time for our wedding, too," Tommie said. "We haven't set a date, as yet. We can't until we find out exactly when my father is going to arrive, but we're expecting him any day. We've been in touch with him by telegram, and he has rearranged the schedule of his ship, the *Big Muddy*, so he can return in the near future. He is as anxious to be here as we are eager to have him—and the sooner the better."

"I don't know of anything that will give me greater pleasure than to see Edward married," Toby replied. "Unfortunately, my time isn't completely my own. The length of my stay here depends on how soon I'm able to establish contact with a Chinese man named Kung Lee."

His listeners' faces were blank; it was plain that none of them had ever heard of the head of the tong. So Toby told them about his encounters in San Francisco with Kung and his bodyguard Ho Tai and how it was that he had followed the Chinese tong leader to New Orleans. "Tomorrow," he said, "I'll go to the army garrison here in New Orleans and seek the cooperation of the new commandant."

Now his friends explained to him the dramatic events in their lives since they had come to the city.

"It appears to me that this fellow Kellerman is a bad apple," Toby commented.

"He's as bad as they come," Jim agreed.

"We've been staying in Louisiana for two reasons," Edward added. "One is that we're going to attend Millicent's wedding. The other is that we hope to nail Kellerman—or at least Wallace Dugald, Kellerman's one-time partner, intends to nail him. He forced us to promise him that once we find Kellerman, we'll let him confront the man face to face. I'm sure that will take care of the problem."

"If I should learn anything about him in my own investigations," Toby said, "I'll let you know at once."

While they were still at the table, a note in a flowery, feminine handwriting was delivered to Toby by their waiter. It read: *Meet me in the lobby of the hotel after supper to discuss a matter of mutual interest.* The communication had no salutation and no signature.

It was possible, Toby thought, that he was being led into a trap of some kind, but there was only one way to find out. Telling his companions only that the message invited him to meet with someone who might shed some light on his quest, he dropped the folded paper into a pocket and went on with his meal.

After supper the others retired to their rooms while Toby went to the hotel lobby. There he sat on a brown sofa in a corner of the room.

He did not have long to wait. Within a few minutes, a striking green-eyed redhead, with hair streaming down her back, her snug-fitting dress emphasizing her curvaceous figure, came into the lobby, looked around, and headed straight for Toby. A score of eyes watched her hip-wiggling walk as she approached him.

"Mr. Holt?" she asked politely in a musical voice, extending a gloved hand to him, and then continued without waiting for an answer. "I'd know you anywhere from the pictures I've seen of you."

References to his fame invariably embarrassed him. "Won't you sit down?" he asked her, aware of the fact that she had not introduced herself.

"This is too public a place for a confidential talk," she told him with a laugh. "Besides, I'm just a messenger."

Not waiting for a reply, she took his arm and led him out of the lobby. At the entrance to the hotel, a large, enclosed carriage pulled by a matched team of horses, with a driver in livery on the box, was waiting for her. The driver tipped his hat, jumped down, and opened the door.

The woman preceded Toby into the carriage, the scent of musk that she wore filling the compartment. The thought occurred to Toby that if Kung Lee was setting a trap for him, he was going to a great deal of trouble. Also, as far as he could see, the woman carried no pistol or other weapons.

The driver shut the door, mounted the box, and the team of horses started off.

The woman appeared to know that Toby was a stranger to New Orleans, for as they rode, she calmly pointed out sights of interest to him. He responded in the same vein, seemingly relaxed while carefully concealing any wariness.

At last the carriage pulled into the driveway of what seemed to be a solid, middle-class home and rolled to a stop under the porte cochere. Not taking any chances, Toby removed one of his pistols from his belt and held it in his hand.

A burly man appeared in the entranceway to the house, saw the pistol in Toby's hand as he alighted, and grew taut.

"Mr. Holt may keep his firearms," the woman said as she took Toby's hand and stepped to the ground. "He has the boss's permission."

Her reference to "the boss" increased Toby's sense of alertness. Kung Lee must have indeed been behind this meeting all along. Well, he was on his guard.

The woman took Toby's arm and guided him through a room filled with plants into a pleasantly furnished parlor. Sitting in an easy chair at the far end of the room, reading a leather-covered book by the light of an oil lamp, was a mild-looking, middle-aged man with gray hair. His face looked thin and somewhat drawn, as though he had been ill, but when Toby came into the room, the man smiled, rose easily to his feet, and extended a hand. "Welcome, Mr. Holt," he said. "I am Domino." His handshake was surprisingly firm.

Now the man turned and called over Toby's shoulder, "That's all right, boys, you can leave."

Toby turned and saw two heavily armed men in the entrance. One of them gestured in annoyance. "He's carrying a loaded gun in his hand, boss, and he has another in his belt."

"That's Mr. Holt's privilege, I believe. I'll let you know when I want something. You're excused, too, Martha," he said to the woman.

She flashed a brilliant smile at Toby, then, still smiling, turned to the older man. "He's my type, Domino."

"We shall see, Martha," he said patiently. "We shall see. Right now I want to have a little private chat with Mr. Holt, if you don't mind."

The woman withdrew reluctantly.

"Sit down, Mr. Holt." Domino was scrupulously polite. "Please accept my apologies for bringing you here under mysterious circumstances. I hope you'll accept something to drink or eat."

"I've eaten, thank you," Toby replied, using an equally polite tone.

"As I say, I am known as Domino," the gray-haired man said. "I am engaged in business locally—I own a number of establishments, including several gaming houses and a number of brothels. I'm also involved in various other enterprises in New Orleans. It's to my advantage to know everything that takes place in the city, which is how I happen to be acquainted with you and your mission. I know why you're here, who sent you, and under whose jurisdiction you're functioning."

Toby's reply was deliberately noncommittal. "That's interesting."

"You and I," Domino went on, "happen to be in positions where we can benefit each other by working together and pooling our resources. I believe we can do each other a great deal of good." He paused and waited for a response.

"I'm listening," Toby said.

"You're seeking a San Francisco tong leader named Kung Lee," Domino said.

Toby stiffened. "Go on."

Domino smiled. "Kung made a very unfortunate error when he first came here. Ordinarily a man in his position would get in touch with me at once, as soon as he entered my territory, and would let me know that he had no intention of interfering in the affairs of my organization. Kung neglected to contact me and to give me such assurances, which I consider a serious lapse in good manners. I've had a discreet watch kept on him, and I believe I'm in a position to tell you what the army commandant and the New Orleans police cannot reveal because they don't know it. Namely, the present whereabouts of Kung Lee."

"That would be very useful," Toby admitted, then added, "What would you expect of me in return for this favor?"

Domino smiled broadly. "Ah, we understand each other, Mr. Holt. It's a pleasure to be doing business with someone as sharp as you. You may have heard of a criminal here by the name of Karl Kellerman."

"I learned a great deal about Kellerman at supper this evening," Toby told him.

A hard edge crept into Domino's voice. "Kellerman not only broke his word to me—something that no man ever does—but he stole a large sum of money and almost succeeded in murdering me. I have a score to settle with him."

"Am I correct in assuming that you want my help in tracking down Kellerman?" Toby asked.

The older man nodded. "Yes, but hear me out first. Kellerman knows I'm looking for him and that I'm not the only one. So are the police, and so are a number of individuals whom he's wronged and who have become his worst foes. He's gone into hiding, and I'm fairly certain he's wearing a disguise. But you're new to the community, and as far as Kellerman knows, you have no connection with me, with the police, or with anyone else. You stand a far better chance than any of the rest of us in locating him. If you'll agree to conduct an active search for him, I'm sure I can help you locate Kung Lee."

Toby pondered the situation in which he found himself, the strangest he had ever been in. For years his name had been synonymous with obedience to the law, yet here he was being offered a deal, a partnership, by a man who lived and earned his living outside the law.

But in spite of the fact that Domino was the head of a large and powerful New Orleans criminal gang, his offer in no way obstructed justice. On the contrary, Toby realized the cause of justice would be served admirably if he entered into such an agreement. He had everything to gain and nothing to lose. Furthermore, his honor, which was sacred to him, would be untarnished.

Domino handed him a drink.

"Here's to a very odd partnership," Toby said, and raised his glass.

Domino, who was endowed with a keen sense of humor, chuckled appreciatively and raised his own glass in return. "Long may this partnership flourish!" he declared.

They raised their glasses, sipped, and put the drinks down.

"There's a large modern freighter, built at the end of the Civil War, that's currently tied up at the New Orleans docks," Domino said. "Her name is the *Neptune*, and her captain is a penny-pinching Greek named Robin Kayross. She was purchased just recently for utilization in the Orient trade. She'll carry legitimate cargo to China and will return to the United States loaded to the gunwales with illegal Chinese immigrants—who will be overworked and taken advantage of in every possible way by the tong—and with opium. Her owner is Kung Lee, and he has spent time on board her every day since he's come to New Orleans. He usually arrives there early in the afternoon and stays until dark. The ship is still taking on cargo, so if he keeps to his regular schedule, you should be able to find him on board tomorrow afternoon."

Toby thanked him, and they shook hands. Their business, for the moment, was concluded.

"I'll pay the *Neptune* a visit tomorrow," Toby said, "and I'll be in touch with you as soon as I have a lead for you on where to locate Kellerman." They sat back in their chairs, both of them satisfied with the deal they had struck, and as they finished their drinks, Domino said, "If you have nothing to keep you occupied until tomorrow afternoon, you might want to consider spending at least a part of that time with Martha, the girl who brought you here. You'll find her amenable to any activity you might have in mind."

Toby shook his head and smiled. "Thanks all the same," he said firmly, "but I have a wife, and I happen to be a one-woman man."

At breakfast the following morning, Toby told Edward and Jim, "I've tracked Kung Lee to a ship that's anchored at the river docks here, and I'm going to pay him a surprise visit this afternoon."

Both were astonished, and Jim asked, "How did you manage to get a line on his whereabouts so fast? Did it have something to do with that message sent to you at supper last night?"

Toby felt it was necessary to protect the privacy of his agreement with Domino, so he merely nodded but added nothing else.

The cousins, realizing he was reluctant to pursue the subject, did not press him for an answer. After breakfast, Toby excused himself, and a short time later, he was closeted with the commandant of the New Orleans army garrison, to whom he explained his mission and said that he was going to pay a surprise visit to Kung Lee that afternoon on board the *Neptune*.

"I suppose," the commandant replied, "that you will want about a dozen army troops on hand, ready to accompany you on board."

"I think not," Toby said. "I've given the matter considerable thought, and I'm afraid that their mere presence would virtually guarantee a nasty fight. I don't want anyone killed or injured."

The commandant was alarmed. "I realize you've acquired a formidable reputation for yourself, Major Holt," he said, "but surely you don't intend to tackle Kung Lee by yourself! You'd be walking alone into the dragon's mouth!"

"I prefer to try alone in order to prevent bloodshed," Toby said. "But if that isn't effective, I have no desire to be a dead hero. What I have in mind is this: I intend to go on board the freighter alone and to confront Kung Lee. I think—at least, I hope—that he'll be reasonable when he sees that I have a warrant for his arrest. If he does, he'll come ashore with me peaceably, and that will end the crisis. If not—in the event that he tries to kick up a fuss—then I'll need help. So here's what I propose: I'll present myself on the freighter at two o'clock exactly. I'll let your troops show up precisely one hour later, at three o'clock. If I don't appear and come ashore with Kung Lee as my prisoner by half-past three, then I suggest that they force their way on board and conduct a thorough search for me, though I hope that won't be necessary."

"The stories I've read about you in newspapers and magazines haven't exaggerated your courage," the commandant said in admiration, shaking his head. "Obviously you're well aware of the risks that you're taking."

Toby shrugged. "Yes, and quite frankly, I don't think they're very great. You're forgetting that Kung Lee is a civilized man who is anxious to stay on good terms with the United States government. If he behaves in a threatening manner toward me when I serve him with the subpoena, he's going to destroy the façade that he's spent many years creating. I'm not anticipating any trouble, you understand."

"You well might be mistaken."

"I grant you that," Toby said, "and for that reason, your troops will be most welcome. But I believe everything should work out for the best. For all concerned."

Toby ate lightly that noon, then set out for the waterfront, armed with his two repeating pistols and with a knife protruding from his belt. He located the *Neptune* without difficulty and studied her with interest, observing that she was one of the few vessels he had ever seen that was flying the flag of the empire of China. As Domino had indicated, she looked new. She had been freshly painted, and her decks were loaded with boxes and crates of merchandise that, presumably, would be transferred to one of her holds before she set sail for the Orient. A guard, armed with a short, leather-covered club, stood on the dock near the gangway, and another, similarly armed, was wandering about on the deck near the cartons and crates, disappearing and then reappearing again as he made his way between them. Above, on the open bridge of the ship, a man with the tarnished braid of a captain on his uniform was engaged in earnest conversation with someone much taller and huskier. Toby guessed that the officer was Robin Kayross, but he had no idea of the identity of the other man, who was brown-haired, wore spectacles, and had a large, drooping mustache and a beard. Kung Lee was nowhere to be seen.

The pair on deck became conscious of his scrutiny, and the taller man promptly disappeared from sight into the interior of the vessel.

Glancing at his watch and seeing that two o'clock had come, Toby moved swiftly to the gangway and went on board. The guard who had been moving aimlessly on the deck hurriedly approached him.

"I'm here to see Kung Lee," Toby announced in a clear voice.

The man hesitated for a moment. Then, his gaze shifting rapidly, he announced, "I never heard of him." It was plain that he was lying.

Toby had anticipated such a response and had planned on how to deal with it. "In that case," he said, "I must speak with Captain Kayross. Tell him that Major Holt of the U.S. Army is here."

He held his ground as the guard stared at him

for a moment. Then the man bolted and ran up to the bridge. He quickly returned and pointed toward the bridge. "He's up there," he said. "Don't loiter on the way."

Taking his time, Toby sauntered to the short flight of stairs that led up to the bridge, where he could see Captain Kayross waiting for him, obviously ill at ease.

Mounting the stairs, Toby refrained from drawing either of his pistols. This was not yet the time to demonstrate strength. "I am Major Toby Holt, U.S. Army," Toby said as he approached the captain. "I've come to see the proprietor of this ship, Kung Lee."

Beads of sweat appeared on Kayross's forehead. "I'm afraid that Mr. Kung isn't available at present, Major Holt." It was plain that he not only recognized Toby's name, which he spoke with a measure of awe, but that he was very much worried.

"Perhaps you'll be good enough to tell me what time he's expected on board," Toby suggested politely.

Kayross took his time replying. Moistening his lips, he suggested they adjourn to his cabin in order to discuss the matter. Toby was amenable but was very much on his guard.

Kayross headed toward the rear of the bridge's interior, where he opened a door into a combined sitting room/bedroom, simply furnished. He turned to face Toby and spread his hands out in front of him. "To be truthful with you, Major Holt," he said, "I don't know what you're talking about."

Toby remained patient. "You'll admit," he said, "that Kung Lee is the principal owner of this ship."

The words were no sooner out of his mouth than the door behind him opened and five seamen came into the room. Toby whirled around and drew his pistol, but he was too late. Two of the seamen grabbed Toby's arms, and another two held his legs. Meanwhile, the fifth man looped a rawhide noose over his neck and attached the other end of the strand to his arms and wrists, which were bound together. Then his legs and ankles were bound with a separate strand of rawhide, which was also looped around his neck and attached to it. This meant that any violent moves that Toby might make with either his arms or his legs would result in tightening the noose and cutting off his breath. If he was overly active, he could easily choke to death.

The fifth man now took Toby's pistols and removed the knife from his belt.

"Thanks very much, Kellerman," Kayross said. "Major Holt was becoming too damned inquisitive."

Toby turned his head slightly and, in spite of his extreme danger, he carefully scrutinized Karl Kellerman. The man was tall and brawny, and his hair obviously had been dyed, as had his beard and mustache. In addition, he had a pair of spectacles perched on his nose. In all, his appearance, Toby guessed, was very much changed.

Then Kung Lee entered the room. He was very calm, very much in command. "You're wasting time," he announced. "See what documents he's carrying."

Kellerman was the first to obey. Reaching into Toby's inner jacket pocket, he took out a sheet of parchment, which he unfolded. "This is an order signed by Major General Leland Blake, commander of the U.S. Army of the West," he said. "It authorizes Major Toby Holt to apprehend and arrest one Kung Lee for crimes committed against the people of the United States and contrary to that nation's laws."

Kung Lee smiled lazily. "Well, Holt," he said, "it seems that we've turned the tide just in time."

Careful not to move his arms and legs, Toby said, "Kung, no matter what you may do to me, you'll never get away with this. You've broken the laws of the United States for years, but those days are ended. The government has become aware of your crimes and will put you in prison because of them."

"All that you say may be true, Holt," Kung replied gently, "but you won't be alive to see me arrested and to attend my trial. I hope your ghost enjoys the spectacle, because you won't be here." He turned to Kellerman and Kayross. "Captain," he said, "cast off immediately and take this ship out to sea. We're sailing for the Orient immediately."

Kayross was stunned by the sudden, unexpected order. "We're not yet ready to sail, Mr. Kung," he said. "I don't have enough food supplies and water to sail from here to China."

The tong leader gestured impatiently. "We can put into any one of a half-dozen ports as we sail around South America, and we can get any supplies we need at all of them. Do as you're told! Holt isn't stupid, so he certainly didn't come here alone to seek me out. The dock will soon be crawling with U.S. Army troops. I want to be at sea by then."

"Aye, aye, sir." Kayross hurried out to the bridge and began to bark commands into his speaking tube.

"As the junior partner in this venture," Kung said to Kellerman, "you have certain responsibilities for our safety. As soon as we leave the Mississippi River behind us and reach the open waters of the Gulf of Mexico, I want you to dispose of Toby Holt."

"Do you want him shot?" Kellerman asked.

Kung laughed and shook his head. "Certainly not! Use your imagination, Karl! Throw him into the water the way you have him tied right now. If he tries to swim, he'll choke to death, and if he doesn't, he'll surely drown. I'll leave him to contemplate his fate while I go out and enjoy watching us putting out to sea. Join me on deck, Karl, and we'll breathe the fresh air of freedom together." Chuckling quietly, he left the cabin.

Kellerman hooked his thumbs in his broad belt and looked down at Toby, who lay, carefully unmoving, on the floor. "You may be the most famous law-enforcement official in the United States, Holt," he said, "but you really are a damned fool. You should have known better than to have come after Kung Lee single-handed. By the time your helpers arrive at the docks, we'll be well on our way out to sea, and you'll be several leagues below the waves." As he spoke, the Neptune's engine began to rumble and the big vessel trembled as she slowly started to edge away from her dock. Ordinarily her master would have allowed more time for the boilers to build up a larger head of steam, but Captain Kayross was in too much of a hurry to put distance between himself and the land before Toby's reinforcements, whoever they might be, arrived at the waterfront. It was a good thing, Kayross reflected, that he had given orders earlier in the day to fire up the boilers.

Kellerman glanced out the porthole. "Good," he said. "We're under way. I'll leave you to contemplate your fate, Holt, until we reach the Gulf of Mexico." He sauntered out, closing the cabin door behind him.

As soon as Toby was alone, he went into action. He had not forgotten the Cherokee trick that Stalking Horse had taught him many years earlier, and while his bonds were being tied, he had deliberately tightened the muscles in his arms and legs, causing them to swell. By relaxing completely now, they became loose, and he had an opportunity to move without drawing the nooses around his neck tighter.

Wriggling and working his wrists systematically, Toby managed to loosen the bonds sufficiently to free his hands. Gingerly removing the noose from his neck, he untied the rawhide thong that bound his ankles and legs together, and then he slipped that noose over his head, too. He was free.

His mind had been working busily while he had undergone the taunts of Kung Lee and Karl Kellerman, and he knew precisely what needed to be done. Not wasting a single, precious moment, he hurried to the door, opened it cautiously, and when he saw the passage outside was empty, he slipped into it and went to the next cabin. It, too, was unlocked. He looked inside, and on a small desk in the corner he saw a small black notebook. He hurriedly thumbed through it. Several pages were written in Chinese, which he could not decipher, but then he came to a large section of charts with neatly printed words and phrases in English on them. He knew that this notebook was Kung Lee's private property and that he was looking at the entire system for the distribution of illegal immigrants and opium in the United States.

Armed with this evidence, the U.S. government would have no trouble in sending Kung Lee to prison for years or deporting him, whichever course of action the Justice Department chose to follow.

Toby's exceptionally acute hearing, as sensitive as his father's, stood him in good stead. Suddenly he made out the sound of the faint patter of footsteps outside on the deck. Shoving the notebook into his pocket, he stepped behind the cabin door.

One of Robin Kayross's Greek seamen thought he had heard someone in Kung Lee's cabin, and wanting to make sure that his imagination was not playing tricks on him, he had come to investigate. Taking his only weapon, a double-edged knife, from its sheath, he grasped it in one hand and opening the cabin door with the other, stepped inside.

As the door quietly closed, Toby struck, aiming

a blow with the edge of his hand at the back of the seaman's neck. The sailor's peripheral vision was sufficiently good that he caught a glimpse of Toby and turned his head just in time to absorb a portion of the blow on the side of the neck, rather than the back. Therefore, instead of being knocked unconscious, he was merely rendered groggy as he sank to the floor.

Toby well knew that his own life was in mortal danger, and he remembered the advice that his father had always given him: "When the chips are down, forget you're a gentleman. Use any and every means at your disposal in order to win. Just make sure when you get into a fight that you come out of it a winner." Thus, stifling his natural tendency to abide by the rules of fair play, Toby launched a vicious kick that caught the seaman under the chin. His head snapped back hard, striking the floor and knocking him unconscious.

Toby quickly bound the sailor's ankles and wrists, then picked up the knife. At least he was not totally helpless now.

Opening a wardrobe closet, Toby rummaged inside briefly and found what he was seeking—an oilskin coat that Kung Lee undoubtedly had brought with him to wear when the weather was foul. Using the knife, Toby cut a long strip from the hem of the coat up to the armholes about twelve inches wide. Then, after securing the knife in his belt, he wrapped the precious notebook in the strip of oilskin, which he doubled and made sure was tightly closed before he placed it, too, beneath his belt.

Casting a last glance at the unconscious Greek seaman, Toby stepped out of the cabin into the open. The throbbing of the ship's engine was louder here, the trembling sensation more pronounced.

Looking out beyond the starboard rail Toby saw that the *Neptune* was moving slowly down the Mississippi River toward the open sea. The docks had already disappeared behind a bend in the river, and the increasing sparsity of buildings was an indication that New Orleans was being left behind.

Never having visited the area previously, Toby had no idea whether the freighter would reach the open Gulf of Mexico in minutes or hours, but he was taking no chances. After assuring himself that no one was on deck, he began to work his way aft, crouching low among boxes, barrels, and crates of cargo that filled the open deck. He took care to stay behind the bridge, which was one deck higher, so that neither the captain nor any of his officers there could see him on the crowded deck below. Cautioning himself not to rush with freedom already close at hand, Toby made his way forward with extreme caution, making certain that the area directly in front of him and on both sides was unoccupied before doubling over and running to hide in the shadows of another box or crate.

At last, after playing a deadly game of hide-and-seek, he arrived at the aft rail, and as he looked down at the Mississippi below, a new problem presented itself. The *Neptune* was sailing slowly but steadily downstream, and Toby realized that if he were to jump overboard into the river, he might injure himself on the sharp metal blades of the *Neptune*'s propeller. Instead, he moved about ten feet toward the port side of the ship.

Toby was aware that when he jumped into the river below, he would be plainly visible to men on the bridge if they happened to turn and look in his direction. If they should see him, it would be a simple matter for them to halt the *Neptune* and either lower a boat to retrieve him from the water or to use him as a target. Either way, he would be killed. But he had no choice. He had to take his chances.

He estimated that the distance from the *Neptune* to the shore on the port side of the ship was about a half mile in all, and he had no doubt of his ability to swim to land. He was far more at home near the mountains and on wilderness trails than in the water, but he had grown up near the lakes and rivers of Oregon, and swimming presented him with few challenges.

Climbing the port rail, Toby looked swiftly up at the ship's bridge and saw that the three men standing there were looking ahead, down the river, and that none were aware of his presence behind them.

Making sure that Kung Lee's oilskin-wrapped notebook was secure beneath his belt, Toby took a deep breath, then dived out as far as he could into the waters of the Mississippi River.

The force of his dive plunged him deeply beneath the surface, and when he rose to the top again, swimming rapidly, he saw that the *Neptune* was now far ahead of him and that every passing second increased his distance from the ship.

His relief mounting as he swam, he felt the cool air clearing his mind. It was premature to celebrate, but he appeared to have outwitted the most powerful tong leader in the United States.

"There's somebody swimming in the river!" a woman's voice called suddenly. "It's a man, and he's fully dressed! Maybe he fell off the big ship!"

The startled Toby looked up and saw a strange craft bearing down on him. It was a type of raft, made of logs lashed together, and standing amidships was a crude little structure that served as a cabin. A woman wearing a bulky black sweater and men's trousers rested on one knee in the prow of the raft. Even her bulky sweater could not hide her voluptuous figure. With her waist-length, jet black hair, enormous eyes, and scarlet lips, she was very exotic-looking.

"Louis! Charles! Pole more to your left! That's it, get ready to throw him a line, Etienne!"

The raft slowly drew closer to the swimming Toby as it was poled by two burly young men, while the third began to twirl a length of rope. The rope landed within Toby's reach, and he grasped it with both hands.

"All right, Adele, I've hooked him!" the man named Etienne called. "Now what?"

"We'll take him on board, naturally!" she replied, and began to haul in the line, hand over hand.

Etienne did the same, and Toby was pulled to the raft. He managed to scramble aboard without any assistance. Rising to his feet and breathing hard, he found all three of the young giants and the attractive woman staring at him. "Thanks," he said. "I appreciate this."

"I am called Adele," the woman replied, "and these are the Raymond brothers, Louis, Charles, Etienne." Each of the young men nodded as his name was mentioned.

"Did you fall off the freighter?" Louis, the largest of the brothers, asked. "If so, we have a flare in the cabin that we can fire, and I'm sure the ship will stop."

"The last thing that I want on this earth is to halt that ship," Toby said. "I was a prisoner on board, and I'm lucky I escaped with my life."

The woman suddenly became concerned. "You're shivering!" she said. "Etienne! You're smaller than your brothers, so your clothes will be the most likely to fit him. Get him some pants and a shirt, please." She turned back to Toby. "You can go in the cabin and change," she told him, then directed her attention to the pair who were poling the craft. "Pull ashore and start to build a fire," she ordered. "I'm going to make our visitor a good hot meal."

Before Toby went into the cabin to change his clothes, he saw a gleam of jealousy in Louis Raymond's dark eyes.

The interior of the little cabin was as crude as the exterior. Items of clothing were hanging from a number of hooks, and the only signs that a young woman was on board were the presence of a broken mirror, a small jar of lip rouge, and a hairbrush, all of them bunched together on a small, homemade table.

"Here you are, mister," Etienne said, and handed Toby a dry shirt and a pair of trousers.

Toby peeled off his wet attire, changed into the dry clothes, and taking no risks, put the oilskin-wrapped notebook into a hip pocket and then slid the knife he had taken from the unconscious Greek seaman into his belt. When he returned to the deck of the raft, he saw that it had been run aground near a copse of trees and that hanging off the aft end of the ungainly craft were several large nets filled with fish, which moved about helplessly in the shallow waters.

"We've spent a couple of days near the mouth of the river fishing, like we always do," the woman said as she led Toby ashore. "The fish run heavy and good there. Then we were taking our catch back to sell in New Orleans when we saw you in the water behind that big freighter. Tell us what happened to you."

Her companions, who were gathering wood and building a fire with it, stopped their activities to listen.

"My name is Toby Holt," Toby said, "and I went on board the *Neptune* to arrest an international criminal. His men overpowered me, but I was fortunate enough to escape."

The woman blinked at him in surprise and admiration. "You're really the famous Toby Holt?" she asked, clasping her hands together.

It was obvious that Louis Raymond was jealous. "Like hell he's Toby Holt!" he said. "If he's the great Holt, I'm General Andy Jackson." He laughed raucously at his own humor. Toby made no comment. Suddenly Louis, who towered above Toby by at least half a head, drew a knife. "If you're Toby Holt," he said, "let's have us a little duel. I see you have a knife, and I got one, too, so we'll have us a fight and may the best man win."

Toby shook his head. "You and your companions rescued me just a little while ago, Mr. Raymond," he said. "I'd be repaying you rather poorly if I fought you now. I urge you to forget the whole thing."

Louis sneered at him and addressed his brothers, although he was actually speaking for Adele's benefit. "I knew it! The Toby Holt we've read about ain't afraid of nobody or nothing." Then he turned to Toby. "But you got a yellow streak up your back a mile wide, mister. What do I have to do to get you to fight?"

Toby smiled. "If you go about your business quietly," he said, "you'll live a long, happy life down here in Cajun country."

The big man looked disgusted. "Put up or shut up," he growled, and spitting on the ground at Toby's feet, he waved his knife in front of the other man's face. "You hear me? Put up or shut up!"

Toby sighed, then moved with lightninglike speed. Using a trick he had learned several years earlier from the Shoshone Indians of Idaho, he struck swiftly, one hand cracking down onto Louis Raymond's wrist and hand. As Louis dropped his knife into the dust, Toby drew his own knife and held it poised a fraction of an inch from Louis's throat. "I tried to warn you, Raymond, but you refused to listen to me. I hate to repay your kindness by carving you to ribbons, but you're not giving me any choice. Now hear me. I'm tired after a busy and exhausting day. I'm hungry, and I'm looking forward to a night's sleep. I don't want any interference with my dinner or with my night's rest. You'll either behave yourself, or your brothers will be forced to carry you home, and it'll be a long time—a very long time—before you're able to go fishing again. What do you say?"

There was a long moment of silence, and Louis said, "I'm awful sorry, Mr. Holt. I guess I kind of mixed things up when I failed to recognize you. It won't happen again."

The woman laughed and clapped her hands together. "Only Toby Holt could make you back down and apologize, Louis. I never thought I'd live to see the day!" She turned to Toby and put a hand on his shoulder. "You must really be Toby Holt," she said admiringly. "Nobody else on earth could make Louis crawl."

Toby lowered his knife and extended his hand. "No hard feelings, Louis," he said.

"Thanks, Mr. Holt," the big man replied. "From now on we're on the same side."

By now the cooking fire was burning brightly. Adele, who was in charge of preparing the meal, wrapped some sweet potatoes in large, moist green leaves and put them in the coals. Then she went to the nets at the rear of the barge, and from them she took a number of fish, which she proceeded to clean, then to fry, sprinkling them with a pepper sauce that was peculiar to the Cajun country.

While the fish sizzled in two large frying pans, Toby learned more about these backwoods people from Adele. The young woman lived in her parents' house in the bayou country near that of the Raymonds and sometimes went with them on their fishing expeditions. Living in the remote countryside made her restless, and it was her dream to move to the city. Louis, who was eager to marry her, had promised her a home in New Orleans if she would wed him, but she had not yet accepted his offer.

"I've never known anybody," Adele told Toby, "who leads a life as exciting as you do. Will this man you were after be arrested now?"

"Yes," Toby told her, "as soon as he and his companions set foot again on American soil." When that would be Toby did not know, but right then he didn't want to think about it. He was exhausted, and all he wanted to do was eat his meal and get some sleep.

Night had fallen by the time they finished supper. The Raymonds went to check their nets, while Adele went into the cabin on the boat and came out with a blanket and a mosquito net, which she gave to Toby. He spread the blanket on the ground, and when he retired, he put the net over him in order to ward off mosquitoes, flies, and other insects in the humid climate.

Tired after his extraordinary day's exertions, Toby soon drifted off to sleep. When he had been in his early twenties, he would have remained fresh and strong after spending such a day, but now that he was nearing thirty, he found he grew tired and needed his rest. His last thoughts before he fell asleep were of Clarissa, whom he missed desperately.

Later that night—he had no idea of the time—he dreamed that he and Clarissa were making passionate love. He awakened to find himself kissing Adele violently. Their bodies were tightly intertwined, and she had managed to insert a hand beneath his attire and was fondling him.

He was stunned, and his mind almost refused to function, but he knew, nevertheless, that he could not tolerate such a situation. Unless he did something quickly, he would be guilty of infidelity to his wife.

Toby caught the woman by the shoulders and forcibly moved her away. Then he sat up, climbed to his feet, and pulled her upright. Saying nothing for fear of awakening the sleeping Raymond brothers, he walked her to the nearby riverfront and sat her down on a bank overlooking the Mississippi. "You don't want to be doing this with me, Adele," he said. "You're probably only interested in me because you think I'm an exciting, romantic figure."

Adele sat hugging her knees and staring out at the dark, silvery ribbon of the broad Mississippi. She was hurt now and had withdrawn within herself, so she made no reply.

"Let me tell you," Toby said softly, "about Clarissa."

"Who is Clarissa?" she asked in a small voice.

"My wife," he replied. "The woman I love more than I love life itself. She is also the mother, teacher, and nursemaid for our very young son. As for me, I like nothing better than being home with my family, tending to the affairs of my ranch, looking after my horses and my other livestock. You see, Adele, I'm just an ordinary man, married to a woman I love. You should not be interested in me."

Adele was silent for a time. "I'm sorry, Toby," she said at last in a barely audible voice. "I'm truly sorry."

He patted her shoulder. "That's all right," he said. "Everybody makes mistakes, and there's no harm done. You have a good man in Louis. Marry him and live happily ever after, and be glad you have a husband who loves you as much as he does."

IX

The group of officials gathered in the commandant's office of the New Orleans army garrison passed Kung Lee's precious notebook from one to the other. The New Orleans police commissioner, who had also been called in, shook his head, and the director of immigration of Louisiana registered astonishment.

"Major Holt, the detailed information on Kung Lee's illegal immigration network will send him to prison for the rest of his life," the commandant said. "And I'm sure that the data on his dissemination of opium will move the United States Congress to pass laws making the transportation illegal."

"What's more," the police commissioner said, "we have enough evidence about the illegal activities of Karl Kellerman and Robin Kayross to put them behind bars for a good long time—assuming they ever show up here again."

"As in the past, Major Holt," the army commandant said, "you've done the American people great service at considerable risk to your own life."

"When this information is made public," the director of immigration added, "you'll get the recognition you well deserve."

Toby shook his head. "If you please, gentlemen," he said emphatically, "I want no publicity in this matter. I'd appreciate it if not one word appears in print regarding what I've done."

"Aren't you carrying modesty a bit far?" the police commissioner asked.

"This has nothing to do with modesty," Toby replied. "General Blake will want nothing made public until Kung Lee returns to the United States and is placed under arrest. If he's warned, we'll be giving him another opportunity to evade the law."

Each of the officials promptly swore that he would regard the news as confidential.

"I hope, Mr. Holt," the commissioner said, "that you'll stay in New Orleans long enough for us to take you out to supper."

"Thank you," Toby replied, "but I don't think I'll be able to. I have some personal business to attend to, and then I'm going to head back to the West. I promised my wife I'd return home as soon as possible." He deliberately refrained from mentioning that he had made a deal with Domino and that he intended to abide by his end of the agreement. The officials would be shocked to learn that Toby would be going to see the notorious gang leader later that very night. But he had found Kung Lee only with

Domino's help, and now he was obligated to return the favor.

The meeting broke up, and Toby went back to his hotel. Before he had met with the authorities at the army garrison, he had told Edward and Jim about his experiences aboard the *Neptune*, and the Englishman realized that the man who had done him such harm was now out of his reach, on the high seas sailing to the Orient.

"I guess he's in your capable hands now, Toby," Edward said. "Your hands and the government's. But I pity poor Wallace Dugald. When I tell him Kellerman got away from him, he's going to go into a raging fit."

Now at the hotel, Toby found Edward and Tommie awaiting him in great excitement. "We've just had a further telegram from Tommie's father," Edward told him. "He'll arrive in New Orleans day after tomorrow. We've scheduled the wedding for noon that day, and we hope that you'll attend."

Toby knew that Clarissa would understand when he wired her that he had been delayed in his return home because he had agreed to go to Edward's wedding. Saying he would be delighted to attend, he wished the couple the best of everything in the world, and then he went on to supper with Jim, Millicent, and Jean-Pierre Gautier, whom he had not met previously and was eager to know.

Meanwhile, Tommie was totally calm about her upcoming wedding. "My wedding dress is sitting in my clothes closet waiting to be worn," she said, "and

Millicent, as my maid of honor, has her dress. Jim is
going to be your best man, so that leaves just one
thing still to be settled."

"What's that?" Edward asked.

"We'll have to see the minister tomorrow morning," she replied. "Don't you remember? He said he
wanted to have a talk with us on the day before the
wedding, and you invited him to the hotel."

"I haven't forgotten the appointment with the
minister," Edward told her, "but there's one other
thing that's very important."

Tommie stared at him anxiously.

"Fortunately," he said with a reassuring grin, "I
remembered it just in time this afternoon, which is
why I left you for a while. I went to a restaurant in
the French Quarter and made a supper reservation
for us for this evening."

She laughed in relief. "Now you're being silly,
but thank goodness that's all it is! I thought we'd
forgotten something really important."

Her fiancé joined in her laugh but made no
reply. If Tommie had been looking at him, she might
have realized that he was indeed talking about something important, but her thoughts were elsewhere,
and she dropped the subject. She went off to change
her clothes for the evening, and soon thereafter they
strolled from their hotel to the restaurant.

Edward had gone to great pains to make the
evening memorable. When they arrived at their table,
a lovely corsage of flowers awaited Tommie, and a

bottle of imported French champagne was cooling in a silver ice bucket.

Edward had ordered their meal in advance, and as always, his taste was impeccable. The fresh shrimp from the Gulf of Mexico were large and firm; their gumbo was light but not bland; and their main course, fried chicken, was cooked to perfection. Vegetables, roasted potatoes, and a salad of fresh, chilled greens were served with the chicken. When they were finished, Tommie sighed. "I don't think I could eat another thing," she said.

A few moments later, their waiter brought them a steaming deep dish pie, its crust a golden brown.

"A pie!" Tommie exclaimed. "I couldn't eat a bite!"

"This dessert was ordered for you," Edward told her. "Why don't you break the crust to let the steam out and taste a little of it? Then if you can't eat it, you can just leave it."

She glanced at him dubiously, broke the crust on the top of the dish with her fork, and then blinked in surprise. In the center of the dish, beneath the crust, rested a small velvet box.

Tommie stared at it uncomprehendingly. "This is very odd," she murmured.

"Why don't you try opening the box?" Edward suggested. "It shouldn't be too hot to handle."

She removed the royal blue box from the dish, opened it, and gasped. There, nestling in a bed of creamy satin, glistened a huge, square-cut emerald ring, its rich green hues sparkling and shimmering in the candlelight.

"Oh, Edward," she whispered.

"I've been remiss in giving you an engagement ring," he said. "I've had several jewelers looking, but I wasn't satisfied until they came up with exactly the right gem."

"I've never seen anything so beautiful," Tommie murmured. "It's far too good to wear every day."

Edward picked up the box, took the ring from it, and slipped it on the third finger of her left hand. "There," he said. "You'll take it off only once, so that your wedding ring will go under it. Aside from that, I hope you'll wear it every day, as long as you live."

"As long as I live," she assured him solemnly, and unmindful of the other patrons in the restaurant, she raised her face to his. Their kiss was a promise of lifelong love and fidelity.

Tommie was so deeply affected she seemed to have lost her voice. She sat for a long time holding her hand up to the candlelight, moving it closer, then farther, twisting and turning her fingers and admiring the emerald in every possible light and position. "Thanks to you, Edward," she whispered, "this is the happiest day of my life."

"This is just the beginning of our life together," he said, smiling. "Soon we'll have to decide where we're going to live and what enterprises I'm going to get involved in."

She pressed her hands to her temples. "I can't think straight right now," she told him. "My mind is whirling, and this emerald is so bright that it's dazzling me. Give me a little time, and then we can start talking about the future."

He agreed, and they kissed again, then sat back in their chairs and sedately sipped their coffee like a couple who had been married for years.

Neither of them knew it, but the whole scene had been observed closely by two hard-faced men sitting several tables away from them in the restaurant. The pair took special interest in the emerald and exchanged quick, knowing glances, although they said very little to each other. They hurried through their meal, then paid their bill, but nevertheless dawdled over coffee until Edward and Tommie were finished and rose from their table. Then the men departed, too, deliberately staying a half-block behind the happy couple.

Walking arm in arm, Edward and Tommie felt as though they were floating through the air. They took their time, sauntering along, looking up at the moon casting silvery beams through leafy trees that lined the street. They were passing through a neighborhood of large, private homes set back from the road, with high shrubs and iron fences protecting them from the public. It was quiet, and they were so wrapped up in each other that they failed to realize that they seemed to be the only pedestrians abroad at the moment.

Suddenly they were confronted by two men, both of them masked, the taller carrying a cocked pistol, which he pointed straight at Edward.

"If you'll do what you're told without making a fuss," he said, "nobody will get hurt. But if you disobey our instructions, we can't be responsible for your safety."

Edward looked into the muzzle of the pistol and smiled calmly. "What is it you want us to do?" he asked.

"The girl is to stand still right where she is," the robber directed. "As for you, mister, you can back off about fifty feet or so." He turned to his companion. "Go with him and make sure he does what he's told."

Edward smiled at Tommie reassuringly. "Don't you worry, honey," he said, "everything is going to be all right." Making no objections, he accompanied the smaller of the pair until they had moved about fifty feet down the street. He noted that unlike his companion, this robber was armed only with a knife.

They halted, and the man reached out, helping himself to Edward's pistol. Then the man rejoined his companion, who stood near Tommie.

"And as for you, ma'am," the taller of the pair said to her, "you're too young and too pretty to be burdened through life carrying that green stone on your finger, so I'll just take it right now."

Having removed Edward from the immediate scene and relieved him of his pistol, the robbers conveniently forgot his existence for the moment. But Edward was not lacking in resources. At no time did he leave his quarters without carrying ample means of self-protection, and that evening was no exception. He had replaced the weapons that were taken from him when he was abducted, and now as he shook his arm, the derringer he always carried concealed in a special harness up his sleeve fell into his hand. As his fingers closed over the trigger, he felt much more confident.

Tommie was staring in disbelief at the robber. "You would take my new engagement ring from me? I think not, mister! There's only one way you'll get it, and that's over my dead body!"

"Don't make any mistakes about us, lady," the man told her, his eyes narrowing. "We'll get that ring any way that we have to, and if it's necessary to kill you, that's what we're going to do!"

Edward pulled the trigger, and his aim was true. The bullet penetrated the robber's jugular vein, and he crumpled to the ground, dying instantly. Edward continued to brandish his pistol.

"I have another shot left," he called. "Take my pistol from the rogue, Tommie! And while you're at it, help yourself to his knife, too!"

She complied with his instructions, and then he said, "Now move toward me. No rush, one step at a time. That's it."

Little by little she moved toward safety.

"Now then, you scum," he called. "Unless you want to join your friend in a pool of your own blood, I'd advise you to leave and to put as much distance as possible between yourself and us. This is a special evening in my life, so I'm in a particularly benevolent mood. I'll let you off free, provided you make yourself scarce in an awful hurry."

The robber took off, running down the street and disappearing around a corner in record time.

"I'm afraid," Edward said, sliding an arm around Tommie's shoulders, "that we're going to be slightly delayed in getting back to our hotel. We'll have to stop in at the nearest police headquarters and report the unfortunate death of an extremely luckless robber."

She moved closer to him and shuddered. "I was frightened half to death. I was afraid he was going to kill both of us in order to get my engagement ring."

Edward kissed her earlobe as they started off down the street, walking far more rapidly than they had before the incident. "I told you not to be worried, and I meant it," he said. "I waited far too long to get you exactly the right ring, and I was damned if you were going to lose it to a pair of cheap crooks. When you agreed to marry me, I accepted permanent responsibility for your safety and welfare, and I don't intend to let you down, now or ever."

They were still holding each other tightly when they entered the police station moments later to report the incident.

As Toby Holt went down the walk leading to the entranceway of the large house that was surrounded by trees and bushes, two burly men, both of them carrying rifles, appeared out of the dark. One of the men raised a kerosene lantern and held it so it cast light on Toby's face. "It's Holt, all right," he said. "I'd know him anywhere."

"I reckon we'd better let him in, then," the second guard said. "You know how the boss gets when his orders aren't obeyed."

Instead of replying, the first man bowed slightly to Toby and then led the way into the house. "We'll let the boss know that you're here," he said when they were in the hallway, and the two men both promptly disappeared.

Toby was alone for only a few moments. Martha soon appeared in the doorway, her red hair cascading down her shoulders, her voluptuous figure encased in a skin-tight dress that left little to the imagination. She teetered slightly on stiltlike heels, but her hip-swaying walk was nevertheless seductive. She looked at Toby and didn't seem at all surprised that he was on the property.

"Well, hello," she said, a strong hint of intimacy in her warm, welcoming smile.

"Hello, Martha," Toby replied calmly, and the thought occurred to him that the woman apparently had a highly privileged place in the household.

"The last that I heard," she said, "you were going off on a dangerous mission—for us as well as for yourself."

"I've gone, I've attended to several matters, and now I'm back," he said.

"Domino never takes long to listen to reports, especially at this time of night," Martha said, and putting her hands on her hips, she cocked her head to one side. "Perhaps you and I might have a drink together after you're through talking with him. I have the run of the place here, and I have access to some wonderful liquors and rare wines."

"Thank you for asking me," he said politely. "However, I'm not very keen on wines and liquor."

A deep, resonant chuckle sounded farther down the hall. "No doubt Mr. Holt wants to consume nothing that would adversely affect his miraculous prowess," Domino said, appearing from behind some plants. There was no telling how long he had been in the hallway. "Run along now, Martha," he said patiently. "If Mr. Holt is interested, you may see him later."

Annoyed by his tone, Martha flounced off.

Domino approached a large wicker settee. "Once I learned you were here, I took the liberty of ordering us a light supper, Mr. Holt. I hope you don't mind."

"Not at all," Toby replied politely, figuring he had a good appetite and could always eat another meal. "That's very kind of you."

"I heard that you returned unexpectedly to New Orleans this morning on board a fishing barge and that you then held a conference with a number of officials at the office of the army garrison commandant. Obviously you had something of a rough experience, and equally obviously you had some important news to impart."

"Yes, I did," Toby said, and nodded.

"I hope you'll see fit to relate your experience to me."

"Naturally," Toby replied. "It was only through you that I learned of Kung Lee's whereabouts, and I struck a bargain with you. I fully intend to keep my word."

"It's kind of you to honor our agreement, Mr. Holt," Domino said. "After all, we two operate on opposite sides of the law, and it would be easy enough for you to find a simple excuse for breaking your word to me."

"I learned my approach to life from my father, Domino," Toby said. "I never give my word lightly. I always mean it, and I've never yet broken it. I'm in your debt—and I intend to pay off that debt right now. What's more, I hope to work closely with you until both of us accomplish our ends in this nasty business that we're engaged in."

Struck by his sincerity, Domino extended his hand. Toby shook hands with him without the slightest hesitation, and they sealed an unspoken agreement. They had formed a strange partnership that would last until the world was rid of both Kung Lee and Karl Kellerman.

Toby slowly told the story of his experience on board the freighter, *Neptune*, omitting no details. He hurriedly related his subsequent encounter with the Raymond brothers and Adele because that meeting had no real bearing on his visit to Domino.

When he was finished, the gang leader said, "One moment. I want to be sure I have the facts

straight. You say that Kellerman is on board the
freighter and is bound for the Orient at this moment?"

"Correct," Toby said. "From what I learned on
board the ship, he and Kung are traveling to Canton
and Hong Kong in order to pick up a shipload of
illegal Chinese immigrants and as much opium as
they can carry."

"I don't believe in kidnapping or in killing people with drugs," Domino said. "Kellerman is going
to return from the Orient on board the *Neptune*?"

"To the best of my knowledge, he is," Toby
replied. "He has no reason to stay in China, and I
gather that his interests are in this country."

"I appoint myself as chairman of a reception
committee to greet him when he returns," Domino
said, "and no matter in what port he may land, I'll be
notified, and I'll act accordingly. I thank you, far
more than I can ever tell you, for this information."

"Kung Lee, of course, will be nabbed by government authorities the moment he sets foot back in
America," Toby said. "As for Kellerman, the New
Orleans authorities are on the lookout for him, too,
but if you get to him first, you can probably dispose
of him without any help. However, in the event that
you need some assistance, don't hesitate to call on
me. He appears to be an expert at slipping away
once you believe you have him cornered. I'll write
out my address for you at my ranch in Oregon, and
you can always reach me there."

"You're going home soon?"

"Yes, I'm leaving the day after tomorrow, as

soon as I've attended the wedding of a good friend. I'm going by train all the way, first from here to St. Louis and then to Oregon. I'm anxious to rejoin my wife as soon as I can."

Domino smiled broadly. "Do I gather that you have no intention of spending any time with Martha before you head home?"

"I'm grateful for her offers of hospitality," Toby said carefully, "but I'm afraid I won't be able to avail myself of them. I'm one of those strange critters, a one-woman man who happens to be very much in love with his wife."

Domino looked at him curiously. "I've never known a man who would willingly reject the charms of a woman as attractive as Martha," he said. "Now that we've finished our business, I hope you'd have no objection if I invited her to join us for a bite of supper."

Toby shrugged. "By all means, invite her," he said.

Domino tugged at a bell rope and then exchanged some words in private with the man who answered his summons.

A short time later, when he and Toby adjourned to the dining room, they found Martha awaiting them. She had applied fresh makeup to her lovely face, and she looked even more attractive than before.

She devoted her full attention to Toby as they ate, and Domino, casting himself in the role of an observer, sat back in his chair and watched.

Toby seemed to be completely at ease as he

dealt with Martha, answering her questions politely. He suffered her blatant attempts to flirt with him without feeling undue strain, and he initiated as well as responded to her conversation. When the meal ended, he said good-bye to her, then shook hands with Domino and gave the gang leader the address of his ranch in Oregon. He appeared completely unruffled as he took his leave.

"That Toby Holt," Martha said slowly, "is the most incredible man I've ever met."

"Certainly he's the first man I've ever encountered," Domino said, "who failed to respond to you. Holt isn't human—he's superhuman!"

"You've made a mistake," Martha said. "Toby was very much aware of me, as conscious as any man I've ever known."

Domino's interest was piqued. "Really?"

"Absolutely," she replied. "He was so much aware of me, in fact, that he deliberately erected a wall between us, and he hid on his side of it. I had the definite feeling that if he had allowed even a section of his wall to crumble or to fall, he'd have given in to his impulses and would have totally forgotten his principles."

Grinning broadly, Domino murmured, "That's fascinating," and he was silent for a long time, lost in thought.

"I believe I can analyze accurately the way any man responds to me," Martha said. "Toby Holt uses great self-control—greater control than I've ever seen.

That's because he's afraid we'll have an explosive relationship if he doesn't protect himself."

"Do you suppose you can break through that wall of reserve that he's erected?"

"I honestly don't know," Martha said candidly. "I know my own strengths, and I believe I'm capable of breaking down the resistance of most men, but Toby Holt isn't like anyone else I've ever met. I have no idea which of us would win a contest of wills, but I'd love to find out."

"So would I," Domino said, and laughed again.

"Are you planning to set him up?" she asked innocently.

The gang leader smiled slyly. "Holt has done me the greatest of favors, and I'd never harm him or double-cross him in any way. He was loyal to me at the risk of his life, and it's impossible to buy that kind of loyalty. I want to reward him. However, in so doing, I may be able to have a little fun at the same time."

"I hope that I'll be involved in your attempts to 'reward' him, as you call it."

"You shall be, my dear Martha," he replied emphatically. "You most assuredly shall be."

Tommie and Edward received the minister who would marry them the following day and were closeted with him for a long time in Edward's suite. Even Robin Hood, the little monkey who had made himself the couple's inseparable companion, seemed to sense that this was a solemn occasion, and he sat quietly, perched on Edward's shoulder throughout the interview.

"Yours will be no ordinary marriage," Reverend Giddings told Tommie and Edward. "You've already got financial security, and that's a great blessing. On the other hand, you'll find that your separate backgrounds require a greater degree of tolerance and understanding than is required of most newlyweds. You grew up in the genteel Old World surroundings of England, Edward, while you, Tommie, were born and raised on the rivers of the American frontier. That makes quite a difference, and you're going to need a great deal of patience and understanding to compensate for the differences."

"You'll be interested to learn, Reverend Giddings, that I'm intending to apply for American citizenship in the immediate future," Edward said. "I'm also intending to go into the coastal trade. Tommie already knows ships, of course, and I'm convinced there's a great future in it."

Tommie nodded in agreement.

"I wish that every couple I counsel prior to their marriage had prospects equal to yours," the minister said, sighing. "You truly have everything in your favor."

After the meeting came to an end, Tommie and Edward escorted the minister through the hotel lobby, then stood with him for several moments in the entrance to the hotel as they concluded their conversation. They were interrupted when an elegant-looking carriage pulled to a halt in the street in front of the hotel. The coach was pulled by a pair of matching bays, a driver in livery sat on the box, and in the backseat was a gray-haired woman, expensively gowned. Next to her was a little girl, apparently her grandchild.

The lady in the carriage bowed. "Good morning, Reverend Giddings," she called.

The minister brightened. "Ah, good morning, Mrs. Soames." He proceeded to present Tommie and Edward to the woman.

All of them were startled when Robin Hood jumped to the ground, bounded forward, and made a desperate leap that landed him in the carriage.

"Look, Grandma!" The little girl was ecstatic. "Bella has found a new friend!"

The adults were surprised to see a little monkey, smaller than Robin Hood, wearing an ankle-length dress. The creature was seated on the cushioned seat beside the child and was exchanging rapid-fire chatter with Robin Hood.

"Bella found a gentleman friend!" the little girl announced.

"Bella," Tommie said formally, "permit me to present Mr. Robin Hood."

The two monkeys, paying no attention to their human companions, chattered excitedly.

"Can we keep him, Grandma? Please! Can we?" The little girl was so anxious she was on the point of tears.

Mrs. Soames was mildly shocked. "How can you

ask such a thing, Dorothy?" she demanded. "This monkey belongs to Mr. Blackstone."

Edward exchanged a long, significant look with Tommie, and they communicated silently. "If you permit me, Mrs. Soames," Edward said, "my fiancée and I would very much like to make a gift of Robin Hood to Dorothy."

The little girl's joy was unbounded. "Did you hear that, Bella? Did you hear it, Robin? We're going to be together for always! Thank you, ma'am! Thank you, sir!"

"This is too much," her grandmother said firmly. "I simply can't permit—"

"Really, Mrs. Soames," Tommie interjected. "We insist. We want to share our own happiness, and we're sure that Robin Hood will be more than happy with your granddaughter."

"I'll take good care of him," the little girl said earnestly. "I promise!"

Her grandmother wavered. "Well . . ."

"If you please, Mrs. Soames," Edward said gravely. "My fiancée and I will regard your approval as one of the better wedding presents that we've received."

"I cannot refuse a plea of that kind, sir," she said, inclining her head to him. "Dorothy, you and Bella have a new companion. You may keep Robin Hood."

The little girl squealed, the two monkeys chattered more loudly, and the lady ordered her driver to proceed.

"That was a wonderfully kind gesture," Reverend Giddings said as they watched the carriage move off down the street. "You can be sure that your little pet will get excellent care. Mrs. Soames is one of the most upstanding of my parishioners."

"We wouldn't have agreed to part with Robin," Tommie said, "unless we felt certain that he'd have a good home."

"I'm sure," Edward said, "that he's going to be happy living with a little girl who makes an incessant fuss over him and with a fellow monkey who speaks his own language. You may have noticed he was so engrossed that he didn't even look up when they drove off."

Tommie joined in Edward's happy laugh. Looking at them, Reverend Giddings again marveled at how right they were for each other. This, he reflected, was truly a marriage that had been made in heaven.

"Come on, Kale," Cindy Holt urged exuberantly. "Put on your hat, your coat, and your biggest victory smile. Willie Rowe has invited us to get the election results at the newspaper office, where they'll come in first."

Kale Martin demurred. "I don't want to leave Rob just sitting here," she said, "and I haven't made arrangements for anybody to spend the evening watching over little Cathy."

Cindy appealed to her friend's husband. "You can talk her into it, Rob," she said.

Rob smiled at his wife. "Cindy is right, honey,"

he said. "This is a big day for you, and a big day for every woman in Oregon. You'll be in the history books as the first woman to be elected as a trustee of the state college, the first woman to hold a statewide position in Oregon!"

"*If* I'm elected," Kale replied.

"I'm not much of a gambler," Cindy said, "but I'm willing to bet you any amount you'd like to wager that you're going to come in far ahead of Frank Colwyn. After the articles that Willie Rowe wrote exposing him as a crook, he couldn't be elected to dogcatcher or garbage collector in this state. You're an absolute cinch to win!"

"Cindy may have a tendency to paint larger-than-life portraits, but in this instance, she happens to be right, honey," Rob said. "As I've been telling you day after day, I've made it my business to find out how people are voting, and I'm predicting a landslide for you. You're going to win by the widest margin of any officeholder in the state."

"If that's true," Kale said uncertainly, "I'd love to go with Cindy."

"Then get out of here," Rob said, grinning. "Cathy is sleeping, and I'm perfectly capable of looking after her in the event that she wakes up. You deserve to hear the news first, so get along with you and good luck."

Rob almost pushed his wife out the door. Kale, laughing now, allowed herself to be persuaded and, accompanied by Cindy, went off to the newspaper office.

Several large blackboards had been set up in the newsroom and were manned by reporters who changed figures on them as a steady flow of telegrams came in from polling places all over Oregon. Willie Rowe took Kale and Cindy to the board where he himself was chalking up figures. "This," he said, "is the central board. You can tell at a glance how you're doing. As a matter of fact, you're already far ahead of Colwyn. Let's see. You have over one thousand votes to less than two hundred for him."

Cindy cheered, but Kale was embarrassed. "How could it possibly be such a large majority?" she asked. "There must be a mistake."

"There's no mistake," the reporter told her. "People don't want to vote for a crook, and you're the honest alternative."

"Then I have you and Cindy to thank in the event that I'm elected," she replied.

Rowe shook his head. "You have your own efforts to thank. Pure and simple," he said. "The time is right for women to take an active role in politics and to run for public office, and you were smart enough to sense that fact and to act accordingly. You're setting a precedent—not only here, but for women all over the West, and that's why I invited you to watch the returns here. I want to get a victory statement from you that will reflect your feelings on the significance of today's vote, not only in Oregon, but elsewhere."

Kale and Cindy settled down to watch the figures change on the blackboards. Willie provided them with cups of coffee, and as time went on they were fascinated to see the totals mount.

They were particularly impressed by the margin of victory in Kale's favor; at no time was her election in doubt. The state's voters, disgusted with the revelations of Frank Colwyn's wrongdoing, turned away from him in vast numbers, and the vote in Kale's favor was overwhelming. Thus she was not only the first woman ever elected to a statewide post in Oregon, but she was also elected by the greatest majority of any candidate who had ever run for a similar office.

Rowe asked her to write out a victory statement for publication the following morning, and this Kale did. She not only thanked the voters for their confidence in her and for giving her the opportunity to serve them, but she also called attention to the fact that voters in Wyoming and Utah, as well as in Oregon, had already established records by electing women to public office. Kale made the bold prediction that the day would come when women would not only run for such offices as governor, U.S. senator, and member of the U.S. House of Representatives, but actually would be elected to such offices. This hitherto had been a dream that seemed impossible to fulfill.

Returning home, Kale was greeted at the door by a smiling Rob. "Well?" he demanded.

She handed him a slip of paper on which she had written the election returns.

Rob glanced at the returns, then enveloped his

wife in a hug and kissed her tenderly. "You did it, honey!" he exulted. "I'm so glad for you!"

"I'm glad for us," she said, her arms still entwined around his neck. "I'm especially glad for you."

"I wasn't running for office," he replied, somewhat mystified. "The voters went to the polls and cast their ballots for you. The fact that you're married to me was irrelevant. They were expressing confidence in your ability to represent them."

"I know all that," Kale replied, "but there was far more at stake than my election to the board. My past was printed out for everyone to see, and a lot of decent people regarded me as a notorious, fallen woman."

"Which you are not," her husband told her emphatically.

"But which I very definitely was," she replied. "That's all behind me now. It's one of the wonderful things about being an American. As long as one is sincere in one's beliefs and approach, the public will always accept repentance. I'm no longer a pariah. I'm accepted now as a citizen in good standing, and I've been given a position of trust."

She looked at Rob with shining eyes. "I intend to live up to that trust," she said. "I'll be the best trustee on the college board!"

"Just as you're already the best wife and the best mother in the entire Pacific Northwest," he replied.

She threw her arms around him and hugged him again. "This is the happiest day of my life," she said. "Thanks to you and our neighbors and everybody else in the state, I've been rejuvenated, and I'm a new woman!"

It was late when Cindy Holt rode up to the barn behind her brother's ranch house, where she was staying while her mother and stepfather were off again visiting the East, meeting with President Grant. Removing her horse's saddle, Cindy then went to the house itself. She was glad to find her sister-in-law, Clarissa, still awake, and as she put her rifle in the rack that Toby had built for that purpose in the kitchen, Cindy related the election figures.

"I'm so glad for Kale," Clarissa said, "and I'm sure Toby will be, too. In the morning I'll have to send him a telegram in New Orleans and tell him the results before he goes off to Edward's wedding. He'll be anxious to send Kale a wire of congratulations." Cindy nodded but said very little as she wandered aimlessly around in the kitchen.

Her sister-in-law thought she was unusually restless but kept her opinion to herself. "Would you like a cup of hot chocolate, Cindy?"

"Don't bother on my account."

"I won't, but I was making some for myself, and it's just as easy to make two cups as one."

"In that case, I guess I will. Thanks very much." She went to the cupboard and brought out two cups and two saucers, which she gave to her sister-in-law.

While Clarissa poured the hot chocolate, Cindy seated herself at the kitchen table and sighed deeply.

Clarissa stared at her. "Whatever is wrong with you, Cindy?" she asked. "I would have thought you'd be as delighted as I am that Kale won the election."

"Oh, I am," the girl replied. "I couldn't be happier about it."

"But something is wrong," her sister-in-law said.

Cindy stared down at the steaming cup that Clarissa placed in front of her. "Now that you mention it," she said, "I guess there is something wrong."

"If you care to tell me about it, I'll be glad to listen."

"I've been counting the months and weeks and even the days," Cindy said, "until Hank is graduated from the military academy and is awarded his commission as a lieutenant. Until now, I've wanted nothing more than to be his wife, and I can't tell you how much I've been dreaming about the day when we'll be married."

"I know how eager you and Hank have been to be married," Clarissa said, "and I can't blame either of you. It wasn't so awfully long ago, you know, that Toby and I were engaged, and although we got married shortly after that, it felt like we had to wait ages."

"I've always been ambitious, too ambitious for my own good, I suppose," Cindy said, "but that's been one of the penalties of being Whip Holt's daughter. I've always had daydreams about becoming one of the first women lawyers or doctors—or whatever—in America. But once I marry Hank and become Mrs. Henry Blake, pursuing a career of my

own will be out of the question. I realize that one
career—Hank's—in the family will be enough. Oh, I
know enough about the army and army living to be a
first-rate officer's wife, and I'm sure I can be a great
help to Hank in furthering his career—"

"There's no question of that," Clarissa said.

"But," Cindy continued in a voice of doom, "I'm
not sure that will be enough for me. I want to do
what Kale has done, make a mark for myself as a
woman, as a person who has something to offer her
country and her community."

"Has Hank indicated in any way that you have
to be a one-career family?" Clarissa asked.

"Not yet, but he will," Cindy replied gloomily.
"He's a man, and all men expect their wives to stay
at home and raise a family and be nurturing to them."

"Then you don't know men very well," Clarissa
replied, "at least not men like Hank and your brother
Toby." Clarissa put her hands on the younger woman's
shoulders. "Now listen to me," she declared forcibly,
"and hear every word that I say. Like Kale, you are a
woman whose inner needs demand that she find
fulfillment through a career. I happen to be completely fulfilled as a wife and a mother. I admire
Kale, and I respect her for what she's doing, just as
I'm elated over her victory, but I don't envy her, and
I have no desire to change places with her. I'd be
unhappy if I were elected to a post as trustee for the
college, and consequently I'd do a miserable job. I
gain my greatest satisfaction in life," Clarissa went
on, "by doing the very best I can as a wife and as a

mother, and I assure you that doing those jobs is not easy."

Cindy smiled appreciatively.

"My husband knows," Clarissa continued, "that I'm completely devoted to him and to our child, but I can promise you that if I wished to be elected to the United States House of Representatives, he wouldn't love me any less than he does or think I had let him down. He'd give me his full support in whatever I needed to do to fulfill myself as a person, as a woman, as a wife."

"I think I'm beginning to see what you mean," Cindy said.

"Hank will be the same way," Clarissa told her. "Oh, when you're first married, you'll float on a cloud, and nothing will seem important but each other. But then, little by little, the realities of life will begin to seep in, and you'll both realize that you need more to be fulfilled. You and Hank are a new generation, Cindy, and your ways will be different from Toby's and mine. You're both going to need careers that fulfill you, and only in that way will your marriage have stability and peace."

"I can see," Cindy said, "that Hank and I will be carrying a heavy responsibility."

"So you shall," her sister-in-law replied, "but your greatest responsibility will be to yourself. Will you be satisfied—will you find contentment—with life as a wife and as a mother? If you will, you'll make your husband happy, and he'll be equally contented, but if you're bored and restless, he'll become bored and restless, and your marriage will be in trouble. It's up to you. You must not only bolster him in his struggle to make his own career, but he'll have to bolster you as you find just what it is you want for yourself in order to create a good marriage. Wives— women who are just plain, ordinary housewives— have been taken for granted since time immemorial. Well, I say that every last one of us deserves a medal, and I'm sure that a great many husbands will agree. But ambitious women like you and Kale deserve medals, too, and from what I know of Hank, he'll certainly agree." She couldn't help laughing.

The last of Cindy's gloom lifted, and she laughed, too. "You make it all sound so simple, Clarissa," she said.

The older woman shook her head. "Simple, you say! Nothing is simple. It will take work, understanding, patience on both your parts. Just be glad you've got someone to spend your whole life with as loving and as considerate as Hank Blake!"

"Oh, I am. I am!" Cindy said fervently. "That's all that really matters in the whole world."

The corps of cadets of the United States Military Academy at West Point finished their noon dinner in the mess hall and marched off to various afternoon assignments. Some went to classes, while others engaged in intramural athletics. Still others were going to their rooms to study.

Cadet Henry Blake was a member of the group that was bound for their dormitory rooms. He had attended his last class for the day, and since he was a member of several varsity teams, he took no part in intramural sports. He had reading to do, his usual heavy load of reading, which was necessary if he was going to maintain his position as class leader in academic activities as well as in military activities and sports.

A short time after he was at his desk, absorbed in a history textbook, there was a knock on the door. Hank opened it, and he was handed an envelope by a regular army corporal.

Hank tore open the envelope, and his heart sank as he read the message inside. He was wanted immediately at the home of Brigadier General Cavanaugh, the commandant of the corps of cadets. Marcus Aurelius Cavanaugh was a martinet, a taskmaster without equal, and every cadet at the academy was afraid of him. An Indian fighter and scout, he had established an enduring reputation for himself as an infantry leader in the Army of the West during the Civil War, and since that time, he had been making the lives of one class after another of West Pointers miserable.

Leaving his books on the desk, Hank hurriedly left the dormitory and quickly crossed the campus to the commandant's home. He had no idea how he had erred or what he had done wrong, but he would learn all too soon, and he prepared himself for severe punishment. General Cavanaugh was known for treating student leaders far more severely than the academy dullards.

Arriving at the Cavanaugh house, Hank tugged the wrinkles out of his tunic, tucked his garrison cap under his left arm, and standing erect, rang the bell.

A sergeant answered the summons and looked Hank up and down slowly. "You're expected, Mr. Blake," he said quietly. To Hank, that statement had an ominous sound. He expected the general to receive him in the study, which was where infractions or problems were usually dealt with, but the sergeant led him instead to the living room.

As Hank entered the room, a woman, with her thick, dark hair piled high on her head, her violet eyes and trim figure giving her the appearance of someone far younger than her middle years, rose to her feet. At her shoulder stood a distinguished, grayhaired man in uniform who wore the twin stars of a major general on his shoulders.

His heart beating wildly, Hank stood stiffly at attention and saluted. "Cadet Blake at report, sir," he said crisply.

Major General Leland Blake chuckled quietly as he said, "At ease, Blake."

Hank sprang forward and eagerly embraced his stepmother. Until this moment, he had not allowed himself to dwell on how much he missed her.

Eulalia Holt Blake sighed happily. "Every time I see you, Hank," she murmured, "you seem inches taller and pounds heavier. It's remarkable."

Lee extended his hand. "How are you, son?"

"I'm great," Hank replied exuberantly. "I don't think I've ever been better than I am at this moment.

If only Cindy were here with you, my happiness would be absolutely complete."

"Fortunately, for the discipline of the corps," Lee replied, "we had to leave Cindy behind in Oregon. I was called East to a meeting with President Grant, which, as it turned out, was of an informal nature regarding troop dispositions in some of the middle-western states. Now we're on our way back home, but before we head West, we intend to spend the rest of the afternoon and the evening with you."

Hank's face fell. "I'm not sure I can get leave," he said, "even for a few hours."

"You've already been granted leave until breakfast time tomorrow morning," his father said. "General Cavanaugh told me that your record is sufficiently good that you'll lose nothing by being excused for a few hours."

Hank's mind was in a whirl. "I—I see."

"You're coming back to the hotel with us right now," Eulalia said. "And I don't want to hear a word from you about how tough General Cavanaugh is. In my opinion, he's perfectly darling."

Hank had no desire to dispute the point with her or to argue about anything else. The unexpected appearance of his parents made him deliriously happy, and he knew that after their brief visit, he would be much better able to cope with the rigors of academy life. He was learning it was no idle boast that one entered the academy as a boy, and four years later, emerged as a man.

X

Edward Blackstone nervously paced the confines of the living room of the hotel suite. He marched the length of the chamber, wheeled as though on parade, then made his way back to the other end past the oversized couch and the two easy chairs with a lamp between them. When he reached the far wall, he turned without pausing and retraced his steps.

Toby Holt and Edward's cousin, Jim Randall, made no attempt to stop him, but after the one-man parade had gone on for the better part of thirty minutes, Toby decided the time had come to call a halt. "How soon do we leave for the church, Jim?" he asked.

Jim, whose wife Pamela had arrived the day before and was helping Tommie dress, took his time removing his watch from his fob pocket and examining it. "The carriage I ordered will be here in about a quarter of an hour," he said.

"That's plenty of time to relax." Toby's voice became abrupt. "Sit down, Edward!" he commanded.

"I can't," Edward replied. "I'm too nervous."

"Then help yourself to a drink," Jim told him, "or if your hands are shaking too badly, I'll pour it for you."

"No, thank you," Edward replied. "The mere thought of taking as much as a small swallow of liquor makes me ill."

"I suppose we could kill him in cold blood, Jim," Toby said, "but I believe there's a law in Louisiana that prohibits the extinction of bridegrooms one hour prior to their marriage."

"Unfortunately," Jim replied, "that's shortsighted of the lawmakers. My wife is going to be very disappointed in Edward. Pamela has a mental picture of him as being masterful, calm, and always in control of himself and of every situation. I'd hate to let her be disillusioned by seeing him behaving like a gibbering idiot."

Edward halted his march abruptly. "I have not lost control," he said, "and I'm very calm."

"Well, you've succeeded in making us jittery," Toby said. "I don't mind telling you I'm glad I'm leaving by train for home shortly after the wedding. I've been separated from my wife long enough, without extending the time by indulging myself."

Jim nodded understandingly and then turned to his cousin. "Did you hear that, Edward?" he demanded. "Think of the freedom you're losing by voluntarily giving up your bachelor's existence!"

Edward's mental fog wasn't as great as his companions believed. "I don't see either of you giving up married life for the joys of bachelorhood," he said.

They laughed, and Toby pulled out his pocket watch. "It's time to be on our way," he said. "I see you have his ring, Jim. Be sure you don't forget the flower for his lapel. Let's go, Edward. Your misery will soon be ended."

"Those whom God hath joined together let no man put asunder," Reverend Giddings intoned. "Forasmuch as Thomasina and Edward have consented together in holy wedlock, and have witnessed the same before God and his company, and thereto have given and pledged their troth, each to the other, and have declared the same by giving and receiving a ring, and by joining hands, I pronounce that they are man and wife. In the name of the Father, and of the Son, and of the Holy Ghost. Amen."

Edward and Tommie, blissfully unaware of the presence of anyone else, embraced and kissed. Reverend Giddings and Captain Harding grinned at each other, and then the white-haired ship's master kissed his daughter and shook the hand of his son-in-law. It was Millicent's turn next, followed by Jim, and after him came Toby and Jean-Pierre escorting Pamela. The entire wedding party adjourned to waiting carriages, the one carrying the bride and groom decorated with long streamers and with tin cans that rattled on the cobblestones. They returned to Edward's hotel suite, where imported champagne and caviar awaited them, along with huge Gulf shrimp and other delicacies.

The bride and groom were inseparable and stood with an arm around each other's waist as they chattered with relatives and friends. Both were supremely happy. In fact, Toby, looking at them, couldn't help commenting to Pamela and Jim Randall, "I've never seen a bride who looked that radiant."

By now Pamela had had a chance to offer her congratulations to Millicent on her own upcoming wedding. "Jim and I," she said to the other woman, "are happier for you than you can possibly imagine. I wouldn't have missed Edward's wedding for the world, and Jim and I have no intention of missing yours. We're delighted that you set the date for next week."

"Where are you and Jean-Pierre planning to live?" Toby asked.

Millicent smiled broadly. "Jean-Pierre has bought me a new house, or, rather, it's an old house in the French district about two or three blocks from his parents' mansion."

"But it's much smaller and quite modest," Jean-Pierre said hastily. "Millicent and I don't go in much for show."

Toby nodded approvingly and thought that Jean-Pierre was proving to be an excellent stabilizing influence on Millicent. She had grown infinitely calmer since she had been associating with him, and her reckless conduct now belonged to her past. She was once again a modest, unassuming young lady.

There was a subtle difference in her, however.

She had come alive during the preceding months, and her experiences had caused her to develop into a far more well-rounded human being. It was strange, Toby thought, but she had become far more attractive as a woman, too. He would have to ask Clarissa about the phenomenon when he rejoined her. Millicent was not only better looking but was far more confident, far better able to deal with people whom she met.

"I'm afraid I won't be able to stay here until your wedding, but you know that Clarissa and I will be with you in spirit and that we wish you everything good for that day and for the rest of your lives."

They thanked him, then drifted on. Now it was Toby's pleasant duty to offer his own toast to the new bride and groom, Jim Randall having already made his toast. Then Captain Harding drew Toby aside for a private talk.

"My daughter and my new son-in-law have asked me to help them set up a new shipping company in Portland. I'd like your opinion of the idea."

"It's quite feasible," Toby replied. "The mouth of the Columbia River is broad enough and deep enough, as you undoubtedly know, to accommodate oceangoing ships, including freighters that are not only the biggest made but are likely to be the biggest for many years to come. In fact, one of my closest friends is in the business, and I am sure he would underscore the opportunities."

"I'm aware of the physical potentials," Captain

Harding replied, "but I'm wondering about the financial potential."

"I've watched Oregon grow from a wilderness country when I was a small boy into a prosperous, settled, and mature land. I think her financial potential is virtually unlimited. Coastal trade in the Pacific is already extensive and continues to grow rapidly. California has been expanding since the Gold Rush of forty-nine, and not only are towns like Sacramento growing, but new communities, like Los Angeles in the southern part of the state, are mushrooming. The same is true of Seattle, in Washington Territory to our north. Then there's the international trade to be considered. Not four years have passed since Secretary of State Seward bought the Alaska Territory, but the area is already showing signs of promise, and I think there's going to be a considerable trade between the Orient and Alaska. Our trade with Hawaii is also growing, and our business with China and the Spice Islands and India in the Far East is booming, too."

"You're very encouraging, Mr. Holt," Captain Harding said.

Toby smiled. "For whatever my opinion may be worth," he said, "I don't think that Tommie and Edward could have chosen a more promising line of work. I know Edward is already a successful businessman and has money of his own, but I'll gladly invest in their company if they let me, and I can promise them that at least a dozen people whom I know will invest as well."

"It's good to know that my daughter's future is assured," Captain Harding said.

Toby's smile broadened, and he spoke with great sincerity. "Tommie's future," he said, "has never been in doubt from the moment that she agreed to marry Edward Blackstone."

Railroad service between New Orleans and St. Louis was forced to compete for the business of passengers with the great paddle-wheel steamers that plied the Mississippi River, so the trains were more elaborate and luxurious than those found on most American railroad lines. Meals served in the dining car were as delicious and varied as those found in the finest New Orleans restaurants, and the sleeping cars boasted private compartments, which were unknown on the majority of trains.

A private compartment had been engaged by the army for Toby Holt's use, and he also had access to the first-class observation and smoking car at the rear of the train. His train left New Orleans promptly at noon, and he ate a simple but satisfying meal in the dining car and then wandered back to the observation car, where he engaged in amiable, inconsequential conversation with several other passengers. He had left his newspapers and magazines in his own compartment, however, and wanting to read, he wandered back to his own quarters. When he opened the door, he thought for a moment that he had made a mistake and had entered the wrong room. The attendant had made up the bed, and lying on top of

the sheets was a ravishingly beautiful young woman
with red-gold hair that trailed down across her bare
shoulders. She was wearing only a daring, low-cut
nightgown of black silk trimmed with lace, and there
were slits up to the thigh on both sides. The shades
had been drawn over the windows, leaving the room
in semidarkness, but Toby nevertheless quickly recognized the young woman. She was Martha, the
woman who had led him to Domino.

Reacting instinctively, he hastily closed and bolted
the door behind him.

Martha laughed huskily. "Are you surprised to
see me?"

"I'm stunned," he admitted.

Martha extended her arms to him and wriggled
her fingers, beckoning to him.

"Is this a joke of some sort?" he demanded.

The woman's laughter filled the tiny compartment. "A joke? Hardly! We've missed several opportunities to become better acquainted, and I had the
notion—probably false—that you might be avoiding
me. So I deliberately chose this train as the best of
all places to come to know you. There's no way you
can escape from me here, unless you want to jump
from the train." She laughed again.

Before Toby could respond, Martha suddenly
and unexpectedly reached out, catching hold of his
wrists and pulling him closer.

Caught off guard by the unexpected move, Toby
lost his balance, and the motion of the train caused
him to pitch forward.

Martha immediately gathered him in her arms, nibbled his earlobes, and breathed in his ear. Then, in the same continuing gesture, she pressed one hand against the back of his head, and her lips found his.

Her kiss was passionate, and she pressed close to him, caressing him with her free arm as her parted lips were fastened to his mouth.

Toby struggled to right himself, to regain his balance and to sit upright, but Martha remained in control of the situation and gave him no opportunity. Still kissing him fervently, her tongue flicking in and out, probing, exploring, she guided one of his hands inside her nightgown. Instinctively his fingers closed over the nipple of her bare breast. Martha shuddered with pleasure and continued to take the lead in their lovemaking.

Toby had no chance to think, to weigh the situation, or to do anything that would counteract the waves of erotic satisfaction that he felt. Martha's lush body had taken complete control. She knew precisely what she was doing, how to derive the greatest satisfaction out of every movement. In spite of Toby's reluctance to be trapped in the web that Martha was so insistently and expertly weaving around him, he was caught. He was a young, virile male, endowed with natural, healthy desires, and those feelings took possession and swept reason aside. He could not help responding to her in kind, and he stretched out beside her, his own gestures feverish as he began to caress her.

Their mutual lovemaking was leading them toward an inevitable climax when fate—or perhaps the gods who favored fidelity—intervened. Their railroad car suddenly jounced violently as the wheels passed over some ties that had been badly laid, and at the same moment, the engineer blew a long series of loud blasts on his horn.

The intimacy of the moment was ruined. The jolting and bouncing flung the couple apart, with Martha landing against the wall behind her, while Toby was almost thrown to the floor. Certainly the mood in which they had been enveloped was destroyed.

Martha attempted to recapture the mood by reaching lazily for Toby, but the brief respite had given him what he had needed, a moment to regain his composure, a moment to think of the consequences of infidelity. "We went far enough, thanks," he said, and forced himself to a sitting position.

Martha was not yet willing to admit that she had lost the struggle. She pouted slightly, her expression telling him that all he needed to do to make her his was to reach out and take her. But Toby had the inner strength to turn away from her, the character to resist her.

Martha had the common sense to know when she was defeated, the grace necessary to gloss over a defeat and save both of them from embarrassment. She sighed lightly and, without further ado, reached across him for her clothes, which were piled on a small chair that stood next to the bed.

Toby moved to the foot of the bed and raised

the shade partway. In order to give the woman as much privacy as he could in their cramped surroundings, he resolutely stared out at the passing scene while she dressed.

Then, after she repaired her makeup and made herself more presentable, he summoned the attendant, and they moved out into the corridor while the man made up the bed and reverted the room to its daytime status. Only when the man was finished did they return to the compartment and sit in two small easy chairs facing each other.

"We're stopping shortly before midnight," Martha said. "I'll get off and change to a train that will take me back to New Orleans."

"That will give us ample time," Toby told her, "for me to take you into the dining car and buy you supper."

"Thank you," she murmured, smiling lightly, a pensive expression in her enormous green eyes, and her full lips parted in a half-smile. "Never—not even once—in all my life have I been turned down by a man. I didn't believe it possible. I was so sure of myself that Domino teased me about it."

Toby stared at her. "Are you telling me," he asked incredulously, "that Domino knew you were going to come on board this train and try to seduce me?"

Martha laughed heartily. "He more than knew about it, he planned the whole thing."

"This is unbelievable!"

"It's all much simpler than it sounds," Martha

said. "You see, Domino knew that I—well, that I—I found you attractive, and I was sure you hadn't rejected me the previous times we met because nobody's done anything like that to me in all my life. Well, Domino said I was wrong, and he intended to prove it, so he bought my train ticket and gave me the money to bribe the attendant. You know the rest."

"I'm sorry to disappoint you," Toby said, "but it has nothing at all to do with you. I've never met a woman who's lovelier or more appealing or more desirable than you are. It's just that I'm not available. I love my wife so much that I feel it wouldn't be fair to her or to you if I had an affair with you. I've got to admit, I almost gave in and lost my struggle. I came close to giving in, far too close for comfort or my peace of mind, and I know better than to repeat the experiment."

"You've offered me some consolation," Martha said, then sighed. "Even though I wouldn't bet with Domino, he's unhappy unless there's a wager involved, so he made a bet with himself, so to speak. He gave me a gift to present to you in the event that you rejected me. Well, you did, and here's his present."

She fished around in her handbag and came out with a small package wrapped in tissue paper with a ribbon tied around it.

The surprised Toby hesitated, then took the package and unwrapped it. In his hand was one of the most beautiful pieces of jewelry he had ever seen. It was a bracelet made of large diamonds and matching rubies. He knew it was worth a fortune.

Looking at the bracelet, Martha recognized it at once from descriptions she had read in the newspapers just before she left New Orleans, and she controlled a desire to laugh aloud. The bracelet had been taken from the home of a New Orleans society leader, and the city's constabulary had been unable to recover it. Obviously Domino was behind the theft.

"It's gorgeous," Martha said breathlessly.

"I can't accept this as a gift from Domino," Toby said. He meant every word. It was true enough that he had entered into a partnership of convenience with the gang leader in order to capture Karl Kellerman, a goal that remained to be fulfilled, but it would be unethical, wrong in every way for him to accept a bracelet worth many thousands of dollars.

"Domino said to be sure to tell you that it isn't really a gift for you—it's for your wife. He said that if you had the strength to turn away from me, your wife would deserve this gift, at the very least, because she sure has earned it over the years. I'm not certain I know what he meant—"

"I know exactly what he meant," Toby said, interrupting her, "but even so, I can't accept it for Clarissa either."

Martha shook her head. "I've had my orders," she told him. "Domino made it very plain that no matter what you said or did, I'm not to come back to New Orleans with that bracelet. I'm sure you know how nasty he can be when he's disobeyed, so I have no choice. I've got to do as he says."

This put a different light on the matter, Toby

thought. Even though his conscience would not permit him to keep the expensive bracelet, he could not insist that Martha return it to Domino; he knew the young woman would be made to suffer if she returned to the city with it in her possession. He would deal with the problem later, and in the meantime, he dropped the bracelet into a coat pocket and tried to put it out of his mind.

He took Martha to the observation car, where, as other passengers stared at the beautiful woman, he bought her a predinner drink. Then, as night came, he escorted her to the dining car. All of the tables for two patrons were taken, so the chief steward sat them side by side at a table for four, which they found satisfactory. The other two chairs at their table were unoccupied.

As they were looking at the menu, the chief steward approached the table again and seated a middle-aged man opposite them. The newcomer was stocky and of medium height and had gray hair and a bulldoglike face; he was clad in black and wore a clerical collar.

Introductions were exchanged, and the priest, Father Flaherty, speaking in a rich Irish brogue, revealed that he was en route to Independence, Missouri, to take up a difficult new post. As they ate dinner, he spoke freely about his assignment.

For decades, Independence had been the nation's leading starting point for the wagon trains that traveled west across the Great Plains and the Rocky Mountains to California, Oregon, and Washington.

The coming of the railroads had made the wagon trains obsolete, and in recent years, particularly since the end of the Civil War, Independence had been declining in importance.

Nevertheless, a very large orphanage was being organized there. It was surprising, Father Flaherty said, how many children of lost parents ended their travels in Independence, and it was equally surprising how many youngsters were abandoned there by parents who wanted to go West unencumbered by children.

"There is a crying need for an orphanage," he said, "but there are almost no funds to build and to maintain a proper home. We need money for a school, money for good food, clothing, and shelter for the youngsters. We need funds for a staff physician. The list is almost endless. The director-general of my order convinced me that this job was a great challenge, and so I accepted it. But now that I'm actually on the way to Independence, I'm not so sure. The need for money is overwhelming. The director-general says that if I pray hard enough, my prayers will be answered, but to be truthful with you, I've worn out my knees, and I've yet to see a penny."

Toby fell silent as his mind raced. Martha and the priest continued to converse, but he took no part in their talk until suddenly he reached into his coat pocket and brought out the diamond and ruby bracelet that Martha had given him. "This should help to ease your shortage of funds, Father," he said, and handed him the bracelet.

Father Flaherty peered at the gem-laden bracelet, turning it over and over in the palm of his hand. Then, placing it on the table in front of him, he carefully loaded his pipe and lighted it. "A bauble like this," he said, "was made for a pretty wrist. It would grace your beauty, my dear." He bowed his head to Martha.

She giggled and replied, "I gave it to Toby, Father."

The priest looked slightly confused.

"It was intended as a gift for my wife," Toby explained, "but I'll be as honest with you as I can, Father. She has no use for it and would much prefer that you use it for good works at your orphanage."

Martha picked up the bracelet and pressed it into the clergyman's hand. "Please take it, Father," she said, "and when you sell it, make certain that you have the advice of an honest jeweler. This bracelet is worth a king's ransom."

Father Flaherty was so embarrassed that he puffed hard on his pipe, and his face was half-hidden behind a cloud of smoke. "I thank you," he said huskily. "I thank you for myself and in the names of all the youngsters who are going to benefit from your extraordinary generosity."

Domino's laugh echoed and reechoed through the house.

Martha sat opposite him, her hands still tightly clenched in her lap. She was tense and clearly was worried for fear that he had misunderstood her. "I—I hope you understood what I told you," she said nervously.

"I heard every word," he bellowed, "and I'll remember your story as long as I live. There's nobody in the world like that Toby Holt! Obviously he didn't give a damn that planning and executing the stealing of that bracelet cost me a lot of money. I don't suppose he happened to mention why he was so anxious to get rid of it."

Martha explained what Toby had told her.

"He would be like that!" Domino began to chuckle again. "Toby Holt may have nerves of steel, but he can't fool me. He was scared to death of being indebted to me, so he just couldn't wait to get rid of the bracelet." He wiped tears from his eyes. "I just hope that priest gets plenty when he sells it. That'll make the story perfect." He began to laugh once again, and this time, Martha unfroze and joined in the laughter.

After Martha completed her report to Domino, she had one duty left to perform. She changed into less flamboyant attire, then put on a special necklace. It consisted of two miniature dominoes in ivory on a gold chain. In place of the dots on the dominoes were diamonds, five on one half of each and two on the other. The necklace was prominently displayed on the throat of her high-necked, black gown.

Calling for one of the house carriages, Martha asked the driver to take her to a bar located in a workingman's district, not far from the waterfront.

The burly driver raised an eyebrow. "You got your nerve, goin' to a dump like that," he said.

Martha shook her head, her long red hair swaying from side to side. "It's perfectly all right, Don," she said. "It's one of the places that Domino and I visited last year when we toured most of the bars in town. As a matter of fact, something about this joint caught his fancy, and we went there at least twice. I remember the owner well because he was such a fiercely independent little fellow."

"If you say so, miss," the driver said dubiously.

"You'll be waiting for me outside," she said soothingly, "and you can look in through the windows, if I remember the place accurately. If anything bad happens, you can always dash in and be the hero of the night by saving me."

"Whatever you say, miss," he replied, shutting the carriage door behind her.

They arrived at the bar just as Wallace Dugald was about to close for the night. He was living in a state of perpetual agitation since Kellerman had gotten away from him, and he almost didn't care what was happening around him. Nevertheless he was thrown off balance by the arrival of the lovely young woman.

The only women who came alone to his establishment were prostitutes, but he knew at a glance that this woman was many cuts above the streetwalker level. Her clothes were expensive and tasteful. She wore a minimum of makeup, and she had an air of refinement about her that stamped her as a lady of class. He decided to stay open for a time in order to serve her.

Martha ordered a mild whiskey and water, and when Dugald brought it to the table where she had seated herself, she smiled up at him. "You were away for a time," she ventured.

"Some folks," he muttered, "think I went off on a vacation. Some vacation!"

"I'd never make that mistake," she said. "I have a very good idea of what happened to you, and I offer you my sympathies. You've been through a nasty experience."

"How did you hear about it?" he demanded.

By way of reply, Martha fingered her necklace.

As Dugald stared at the two miniature diamond-set dominoes, recognition gradually dawned. "Excuse me, ma'am, but are you the young lady who was with Domino those times that he came in here? I'm sorry I don't rightly recognize you. I was so flustered when I knew it was Domino himself who was sitting here, big as life, having a drink."

"Yes," she assured him with a quiet smile. "I was with him."

"I've been thinking of going to Domino and asking his help," Dugald said. "From what I hear, that no-good rat, Karl Kellerman, has left town, and I'd be willing to pay Domino to let me know when Kellerman comes back. I've sworn to empty a six-shooter into him, and that's one vow I intend to keep!"

"I know Domino won't accept any money from

you," she said, "and if you go to him, I'm certain he'll give you the same advice that I'm going to give you now. Leave Kellerman to him."

"But I've sworn an oath to kill him if it's the last thing I ever do."

"Domino has sworn a similar oath," Martha said. "Kellerman not only broke his word to him, but tried to kill him, and anyone who does things like that to Domino is lost. His days are numbered."

Dugald could only nod.

"Kellerman has another deadly enemy," Martha said. "Toby Holt, from the West. He's sworn to help take care of Kellerman, too."

Dugald whistled softly under his breath. "I'd sure hate to be in Karl Kellerman's shoes," he said. "With both Domino and Toby Holt gunning for him, he doesn't stand the chance of a snowball in hell of surviving."

Now, looking into the deep green eyes of the lovely young woman seated at the table before him, all the venom, all the hatred somehow seemed to go out of Wallace. He knew his enemy would eventually be taken care of, and for the first time in more weeks than he cared to remember, the Scotsman felt peace.

"Ma'am, if you don't mind," Wallace began a bit shyly, "I'd like to propose a toast." When Martha smiled in acknowledgment, the Scotsman ran to the bar and poured himself a drink. Returning to the table and raising his glass high, Wallace said, "To you, to Domino, and to the end of Karl Kellerman for all time!"

Martha, still smiling, raised her own glass and sipped from her drink. Then, her eyes connecting with Wallace's, they both began laughing boisterously.

Toby Holt accepted a second helping of the cherry pie that Clarissa had made for his homecoming, sat back in his chair at the dining room table, and sighed. "You have no idea how good it feels to be home again," he said. "I was away for only a few weeks, but it felt like months."

"I know what you mean," Clarissa replied softly, then asked, "Are you going to be home for a while now?"

"To the best of my knowledge. I've done everything that's been asked of me, and my duty is finished. When I wired General Blake from New Orleans, he wired back intimating that President Grant might wish me to go to Washington soon. But he also mentioned that the President might want you present. So I suspect that there may be more involved than meets the eye."

"I just hope," she said, "that he doesn't have some new task that's going to take you away from home again."

"All I can say is that if he does, my mother and General Blake don't know about it because they certainly would have mentioned it to me."

"I realize I'm borrowing trouble," Clarissa said,

"but it occurs to me that every time the United States needs help, the government calls on you."

"I suggest," he said, "that we live in the present. "I'm home now, and to the best of my knowledge and belief, I'm here to stay. Let's make the best of it."

Clarissa went off to the stove in the kitchen for the coffee pot, returned with it, and put it on the dining room table. Then she bent down and kissed Toby before resuming her seat.

"I like that," he said, grinning.

"So do I," she told him.

In the next day or two, he decided he would tell her the story of Martha and of the bracelet that Domino had given him, but such things could wait.

Meanwhile Clarissa tried hard to banish her worries from her mind. Toby was right; it was enough that he had come home, and she would be wise to let her worries fade while she enjoyed their reunion.

As the freighter *Neptune* plowed southward through the waters of the Caribbean Sea, the weather worsened, with rough seas and heavy rains.

In late morning, the weather having cleared, Captain Kayross held the bridge for the current watch, and the ship's first and second officers, Davis and Symes, sat in the officers' wardroom, drinking coffee with Karl Kellerman. Davis rose, took the coffee pot from the adjoining serving table, and refilled their cups.

Kellerman, wearing an open-throated shirt with

the sleeves rolled up, sprawled in an armchair and appeared to be very much at ease. His eyes were alert and bright, however, and he missed nothing that was said.

He had good cause to be awake to possible dangers: Kung Lee, the powerful head of the most prominent tong in all of North America, was also on board the *Neptune*, very much annoyed with him. Kung claimed that Kellerman was solely responsible for Toby Holt's escape. As a result Toby presumably was still alive, able to cause further troubles for the tong and for Kung.

What Kung failed to realize, Kellerman reflected, was that he himself also stood to lose by Toby's escape. Holt had a bulldog quality to him, and Kellerman felt reasonably certain that he would reappear at some time to cause more headaches. Therefore, Kellerman was also highly annoyed with himself for having been negligent and allowing Holt to set himself free, though to give the devil his due, Holt was as slippery as an eel and had the proverbial nine lives of a cat.

Kellerman was not for an instant forgetting that he had invested one-third of the money necessary to take the *Neptune* to China, where her cargo would be exchanged for illegal immigrants and opium to be brought to the United States. It was for the sake of the investment, as well as because of Kung Lee's annoyance with him, that Kellerman was currently courting the two ship's mates.

"Let me show you something, lads," he said,

and removed a roll of paper money from an inner pocket.

The two ship's officers were very much impressed, having no idea that Kellerman had prepared the roll in advance, placing several fifty-dollar bills on the outside and filling the better part of the interior with one-dollar bills.

"I'm not ready to make an independent move yet," he said, "and I won't be until we've been to China, picked up our cargo there, and are returning to the United States with it. That's when I'll make my move. I'll want help—a great deal of help to take over this ship, and I'm prepared to pay well for it."

Avarice shone in the mates' eyes, but before they could speak, the door behind Kellerman opened, and Kung Lee stood in the frame. The two officers froze.

Kellerman looked back over his shoulder, deliberately sipped his coffee, and said casually, "Morning, Kung." He felt himself growing taut but would not show it, no matter what might happen.

Symes hastily muttered an excuse, which Davis quickly echoed, and the two officers left the wardroom in a hurry, pushing past Kung Lee in their haste to depart.

Kung Lee took his time, helping himself to a cup of coffee. As he sat down, a thin smile creased his face. "The mates," he said, "were in a great hurry to depart. My experience tells me that I interrupted a conspiracy of some sort."

"That's a lot of damned nonsense," Kellerman

growled. "You're always imagining some kind of conspiracy or other."

Kung measured a tiny quantity of sugar onto a teaspoon and dropped it into his coffee. "If I wished," he said, "I'd have Captain Kayross clamp you into irons, and then I'd go to work on you myself with a knife. You'd confess your conspiracy soon enough." He paused, looked out at the sea through a porthole, and then went on. "Fortunately for you, I am relaxing on this voyage, so your ugly little secret need not be revealed, at least for the present. But let me tell you something, Kellerman. Even though I accepted you as a partner for this voyage, I still don't trust you."

Kellerman boldly returned the Chinaman's icy glare, his own expression insolent, his manner daring Kung Lee to halt him.

"I will be watching you with great care," Kung said, "and when you step out of bounds—when you overstep the mark by a mere fraction of an inch—I will strike, and you shall suffer the fate from which you so stupidly allowed Toby Holt to escape!"

There was no sound in the office of the superintendent of the new orphanage in Independence except for the scratching of Father Flaherty's quill pen as he wrote to the director-general of his order.

Work has been completed on the new wing, and the population is now one hundred and sixty children, which is our capacity.

We have hired the best cook in the state, and he's filling our larder with provisions of every sort. No one here will ever go hungry.

We have purchased two complete changes of clothing for every child, one to use on school days, and the other for Sundays, holidays, and vacations. I am pleased to report that our faculty is now complete. A full list of teachers and their credentials accompanies this report.

He lighted his pipe, sat back, stared at the ceiling for a time, and then added a final paragraph.

You told me repeatedly that if I prayed hard enough, the Lord would provide. So he has.

Father Flaherty puffed on his pipe, and clouds of fragrant smoke drifted toward the ceiling. He chuckled as he reread his report, and the sound filled the room.

★ WAGONS WEST ★

A series of unforgettable books that trace the lives of a dauntless band of pioneering men, women, and children as they brave the hazards of an untamed land in their trek across America. This legendary caravan of people forge a new link in the wilderness. They are Americans from the North and the South, alongside immigrants, Blacks, and Indians, who wage fierce daily battles for survival on this uncompromising journey—each to their private destinies as they fulfill their greatest dreams.

☐	26822	INDEPENDENCE! #1	$4.50
☐	26162	NEBRASKA! #2	$4.50
☐	26242	WYOMING! #3	$4.50
☐	26072	OREGON! #4	$4.50
☐	26070	TEXAS! #5	$4.50
☐	26377	CALIFORNIA! #6	$4.50
☐	26546	COLORADO! #7	$4.50
☐	26069	NEVADA! #8	$4.50
☐	26163	WASHINGTON! #9	$4.50
☐	26073	MONTANA! #10	$4.50
☐	26184	DAKOTA! #11	$4.50
☐	26521	UTAH! #12	$4.50
☐	26071	IDAHO! #13	$4.50
☐	26367	MISSOURI! #14	$4.50
☐	27141	MISSISSIPPI! #15	$4.50
☐	25247	LOUISIANA! #16	$4.50
☐	25622	TENNESSEE! #17	$4.50
☐	26022	ILLINOIS! #18	$4.50
☐	26533	WISCONSIN! #19	$4.50
☐	26849	KENTUCKY! #20	$4.50

Prices and availability subject to change without notice.

**FROM THE PRODUCER OF WAGONS WEST
A SWEEPING SAGA OF WAR AND HEROISM
AT THE BIRTH OF A NATION.**

THE WHITE INDIAN SERIES

Filled with the glory and adventure of the colonization of America, here is the thrilling saga of the new frontier's boldest hero and his family. THE WHITE INDIAN SERIES chronicles the adventures of Renno, his son Ja-gonh, and his grandson Ghonkaba, from the colonies to Canada, from the South to the turbulent West. Through their struggles to tame a savage continent and their encounters with the powerful men and passionate women in the early battles for America, we witness the events that shaped our future and forged our great heritage.

☐ 24650	White Indian #1	$3.95
☐ 25020	The Renegade #2	$3.95
☐ 24751	War Chief #3	$3.95
☐ 24476	The Sachem #4	$3.95
☐ 25154	Renno #5	$3.95
☐ 25039	Tomahawk #6	$3.95
☐ 25589	War Cry #7	$3.95
☐ 25202	Ambush #8	$3.95
☐ 23986	Seneca #9	$3.95
☐ 24492	Cherokee #10	$3.95
☐ 24950	Choctaw #11	$3.95
☐ 25353	Seminole #12	$3.95
☐ 25868	War Drums #13	$3.95
☐ 26206	Apache #14	$3.95

Prices and availability subject to change without notice.

Special Offer
Buy a Bantam Book
for only 50¢.

Now you can have Bantam's catalog filled with hundreds
of titles plus take advantage of our unique and exciting
bonus book offer. A special offer which gives you the
opportunity to purchase a Bantam book for only 50¢.
Here's how!

By ordering any five books at the regular price per
order, you can also choose any other single book
listed (up to a $5.95 value) for just 50¢. Some
restrictions do apply, but for further details why not
send for Bantam's catalog of titles today!

Just send us your name and address and we will send
you a catalog!